PRAISE FOR KARLA SORENSEN

"Karla Sorensen's books are pure magic!"

—Penny Reid, *New York Times* bestselling author

"An expert at her craft, no one writes heartwarming characters with emotional depth like Karla Sorensen. She's a perfect fit for readers who love to laugh, build a found family, and fall in love."

—Kandi Steiner, *USA Today* bestselling author

"If Karla writes it . . . I'm reading it."

—Devney Perry, *New York Times* bestselling author

"It was beautiful, heartbreaking (yet it put me back together, too), and the perfect mixture of spicy and sweet."

—Megan Reads Romance on *The Best Laid Plans*

"Sparkling tension between our main characters, a slow burn that doesn't leave you unsatisfied for too long, witty and smart banter, all blended together with romance that feels right and natural."

—Helpless Reads on *The Best Laid Plans*

"A perfect blend of raw emotion, tension, and humor, it was everything I didn't know I needed."

—All in with A on *The Best of All*

"With a torturous slow burn that finally snaps with the most electric kind of tension, a seriously swoony tortured hero, and a storyline that made my chest ache, this was even better than I expected."

—Jeeves Reads Romance on *The Best of All*

SINGLE DAD

Dilemma

DISCOVER OTHER TITLES BY KARLA SORENSEN

The Wilder Family

One and Only

Head over Heels

Promise Me This

Forever Starts Tonight

This Wild Heart

The Wolves: A Football Dynasty (second gen)

The Lie

The Plan

The Crush

The Ward Sisters

Focused

Faked

Floored

Forbidden

The Washington Wolves

The Bombshell Effect

The Ex Effect

The Marriage Effect

The Bachelors of The Ridge

Dylan

Garrett

Cole

Michael

Tristan

Three Little Words

By Your Side

Light Me Up

Tell Them Lies

Love at First Sight

Baking Me Crazy

Batter of Wits

Steal My Magnolia

Worth the Wait

The Best Men

The Best Laid Plans

The Best of All

The Kings

Lessons in Heartbreak

SINGLE DAD *Dilemma*

The Kings, Book 2

KARLA SORENSEN

This is a work of fiction. Names, characters, organizations, places, events, and incidents are either products of the author's imagination or are used fictitiously. Otherwise, any resemblance to actual persons, living or dead, is purely coincidental.

Published by Montlake, Seattle
www.apub.com

EU product safety contact:
Amazon Media EU S. à r.l.
38, avenue John F. Kennedy, L-1855 Luxembourg
amazonpublishing-gpsr@amazon.com

ISBN-13: 9781662526770 (paperback)
ISBN-13: 9781662526763 (digital)

Cover design by Letitia Hasser
Cover photography by Michelle Lancaster PTY LTD
Cover image: © Pasta La Vista / Shutterstock

Printed in the United States of America

SINGLE DAD
Dilemma

Chapter One

Lily

New people, in general, were not my favorite thing in the world. Some could be nice. Friendly and genuine and all that shit. Their desire to get to know you was well intentioned and everything, but in order to do that, God, it involved questions and conversation, and I'd never been all that good at either of those things.

My dog—little asshole that he was—was a phenomenal conversationalist. Well . . . a great listener, maybe. I'd long begun to suspect he was an introvert too.

He wasn't friendly. When approached by someone new, he'd do this little brow-furrowing thing and back up a step. There was no tail wagging, no jumping up and down at the attention from a stranger. Usually, he'd just give me a long-suffering look that conveyed a general sense of *Why the ever-loving hell are you letting them touch me, human?*

In my head, Larry swore a lot. Not that anyone else could know this about him. All they saw was his fuzzy little face, and they lost all sense of polite personal boundaries.

It didn't matter where we lived, people *always* wanted to meet the dog. It didn't matter that I could've won every award in existence for

Resting Bitch Face, or that I put out the welcoming energy of a cactus—the dog fucking reeled them in.

In general, I was convinced that people could not help themselves, given that he looked like a troll doll/gremlin hybrid on a leash. Fluffy, weird hair. Big, buggy eyes. So ugly he was cute. Sort of.

And it's why, at the moment, there were two small human faces staring at me through the fence separating my current living situation from the neighbors'. For a while, they'd played coy, acting like they weren't desperately trying to get the dog's attention while I walked him around and pleaded with him to do his business out on the grass.

Larry did not feel much like listening to me. We were still in a tiff from earlier in the day.

He was old as shit, and we'd long since passed the time when wearing a diaper was the best bet to avoid public embarrassments, and I'd been on the receiving end of more than one Larry glare when I affixed it to his little ass.

"It's cold," I told him. "I know it's cold, you know it's cold, let's just move on and not make a big thing of it, okay? This is far more dignified than me changing your diaper, don't you think?"

Larry looked up and stared at me, unmoving. Like literally, he would not move, and I know his dime-size bladder had to be full. My eyes narrowed, but he didn't do shit. I could practically hear him: *You're the genius who took a new house-sitting job in Buffalo, New York, in December. Of course it's fucking cold, but I shouldn't be expected to pay the price for that.*

Basking in the sun like a cat was more Larry's style, but unfortunately for him, there'd be a bit less of that during our time here, what with the ever-present cloud blanket that never seemed to go away. I sent an ineffectual glare in the direction of that cloud and shifted on my feet, praying that when I looked back down, Larry would be doing his little forward-lean pee stance.

"Your dog is really cute."

There it was.

The fence kids had finally saddled up enough courage to say something. I raised an eyebrow and glanced over. They were tall and gangly, all long legs and big eyes and brown hair. Sort of like Larry, except the kids were cute and not terrifying. The girl had a white hat shoved on her head, and the boy wore a similar style in blue.

"Thanks," I told them. "He knows it too."

The boy sniffled, likely from the cold, and ran a hand under his nose. "Why isn't he moving?"

"Because he hates me."

They both laughed, unaware that I was telling the honest-to-God truth.

It was one of those incontrovertible facts of life, like gravity. The sun rose in the east and set in the west. And Larry lowered his personal standards to tolerate me, simply because I was the one who fed him, sheltered him, and clothed him (see previous comment about the diapers). I even bought him the fancy dog food that had to stay in the fridge, because his old-man teeth couldn't handle kibble.

"No, he doesn't," the girl said on a giggle.

"Sure he does. Watch." I crouched down and extended my hand. "Come here, Larry," I cooed in the nicest voice I could manage. "Come here, little man. Let's cuddle."

He plopped his ass down in the cold grass and gave me a haughty look.

I glanced over at the kids. "See? A cold heart in this one."

"Can we try?" she asked. "Maybe . . . maybe he likes kids?"

For a second, I stared at her, a dangerous cavern opening up in my chest. I didn't want to prod at what was hiding there in the dark, but even with my aversion to new people, I found myself nodding. "Yeah, you can try."

Her brother whispered something fiercely, and she paused with a great heaving, dramatic sigh.

His little chest puffed out. "We don't know who you are. You might be a kidnapper. Dad always tells us to be careful about strangers."

"Your dad is pretty smart," I said, standing up and wiping my hands over my leggings-clad thighs. "Not a kidnapper. I'm house-sitting for your neighbors while they're gone."

The girl's eyes narrowed. "What are their names?"

"Scott and Patty."

Their heads leaned toward each other as they discussed.

"Where did they go?" the boy asked.

"Arizona. They'll be back the middle of February, which seems counterintuitive to me because it'll still be cold as f—" I stopped, tilting my head to readjust my rusty conversation skills to be little-people appropriate. I settled on, "It'll still be really cold. Something about a friend's seventy-fifth birthday."

Apparently this was the right answer, because the two gave each other a wordless look of understanding—sibling agreement that I wasn't a psycho—and immediately slid through an opening in the fence, the girl coming through first.

Larry tilted his head and watched them approach. To their credit, they moved slow, not wanting to scare him.

"I'm Maggie," the girl said. "Maggie King. And this is my older brother, Bryce."

"I'm almost twelve," he pronounced, but his eyes were locked on the dog when he said it.

"A good age," I replied. "I'm Lily. It's nice to meet you."

Maggie wasn't paying as much attention to the dog, her big eyes occasionally darting up to study me. "You have blue hair."

My hand moved to the hair in question. "Sort of. I'm growing it out. Just blue on the ends right now." My natural black was covered by the hat I'd worn to avoid hypothermia while Larry took his sweet fucking time to . . . not pee, apparently.

Bryce was sitting on the ground, leaving his hand outstretched. Larry's head inched forward, and I found myself holding my breath.

"His name is Larry," I told them. "Don't take it personally if he doesn't react much. He's kind of like a grumpy old man. He's not very friendly with new people."

"Sounds like our dad," Maggie giggled.

My eyebrow quirked. "Your dad's old?"

Bryce shrugged. "Sort of. He's in his thirties."

I rolled my eyes. "Kid, that is not old."

He gave me a curious look. "To me, it is. How old are you?"

"Twenty-eight." I tilted my chin toward the dog. "He's fourteen."

"Whoa," Maggie breathed. "He's ancient."

Look at me, talking to brand-new people. Maybe it was easier because they were little people.

"Do you need to ask your parents if it's okay to be over here?"

"He's at work," Maggie said. They shared a look. "He's *always* at work this time of year."

"What about your mom?"

"Oh, they're divorced. She moved to Los Angeles last year. We live with our dad because he wanted us more." Bryce gave me a matter-of-fact shrug. "It's better this way."

Open little shits, weren't they? If I wanted to, I could probably get their entire life story with ease. "So you have no one watching you? You seem a bit young for that."

"Miss Jill is there, but she doesn't care what we do," Bryce added. "She's not very fun."

My gaze cut over to the house in question. "She doesn't sound like a very good nanny."

Bryce shrugged. "Our last nanny quit—"

"She was *awful*," Maggie interjected.

"—and my dad offered Miss Jill extra money to help with us. I don't think she really wanted to, though."

"A lot of money," Maggie said with big, serious eyes. "And she's not technically a nanny. She's the housekeeper."

The housekeeper. It was one of those things kids said, not realizing they were giving *we're rich and I'm completely unaware* vibes.

The houses in this neighborhood were on the big side, but not mansions by any stretch. More like, people with money who kept more of it in the bank than in real estate. The cars were all nice and shiny. The landscaping immaculate. Or it would be, if everything wasn't frozen to shit. Lots of brick lined the street, as well as big, tall trees that would give plenty of shade if it weren't an arctic tundra. As it stood, their spindly branches didn't do much to block out the irrepressible gray.

"I like your sweatshirt," Bryce said. "But you should probably be wearing a coat. My dad always tells me that sweatshirts don't count." He sighed. "I think they do, though."

I almost laughed. Almost.

Between Larry and the sweatshirt, I should've known I would reel someone in. Half the conversations people started with me in this general area of the United States was when I was wearing the damn thing.

"It was my dad's," I told him, keeping my voice even. "He, um . . . he loved the Celtics."

It was ancient, fading and falling apart. Older than me by a healthy number of years. There were holes in the sleeves where I shoved my thumbs, and it hung over my thighs, far too big for me. There wasn't a lot about me that people would call *soft* or *cozy* or *warm*, but the sweatshirt sure had people fooled. Maybe it had me fooled, too, and that's why I wore it.

What it *wasn't* was a coat, as Bryce so astutely pointed out, and I couldn't help but shiver. Maggie was whispering to Larry, speaking so quietly that I couldn't understand her, but even though he pretended like he couldn't hear my calling for him half the damn time, that dog stood back up and his stubby tail wagged. Just a little. As my mouth went slack, my jaw made a soft clicking noise.

He took a couple of tentative steps closer and deigned to allow Maggie to scratch his head, which she did with absolutely heartbreaking gentleness. She smiled up at me, and I lost my breath a little at the sight of it.

"He likes you," I said quietly. "He doesn't like many people."

I pulled in a quick breath, fighting another shiver when the wind picked up.

Bryce watched me for a moment. "Can we maybe play with him a little? If you're cold, you can go inside. I'll hold his leash really tight."

Maggie's face lit up. "Yeah, we'll bring him inside. We promise."

"Oh, I can't leave him out here too much longer, kids. I'm really sorry. He needs some medicine before I feed him dinner."

Immediately, they deflated. Then Maggie perked up. "Can we play with him inside? We'll be super good. I promise we won't break anything inside their house."

"Do you usually?"

They traded another look. "No?" Bryce said haltingly.

Blowing out a harsh breath, I looked over at their two-story brick home, slightly larger than Scott and Patty's. "You should tell your housekeeper where you are."

Bryce whipped out a phone. "I'll text her."

Maggie gave him a quick glance, then grinned up at me.

Something about that grin found a foothold in my usual reserve, like she'd pried her cute little fingers into a crack and pulled really fucking hard.

"Do you guys like oatmeal-raisin cookies? I just took some out of the oven."

The words were out before I could stop them, and a string of expletives spun through my head. Later, I'd blame my offer on the cold. Or I'd blame Larry and his uncharacteristic friendliness.

Their eyes brightened, and they stood to their feet immediately. "Yes," they said in tandem.

What the *hell* was I doing? It was too late to take it back, and the two of them ran onto the deck and let themselves into the house, clearly comfortable with their neighbors.

I gave another quick glance back at the house, then down at Larry.

He blinked.

"I don't fucking know, Larry," I replied. "It's your fault. You always bring in the friendly ones, but *I'm* the one who has to deal with the consequences. We're gonna talk about this later."

Instead of moving, he just stared up at me, and with a sigh, I reached down and scooped him up in my arms. He made a grumbling sound, like he paid a mortgage and taxes and worked fifty hours a week. I rolled my eyes.

"Yes, your life is very rough, you little freeloader."

Chapter Two

Barrett

During the regular season, my entire life boiled down to fifteen-minute increments. It didn't sound like much, but with a hundred and sixty-eight hours in every week, that gave me six hundred and seventy-two chunks of time to manage my life.

Fifteen minutes to debrief with my assistant, Bridget, every weekday morning at six thirty. Bridget knew every minute detail about my life, down to the way I liked my eggs at breakfast, that I was allergic to cashews, and wanted extra starch on the collars of my dress shirts when I had occasion to wear them.

If I thought about it too hard, she also probably knew I hadn't gotten laid since the last time I'd touched my ex-wife, which was why she gave me sad eyes when she thought I wasn't looking.

My assistant coach, as well as my offensive and defensive coordinators, received daily meetings as well, something that wasn't typical for most NFL coaches, but mine carried a slightly heavier load than most after my divorce had put me firmly in the single-dad club.

The team's general manager got two of those chunks every Monday, once I'd finished breakfast with my team captains.

Pearl, the octogenarian owner of the team, received another two. Sometimes more, if she was feeling particularly chatty. And the last few weeks, I couldn't blame her. When the new head coach and the new quarterback were butting heads, I'd have a few extra words in my daily allotment too.

Archer, the quarterback in question, avoided getting on my schedule as much as possible, which was part of the problem.

Sorry, Coach, can't make it today, he'd said earlier, his phone tucked up to his ear and a smirk on his face as he tapped a fist with the guys who passed us in the hallway. *Promised I'd do a polar bear plunge with a local sorority for charity.*

When all I did was raise my eyebrow, he laughed under his breath. *Don't worry, I still know how to throw the ball. We'll be fine this weekend.*

Then he walked away, hands tucked into his pockets, whistling as he did, and I tried to decide how long I wanted to let this slide before I benched him.

It was moments like that, I wondered why the hell I wanted to be a coach in the first place. Most of the time, it was amazing. Rewarding and fulfilling, and it kept my feet planted in a world that I loved. But when you're watching the retreating back of the guy leading your team so he can go swimming with a sorority, knowing he had a guaranteed thirty million from a four-year rookie contract that I still wasn't sure he deserved, it left me asking myself a lot of questions.

Questions that, unfortunately, didn't have many answers. Or not yet, at least. Just like anything worthwhile, building up the right foundation for this team would take time, and I hadn't had much of it yet.

It was one of a million things weighing on my shoulders, and no matter how many deep breaths I took, that weight never dissipated.

A text from Bridget lit up my phone.

Bridget: Do we want to comment on this?

Included was a link to an article with the headline: Buffalo's Power Struggle: Can Coach King Wrangle the Talent?

And then below: Based on this season, and what we're hearing from the locker room, we're not so sure.

Reading anything else would simply ruin my already tenuous mood, so I clicked away, a familiar sensation churning in my gut. Failure didn't sit well with anyone in this industry. Competition was in the driver's seat at all times, the thing that drove every single person who walked through the doors: from the owner to the front office staff to the staff who painted the lines on the field every week. We all wanted to win.

But when I felt like I was failing—at anything—it was like a bug was stuck in my ear, buzzing and buzzing and buzzing until I was halfway to crazy before I could tear it out. And lately, those failures just kept piling up, recycled into catchy headlines meant to garner clicks.

Me: I say no, but send it to PR and get their take.

Before she could respond, I set my phone down and tried to refocus.

The clock on the wall of my office ticked more loudly than usual, grating on my already exhausted nerves as I tried to pay attention to the screen in front of me.

Other than the time I took to sleep—and yes, I had to schedule that too—it was reviewing film that took the single biggest amount of time. Outside of that, it was meeting upon meeting upon meeting.

But of all the things I scheduled into my day, there was one fifteen-minute slot that was my favorite. It always went by too fast, and when it was done, I'd give myself another minute to fight the guilt of how much I was forced to leave them alone.

At 3:30 p.m., my phone would ring with a video call, and the two faces I loved most would fill the screen.

Bryce was almost twelve, Maggie almost eleven, and they were old enough now to remember to call as soon as they got off the bus. Our conversations were often mundane—discussing homework, telling them to stop arguing with each other, and reminding my daughter that she was not, in fact, allowed to try to access government databases in her spare time.

Prior to that 3:30 phone call, it was rare for me to hear from them, unless someone was sick or—as they'd done time and time again since my ex, Rachel, had moved across the country with her healthy alimony payment—they'd successfully run off another nanny, housekeeper, or tutor.

It was during one of the later fifteen-minute increments, just past 5:00 p.m. on a Wednesday, that my phone began ringing.

It wasn't either of the kids, and it wasn't from the house phone, so I silenced the ringer and returned my focus to the front of the conference room.

Wednesday evenings, I tried to sit in on positional meetings; today, I was in the running back's meeting. Miguel, my running back's coach, had some film from last week's game up on the screen, pausing it to show a breakdown in one of our routes, when my phone rang again.

Everyone turned to look at me.

I cleared my throat and silenced the ringtone again, eyeing the same number with a growing sense of unease. When a voicemail came through, I muttered an apology and brought the phone up to my ear.

"Mr. King, it's Jill. I'm sorry for bothering you again, and I apologize for not giving you my new cell number, but I have no idea where the kids are, and they're not answering their phones. Again. This is the fourth time this has happened in the last two weeks, and with all due respect, sir, you do not pay me enough to keep track of them like *this*."

I let out a slow, deep breath, disconnecting the call with a firm tap of my thumb. "My apologies at having to leave early; I have something that needs my attention at home."

My offensive coordinator, who'd worked with me for the last five years, gave me a curious look. "Everything okay, Coach?"

I managed a tight smile. "My children seem to be missing."

No one was fazed by this information.

Miguel snickered at the front of the room. Darius, our leading rusher, smothered a smile behind his hand. My OC nodded slowly. "Maggie must've been bored again."

"Looks to be that way," I said, tone even despite the surge in my blood pressure. "If you'll excuse me."

The walk back to my office was blissfully uninterrupted. Most of the front office staff knew not to stop me unless they'd gone through Bridget to find a fifteen-minute slot. With only two games left in the regular season, the offices were drenched in Christmas decor—gold and white and silver seemed to be the theme this year, contrasting with the red and white of the Buffalo logo.

In my hand, my cell phone got heavier and heavier the longer I walked, but I would not be having this conversation within earshot of anyone besides Bridget. I turned the last corner, entering the lobby for my office, as well as the offices for the offensive and defensive coordinators, and my assistant coach.

Anchored in the middle of the space of lush carpets, deep leather chairs, and a silver version of the logo on the wall was Bridget's command center—a massive desk that dwarfed her petite frame. At the moment, it was empty. A glance at the clock told me she was likely eating dinner. She usually did from 5:00 to 5:30 when I was in position meetings.

The moment I cleared my office door, I stopped short. There was a full-size Christmas tree in the corner—half covered with red, silver, and white ornaments—and another smaller one with bare branches. I pinched the bridge of my nose and pulled up Jill's number.

"Mr. King," she answered, the irritation bleeding into every individual letter of my name.

"I'm sorry for the delay; I was in a meeting and didn't recognize the number. Did you find them yet?"

She let out a disgruntled scoff. "Yes. They're at the neighbors' house."

My brow furrowed. "Which ones? Scott and Patty are gone until February, and they're the only neighbors they know."

"Well, Scott and Patty have a *very* friendly house sitter who has a dog, so . . ."

I tipped my head back. "So my kids are playing with the dog."

She made a tight, uncomfortable sound. "They've informed me they're not coming home. So *I'm* informing *you* that I quit."

My jaw clenched tight, and I let my frustration escape in a tiny, harsh puff of air. "Jill, please just give me through the end of the week."

"You hired me to be a housekeeper. You also told me your kids would need very little supervision once they were home from school, and that is not the case." She cleared her throat. "I have no desire to be a babysitter, sir, especially not for *your* kids, no matter how much you pay me."

As I took a seat in my leather chair, I glanced at the rest of my carefully constructed schedule and mentally delegated about half of it to my assistant coach, who hopefully would forgive me. "I can be home in an hour. Please . . . just . . . give me an hour."

"They'll be at the neighbors' with their house sitter when you get home," she informed me. "Who was not very friendly to *me* when I tried to get the kids to come back. Not the kind of woman I'd want my kids around."

"And yet you're leaving mine there?" I asked incredulously.

Jill snorted. "You say that like I am capable of dragging those two back home. Mr. King, I appreciate that you give me that much credit. It's been an enlightening month in your employment, and I don't mean that as a compliment. If I were you, I'd think about finding a new job so you can deal with them yourself."

And with that, she hung up.

I stared, slack jawed, at my suddenly black phone screen.

"What the hell?" I breathed.

The door to my office swung open, Bridget barging in with a furrow in her brow. "You're not supposed to be here right now. Why aren't you in your meeting?"

I held up my phone. "My children—"

"Are at the neighbors'," she finished. "I know."

Slowly, I leaned back in my chair and fixed her with an incredulous look. "And how do you know that?"

She merely smiled, pulling out her cell phone to reference something on the screen. "Maggie sent me a picture of a dog and said, *Will you help me convince Dad that I need one?*" I muttered something under my breath, but she ignored it and kept reading. "To which I replied, *Maggie, darling, whose dog is that and whose living room are you in?*"

I slicked my tongue over my teeth. "Keep going."

"The house sitter is *supercool*, according to your offspring," Bridget said. "Maggie met her in the backyard when they were *hiding from that b-i-t-c-h Jill*," she read, glancing over the rim of her glasses to make sure she read it correctly. "And yes, she spelled it, because your daughter is nothing if not conscientious of following the house rules about swearing."

With jerky movements, I shoved my laptop and my tablet into my bag. "Doesn't follow any other rules, apparently." I paused, glancing at the boxes of ornaments. "Why are there *multiple* Christmas trees in my office?"

She folded her arms over her chest and quirked a brow. "To let everyone know that you're full of Christmas cheer and not even remotely a grump." She pursed her lips. "Jury is out on whether it's working or not."

I gave her a long look, and Bridget rolled her eyes.

I'd only met one other person in my life who dared to do that when I was in one of my moods—my twin brother. It wasn't a talent specific to him; I was just as skilled in the reverse. There was a span of time when I was certain my brother disliked every single thing about me.

It didn't feel quite like that anymore. We were *trying*, for lack of a better term, after a solid decade where even that felt impossible. Being separated from your twin was weird.

There was always an awareness of him, a heaviness I'd never really been able to shake, and no matter how the press liked to pit us against each other—the Brain and the Brawn, the serious twin and the fun twin (no need to guess which one I was)—I still loved my brother. I worried about him.

Figuring out how to show it in a way that didn't feel like I was trying to tell him what to do had eluded me thus far, something I seemed to be carrying over into my parenting skills, apparently, judging by how often my children acted out.

They'd all probably call me a Grinch, say that my heart was two sizes too small—and that was on a good day.

My kids did love me, but I worked so damn much they felt ignored, and I couldn't even blame them.

A headache bloomed at my temples, and I rubbed the back of my neck. My heart wasn't too small, but it did feel like it was stretched so thin that it was close to snapping around inside my chest if pulled any tighter.

With a heavy sigh, I closed the bag and slung the strap over my shoulder. "If you could please ask Mike to handle the two meetings on my schedule after dinner, I'll finish watching film at home and connect with him there, if you don't mind setting up a virtual meeting room for the next few hours."

"You got it, boss." She paused after she cleared the door, her red braid swinging over her shoulder as she poked her head back into my office. "Thank you for the Christmas bonus, by the way. Someone was in a generous mood when they wrote out the checks. The other assistants started crying when they opened theirs."

I grunted. "Your wife told me you don't take enough trips, so I figured if I pay for it, you might actually go."

"True," she mused. "Now I'm going to be stuck on a beach somewhere after the season is done, with a horrible fruity drink in my hand, and Janie will be reading her fairy-smut books while I beg to go do something active."

I gave her a serious nod. "Sounds miserable."

"Indeed." She tapped the doorframe. "Pearl wants a quick meeting in the next few days if you can manage it."

"Pretty sure I pay you to decide those things for me."

She smiled smoothly. "You don't really have the option to say no to her."

"Considering she signs my paychecks, you're right," I said. "She's scary, isn't she?"

"Are you kidding? She's terrifying." Bridget grinned. "I want to *be* her when I grow up."

My eyebrows arched slowly. "You're well on your way."

Bridget laughed. "Good luck with the kids, and . . ." She paused.

"And what?"

Bridget gave me a stern look. "Don't be too mean to the neighbor."

"I'm never mean," I said evenly. She pursed her lips, and I gave a slight eye roll. "I'm just not . . . warm. There's a difference."

Bridget gave me a condescending pat on the shoulder as I passed by. "Mm-kay."

The drive home from the facilities took forty-two minutes instead of the normal twenty-five, considering it was at the peak of rush hour as opposed to my usual nine-thirty arrival during the weekday. Most coaches didn't get home that early during the regular season, but this was the sole reason I'd made the move to Buffalo, a family-friendly atmosphere and an owner who promised me flexibility to be home, at least a little bit more time for my kids. Pearl Pennington may be the most intimidating woman I'd ever met, but she was also a devoted mother and grandmother.

Even though the streetlights came on earlier in the winter thanks to daylight savings, there was still a hint of light in the sky when I turned my truck onto the curved street of the two-story brick home in East Amherst I'd bought when I signed my three-year contract in Buffalo.

My ex-wife would've hated it.

Not big enough. Not fancy enough. And maybe that was why I loved it so much and placed a cash offer the day we walked through.

It was a little outdated—something I'd address eventually—but we had room to grow, and I liked the tall trees weaving through the neighborhood, offering us a modicum of privacy from the homes behind us and to the left. On the right, though, we had less privacy. Only a wooden fence running through a backyard that needed updating and some oak trees that provided shade for our lawn, though the thick trunks took up residence in Scott and Patty's yard.

The retirees were kind and friendly, giving us a warm welcome when we moved in, in the form of baked goods and the offer to let my kids use their pool anytime they wanted in the summer. This year, though, they'd decided to winter in Arizona, escaping Lake Erie's brutal lake-effect winters until the middle of February.

The lights on inside their house drew a narrow-eyed gaze from me as I turned my car into my own driveway.

Don't be too mean to the neighbor.

Even if she'd meant it as a joke, the admonishment from Bridget stuck like mud in my throat. I was so frustrated over this entire turn of events that I could feel my temper lifting the hairs on my arms as I climbed out of the truck and slammed the door hard enough that the truck rocked a little bit.

My ability to stay calm under pressure earned me the nickname Ice Man in college. Nothing—and I mean *nothing*—got under my skin to the point where I couldn't keep my cool. If I could bottle that up and sell it, I'd never need to work another day in my life, but unfortunately, no one had figured out how to extract that personality trait straight from the source.

At the moment, I found my patience rather thin, temper bubbling dangerously as I crossed the yard between our house and the neighbors'.

Every light was on, and as I drew closer, the loud thump of music from inside had me clenching my teeth.

A shriek of laughter pierced the air.

Maggie.

I pinched my eyes shut. When was the last time I heard her make a sound like that?

They were always begging to do something fun. Begging to go visit Uncle Griffin, and I damn well knew why.

He was the fun one. The guy who let them make a mess. Who bought them frivolous toys and spoiled them rotten.

Before she'd left, my wife accused me of being stingy. Not just with my spending habits but also with my time, with my affection.

Cold-blooded, she'd said. I wasn't—or at least, I didn't think I was. But something needed to change. The thought hung heavy in my brain, and I struggled to breathe through the sludge of failure again, a running list of all the places I fell short.

As a husband.

A coach.

A housekeeper lecturing me on how I needed to parent.

Now I had a fucking stranger making judgment calls on behalf of my kids. It was all too much. The helpless feeling of wanting to do something well, something right, turned the corner into heat and anger and frustration.

I took a pause on the front step and tried to rein in the out-of-control feeling kicking my pulse dangerously high.

It didn't work.

I knocked on the front door, tipping my head back to stare up at the darkening sky.

The music kept playing. Another scream of laughter and a loud thumping sound had me cursing under my breath.

I knocked again. Louder.

No change from the inside.

Heat crawled across my neck, a dull burning sensation that could either be the beginnings of a heart attack or flames threatening to split my skin open.

Whoever this woman was . . . she would hate me by the time this was over, and I couldn't even bring myself to care.

Chapter Three

Lily

"Are you sure this is a good idea?" I asked, peering over Maggie's shoulder.

"Yes," she answered with an emphatic nod.

"I guess we'll find out when we get to the bottom." I tapped her arm. "Helmet."

"Do I have to?"

"Oh yeah." I tucked some hair behind my ears. "And you guys do this at home?"

The kids shared a look. "Yup," they said in tandem.

"Why do I feel like I'm getting manipulated right now?" I muttered.

Bryce handed his sister a bike helmet—the one he'd snagged from their garage about thirty minutes earlier, when they'd convinced me this was *the best idea ever*—and she tugged it on, buckling the strap under her chin.

The moment they turned those big dark eyes in my direction, I was a fucking goner. As a kid, this was exactly the kind of thing I would've wanted to do, if our house had an entryway like this.

The staircase was big, the kind of sweeping, grand thing that dominated all the homes built in that time period. Scott and Patty had told me to make myself at home when I arrived.

Was this what they had in mind?

Highly doubtful, but with Maggie's concussion risk minimal and me holding her tight from behind to bear the brunt of any unforeseen carnage, I decided this was exactly what I'd be doing if I were babysitting two adventurous preteens in my own home.

I mean, my home didn't exist, because the nomad lifestyle didn't really jibe with a mortgage, but *if* I had a home, and *if* I had a big-ass staircase, I'd do some mattress surfing in a heartbeat.

"Ready?" I asked.

She wiggled herself farther down onto the mattress, nodding over her shoulder. "Ready."

Bryce must've turned up the music, because the heavy pop bass echoed through the entryway as I pushed us off from the top step. They were fun kids, but holy hell, the music choices of this generation left something to be desired. I'd have to pour bleach down my ear canals before the night was over.

I pushed off, and Maggie squealed as the mattress slid down the wooden steps, the jarring bounce, bounce, bounce left me laughing breathlessly and in possession of a bruised tailbone when we came to a halt as the front of the twin mattress hit the ground. We toppled forward, ass over teakettle, and Bryce pumped his fists in the air, running down the steps after us.

"That was awesome!" he yelled over the music.

I flopped onto my back with a groan. "I'm too old for this."

"Can we do it again?" Maggie's face hovered over mine, her grin almost impossible to resist. "That was the funnest thing I've ever done."

As I pushed up to a seated position, I gave her a droll look. "I thought you did this at home."

Her eyes widened. "Oh, um, yeah, but our staircase isn't this big."

"Hmm." I rolled over onto all fours and took stock of the bruises I'd likely feel the next day. "I'm not convinced, young lady."

A sound came from the front door, a tapping barely heard over the music. "Bryce, can you turn that down, please?"

The music cut off immediately.

Bang, bang, bang.

"Oh shit," Maggie muttered.

My eyebrows raised. "You allowed to say adult words like that?"

"No," she hedged, her attention fixed on the front door. "Bryce," she said in a resigned tone, "I think we're about to get grounded for life."

"Your dad?" I asked. Maggie nodded. "He can't be *too* mad, right? You told me he'd be fine with you staying here." My gaze darted between them. "*Totally cool. The coolest.* Those were your exact words."

They didn't answer, and boy, that did not bode well for me.

Exhaling heavily, I stood up, hopping over the edge of the mattress. In the mirror on the wall, I couldn't help but groan at the mess of my hair, half falling out of the braid I'd done that morning. There was more angry banging at the door, which meant I was going to meet the dad with shitty-looking hair and the fresh knowledge that his kids had totally played me.

"Coming!" I yelled, almost tripping on one of the dog's toys. "Bryce, can you hold on to him so he doesn't run when I open the door?"

Both kids were sitting at the bottom of the stairs, Bryce with a firm grip on Larry's collar. Larry gave me a droll look. *Please,* that look said, *like I'd go anywhere.*

I took a deep breath and pulled the door open, pasting a friendly smile on my face.

It dropped immediately because *Oh shit* was right.

The man standing at the door was big and hot and frowning. I had to admit, his resting bitch face was even more frightening than mine, because boy oh boy, there was intent behind it. When he leveled those eyes on me, I had to fight every instinct not to take a step back.

His gaze traveled to his children, and the momentary relief on his face was the only thing to convince me that I didn't need to be all that intimidated.

"Hi, Dad," Maggie said quietly. "Did you have a good day at work?"

"Maggie, Bryce, get your things." A muscle in his jaw twitched. "Right now."

They didn't move, and I cut a quick glance over to Hot Angry Daddy. God, he was a specimen, wasn't he? Sharp jawline. Straight nose. Long eyelashes. Dark hair in need of a haircut. A broad chest and heavily muscled arms covered by a black quarter-zip with a sports logo on the chest, the kind that a million dude bros would wear running errands on Saturday. Tall too. All in all, he was exactly the kind of man one would think of when you said he was *climbable*.

Not that *I* wanted to; it was just a general observation. There were all sorts of people in the world who liked to climb things. Mountains. Stair machines. Tall people. Sounded like way too much work to me, thank you very much.

His gaze didn't move from his kids, probably because they were doing an excellent impression of children who did not want to go home.

"I told Bridget where we were," Maggie insisted. "It's not like we hitchhiked across town or anything."

Bryce muttered something about a flight under his breath, and she elbowed her brother. Hard.

Hot Angry Daddy was not particularly swayed by this argument. "As much as I'd love to trade stories of the things you *have* done the last year, I am not in the mood right now. I had to leave work before I was supposed to because I was worried out of my mind not knowing what happened to you two."

Guilt gnawed at my stomach, but I kept my mouth shut.

"But I—" Maggie interjected.

"*Now*, Maggie," he said firmly.

The kids stood, even though their movements were sluggish and slow, and when Bryce let go of Larry to get his backpack, the dog did exactly as I'd feared, darting straight past me to march up to our newest guest and let out a growly little bark.

Larry's bitch face wasn't bad either.

"Larry," I admonished, "get back here."

Naturally, Larry did not feel like listening to me, because why would he? Now he wanted to go outside, trotting his little ass toward the open door.

Their dad leaned over and grabbed the dog's collar, and Larry growled ominously in his throat.

Well, as ominous as a fifteen-pound dog wearing a diaper could sound.

When Hot Angry Daddy lifted his head, the annoyance lighting his eyes made me swallow against a dry throat. "Please take the animal," he said calmly.

Our fingers brushed when I took hold of the collar, and the heat of his skin had me rolling my lips over my teeth. My fingers hadn't thawed out since I got to this frozen wasteland called Buffalo, and it was really tempting to ask him if he'd let me put my hands underneath his shirt just to warm them up a little bit.

The impulse was so strong, imagining his horrified reaction so amusing, that an ill-timed laugh bubbled its way up my throat. I covered it with a cough. Barely.

His gaze turned to me and narrowed dangerously.

"I'm Lily," I said. "I'm house-sitting for Scott and Patty."

"I know."

That was it.

Nothing else.

No name, no attempt at niceties—and you can bet your ass I narrowed my eyes right back. He saw it, too, and I swear there was a flash of a challenge in his eyes, like he was daring me to push him.

There was no way he could've known, of course, that a challenge of that nature was like waving a red fucking flag in front of a bull.

Because the kids were gathering their coats from the kitchen, we were left alone in the entryway, and his eyes tracked over my messy hair, dipping briefly to the flash of ink under my collarbone and the other on the inside of my arm.

No one—not even Hot Angry Daddy—was going to make me feel self-conscious. I got looks like that all the time. That was the other thing about people. They were so painfully predictable that I just barely stemmed the eye roll. Judgment left me feeling cold, too, the frigid blast of air coming from this guy cutting straight to the bone, much in the same way the weather did.

One was natural. Something we couldn't control.

The other was man-made, and ugly when unleashed simply because someone couldn't control their reactions to a person whom they knew nothing about.

Bryce hitched his bag over his shoulder and stopped to give me a high five. "Thanks for letting us wreck your house," he said, his adorable little half smile melting my heart.

"Anytime."

Maggie's eyes were red rimmed, and she flung herself against me for a hug, which I returned with an awkward pat on her back. "This was the best afternoon of my whole life," she said between sniffles.

In response to the slightly dramatic statement, her dad looked skyward, his chest expanding on a deep breath.

I cleared my throat. "It was great to meet you, Maggie. Come play with Larry anytime, okay?"

Oh, he did not like that I said that.

His gaze locked on mine as his children marched through the door and headed back to their home.

Larry growled in his direction again, and I turned, opening the door behind me to set him in the office. Instead of an annoyed bark, Larry gave me a look like *Is this completely necessary*?

The silence between us stretched into something horrifically awkward, and when I finally quirked an eyebrow, his expression flattened.

"I was waiting for an apology, but I guess that's not coming," he ground out.

Slowly, I folded my arms over my middle and stared him down. "An apology? For what?"

"Oh, I don't know—keeping my kids without permission? You're a stranger; you could be a serial killer, for all I know."

I smiled. "Only for overbearing men who have the social skills of a potato."

"A—"

I took a step closer, and his eyes flashed. "You should be thanking me."

"Thanking you? Are you drunk?"

"No," I answered smoothly, "but at the moment, the desire is high." I cocked my hip out. "You could thank me for playing with your kids all afternoon—and they're delightful, by the way. They must take after their mother." His eyes flashed, but it was going to take a hell of a lot more than that to stop me. "I have a strong suspicion they lied to me about being allowed to ride a mattress down the stairs, but . . ."

His gaze was relentless. "And what made you come to that astute observation?"

My eyes tracked every inch of his body—head to toe and back up again—and that felt like a good enough answer. His nostrils flared, and he took a step closer too.

"They should have been at home. The moment the housekeeper came over here and told them they weren't allowed to stay, any adult with a modicum of rational thought would've sent them back home with her."

"Oh, believe me, my ability to think rationally was in short supply when that woman opened her mouth." At my icy tone, his head reared back slightly. "She was lucky I didn't break her fucking nose, the way she spoke to them."

His eyes flickered, but he didn't ask.

I tilted my head. "So no, I didn't send them home with her, because she was a bitch who shouldn't have been responsible for anyone's children." I smiled again. "So I let them stay here. We played. We made a mess. I fed them dinner. And now they're all yours, asshole. *You're welcome.*"

With that, I yanked on the door, ready to slam it in his face. His hand smacked against the surface, and I let out an incredulous huff.

"Wait," he growled, color high in his cheeks. "Just . . . hang on. I was frustrated and worried, and maybe I . . ."

His deep voice trailed off, like the words were physically hard for him to say.

"Maybe you jumped to conclusions and snapped at me for something that wasn't actually my fault?" I asked.

He licked his bottom lip. "Maybe," he said between gritted teeth.

"If that's your attempt at an apology, we've got a long way to go, buddy. Now, if you'll excuse me, I have a house to clean up, and you've pissed me off enough for one night." I stepped forward and knocked his hand down, taking unholy, leg-shaking, orgasm-level satisfaction at the way his hard features slackened with shock, right before I slammed the door in his face.

Chapter Four

Barrett

"I'm not quite sure where we went wrong with you two. Were we too strict? Not strict enough?"

I laid my head back on the couch and sighed. "You were plenty strict, Mom. I think it just . . . happened."

She snorted. "This does not *just happen*, son. I saw one of those videos online; people are so clever with what they notice, you know?"

"So I've been told." I tried not to sigh again, but when one calls their mother for advice on how to handle the kids who are pissed at him, this is not the direction one wants the phone call to go in. Suggestions of help were the expectation; instead I was getting a full breakdown of why I was so uptight.

"These two girls—women, I suppose—have a whole channel—or profile, whatever you want to call it—dedicated to just you and your brother. Isn't that something?"

I smiled grimly. "It's something, all right. I don't think I want to know what they were talking about."

"Oh, it wasn't bad. After the game on Sunday, one of the girls made such a fuss about how she saw you smile at one of the players, and she went back and compiled footage of every time you've smiled on camera in your professional career—even when you were still playing. Can you believe it?"

"People are incredibly bored and have developed a crippling need to be seen online because it makes them feel significant to a toxic degree. So yes, Mom," I said evenly. "I can believe it."

There was a slight pause. "Aren't you going to ask how many times you've smiled on the sidelines?"

"No."

"It was a short video, son." She made a concerned humming noise. "I don't remember you being like that when you were younger. I have lots of videos of you in college; when you and your brother played at Oregon, you smiled all the time. Maybe I should send her some of that." She paused.

I focused my attention on deep-breathing exercises. I could list plenty of things that had changed since then, since a time when I'd smiled more. Smiled easily.

Tenuous though it was now—like we were inching out onto an iced-over lake and hoping it wouldn't break—in high school and in the early years of college, I still had a decent relationship with my twin brother. I hadn't married Rachel yet; that came right after college, when she told me she was pregnant with Bryce. She had changed things between us more than anything had.

It was difficult for me to extricate my feelings toward my ex or label them properly. Our marriage, though it had lasted close to a decade, was like navigating an abandoned minefield, except I was the only one setting off explosions.

I didn't hate her, but if we'd been married much longer, it might have danced right up to that edge. But even admitting that made me uncomfortable. The sound of my kids upstairs in their bedrooms filtered down into the family room. Bryce laughed at something, and I closed my eyes.

I couldn't ever really hate Rachel, because she'd given me the two best things in my entire life.

"I'm failing them, Mom," I admitted. "That whole situation with Jill and then the neighbor just made it impossible to ignore. What if I don't know how to do this by myself?"

"Oh, nonsense. You're not failing anything. You have two wildly intelligent kids who can run circles around most adults, and they know they're safe with you. Why do you think they act out so much?"

A wry laugh escaped before I could stop it. "Is that why?"

"Yes," she insisted. "They know, deep down, you'll always be there for them. You won't send them off to live with Rachel, because you love them more than anything in the world."

I thought about Maggie's face when we'd gotten home a couple nights earlier. I'd tried to apologize to them, too, but she merely swiped at the tears on her cheeks and marched up to her bedroom, saying she had homework to do and it wasn't necessary to tuck her in.

I'd waited, of course, until her lights were out and I knew she was sound asleep before quietly entering her room. Crouching next to her bed, I'd swept the tangled hair off her face and watched her sleep for a few minutes, my heart breaking into a million pieces for her and her brother.

"How are they supposed to know that?" I asked. "I work a hundred hours during the season, Mom."

"Because you found a place that would allow you to be home for a good chunk of those hours. Took less money, too, didn't you?"

"A bit, yeah." I scrubbed the side of my face, unwittingly thinking about the slew of articles at the end of a rough season. "Though if you ask anyone, it was probably a mistake and I'm ruining Buffalo because of it."

"Nonsense," she said again. "You just need some more time to settle in. And that has nothing to do with your kids."

"Doesn't it?" I sighed.

"Barrett, your kids act out because that is what children do at their age. They think they're almost adults, so they test the limits of everything. You and your brother did the same thing."

"I know Griffin did," I answered dryly. "Not sure I followed in his footsteps."

"No. You never dared break the rules, always wanted to do things the right way because you were afraid of what would happen if you didn't," she said, and it sounded just sad enough that I felt a lump in my throat. "Have you talked to your brother lately?"

This was the minefield my parents had to navigate, and guilt over that gnawed at my insides. "No," I admitted. "I, uh, messaged him when he broke his arm in the preseason, and we've texted a few times since then, but that's about it. He's busy. He's got Ruby now, and he's back on the field. You know I'm the last person he wants to hear from."

"I don't know that, no. I think you'd be surprised at the reaction you'd get if you tried." She sighed. "The kids text him; he's told me that. I know he'd love to see them again once the season is done."

"I have to get through the next two games first, Mom. Figure out what I'm going to do with the kids. I hardly have time to sleep, let alone interview someone else to watch them until the season is over."

"Well, your father and I can fly in the day after Christmas. I leave tomorrow to help your aunt Billie after her surgery for a little bit, but as soon as I'm back from that, we'll get a flight to Buffalo."

One of the kids ran down the hallway upstairs, and a door slammed, the muffled sound of their voices filtering downstairs. "Thanks, Mom."

"They do all right at the office this weekend?"

"Yeah. Bridget already told me she's getting a massive raise if childcare is now part of her job description, but they love her, so it went fine. Bryce was asleep on my office couch when I got done with film Thursday night. Reminded me of when he was a kid and I could never wake him."

She hummed. "And they sat in the box at the game today?"

"Yeah. With Bridget and Janie."

"It was a tough loss, son."

"I know."

There was a telling pause, and I stared up at the ceiling, waiting for what was undoubtedly coming next. "Your quarterback stepping in between two guys taking swings didn't help my nerves. Especially when he shoved that lineman twice his size."

I closed my eyes. "Mine either."

"Still think it's unfair they gave him a flag for that." She sighed. "You didn't look too happy with him on the sidelines."

Only my mother would've been able to see through that. Archer, hot off the fight and the flag—both of which triggered his impulse-control problem—came jogging off the field with his fist raised like he'd scored a fucking touchdown instead of costing us fifteen yards.

He'd met my gaze unflinchingly, only dropping his when my jaw clenched ominously and one of the veteran players pulled him aside. I was not the coach who'd get in his face, yelling and screaming. Public berating wasn't my style, but most guys who'd played under me for a long time knew that my silence was sometimes far, far worse.

"I need him to be a calming presence in moments like that," I said. "Not make things worse. The second he interjected himself, the entire offensive line got involved."

"Your brother was always the one stepping in the middle of the fights," Mom said lightly. "You always stayed back and pulled your teammates away."

Another difference between us.

"It was messy at the end of the game, but they're a young team." I rubbed the back of my neck. "Still learning how to keep composure in big moments."

"And afterward?"

I snorted. "I'm assuming you saw my postgame press conference?"

"Maggie is a natural with the media," she answered diplomatically. "My personal favorite was when she started choosing which journalists asked questions and then answering them for you."

"Yeah, everyone loved that. But she wasn't supposed to be up there with me, and she knew it the moment she marched up to my chair."

"She still punishing you?"

"With every inch of her being," I answered wearily.

Mom hummed. "She must have loved that neighbor."

My jaw tightened instinctively. An unwilling image of Lily's face played like a movie in the back of my head—flashing, angry, dark eyes and full lips on an irritating loop that I couldn't rip from my subconscious. "That makes one of us."

"Oh, come on, how bad can she be?"

"She slammed the door in my face when I tried to apologize. She was letting them ride mattresses down the stairs. Who knows what else they did. She's a menace," I said hotly.

"Dearest son, one of the great loves of my life, I have seen you try to apologize," Mom said with a smile clear in her voice. "You are good at a lot of things, honey. That's not one of them."

I stood from the couch and walked over to the sliding glass door that overlooked the backyard. Without permission from my brain, my eyes flicked over to the house to the right. Lights blazed from just about every window, just like they had the other night. An unfamiliar sensation churned through my stomach, and I turned away. Because we had an early game today, we were home just before dusk. Now the sky had darkened, and the neighbors' twinkling Christmas lights flickered through the trees.

We didn't even have a tree up at our house yet.

Too busy. Always too busy. Working my ass off at a job I loved, to make sure my children had everything they wanted in life—but stretched so fucking thin I could hardly take the time to enjoy it.

The sound of footsteps descending the stairs pulled me back to the present. "Mom, I'm gonna go talk to the kids. Text me if you book flights."

"Love you, Barrett."

My eyes closed. "Love you too," I said gruffly.

The kids whispered urgently to each other, and when I turned around, Maggie was connecting her school laptop to the TV screen in the family room.

"Hey," I said gently, not wanting to run them off now that she was finally willing to talk to me again. "What have you two been doing up there?"

Bryce cleared his throat, shuffling some note cards in his hand. My eyebrow rose at the way he'd slicked his hair back like mine. "Working on something," he said. His skinny chest puffed out. "We have a presentation for you."

"Do you?"

Maggie was in one of her best dresses, a pleasant smile fixed on her face, but her eyes looked a little manic. "Won't you please take a seat, Father?"

"'Father'?" I repeated under my breath. "What do you two want?" Just before the screen flickered to life, I sighed. "Maggie, if this is about getting a dog again, you know we are not in a position to have something that requires that much responsibility. Someday—"

"It's not," she rushed to interrupt. "It's not about a pet, I promise."

I glanced at Bryce, and he beamed. It did nothing to quell my suspicion. I took a seat on the couch and gestured for them to continue. "Let's hear it."

They stood together at the front of the room, whispering something I couldn't hear. Bryce showed her something on his note cards, and she nodded.

Maggie pressed the button on the remote and the TV flared to life. The title made me raise my eyebrows.

The FOOLPROOF post-school plan to make Dad's life as easy as possible!

by Bryce and Maggie King

(we are listed in alphabetical order even though I, Maggie, did most of the work)

"Foolproof, huh?" I asked.

Bryce nodded, then cleared his throat. "It's estimated that as many as fifteen million kids in America are left unsupervised in the hours between when school lets out and when their parents return home from work," he read, voice a touch robotic. "The gap in after-school care is a m-major crisis, as most programs focus on elementary-age kids and have strict ele-eligibility requirements."

I covered my mouth with one hand, hiding the beginnings of a smile, while Maggie mouthed the words along with him as he read.

She took the stack of cards. "According to a research study at Princeton, the key to successful after-school care for middle school–age kids"—she gestured between herself and her brother—"is strong interpersonal relationships"—her eyes flicked up to mine—"a focus on the kids' individual interests, and excellent group management by supportive, friendly adults."

Sitting back against the couch cushions, I let my hand drop, and the sight of my begrudging smile bolstered both of them. Bryce took the cards from his sister and told her to flip to the next slide. But before she did, they both gave me a breathless, questioning look.

"I'm listening," I said gently. Knowing Maggie, she'd have a program outlined for the front office at work, along with a preliminary budget and a place at the team facilities where this program would be taking place. She'd probably try to rope the players into being group leaders or something, under the guise that it would help them on the field too.

The first slide included their school pictures, and underneath, a bullet-point list of what they were most interested in.

Maggie rattled off her list in a rushed exhale. "I like dogs, kittens, music, drawing, and nice, friendly people who let me do crafts and could maybe teach me how to bake."

My left eyebrow quirked at the specificity.

Bryce stepped forward. "I like dogs, playing soccer, watching sports, and nice, friendly people who also like dogs and are super fun to play with and don't yell at us for talking."

My brows flattened.

Maggie gave me a nervous look. "In light of our interests, we've done extensive research on our proposal." Briefly, she rolled her lips between her teeth, then pressed the button to go to the next slide.

Lily's picture was right in the center. Her hair was down around her shoulders—*so* much hair—and she stared straight into the camera with a tiny smile playing around her lips, which was an expression I'd definitely not seen on her the other day.

That woman would only smile at me if I were on fire.

"Absolutely not," I said.

"Dad," they both said.

"You said you'd listen," Maggie continued.

"Yeah, you promised," Bryce said.

I folded my hands in my lap and prayed for patience. "Where did you get that picture?"

Maggie and Bryce shared a look. "The internet?" Bryce answered.

"Where on the internet?"

Maggie straightened her shoulders. "Her social media. She's not very active. She hardly posts anything. But *no one* can hide online, Dad."

I dropped my chin to my chest and tried to keep breathing. "All right. Keep going."

"Lily Townsend is twenty-eight years old, never been married, no kids, and comes *highly* recommended," she said.

My head snapped up. "From who?"

"Scott and Patty," Bryce answered. "We have text messages of them giving her a glowing recommendation." He elbowed his sister.

The next slide was screenshots of their texts with our neighbors, and I read the exchange with a growing sense of despair.

They loved her. Said she'd be phenomenal at taking care of them. She was smart and polite. Even though she kept to herself, they absolutely fell in love with her when they met her in Phoenix on their winter visit last year. She was house-sitting for someone there, and the rest, it seemed, was history.

"Lily loves to bake, and you know I've been wanting to learn." My daughter clasped her hands together over her chest. "It would be *educational*, Dad."

I closed my eyes. "That's a stretch, and not nearly enough to convince me it's safe to let her watch you. We don't know her."

"You didn't know Jill when you hired her, either, and she was horrible."

My eyes opened, landing unerringly on my son. "She came highly recommended from her agency, and they have a thorough vetting process."

The kids looked at each other meaningfully, which honestly, never boded well.

The next slide had me leaning forward. "Maggie," I said in a warning tone. "Where did you get that?"

"Well, it's not *hard* to run a background check on someone," she hedged. "She doesn't have a criminal record. Not even a parking ticket, Dad."

I pinched my eyes shut. "Kids, I appreciate how much work you put into this—"

"Dad, please," Bryce begged. "We really like her. She didn't treat us like little kids or try to play stupid games. And she's next door until Mr. Scott and Mrs. Patty get home in February. It's not a forever thing, you can find someone else; but until we're on Christmas break and Grandma and Grandpa can come, this could work. Then you're in the offseason and you're always home when we get off the bus. This is a good compromise, and—and you know what, um, John F. Kennedy said about compromise, right?"

"I can't say that I do."

"Compromise does not mean cowardice," he told me. "I learned it when I did that project last month."

Slowly, I sat back again, watching incredulously as Maggie's eyes filled with tears that she tried to blink away and Bryce's cheeks pinked with his vigorous defense of their idea.

"We can stay over there until you're home," Maggie said in a trembling voice. "She was nice, and she didn't make us feel like bad kids. Half the people we've hired always remind us how much trouble we're always getting in."

Her eyes. God, the way she was looking at me cut me straight through to my ribs.

"Please, Dad," Bryce whispered, clearly trying his hardest not to get emotional. "It's just for a couple weeks. When you're done with the season, we won't need her help—but you're gone so much. We just want to like the person who's taking care of us."

I couldn't remember the last time I'd cried. When I even came close. When they were born, maybe?

But the sight of them begging me for this had a lump building dangerously in my throat.

"Will you just . . . just talk to her?" Maggie asked. "Please?"

There was no other answer for these two, who held my heart in their hands and didn't even realize it. "Yeah, I'll talk to her," I managed in an uneven voice.

They were on me in the next heartbeat, laughing and whooping, and I wrapped my arms tight around them, pressing my face into the tops of their heads.

"Thank you, thank you, thank you!" Maggie gushed.

Bryce squeezed me tight, the kind of hug I hadn't gotten from him in so long. "Thank you, Dad."

I swallowed around the lump and forced it down, forced it somewhere safer. "She may not say yes," I reminded them gently. "But I will ask."

Maggie lifted her head, happy tears making her eyes sparkle. "Right now? Then we don't have to come to the office tomorrow after school. Bridget said she was going to put us to work, and I don't know if she was serious, but I don't really want to find out."

I exhaled. "Yeah, I can go ask her right now. But that means you've got to let me up."

They jumped off the couch, still whooping in glee. "She's totally going to say yes," Bryce said. "I just know it."

I ran a hand through my hair and straightened my game-day Henley—the black long-sleeve I favored for home games, though it usually stayed hidden underneath my coat. "All right, all right. I'll, uh, I'll go now."

My kids couldn't be happier. But as I walked through the front door and stared across the expanse separating my yard from the one temporarily serving as hers, my face flattened.

Knowing my luck, she'd see it was me and slam the door in my face. Again.

"Be nice to the neighbor," I said under my breath, and exhaled heavily as I strode toward the house. "I'd love to hear your advice now, Bridget."

Music was audible again as I approached the front door; the recognizable strains of old Christmas songs had me sighing.

Get a fucking tree for your kids, I chastised myself. No wonder they were seeking out someone else's company. I swiped a hand over my mouth, took a deep, fortifying breath, and pressed the doorbell.

"Just a second," her voice called through the door, punctuated by the dog's gruff, growly attempt at a bark. The furry face appeared in one of the windows flanking the door, and I swear that animal glared at me.

The door opened, and the sight of her polite smile made me blink, but the moment she saw that it was me, the smile disappeared like someone flipped a light switch.

"Oh, it's you." Her arms immediately crossed over her chest. She wore all black—leggings molded to her long legs, a slinky shirt clinging to her torso, and a fuzzy Santa hat on the top of her head. "What do you want?"

It was on the tip of my tongue to tell her that I wanted to be anywhere in the continental United States than right there, but I didn't think it was wise. Her dark eyes were heavily lashed, but her face—high cheekbones and a delicate jawline—was free of makeup.

Underneath her collarbone, I saw that flash of ink again, but given the amount of cleavage on display in the deep V of her shirt, I kept my eyes right on hers.

Something about her was disconcerting enough that I almost spun on my heel and marched right back home. The thought of my kids was the only thing that kept me in place.

I exhaled slowly, dredging up the words even though they were the last thing I wanted to say. "I'd appreciate if we could have a moment to talk." I licked my lips and kept my face even, despite the anxious coil growing tighter and tighter in my chest. "I have a proposition for you."

Chapter Five

Barrett

"I'd tell you to make yourself at home, but . . . I don't really feel like having guests."

Lily hopped over a pile of tangled Christmas lights, and while she let the dog out of the office, I eyed the stacks of clear bins everywhere. Literally everywhere.

A nine-foot tree stood in the corner of the living room off to the side—branches empty except for the white twinkling lights. Bins of ornaments sat on the floor around it.

The mantel was covered in thick garland, lights peeking out between the green, red, and gold ornaments affixed to the branches. A collection of nutcrackers in varying shapes and sizes stood at attention on the dining room table.

"These are all Christmas decorations?" I asked.

Lily let out a low laugh, and the sound of it made me grit my teeth. "There's more in the basement, but I'm just starting with the basics. Seems like they go all out."

"I wouldn't know," I admitted. "We moved in last spring." Released from its prison, the dog trotted over in my direction, his underbite surprisingly menacing, considering his size. "Your dog is wearing a diaper."

"Is he, now?" she said dryly. I gave her a look, and she shrugged one shoulder lightly. "He's old. Sometimes they need one."

The dog growled under his breath, and I held up my hands. "I'm not judging. Calm down. God, you two are a friendly pair, aren't you?"

The expression on Lily's face might have been a smile on anyone else, but on her, it looked more like a threat. "I know you didn't come to talk about the dog."

"No, I didn't." I straightened, crossing my arms over my chest. "I've heard a lot about you from my kids this week, Lily Townsend."

One dark, graceful eyebrow arched slowly. "I didn't tell them my last name."

"No, but Scott and Patty did." The rest of that story could come later.

For the moment, that seemed to appease her. "Wouldn't it be nice if I also knew yours? I came up with all sorts of clever nicknames the other night, but I'm not sure if any of them are fit for repeating publicly."

I mimicked the rise of her eyebrow with one of my own, and her lips curled into a tiny little smirk that had a tremendously strong effect on my blood pressure.

"I'm Barrett," I said. "I thought maybe Maggie and Bryce gave you their entire life history when they were here."

"I know a few things." She strolled past me into the kitchen, smelling faintly like gingerbread cookies and something even sweeter. "They have an uncle that they love but never see; his fiancée, Ruby, is funny, according to Bryce. They're getting married this spring. You're divorced. Ex-wife lives in California, and the kids see her for two weeks during the summer and every other Christmas. Your parents moved from Michigan to Arizona when they retired, and they're the *best grandparents ever*. Also, they want a dog and you keep saying no."

My brow furrowed briefly, an unfamiliar kind of vulnerability leaving me twitchy. Unfortunately for Lily, it also left me feeling a little snappy. "Where are you from?"

She paused at the change in my tone, doing a slow pivot in the kitchen once she was on the other side of the island. "All over, but I was born in Texas. Haven't lived there in about ten years, though."

"Where have you been living since then?"

Her tongue peeked out, licking lightly at her bottom lip as she started unpacking a bin of angel figurines. "All over," she repeated. "I tend to get restless if I stay in one place for too long. I like experiencing different places, different people. Though I could pass on the people most days."

"How did you meet Scott and Patty?" I asked, walking closer to where she stood.

"I was house-sitting in Arizona and met them at the neighborhood pool. It's one of those communities with all the activities, you know—pickleball, shuffleboard, pools, all that jazz." From the bin, she pulled out a tiny gold angel playing a trumpet, setting it carefully on the counter. "I know this will shock you, but they liked me. So they asked if I'd be interested in watching their house for a couple months. While they were gone last year, they had a water leak—came home to a big old mess in their kitchen and didn't want to risk something like that happening again."

Lily's movements were slow and careful, treating each item like something breakable, even if it wasn't. She took the time to study each one. In turn, it gave me the opportunity to study *her*.

The name didn't fit, I decided. *Lily* gave the impression of something delicate and feminine. But that wasn't her. Her arms were toned, strong. Her features sharply defined. Despite the ease in which she got under my skin, some long-neglected part of me could admit that she was, in fact, beautiful.

Uncomfortably so. It wasn't an approachable kind of beauty. Like, she'd stab the shit out of you if you came too close.

The last item in the bin had her movements slowing, a snow globe wrapped in packing material. Inside it was another angel, with wings spread wide, and Lily seemed to forget she wasn't alone for a moment, watching the little bits of white float through the water. Her eyebrows furrowed, a wrinkle appearing between her eyes.

My notice of her, all those little details, the irrational desire to ask her what it was about that thing that made her uncomfortable, made my skin tight and itchy and, as a result, more than a little pissed off.

"So you just, what? Job-hop until you find someplace you want to stay?" I asked, tone giving away just a hint of my disbelief.

Her shoulders stiffened, defensiveness drawing her up a couple of inches taller.

She unpacked the last angel and set it carefully next to the others, closing the lid on the bin with a sharp click and moving it off to the side. "Not everyone wants to be anchored down."

"How do you afford that?"

"Why, do you need a sugar momma?" Her eyes met mine, a dangerous gleam setting my teeth on edge. "I like my men more pliable."

"I bet," I answered smoothly.

Lily held my gaze for another beat, then picked up a bag of frosting, leaning over a cooling rack full of cookies. In fact, half the island was covered in cookies. Dozens of them, cut in various holiday shapes. Most were bare, but about ten were decorated so perfectly that I found myself blinking repeatedly.

While I watched, Lily's hands moved in smooth gliding motions, draping a thin white line of frosting around the edges of a cookie cut into a snowflake. The song in the background changed, a Bing Crosby song that my mom loved filling the room, and it was all so unbearably nostalgic that I forgot what I was doing there.

She switched bags, piping thicker lines of white until the thin outline was completely filled. "Did you come for a purpose, or did you just want to ogle my cookies, Barrett?"

At the innuendo, my face went a little hot. "I came for a purpose."

"Oh, goodie. I'd love to hear it."

But still, Lily didn't give me her attention, instead focusing on the frosting she'd just piped with a thin metal tool that left the surface perfectly smooth. When she sucked on the tip of her finger, I saw a tiny tattoo inked on the inside of her middle finger.

"Who are you making cookies for?" I asked.

"Your kids," she answered distractedly, picking up another bag filled with pale-blue frosting for the next cookie. There was another small tattoo on the inside of her bicep, half hidden by the sleeve of her shirt. Before I could stop myself, my eyes lingered on it, trying to decipher the shape.

"I'm surprised you'd give me anything, after what happened the last time I was here."

She paused, her eyes flicking up momentarily. "I said your kids, not you."

I managed to stifle an eye roll. Barely.

"What do you want, Barrett? All your man-looming is making me twitchy, and if I fuck up these cookies now, you're really going to piss me off."

"You swear like this when my kids were around?"

"Oh yeah, if you'd shown up ten minutes later, we were going to do a lightning round to see how many curse words they could use correctly in a sixty-second span."

My smile was tight. "You're making this so easy on me, thank you."

Finally, she let out a huff and straightened, tossing the frosting bag back onto the counter. Her hands went straight to her hips, gaze locked on mine. "Make what easy on you? I don't know why you're here, except to annoy the hell out of me and make this feel like an interrogation."

"In a way, it is."

Her dark eyes narrowed. "Explain."

Could I actually do this?

In the last few years, I'd had to tolerate a lot. A wife who slowly learned to hate me because I didn't meet her expectations. A brother who thought I'd ruined his life. Kids who consistently pushed every boundary erected to keep them safe. And now I was voluntarily putting myself at the mercy of the blue-haired siren with more ink than manners and an attitude that made me want to break something.

Then I thought of their faces. Thought of how badly they wanted this.

"I'd like to offer you a job."

Her features froze; then Lily blinked. Blinked again. "I'm sorry," she said slowly, tilting her head to the side. "Can you repeat that?"

I sighed heavily. "If you're available, I'm wondering if you'd be willing to watch the kids after school and the first couple days of their Christmas break. I'll pay you."

Her mouth fell open. Then snapped shut. "Is this a joke?"

"Believe me, my sense of humor isn't that good."

Lily's gaze tracked over my face. "Now, *that* I believe."

This time I *did* roll my eyes. "Can you do it or not?"

"I can, but that doesn't mean I'm saying yes." She crossed her arms and kept studying me like I was a puzzle she couldn't quite piece together.

"I'll pay you well." I told her the hourly wage the last housekeeper had made, and her eyebrow quirked again.

"I didn't ask about money. That's not why I'd say no."

I let out a harsh breath. "Then why?"

Just like the other day, she took a leisurely glance from the top of my head, down to my feet, and back up again, ending with a pointed look at my face.

Because of me.

Right.

Undoubtedly, my cheeks were flushed by her thorough gaze and just . . . her.

"I don't like most people, but I like your kids," she said. "And I know they liked me. What I can't figure out is why you'd agree, given . . ." She gestured to her general person, like she was an explanation in and of herself.

And in a way, she was.

Everything about her set me on edge, and not in a good way. Not because of her hair, not because of her little tattoos everywhere. It was just . . . her.

"You made my kids happy," I said as evenly as I could manage. "And when I have happy kids, they pull a lot less shit on the person in charge of them."

Lily laughed, a bright, tinkling sound that didn't match her at all. "Oh, come on. How bad can they be?"

Slowly, I raised an eyebrow. "Well, as part of the slideshow my kids created trying to convince me you're the perfect person to watch them after school, Maggie included the federal background check she pulled on you."

"What?"

"Believe me, that's the tip of the iceberg with that child. She is terrifyingly smart, and underestimating her would be the biggest mistake of anyone's life." I shook my head and sighed. "Bryce is smart, too, he's just . . . less scary than her. They're both good kids. Well mannered, respectful—but when they're bored, they come up with horribly reckless ideas. My hope is that if I compromise with them on this—on *you*," I amended, studying the flicker in her eyes when I said it, "they'll compromise back by not breaking any laws for the next couple weeks."

For a moment, Lily didn't speak. Then her eyes narrowed. "What kind of laws?"

"Do you want a list?" I asked dryly.

"If I'm going to be responsible for them? Yeah, maybe. I'm not . . . I'm not a nanny. I've never babysat anyone's kids."

For the first time since I'd walked in, Lily's demeanor held an air of discomfort. Or that's how it looked, at least.

"I don't need a nanny. I just need someone to hang out in the same place as them after school. Make sure they don't eat sugar all night, do their homework." I wiped a hand over my mouth, letting my arm fall back to my side. "I work a lot. My job—especially right now—is very demanding. But I'll be in the offseason in a couple weeks, and a lot more available."

"What exactly do you do?" she asked.

It had been so long since anyone didn't know me—as a player, then as a coach—that I'd almost forgotten what it was like to just be Barrett.

"I'm a coach," I told her, watching her reaction carefully.

"Huh. What kind of coach?"

"Football. For the professional team here in Buffalo."

She blinked. "Yeah, right."

I pointed to the logo on my Henley. "I'm the head coach for the professional football team in Buffalo."

"I thought head coaches lived in giant glass mansions and had a fleet of staff running their life."

"You know, I've tried, but they keep quitting."

Her eyes narrowed. "I think you're screwing with me."

"Trust me, I have better things to do with my time than lie about my job."

"So you're, like, famous," she said. "People want your autograph and shit."

I held her gaze. "Yes."

Lily was unimpressed by this. "I suppose there's no accounting for taste. So your entire week, all those hours you're working, revolves around telling people what to do, and they listen. You say jump, et cetera, et cetera."

Ah, so we were playing the subtext game? Got it. I let out a painfully slow, deep breath and tried valiantly to tamp down the surge of annoyance flickering in my chest. "With a few notable exceptions, yes, I suppose so."

She nodded seriously. "Obviously, I'm counting your kids as those exceptions, because . . ." She gestured between us, leaving the implication hanging like an unpinned grenade. A habit of hers, I was finding.

I licked my bottom lip. "My kids listen to me most of the time. I meant the owner of the team. The GM. That sort of thing. They don't answer to me."

"That must be trying."

A shocked gust of air left my mouth as I stared at this woman. It was strange—almost uncomfortably so—to have someone meet me head-on with such . . . I didn't even know. Audacity?

Deference, I was used to. A certain level of respect afforded to me because of my position, even when the players did stupid shit like start fights and skip meetings. But based on the absolutely unbothered way she spoke to me, she *wanted* to piss me off. There was a distinct tightening in my stomach, and I ignored it.

"I'll survive," I answered dryly.

"Oh, goodie." She picked up the bag and finished frosting another cookie, then wordlessly moved on to the next. How did she keep her hands so steady? They were all *perfect*. "You know, I think I've changed my mind."

"What?"

Her eyes moved up to mine. "Don't blow a gasket. I changed my mind about the pay."

"Are you negotiating for more?" I asked incredulously.

After another beat, her gaze returned to the baked goods. "Tempting, but no. I don't want you to pay me at all."

I pushed my tongue into the side of my cheek. "Don't be ridiculous."

Her hand made this seemingly innocuous little swirling motion on the frosting bag, and the result had me leaning in a little bit. How was she doing that?

"It strikes me as a horrible idea to put the two of us in a transactional relationship," she said calmly.

One eyebrow arched slowly. "Does it?"

"You're witnessing this, right? I'm no friendlier than you, cupcake, and my verbal filter is low on a good day, which is why I typically avoid people as much as possible."

"So it's not just me," I mused. "I'm unbearably touched."

Lily let out a small laugh. "Oh, it's you." Her eyes flicked between mine. "When someone tells *me* to jump, I don't have the best track record."

"You don't say," I said in mock disbelief.

In that woman's mind, she was flipping me off with the biggest middle finger she could conjure. I could see it in her eyes. "I don't *people* if I can help it, but I liked your kids. And since I spend most of my time alone, it won't hurt me to, you know . . . socialize or whatever for a couple weeks. Maybe I'll come out of this a friendlier, warmer Lily, who knows."

"Not sure my kids are that powerful," I muttered.

Her lips pursed slightly, but she didn't respond right away.

"You must be nicer at work than you are to your neighbors."

"I'm nice to Scott and Patty."

"If you think I'm not asking them questions about you after this, you're out of your mind. How am I supposed to know *you're* trustworthy?"

"You don't," I told her unflinchingly. "But you can trust that I'm honest. I don't want to be here asking you this. I want to be at home with my kids because I don't get very many nights like that this time of year. Even being home before they go to bed is a fucking miracle in this job, and that's because I've had to fight for it. If you say yes to this, you're doing me, and my kids, a massive favor. I don't like asking favors of anyone outside of my parents, because then I feel like I'm in their debt. It makes me uncomfortable, but I'm here because they matter more than that."

It was so much more than I wanted to say. And judging by the look on her face, she could tell. There was a slight softening, but other than that, Lily Townsend, with the bright hair and the tattoos, did a good job of keeping her facial expression locked down.

"Starting tomorrow, I'm assuming?" she said.

Relief had me exhaling heavily. "If you're available. I'll text you when I'm almost home, and you can send the kids over. You won't even have to see me."

She tilted her head. "Well now, that's the perk you should've started with. I would've accepted immediately."

"I'll keep that in mind the next time."

With brisk movements, Lily slid a dozen cookies into an airtight plastic container, the layers separated by wax paper.

"I'll have some rules," I told her.

Her full lips tipped up at the edges. "Of course you will."

Her big dark eyes met mine as she pushed the cookies in my direction.

"Does that mean I get to eat some since I'm carrying them back home?"

"No."

My jaw clenched, and she noticed, her smile deepening like she couldn't help it. On both sides of her cheeks were the tiniest little dimples, and my stomach went tight that I'd even noticed.

"Regretting the offer already?" she asked, fake sweetness dripping off every inch of her tone.

"Yes," I answered grimly.

Chapter Six

Barrett

If there weren't three perfectly serious women staring back at me across the conference room table, I'd have thought the entire thing was a joke.

I schooled my expression and took a quick glance at the clock. Eight minutes left in this meeting; then I'd need to be back in my office to take the call from the kids.

Pearl noticed. Her hawklike features sharpened at the small tell.

"You're being awfully quiet about this," she said. "Even for you."

"I'm . . . thinking."

Bridget cleared her throat delicately. "That means he hates it."

The marketing admin next to Bridget . . . I couldn't remember her name, but she had a mass of curly brown hair and a small nose piercing that winked underneath the overhead light. "No, he doesn't hate it. That's just his uncomfortable face."

I wasn't entirely sure I'd ever had a conversation with her before in my life, but apparently she knew me well enough to have me pegged on that one.

"And you all think this is a great idea."

"Yes," they answered in unison.

Curly Hair slid a folder across the table. "Our social media reach went up by forty-two percent when we shared those clips."

Jaw tight, I opened the folder and glanced at the numbers she'd shared. It was all neatly displayed in bright colors. Maggie would've loved it. Proof that her impulsive decisions yielded incredible results. With a flick of my thumb, I closed the folder, tented my hands on the table, and stared back at them.

When I didn't say anything, the three women shared a look. Finally, Pearl rolled her eyes and slapped the table with her open palm, the bottom of her wedding ring clinking loudly against the surface. "If you take too much longer, I may die sitting here waiting, and I cannot tell you how pissed off I'll be if I die in the middle of a marketing meeting."

I exhaled slowly. "I hate it."

Bridget smirked. The marketing admin deflated in her chair, and Pearl narrowed her eyes.

"Why?" she asked. "If you're gonna break Wren's heart, you might as well give her a good reason."

Wren. Got it.

The woman in question pursed her lips, trying and failing to hide her annoyance.

"Wren," I said as gently as possible, which is to say I was also failing, "I'm not sure I'm comfortable putting my daughter out there like that."

She straightened in her chair and pulled another folder out, sliding that in my direction too. "I can understand that—but with all due respect, Coach, she's already in the public eye. Last week, they showed her on *SportsCenter*'s top ten plays of the day when she took over your press conference." I pinched my nose and sighed. Wren shared a look with Bridget, who nodded. "She's a scene stealer. If we do something like this, we can control the narrative of how she's featured in the public eye. We can highlight what makes her so great—her intelligence and her humor and the amazing relationship she has with the players."

The second folder wasn't data or neatly printed bar graphs. There were logo mock-ups, and a sketch of a set that looked like a talk show.

The yellow background had me lifting my eyebrow at Wren. "Yellow, huh?"

Bridget smiled. "I know everything."

I gave my assistant a dry look. "I'm aware." I glanced back down at the proposal.

Midfield with Maggie—a recurring social media series featuring Maggie King, an informal question-and-answer segment featuring three to four players each week.

Pearl cleared her throat. "It's a good idea," she said. The diamonds on her rings sparkled, and I had to wonder if the jewelry she had around her fingers and neck and ears were worth more than my house. "It gets your kids involved."

"Bridget's already planning to blackmail me for more money if she has to watch them again."

Bridget pursed her lips. "I did say that, didn't I?"

"More than once, actually."

"In my defense," she sighed, "Maggie was showing me how she learned to forge your signature, and I didn't particularly feel like having that knowledge inside my head. She would love something like this," she pointed out, giving me one of those stern looks that didn't leave me much room in the way of arguing.

"So let them be here more," Pearl said. "You think I'd walk all the way down here for a shitty idea, King?"

"No, ma'am."

"All our competitors will be jealous they didn't think of it, and I love making people jealous. You gonna deny an old lady what few pleasures she has left in life?"

Bridget smothered a smile. Wren bit down on her bottom lip, and I cleared my throat.

It didn't seem like a great time to remind her that she was a billionaire who could buy whatever pleasures she wanted.

"No, ma'am."

She waved her hand. "Would you quit calling me *ma'am*? Makes me sound old."

Bridget widened her eyes meaningfully, flicking them over to the clock.

Five minutes.

I tapped my thumb against the table and stared down at the logo.

"And if the narrative shifts in a way I don't like?" I asked. At any given moment, I could conjure two dozen headlines that lingered painfully long after they were published . . . the ones that had pitted me and my brother against each other, had made my divorce tabloid fodder. The thought of my daughter risking any of that was worth pissing off the boss.

"Then we stop," Wren said. "Right now, it's something fun and lighthearted. And if Maggie stops having fun, if you have any concerns that the marketing team doesn't notice first, we're done. No questions asked." She looked to Pearl, who gave a short nod. "We're just doing this as a test run."

I was so used to having eyes on me, dissecting things like how often I smiled on the sidelines, when I got visibly angry during a game, if I was making the right moves as a coach. But this wasn't that, and I didn't want to be the kind of father who applied my own shit to my kids' lives.

My daughter would perish from excitement. I gave them a weary nod. "Fine."

Wren smiled widely. "Thank you. We'll do one feature before the end of the season and see how it lands. If it does what I think it will, we'll run it maybe once a month during the regular season so it doesn't take up too much time during practice."

"During practice?" I asked incredulously.

"What do you think *midfield* means?" Pearl barked.

"End of practice," I countered.

Wren looked a lot tougher now that she'd gotten her way, crossing her arms and lifting an eyebrow. "Last thirty minutes. I want chaos in the background; that's what will make it even funnier. Players will spend less than a minute with her for each rapid-fire round. If we get to the point where it's too much, we'll schedule separate filming."

I slicked my tongue over the edge of my teeth. "Fine."

Pearl reached out, patting Wren's arm. "I told you he'd come around."

"Did I have a choice?" I asked dryly.

"Of course. If you'd said no, we would've asked someone else. But like it or not, you've got a daughter who's so great at this, she can't seem to help herself."

"And if I change my mind now?"

She arched a silver eyebrow. "Too late for that, King. Now your choice is gone."

My entire life seemed to be comprised of women meant to humble me, and I tried not to think about what universal meaning I was supposed to glean from this. Bridget was no help; she watched the exchanges with the bright glint of humor in her eyes, no doubt recalling every minute detail so she could go home and tell Janie the best part of her entire day.

"When would you like to do this, Wren?" I asked. "I need to coordinate with my parents since they'll be watching the kids."

"I thought Bridget was doing that?" Pearl asked.

Bridget shook her head. "Oh no, he has a neighbor who's helping until his parents get here."

"Ah."

"She hates him. Like, *a lot.* But still she's helping."

I gave Bridget a quelling look, but she ignored it.

Pearl glanced between us. "Why does she hate you?"

"Why *doesn't* she hate me might be a better question," I answered, exhaustion pulling at my frame. "My very presence seems to offend her."

Pearl sighed. "I know a few men like that."

I cut her a questioning look.

"Not you, Mr. King." She adjusted the diamond pendant around her throat. "If you made me want to claw my skin off because you breathed too loudly, I'd have fired you already."

"Good to know."

Bridget slapped a hand over her mouth to stem the laughter.

Wren stood, stacking her folders into a neat pile, then tucking them beneath her arm. "I'll email you some dates, Coach."

I rubbed my hand over my jaw. "Thank you, Wren."

Just as she turned to leave the conference room, the door flew open and six feet four inches of quarterback barreled her over. Wren shrieked, papers went flying, and Archer's arms darted out to keep her from toppling onto the floor.

"Oh fuck, sorry—wasn't watching where I was going." He set her back to see if she was okay.

Wren's cheeks were pink, and she ripped her arms away from Archer's grasp. "It's fine."

He scratched the side of his neck; then Pearl stood up and smacked him on the back of his head. "Help her pick up the papers," she snapped.

Archer was a bit too slow to move, and Pearl muttered something about idiotic young men, giving him a steely-eyed glare. "Wren, come see me tomorrow morning. I've got some other ideas," she called, just before stalking out of the room.

"Okay, Pearl."

"You call her *Pearl*?" Archer asked. "Aren't you scared?"

Wren barely stifled a sigh. "No."

He picked up a single sheet of paper and held it out to her. She didn't meet his eyes, but her lips were set in a firm line as she snatched it out of his grasp.

I'd already come around the table, joining Bridget to help gather the remaining pieces on the floor. I handed Wren the folder once we had them gathered, and she gave me a tiny smile.

"Thanks, Coach."

Bridget tapped her watch before she left the room, and I nodded, folding my arms over my chest before turning to face Archer, who was still watching Wren as she hustled down the hallway.

"She hates me."

"Well, you did just about give her a concussion, so I'm not sure I can blame her."

He crossed his arms, too, mimicking me, and I took the measure of his facial expression.

"You were supposed to come see me this morning," I said.

Archer's jaw was tight, his mouth firm, and his stance prepped for a lashing. "Got busy in the weight room. Saw you in here and thought I'd see if you can talk now."

"I can't," I told him. "I always take a call from my kids at three thirty, and I never miss it."

"Look, I know you're pissed at me about the game," he said, dropping his arms and setting his hands on his hips, a defensive gesture that wasn't lost on me.

"I'm not pissed, Archer."

He lifted an eyebrow. "You looked pissed."

"I was disappointed," I amended.

His eyes flickered, face closing off immediately. "I was standing up for my team."

"And I need you to be a leader. Not an instigator." I dropped my arms, too, hoping that instead of defensiveness, he saw it as a softening. "We can't always do whatever we want out there. Your teammates require a level head for game management. Preparation during the week so that you can override the impulses and rely on your training."

"Aren't my instincts what got me here?" he asked with a slight tilt to his head. "No one's questioned them until *you* got here."

"Yes. And as we get older, we hone those instincts until they're a weapon. If we don't, it's just unrealized potential."

He let out a short scoff, frustration weighing down the sound until it dropped like a lead weight between us.

"You're the last player in every morning. You spend half the time in the film room that you should. You've missed meetings," I told him. "We've had to fine you multiple times for other offenses too."

"And last season, the team had three wins." His chin jutted out. "We'll finish over five hundred this year if we win out, and we have a shot at the playoffs."

I held his gaze. "And that's great progress, Archer, but I'm not satisfied with just over five hundred—*or* relying on other teams to lose in order to *get* that playoff shot. I want championships, and I think you do too. You and I have to work together if we expect that to happen, and you cannot keep skating by on your arm alone."

"And my legs," he said lightly. "They're not bad."

Irritation flared, and I had a memory of a conversation like this with my brother in college. He never seemed to take things seriously, and I'd never been able to wrap my brain around that.

"I need you to do better, Archer," I told him, voice low and serious. "Not because they're paying you an unholy amount of money, but because you are smart and fast, and were born with the kind of talent most guys can only dream of. And because you don't want your legacy in this league to be a guy who peaked in college and couldn't put in the work once things got serious. It's never going to be easy. It shouldn't be, not if you want to be the best. But right now, I can't tell that you want much of anything except a paycheck. And you get that whether you're on the field or not."

The arrow hit its mark, color creeping up his cheeks and his mouth flattening.

"I'm still the starter," he said. "As long as you're here, your wagon is hitched to mine, Coach."

My eyes narrowed slightly. "You're the starter . . . for now."

He exhaled in a short burst. "You wouldn't bench me."

"Wouldn't I?" I crossed my arms and held his gaze.

Archer let out a quiet laugh. "No, you won't. Because everyone would question your sanity if you did. You wouldn't risk your job—or your reputation—to prove that point. You want everyone to think you're perfect."

The sharp thwack of his comment caught me somewhere between my ribs, dead center bull's-eye, but I kept my face impassive.

"My kids are going to call any minute," I told him. "If you want to join me tomorrow morning, I'm having breakfast with your receivers. I think we're done here."

He didn't answer, simply looked down at the ground for a second, then shoved the conference room door open and stormed back out into the hallway.

I sank into a chair, braced my elbows on the table, and let my head rest in my hands.

Chapter Seven

Lily

At 3:25 p.m. the next day, Larry lost his shit at the front window, heralding the arrival of my two new afternoon buddies. By the time I opened the door to make sure they remembered to head in my direction, Maggie and Bryce were already sprinting up the driveway. In their hands were bags full of winter gear for recess, even though there was hardly any snow on the ground, their cheeks were flushed, eyes bright with excitement.

"Well, hello," I greeted them.

"Hi," Maggie said. "What's your favorite color?"

I blinked. "Favorite color to wear and use in everyday life? Or just in general? Because there's a difference."

Maggie peeled off her yellow coat to reveal a yellow shirt. "To wear," she stated.

"Black," I said on a sigh. She did not look impressed by this answer. "Boring, I know, but it goes with everything."

"Huh." Then she shrugged. "Mine is yellow. My bedroom is yellow, and my bedspread is yellow. I tried to get Dad to paint the family room yellow, too, but he said no. I'd have yellow everything if I could get away with it."

I smiled. "How's it going, Bryce? How was your day?"

"Stupid. We didn't learn anything." Bryce dumped his backpack onto the floor, tossing his winter bag on top of it. "I don't understand why we can't just do, like, a four-hour school day. I think the teachers would be happier too."

"Wouldn't you learn less if you were only there for four hours?" I asked.

Maggie unloaded her mountain of crap in the same pattern as her brother. "It's impossible not to learn *anything* at school. You're just not paying attention, which is why your grades aren't as good as mine."

Bryce rolled his eyes but didn't seem too bothered by his sister's ribbing. He sat on the floor to greet Larry, grinning when he received a small lick on the hand for his efforts. The kid was gentle, I'd give him that. I figured a preteen would come in like a freight train, but he was surprisingly careful when he reached forward and scratched Larry on the top of his head. Then he straightened, taking a deep inhale. "Did you make cookies?"

"Of course. It's the greatest thing I can contribute to society as a whole—fresh-baked cookies on a cold school day."

His eyes rolled back in his head like he'd already bitten into one. "What kind?"

"Chocolate chip," I whispered.

He was halfway to the kitchen when he called over his shoulder, "Can I have however many I want?"

"Let's start with two and work from there, okay?"

Maggie tugged off her winter cap, her shoulder-length hair lifting into the air from the static electricity. I shook my head and tried to smooth it down. "And your day, little miss?"

"Good," she stated with a shrug. "I like school. It's easy."

"The smart kids always say that," I whispered.

"That's what my dad says too." She paused. "Or that I'm too smart for my own good."

"Yeah, you and I are going to have a chat about the background-check thing."

Maggie scrunched up her face. "Sorry."

I squeezed her shoulder. "It's all right. Just don't go spreading it around the neighborhood, okay?" When she nodded solemnly, I nudged her toward the kitchen. "Go get a couple cookies before your brother eats them all."

There was something a little magical about making good food for people. I was no chef, and I ate takeout more than I should, but even for someone like me—a wanderer who spent more time alone than not—I could've sat in that kitchen all day to watch them eat those still-warm cookies.

From the opposite side of the island, I watched them do a video call with their dad. The kids chattered happily, telling him about school and what homework they had. Bryce showed him a close-up view of the cookies, and I fought a smirk over the fact that Barrett might go his entire life never tasting my baked goods. After about fifteen minutes, they hung up, eyes already wandering to the rest of the cookies.

Bryce had chocolate in the corners of his mouth, but all it took was one pleading expression and I let him have a third. Maggie too. While they finished those, I poured them both a glass of cold milk.

"Feel better?" I asked when Maggie patted her belly. She nodded, then let out a contented hum.

Bryce burped, then gave me a panicked look. "Sorry."

"I told you to stop at two," I sighed. "The youths never listen, do they?"

The kids laughed.

Bryce called for Larry, then paused at the slider. "Can I take him outside?"

"Larry doesn't really play," I warned him. "But yes, use that green leash by the door. Put your coat on, though; it's cold."

He groaned. "I'm wearing a sweatshirt. I'm fine."

"Coat," I instructed. When he begrudgingly did as I asked, I gave Maggie a look. "That's the sort of responsible-adult thing I'm supposed to say, right?"

His sister grinned. "Yeah."

I made a swiping motion across my forehead. "Whew."

She gave me a shy look, then flung herself against my midriff, wrapping her arms tightly around my middle. "Thank you for saying yes," she said.

"You're welcome," I answered, almost unbearably touched. That pesky feeling stuck in my throat, unwilling to be pushed down with a firm swallow.

Maggie didn't make eye contact when she pulled away, just darted off to dig something out of her backpack. From the front pocket, she extracted an envelope, and once it was in my hand, my stomach flipped at the sight of my name in blocky masculine handwriting.

"My dad wanted me to give you this," she said. "Can I go outside with Bryce?"

I nodded absently, my thumb running over the edge of the envelope. "Don't forget your coat."

When Maggie was out of the room, I took a seat at the island and tucked my thumb under the edge of the flap, pulling it across to tear open the envelope.

Inside was a piece of paper with the football team's logo.

Barrett King, Head Coach.

God, he was so official. This job of his told me a whole hell of a lot.

Competitive. Organized. Demanding. Intensely focused.

It made a whole lot of sense after my two interactions. I tried to imagine him giving a motivational speech, and snorted.

Don't lose, because I said so. Growl, growl, look at my hard jaw and scary dark eyes.

He'd cross his big, muscly arms and glare around the room, and do it so effectively that all the overgrown man-children playing ball would do his bidding out of fear for what would happen if they didn't.

But I had to admit, he clearly loved his kids, because there was no fucking way he would've asked me to help out otherwise. With his list of rules clutched in my hand, I watched them try to play with Larry, a smile tugging at my lips when the dog did nothing but sit down and stare up at Bryce. He laughed loudly enough that I could hear him through the closed slider.

They'll be hard to leave, a little voice whispered. My eyes felt a little gritty, and I blinked repeatedly.

Eventually, I'd move on from this place. I always did.

As the years passed, it got a little harder, a little bit more tiring. Each time I packed my bags, I had a lingering sense of disquiet, an insistence I wasn't quite ready to heed that said I should stop.

That I should find a place that feels like home and allow myself the freedom to stay.

For a few more moments, I watched the kids play and let that insistence spread, just a little bit further. I pinched my eyes shut and let out a shaky breath.

When I opened them, Barrett's handwriting came into view.

"He was not joking, was he?" I murmured.

After-school rules

1. Homework done before dinner

2. No screens until after dinner

3. Dinner should have protein, fruit and veggies. No treats until all of that is finished. I will be reimbursing you for groceries, so please keep receipts.

There was more, but I just . . . stopped reading them. He underlined *will* twice, which had me rolling my eyes.

"Quit yelling at me, Coach," I muttered.

With my brow pinched, I folded up the letter and put it right back into the envelope. The kids came inside with Larry tucked in Maggie's arms. I swear he gave me a look like *See? She likes carrying me*. He was always happiest when someone else did the walking, lazy little brute.

"Do you guys have homework?" I asked. "Should you do that before dinner?"

I could practically hear the man shouting about rule number one in my ear.

This is why there are rules, growl, growl. This is why I should've paid you.

And it was precisely why I *didn't* want him to pay me. Having that man as my boss would give me hives.

They looked at each other. "Can't we do it later?" Bryce asked. "I've been doing schoolwork all *day*."

For a moment, I thought about what I should do. What a responsible adult might choose in this moment. But even using the word *responsible* felt like dismissing an entire gray area when it came to preteen best practices. In a situation like this—to do the homework now or later—there was no such thing as right and wrong. Barrett would disagree, of course, but Barrett wasn't here, was he?

Maggie and Bryce were young, and when I was their age, the last thing I wanted was to go straight from school to doing homework. It was a fight oft repeated during my childhood.

It would be so much easier if you just got it done. You always want to do things the hard way, don't you?

I blinked the memory away, fighting a different kind of tightness in my throat.

"Yeah," I said, giving him a smile. "You can do it later. Anyone up for a *Mario Kart* battle before dinner? I can order some pizza, if that sounds good."

They whooped loudly, flinging off their coats to run into the family room.

◆ ◆ ◆

True to Barrett's word, I never saw him. The whole week passed in a pleasant blur of my new routine: ease into my morning with a cup of coffee, do yoga in the family room, run on the treadmill downstairs, beg and plead for Larry to pee outside while we both froze our asses off, then make some lunch. I'd usually read or, if it wasn't too cold, explore the area until it was almost time for the bus to pull to its squeaky stop in front of the house.

What shocked me most was how much I looked forward to them getting dropped off every day.

Even though he'd be embarrassed to have me admit it out loud, Bryce was one of the sweetest boys I'd ever met. He asked for my advice about things at school—drama with friends and a girl he thought was pretty. He checked in to see if he could help clean up dishes after dinner. And as much as he teased his sister, he was constantly looking out for her, in little ways that had me on the edge of melting into a happy pile of goo.

At the base of whatever smelly-preteen-boy antics he participated in, Bryce was kind, and that was the best sort of kid to have around.

And Maggie?

I'd decided quite quickly that Maggie was my platonic child soulmate.

She was adventurous and quick-thinking. She had a voracious thirst for knowledge and wanted to know how and why I did everything. The moment I suggested anything, she was instantly game. And she was constantly asking about the places I'd lived, the things I'd experienced.

"Whoa, what's this?" she asked, scrolling through the pictures on my phone.

I nested in next to her on the couch. "That's Sedona. Beautiful, isn't it?"

She nodded, zooming in on the shots I'd taken of the red rock formations. "You like hiking?"

"Sometimes." I tapped on another one. "That was too hard for me, so I didn't make it all the way up, but the view at sunrise was incredible."

"Wow," she breathed.

Bryce popped up from his spot on the floor. Larry had inched close enough that Bryce could gently scratch his back.

"What's that?" He pointed to another series of pictures higher up in my camera roll as his sister scrolled.

"That's the lighthouse in Holland, Michigan." I picked one of the pictures so he could see it. "Lake Michigan was pretty rad. I visited a couple years ago when I was trying my hand as a travel influencer."

"My dad and uncle were born in Michigan."

"Yeah? I liked it there. People were nice. Only spent a few weeks along the lakeshore and then made my way back down into Chicago for a while. Turns out, I hate social media, so I didn't last very long and I sure didn't make any money doing it."

Maggie nodded, eyes wide. "It's a jungle out there."

"What did you do in Chicago?"

I smiled. "Worked as a barista for a few months. A friend of mine from high school let me crash at her place; then when the weather started turning cold, I hightailed it back south. Stayed in New Orleans for about six months."

"I think I'd forget all the different places if I moved around so much." Bryce lingered on a photo of the beach, zooming in on the swell of the waves and the blood-orange sunset that made the water glow.

"Sometimes you forget details, yes."

"Don't you want to remember everything?" Maggie asked. "I would."

"Every new place I go—even if I'm just visiting for the weekend—I get a postcard," I told them. "I have a book I can take with me because it's easy to pack. And on the back of each postcard, I write down my favorite things from that place. Memories I don't want to forget."

"Cool," Maggie breathed. "Can we look at it sometime?"

"Sure."

"Where's your favorite place you've ever lived?" Bryce asked.

"That's a hard question to answer," I told him. "They're all really different. The sights, the food, the people."

"Where are people the nicest?" he asked.

I pulled in a deep breath and let it out as I thought about that. "I tend to find a few nice people everywhere I go," I answered. "But I spent about five months between Michigan, Illinois, and Iowa. They were really friendly. Big fans of bringing over casseroles when they see someone new in the neighborhood." I tilted my head. "And banana bread."

He leaned down to kiss the top of Larry's snout, and that little shit dog gave him such an adoring look, I couldn't help but shake my head. If I tried that, he'd probably bite my face off. "Why didn't you stay there?"

"Winter," I said seriously. "I've made it this long in my life avoiding it."

The kids looked at each other. "Lily? I hate to break this to you . . ." Maggie said slowly.

"I know. Why did I come here?" I glanced outside, where a few inches had fallen overnight. It was beautiful, sure. Everything was blanketed in white, fluffy shit, and yes, I could admit that it did make the Christmas vibes stronger. More Christmas-y. "I guess I wanted to try something really different this time. Even if it means all that cold stuff."

"Dad told us all about lake-effect snow before we moved here. He used to live in Michigan, so he knows all about it."

"Yeah, I don't know what that means." I glanced between them. "Isn't that just normal snow?"

They shook their heads. Profusely.

"Huh. Well, I guess I'll figure it out, won't I?"

"It's a Great Lakes thing." Bryce hopped up and transferred Larry to his lap. "At least you can go sledding in snow. Can't do that anywhere else."

"I've never gone," I told them.

Oh, how their little eyes brightened. "You've never gone sledding?" Maggie asked. "Can we go now? There's a super-fun hill a few blocks over behind a church."

I glanced between them. What was it with these two? They held a strange power over me, and I wasn't quite sure how it happened. "We have a few hours until your dad comes home," I said slowly. "And you still have to finish homework." They held their breath. "But yeah, let's do it."

Which was how we found ourselves walking home six blocks in the dark, our winter clothes soaked and heavy, my feet giving the distinct, prickly feel of hypothermia or . . . whatever happened to people who didn't know how to dress for snow.

"I can't believe you wore those shoes," Maggie laughed, most of her face covered by the red-and-white scarf tied tight around the bottom half of her face. Her snowpants made a loud *swish, swish, swish* sound as we turned onto their street.

"I thought they were waterproof," I told her.

"That doesn't mean they're winter boots."

"Well, I know that *now*."

"You could've borrowed some of ours. My dad has boots in the mudroom," Bryce said, scooping up some snow and packing it into another snowball, which he tossed into the sled he was dragging behind him.

"I think they would've been a little big for me, dude." I shivered. "How do people survive in this weather? I think my feet are going to fall off."

"Can we go to our house?" Maggie asked. "I know it's not close to bedtime, but we should put our coats and stuff into the dryer so they're ready for school tomorrow."

Bryce's eyes widened as he slowly came to a halt. "We haven't even done homework yet. Dad's gonna be pissed."

"Your dad won't be home for a while," I assured him. "We've never missed getting it done, right?"

"Right," they answered. Bryce jogged ahead, hitting a bump in the sidewalk that sent his pile of snowballs flying.

"I've got the key," he yelled.

As Maggie and I walked up the driveway, I tipped my head back to study their home. There'd been no need for me to go in there yet. All week, Barrett had made a concerted effort to be home in time to get them showered and in bed. I'd get his text around 8:30; then the kids would pack up their stuff, trudge across the yards, and wave when they'd unlocked the door. I'd watch from the front window until Barrett's headlights appeared on the street before retreating back into the suddenly quiet, empty house.

One week, and it was starting to feel weird when I was there by myself.

That feeling would pass, eventually. It was just part of my normal routine: miss the place I'd left and let the next fill that gap.

The gap left by these two would be bigger, though. A scary sort of big I'd never encountered.

I shoved that thought aside, refusing to follow it any further.

Bryce held the front door open as we toppled into the house, and Maggie and I shimmied out of our boots on the large rug in the entryway. The warm air had me moaning in relief. *My* kingdom *for a hot bath.* I thought about the large soaking tub in Scott and Patty's bathroom and made a mental note to try it later.

The kids disappeared into the mudroom, and I carefully shrugged off my puffy coat—which was far more fashion forward than it was functional, as it turned out—and rubbed my hands together once I'd set my wet gloves on top of the coat.

It was a two-story entryway with a large staircase leading up to a second floor—wood floors and trim stained in a warm color, and nondescript tan walls that could stand a freshening up. The room to the left was set up as a den of sorts, or maybe an office—two walls of bookshelves and an overstuffed leather couch facing a TV mounted on the wall. A desk was tucked against the other wall, but nothing on its surface gave away any hint of who might use it.

There wasn't much in the way of art that I could see on any of the walls, but on the shelves, there were framed pictures of the kids. Maggie and Bryce as toddlers, with missing teeth and painted faces. At a beach, their arms slung around each other. In front of a Christmas tree, holding matching stuffed animals.

I rubbed my hands up and down my arms and shivered, glancing longingly at a fuzzy blanket draped over the arm of the couch.

"Fuck it," I muttered, pulling it off and wrapping it around my shoulders. Next to the couch on the floor was a pair of overlarge house slippers, lined with sherpa and covered in soft black material. I shoved my feet in and sighed at how much warmer they made my poor little toes.

"We're gonna go change, Lily," Maggie called, the sound of their feet pounding up the stairs drowning out my murmured reply.

The pictures were mostly of the kids, Barrett rarely appearing in any of them.

Because he was behind the camera? Or because he wasn't there?

More than once, I'd stopped myself from googling Barrett King. Nothing good would come from it, I thought. It was hard enough not to pepper his children with questions about what kind of father he was. They were so sweet and smart and funny. He couldn't be a total asshole, right? Curiosity in any one person didn't typically yield the kind of fruit I was looking for, not given the life I'd led.

It wasn't like I was devoid of male companionship in my travels. I'd had some great companionship. Didn't-even-have-to-fake-it-with-anyone kind of companionship. But in general, I didn't chase it. I didn't care enough to chase, because that was just one more thing that might make it harder to leave, and no one had time for that shit.

Me. I was no one.

I stopped, studying a framed photo of a slightly younger Barrett wearing a football uniform, face stoic as he stood in between an older couple that must be his parents. The chiseled features were sweaty and dirty, black streaks under his eyes, and the curves of the muscles in his arms covered in streaks of green from the grass. Even then, not a smile in sight.

Maybe his face would break if he tried. Shatter from the force of trying to use muscles that never got used. Then I snorted, because what a fucking hypocrite I was. Like I was any better.

There was a side effect to living the life I led. Meeting people all over the country, from all walks of life, you started recognizing patterns. You could see things that others might not always see so quickly. And in Barrett King, I could see, quite clearly, someone who'd work himself to the bone trying to prove . . . something.

I wasn't sure what; I didn't know him well enough. But it was enough of a mystery that the seed of interest had been planted and bloomed before I could do a damn thing to stop it.

There was a shuffling sound behind me, and I tilted my head as I continued to study the picture in front of me.

"Does your dad *ever* smile?"

There was a beat of silence.

"Sure," answered a deep voice. "Just usually not at prickly neighbors with the social skills of a potato."

The sound of Barrett's voice—low and measured and just that hint of annoyance—had me pinching my eyes shut and fixing my face into an approximation of a polite smile before turning.

There was no way it worked. I probably looked like I'd chugged battery acid instead.

How did a man that big ninja-sneak into a house? From the size of him, he should have heavy footsteps, a telltale slam of the door. Something to prepare a girl to, you know, not be snooping in his shit.

"You're home early," I said slowly, absolutely hating the blush flooding my cheeks. Blushing! For fuck's sake. I couldn't remember the last time I'd been embarrassed by anything, and the fact that this time it was him made me want to scream into a pillow.

"I did text you."

"I didn't hear anything," I hedged, shifting away from the bookshelf like I hadn't been two seconds away from riffling through family albums.

Of course I hadn't heard anything. My phone was in my soggy-ass coat.

"It's not my fault you ignored your phone." It was the utterly unrepentant gleam in his eyes that made my cheeks feel hot. Maybe I wasn't the only one who liked pushing buttons. "Just keep in mind who's breaking the rules here. I did uphold my promise that you'd never have to see me."

"You didn't say I could never come over," I argued. "Should I have left your kids in their freezing-cold clothes?"

"No." His eyes started at the top of my head, which was covered in a black beanie with a fluffy white pom-pom on top, to the blanket around my shoulders, stopping on my feet—the feet currently wearing his slippers—where they narrowed imperceptibly.

I swallowed. "My feet were . . . cold."

"Apparently. Do you always help yourself to strangers' clothing?"

"Only when absolutely necessary." I tilted my head. "I wasn't sure you wanted my little piggies falling off in your entryway, what with the impending hypothermia and all."

"How long were you outside?"

"About an hour and a half."

He let out a disbelieving scoff. "Unless you were out there half dressed, you aren't at risk of hypothermia. It's in the high twenties."

"Fucking freezing," I amended.

"Can't hack it? You're in the wrong place for winter, then."

"Yeah, lake effect, whatever, I heard all about it." I tightened the blanket around me as the tiniest shiver racked my frame. He noticed, his gaze dragging from head to toe again, like he was scanning for injuries. "It's snow. I'll be fine."

"I'll remember that when we get eighteen inches in a weekend." I narrowed my eyes, ready to call bullshit, but Barrett glanced up the stairs. "What are they doing up there?"

"Changing their clothes."

Just like he had the first night I met him, Barrett wore a black quarter-zip that stretched across his heart, the red-and-white logo over his chest.

"There are sleds in the driveway," he said, crossing his arms.

I nodded seriously. "Personally, I wouldn't recommend going sledding without them."

"And where did you manage that? We have a flat backyard, and it was in the rules not to take them anywhere," he said, his gaze colder than the glacial air outside.

Heat crawled up my neck as I remembered the rest of his note that I just . . . ignored. My chin rose a notch. "We stayed in the neighborhood. There's a good hill behind that church a few blocks over. Their school friends told them about it."

Barrett hummed. "So their homework is done already?"

I slicked my tongue over my teeth. "It would've been before you got home." I kicked off the slippers, tucking them back into place. And even though I wanted to weep sad, cold tears at the thought of putting my wet, soggy coat back on, I pulled the blanket off my shoulders, kept the visible shivering to a minimum, and laid it in a neat pile on the couch. "I'll just head back home. Tell the kids I'll set their backpacks by the door when they're ready to come get them."

His hand shot out and grabbed my elbow. Not a hard, mean sort of grab. If it had been, I probably would've kneed him in the balls as a reflex. The pressure of his palm was just enough to stop me. The heat of his fingers seared through the thin layer of my long-sleeve shirt.

"I had rules, Lily. That was our agreement."

"I saw them." When he gave me a disbelieving look, I bit down on my bottom lip, trying my very best to look contrite. Based on his reaction, it wasn't working, which was probably for the best because I didn't actually feel bad. "Most of them, at least."

His jaw tightened, and goodness, if there was such a thing as an ominous muscle tightening, this was it. Like a siren blaring before a storm, cutting through the air like a scream.

"And you just . . . chose to ignore them? I said I didn't want you taking them anywhere."

I ignored a lot of shit out of a resolute sense of self-preservation. A therapist would have a field day with someone like me.

What do we do when we're scared of our big feelings, Lily? they'd ask.

We run away and distract ourselves with new experiences. We pretend like those feelings don't exist because it's a million times easier than dealing with them.

There wasn't a shrink's couch in the continental United States that could hold all my baggage.

I gave him a hint of a smile, and his eyes never wavered from mine. "Flexibility isn't a bad thing. Sometimes we're better off breaking the rules."

He released his grip on me, and I fought the urge to shake my arm out. It tingled where he'd held it. Good tingles, which I hadn't gotten from a man in a very long time.

No. Bad tingles. Very, very bad tingles.

"Not the way I live," he said. "Everything will fall apart."

I quirked an eyebrow. "My goodness, I didn't take you for the overly dramatic sort."

"My life is held together by rules," he said in a low voice. "Theirs is too. I didn't ask for your help to have you dismantle it. They need structure. Routine. And so do I."

"Sounds like my nightmare," I said lightly.

He let out a quiet huffing sound, almost a laugh but not quite. "My entire day is lived fifteen minutes at a time. I don't have a single minute unaccounted for. If a piece falls out of place—one single piece, a domino knocked over when it shouldn't be—everything comes crashing down."

Lord, I wanted to muss him up. There was something about this man. It was that serious air, the unshakable focus, that sent an itchy little urge under my skin to see if I *could* shake him. Just a bit.

"Fifteen minutes," I said quietly, taking a step closer and glancing up at him with a guileless expression. "Can't really accomplish anything fun in fifteen minutes, can you?"

There was a flicker in his eyes, but he didn't say anything. In fact, it didn't even seem like he was breathing. His body was so close to mine—he smelled clean and crisp, scents and notes that I couldn't place. Like anyone actually knew what bergamot and sandalwood and citrus smelled like unless they read it on a bottle somewhere. Anyone who said otherwise was full of shit.

Good. He smelled really fucking good. And that gave me unfortunate little tingles too.

I brushed past him, pausing momentarily to see if he'd react, and when he didn't, I walked over to my coat and gloves.

He was still facing the den, and the only sign he'd even heard me, that my words had registered at all, was the way his hand tightened into a fist at his side. I couldn't help it; it made me smile.

"Barrett?"

His head turned but he kept his body facing away. The harsh lines of his profile would photograph like a fucking dream. But that was neither here nor there.

"You'd be so much prettier if you smiled more," I said silkily.

He let out an incredulous huff, big body finally turning in my direction. "Excuse me?"

Putting on my coat felt like draping a wet towel over my shoulders, but I kept my face even, pulling my hair out from underneath the collar. "What? You don't like it when people say that to you? Weird. I *love* it."

An almost imperceptible narrowing of his eyes was the only reaction I got. After I turned around to slip my shoes on, I let out a low, controlled breath. Probably not smart to poke the bear, but he was so fucking *pokeable*.

"Have a good night, sunshine," I said, then let myself out the door without waiting for a reply.

Chapter Eight

Barrett

An alert went off on my phone. Again.

I jammed the button to turn it off and swore under my breath.

"Bridget," I barked.

She popped her head into my office. "I just love when you ask for me in such a nice, friendly tone," she said, raising her eyebrow meaningfully.

I set my hands on my hips and let out a deep breath. "Bridget," I said more calmly, "thank you for taking time out of your busy schedule to come into my office."

"You're very welcome. How can I help you?"

Then she smiled, a placid smile so full of shit that I worked my jaw back and forth before speaking again.

"Why is my phone alert going off every fifteen minutes?"

"So you don't forget Maggie's Christmas concert," she explained, slowing her speech and over-enunciating the words. "That's why the alert says *Maggie's Christmas Concert.*"

I pinched the bridge of my nose. "Right. I didn't really . . . look at the screen, I just wanted it to stop making noise. I haven't slept well the last couple nights, and I'm a tad irritable."

The small humming noise she let out could've been one of sympathy and understanding, but coming from her, it had more of an *I don't give a shit* tone to it. "Concert is at seven. Once your next meeting is done, you have time to grab a quick dinner with your coordinators and then an hour to review film. You have to be out the door by 6:20 in order to make it to the school on time."

My brows furrowed. "Who's bringing her to school?"

"Daisy's mom. She's picking her up at the house at 6:15—and yes, Lily knows."

"You're texting with her too?" I gave Bridget an incredulous look. "How did you get her number?"

"It is wild that you're still underestimating me after six years of running your life," she said, walking into my office to slap a folder on my desk.

"I really shouldn't," I sighed. "Before, it felt more . . . normal, I guess. You always coordinated with Rachel."

At the sound of my ex's name, Bridget scrunched up her face like she smelled something rancid. "And what a pleasant experience that was. I can honestly say I'd never been happier to see paperwork in my life than when you signed those divorce papers."

I grunted, tapping the screen of my computer to life. "What's next?"

She glanced at her watch. "Archer should be here any minute so you can talk about the game on Sunday."

"Should be a fun one," I muttered.

"He keeps rushing out of the pocket instead of letting the plays develop," she said. "He's good, but he's impatient. You don't like it when people change the plan on you."

I raised a brow. "Should I be adding you to the coaching staff?"

"Would it come with a raise and less hours?"

For a second, I mulled that over. "Yes to the first. No to the second."

"You know, I already deal with enough men in my life. I think I'll pass."

"Wise move," I murmured.

"What are you going to say to him?" she asked.

"Still trying to figure that out. It's not even about the rushed plays," I admitted. "Though that is a problem. It's everything. He doesn't want to be coached. Doesn't want to prepare the way he should."

"That's what makes the great ones great." She folded her arms. "I remember your rookie year. You were always the first player in the building. Every single day."

I gave her a wry look. "I was not one of the 'great ones.' My knee blew out too soon to even come close to that conversation."

"Maybe not," Bridget conceded, "but every single person in that building trusted you. Archer doesn't have that."

Another reminder for the concert popped up on my phone, and Bridget smothered a smile when I tapped the screen far harder than necessary. "Yeah, it's nice when people trust you to remember things, isn't it?"

Instead of leaving my office, Bridget gave me an appraising look. "Speaking of Lily, how's it going there? She hasn't murdered you or quit—I was expecting one or both by the end of the first week."

I'd expected the same, but I kept my mouth shut.

"Plus," Bridget continued, "my text thread with Maggie has been conspicuously quiet, which would worry me under normal circumstances. But you haven't had to sprint out of the office in search of your children, so it seems like a step in the right direction."

Was I ready for this conversation? Bridget knew me better than just about anyone, something she loved to rub in my face on a weekly basis. Which meant it was pointless to lie.

I carefully closed my laptop, sat back in my chair, and laid my folded hands over my stomach while I stared at her.

She nodded seriously. "That bad."

Long ago, I'd learned that yelling and cursing when you're upset does absolutely nothing. It doesn't lessen your pain, it doesn't make the situation disappear. Creating the energy I wanted around me was paramount to my coaching strategy—to my parenting strategy too.

Used to drive Rachel insane. She wanted me to fight with her. Fight and yell and get upset when she pulled shit on me. And I never did. Not with my team either. I wasn't the guy screaming in their faces, but they knew exactly what I demanded of them, even when I remained quiet.

And if I could harness that tone when discussing *Lily*, then I could manage it anywhere else.

"She drives me insane," I said in an even tone.

"Does she?" Bridget folded her arms. "In what way?"

"Pretty much every way that exists. She doesn't listen to me. Doesn't follow my rules. She's constantly trying to push my buttons."

If I thought too hard about the *fifteen minute* comment, I'd lose my tenuous grip on my emotions. I almost had when she'd said it. I was too tired to think too much on the sex I wasn't having, and hadn't had in the couple years since Rachel and I last . . . tried. Leave it to *this* woman to make me think about it.

"So," Bridget drawled, "your quarterback and your nanny are putting you in the same corner, it seems."

My eye twitched. "Apparently."

She grinned. "How's that feel, boss?"

"About as great as you can imagine."

Bridget laughed. "Oh, come on, she cannot be that bad."

I let out a weary exhale. "She is. But my children adore her, so I just have to . . . deal with it. With her."

It was the slight narrowing of Bridget's eyes and the thoughtful purse of her lips that made me shift in my seat. "Interesting," she mused.

"It's not *interesting*. It's fucking annoying."

Her eyebrows shot up. "And she's making you swear. *Very* interesting."

I rolled my lips together and sat up in my chair, opening my laptop with a brisk movement. "Whatever you say. I don't need her help much longer. My mom will be here . . . soon."

Lord, let her be here soon.

"She pretty?" Bridget asked with an innocent widening of her eyes.

"I didn't notice," I lied. Based on the wry arch to her eyebrow, I wasn't all that convincing.

She paused again by the entrance to my office. "Barrett?"

I gave her an annoyed look.

"Don't forget Maggie's concert," she said sweetly.

◆ ◆ ◆

The parking lot of the school was full by the time I arrived, and I jogged inside the one-story brick building to get out of the cold. It hadn't snowed in a few days, but the temps continued to drop, the windchill enough to make your skin hurt if you stayed out in it too long.

I was stomping the slush off my boots just inside the door when a couple of boys ran up to me.

"Hey, Coach," they said, holding out their fists for a tap, which I gave them.

"Hey, guys." They might have been in Maggie's grade, but I didn't recognize any of her classmates yet.

Despite the fact that I wasn't the dad who could come to field trips or PTO events or classroom parties, I was probably the most popular parent in the middle school, at least according to Bryce.

"We gonna win this weekend?" one of them asked, eyes bright and cheeks a little flushed.

I gave him a small smile. "Hope so. Excuse me, I need to go find a seat," I told them.

They ran off, and I glanced around, trying to find Bryce. The text on my phone said he'd be waiting for me outside the doors of the gym after he saved us some seats.

His head popped up between a group of parents chatting by the door, and I nodded, making my way through the crowd. A few people said hi, most of them just smiled or cut me a wordless look, but no one stopped me before I reached Bryce.

"Hey, kid. You look nice," I told him.

He ran his hands over the front of his button-down shirt. "Thanks. Lily told me it's good to dress up for special occasions, even if they're not ours."

The sound of her name had me gritting my teeth. "Did she?"

"You like it?" he asked shyly. "And I, um, I tried to do my hair like yours."

Bryce didn't look exactly like me when I was younger, but it was close. He had the same height, the same build as me and my brother. He'd be tall and strong, already showing signs of being a natural athlete, even if he preferred soccer to football. And in his jaw, the line of his nose, and the slight curl of his hair when it got too long, I saw glimpses of myself I hadn't noticed as strongly when he was younger.

My smile was bittersweet. "Looks good, son."

He let out a small exhale, face breaking open into a wide smile. "Cool. Our seats are over here. She's already sitting."

My brow furrowed. "Who is?"

But Bryce was already bounding ahead. With each step, a growing sense of unease rolled around my stomach and up into my chest, breaking open into something else entirely when I saw her hair from behind, a chair open on either side of her.

She'd curled it today—big, loose curls that fell down past her shoulders. Her hair was a deep, glossy black, except for the last few inches, which were still a shocking blue. As I stared, heat built on my neck.

With my hands on my hips, I paused before walking into her eyeline, tipping my head back and staring up at the ceiling for a moment. There were eyes on me in situations like this; I'd have to be careful. Bryce slid past her and took his seat, immediately talking with a tall, skinny boy next to him. They leaned their heads in and laughed, so he must have been a friend of his from school.

When Lily's face was visible in profile, I slicked my tongue over my teeth and walked over to the open chair at the end of the row, taking a seat wordlessly.

Her bare arm brushed against mine, and I kept my eyes forward, staring blankly at the stage covered in trees and garland and lights, the empty risers waiting to be filled with nervous students.

Mine wouldn't be nervous, of course. But someone's kid was.

Next to me, Lily shifted, and I desperately wished I'd changed from the short-sleeve polo I'd chosen that day.

Her skin was warm. Soft. And without me giving them explicit permission, my eyes darted down from the stage.

She was wearing dark jeans and a soft-looking charcoal sweater with short sleeves, combat boots with a chunky heel on her feet. Around her wrist was a bunch of delicate little gold and silver bracelets.

There was another tattoo just on the inside of her wrist, but in my peripheral vision, I couldn't see what it was.

Finally, she turned in her seat and pinned me with a stare that I tried very, very hard to ignore.

"I'm concerned about you," she said.

"Why's that?" Even though every atom of my being implored me to look in her direction, I kept the impulse lashed down.

"Is it a small-talk thing? I hate it, too, don't worry. But it's common to say hi. Polite, even. Then I'd say hi back. Maybe a *What are you doing at my daughter's Christmas concert?*" Her attempt to sound like me had me closing my eyes for a moment so as not to threaten the structural integrity of my retinas because of the mighty eye roll wanting to be unleashed. "Or are you afraid of women? Divorce can do a number on a man's ego sometimes, and given your personality deficiency, I could understand if that was the problem."

My eyes snapped open and I slowly turned my face toward hers. Immediately wished I hadn't. Her eyelashes were darker and thicker. Her cheekbones looked . . . shimmery, chiseled features of her face seemingly amplified by whatever simple makeup she'd added. Her lips, already full, were glossy. Shiny. A shade darker than her normal color.

It took me only a single heartbeat to realize I hadn't lied earlier. Lily *wasn't* pretty.

She was so beautiful that it made my chest hurt.

"Hi," I said simply. Her eyes blazed with heat. "What are you doing at my daughter's Christmas concert?"

Lily quirked an eyebrow. "She begged me to come. I told her you wouldn't want me here, but she was insistent that that was not the case." Why was her skin so perfect? This close up, I could see everything, every little fleck of color in her eyes, and I realized they were a deep blue. I'd never seen eyes that color before in my life. "I'm not in the habit of breaking a kid's heart if I can avoid it. So even if you hate that I'm here, I think you and I can play nice for the next hour, can't we?"

I ran my tongue along the bottom edge of my teeth, and she inhaled slowly.

"I guess we're about to find out," I told her.

Lily turned in her seat with a sharp pivot, and her arm moved away from mine. Bryce leaned forward, gesturing to his friend.

"Dad, this is Booker. He's the friend I told you about."

I managed a small smile, holding my hand out. "Nice to meet you, Booker. Thanks for hanging out with Bryce at school. I know he's a little hard to manage sometimes."

My son groaned, allowing a good-natured eye roll.

The boy smiled, clearly a little starstruck. "N-nice to meet you, Mr. King. Um, can Bryce maybe come over to my house over Christmas break? My mom said it's okay."

A friendly-looking woman with a big smile leaned forward, her waist-length braids shifting over her arm when she extended it to shake my hand. I managed to return the handshake without touching Lily, which might go down as my biggest win for the night. "I'm Booker's mom, Imani. We can trade numbers if that sounds okay to you."

I nodded. "Sounds good. Bryce, why don't you go ahead and give it to her."

The boys immediately started planning, and I leaned back in my seat, expelling a quick sigh.

Lily gave me another pointed glance. "Well, I stand corrected. You *can* be friendly to people."

"On occasion." I flicked my gaze briefly in her direction. "I've yet to see you do the same thing, you know."

"What?"

"Be friendly. I imagine you hissing at everyone new, smacking their hands off doors and trying to glare them back to a safe distance."

"Are you saying people don't like that? Weird. Maybe that's why I don't have any friends," she mused. "Maybe I'll work on my hissing technique," she whispered, leaning in toward me like she was telling a secret. "Do *you* have friends, Mr. King?"

Before answering, I tried to count to ten. I made it to four. "I don't have time for friends."

To my utter surprise, Lily didn't have a response to that. She merely sniffed, adjusting her long legs, crossing one over the other, the combat boot on her left leg bouncing slightly as we waited for the concert to start.

I recognized a couple of faces in the row in front of us. One of the dads from Maggie's class glanced back and stared at Lily's legs, his gaze slowly dragging up to her face, where it lingered. I crossed my arms, narrowing my eyes in his direction, and as much as I wanted to stop the scowl on my face, there was no helping it.

He caught my expression and blinked guiltily, giving me a little wave and a lift of his eyebrows.

Lily made a small sound just shy of amused. Could've been annoyance, but it was hard to tell. "Now, why you'd do that? Maybe I wanted to talk to him afterward."

Watch the fathers of my daughter's classmates fawn over Lily in public? I'd rather shove bamboo splints under my fingernails.

It wasn't jealousy. There was nothing to be jealous of. I tried telling that to the fire lodged under my ribs, but each deep breath seemed to inflame it more. God, she was driving me out of my fucking mind, one interaction at a time. A couple more weeks and I'd need to be institutionalized.

"Trying to make some new friends?" I asked, choosing my words carefully.

"Maybe." She sniffed, tossing her hair behind her shoulder. It smelled like vanilla. Why the hell did she always smell like cookies? "He's cute. I bet he likes to be smacked around a little, don't you think?"

The not-jealous burning sensation flared hot. I'd trade half my savings account for some TUMS. I needed to ask Bridget to start stocking them in my desk.

"He's a spineless little dweeb," I said, keeping my voice remarkably even. "You'd eat him alive."

"Maybe that's exactly my type."

Now it was my turn to stare at her profile while she looked ahead. "No, it's not," I said in a low voice.

Her throat worked on a swallow, a flicker in her brow that conveyed surprise, maybe? Yeah, join the club, Townsend; I was even surprising myself.

"How would you know?" she replied quietly. Not just quietly, but there was a split second of unsteadiness in her voice that sent an unholy streak of satisfaction screaming through my veins.

Satisfied for what, exactly? That I wasn't the only one affected? I didn't want to dwell on that for too much longer.

It was on the tip of my tongue to say something dangerous and stupid, like she needed a man who knew how to handle her. A man who wouldn't try to tame her but wasn't afraid of her either. A man who would take much, much longer than fifteen minutes.

But all those words stayed locked down, safe behind my well-honed discipline.

"He's also married," I said instead.

She made a disappointed clicking sound with her tongue. "Yeah, that'll do it. Otherwise, I love a spineless dweeb." Her face turned, her eyes locking on mine until my heart thundered in my ears. "They're so malleable."

Before I could respond, the lights dimmed, and the first class marched out onto the risers. Lily faced forward, tilting her chin up and focusing on the little faces in front of us like nothing had happened.

It took me thirty minutes to get my pulse under control, and my hands finally relaxed when Maggie's class took the stage.

I couldn't keep doing this. Even having her on the periphery of my life for another day felt like too much. Something needed to change.

Immediately.

Chapter Nine

Barrett

With my head down and my focus on the notes for my next meeting, I hardly noticed Bridget trying to flag me down. When I finally glanced up, I looked around her desk area. Her *empty* desk area.

"Where are my kids?"

She set her hands on her hips. "You give me too much credit, boss. Maggie crashed the defensive-line meeting, and I haven't seen her for at least an hour." Her head tilted toward the office across the way from mine. "Bryce is in Mark's office; he's either asleep on the couch, or he's helping him with play selections for our last game. Hard to say."

I rubbed the back of my neck. "Okay. Wait . . . Maggie's doing what?"

She laughed. "You should go check. Wren is having a field day with this."

"Shit," I muttered.

"Why are they here again? I thought the neighbor was watching them today." She quirked a knowing brow. "Last day at the office before Christmas break, and all."

The way our last two games were scheduled out, we had an eleven-day stretch between. Great for resting injured players. Great for giving the guys a couple days to enjoy the holidays with their family. Absolute havoc for guys like me, who had kids out of school and couldn't wrangle his mental stability long enough to let Lily watch them for a little bit longer.

"My parents are flying in after Christmas," I answered gruffly, immediately cursing the defensive edge to my voice.

"Ah. It's too bad there's not, like, a person in your neighborhood who could help." Without looking at me, Bridget pretended to skim the notebook in front of her. "Like, next door or something."

"We needed to give her a break," I said. The words came out clipped and terse.

"'We'?" she asked slowly.

The times I'd lied to Bridget could be counted on one hand, and two of them had been about Lily Townsend. That alone should've scared the shit out of me.

I needed a break. I needed a break from her eyes and her hair and her snippy little comments. From that fucking mouth. Because that mouth . . .

When I realized Bridget was waiting for me to respond, I blinked rapidly, tucking my folder underneath my arm. "Yes. She helped a lot the last week and a half."

"And one more day was too much for her," Bridget added. There was nothing inherently skeptical about how she said it, but I knew this woman. "You're off tomorrow. And the next day. Like, completely, totally off, and she needed a break from watching them for one day. Am I getting that right?"

"Don't you have work to do?" I asked her.

"Yes, I'm terribly busy and important at all times." She sat in the big, expensive leather chair she'd requested when we started in Buffalo, then shooed me away from her desk. "Speaking of which, go find your own kids. I know you have fifteen minutes until your last meeting."

When her chair angled smoothly in the opposite direction, I was effectively dismissed. "You know, I bet there are head coaches in this league who have executive assistants who respect them."

"Oh. Are you still here?"

I sighed, walking to Mark's office, where, sure enough, Bryce was studying schemes on the giant whiteboard on the far wall.

"Do you need me to remove this small human from your office?" I asked Mark.

They both turned, and I smiled. Bryce was wearing a prototype jersey about three sizes too big. "I'm helping," my son insisted.

Mark grinned. "He's fine."

"Thanks, Mark." I tapped my watch. "I'm going to find your sister; then I have one more meeting and we can go home, okay? Be ready in about forty-five, Bryce."

He gave me a crisp salute, then turned back to the board.

The conference room where the defensive line was supposed to be meeting was empty, so, with another sigh, I turned to take off down a few more hallways. They weren't in the locker room. Not in the weight room either.

One of my defensive backs found me standing, hands on my hips, trying to decide which direction to go next.

"Looking for a girl about this tall?" Travis asked, holding his hand up to his midsection. "Likes bossing people around?"

My mouth tugged into a reluctant grin. "Yes."

He tilted his head down the hallway to the right, which led to the main practice field "Down there."

"I'm scared to ask why," I muttered, and it made him laugh. It wasn't the typical Saturday for us, with no game on Sunday. On a normal week, we'd do walk-throughs of all the plays, gearing up for travel if it was an away game. Because of the holiday and the longer-than-usual break between games, the schedule wasn't as grueling. A good number of the players were already home for the day after reviewing film and spending time with their coordinators. Some would've come in for treatment too; everyone was a little banged up by this point in the season.

This time of evening, just past dinner, there weren't usually players on the field anymore. I made the last turn, and when I let myself through the first door that led to the field, I couldn't help but let out an incredulous laugh.

Maggie stood on a step stool, a megaphone to her mouth.

My entire defensive line was practicing dance moves while she instructed them on what to do next.

"No, no, everyone on the left, you need to *pirouette*," she said in exasperation. "Look at Keshawn; his is so good."

I covered my mouth with my hand as one of our team captains, an absolutely massive guy, one of the stalwarts of our defense at six five and with inked arms the size of tree trunks, executed a perfectly graceful ballet move, his hands arched above his head.

The other guys clapped and whistled. "How can you do that so well, man?" someone asked.

Keshawn shrugged. "My daughter is in ballet. I help her practice sometimes. You gotta *feel* the move."

Wren was off to the right, directing the intern who was filming every bit of this, and I could only imagine what would end up on the team's social media.

I cleared my throat, and Maggie whipped around. "Dad! We're making content. They're gonna give me my own *show*."

I raised an eyebrow. "So I heard. Are you keeping these guys from doing their work?"

"Aww, come on, Coach," Keshawn said. "Five more minutes? We almost got it that time."

"Yeah, Dad, can we have five more minutes?" Maggie asked, bouncing slightly on her toes.

"Five more minutes," I told her, my lips curving into a helpless smile. "Then make your way back to my office, okay?"

She held her hand out, and Keshawn gave her a high five. Then she brought the megaphone to her mouth. "You heard the man. We have five minutes, so let's do two more takes." She swiveled in my direction, still speaking into the amplifier. "Dad, can we watch a Christmas movie and eat cookies when we get home?"

Every eye on the field was on me. "Uh, yeah, that's fine."

"Can we come, too, Coach?" someone asked.

I smiled wryly. "Not tonight, no."

Maggie turned again, pointing at one of the tackles at the end of a line, megaphone to her mouth. "Justice, if you can't get that pirouette on beat, you're off the video."

"I'll get it," Justice promised. He gave me a meaningful look. "She's scary, Coach."

"Trust me, I'm aware."

"Christmas break is the best," Bryce sighed. "No school for two weeks."

"Totally the best," Maggie agreed. We were halfway through *Home Alone*, Maggie lying on the floor with a pile of pillows from her bed, her legs kicking back and forth in the air. We'd finally taken some time to put up a tree when we got home from the facility, though the kids lost interest in hanging the ornaments about halfway through the process. Bridget assured me that all their presents were wrapped and ready to put under the tree—hidden in the storage room in the back of the extra garage stall. She'd snuck them in earlier that day while I was in a meeting.

Bryce's chest was covered with cookie crumbs, leftovers from the most recent batch brought home with them from Lily's. The best cookies in the entire world, according to my children.

I'd yet to try one. Knowing her, she'd slipped a camera into the takeout container and the entire thing would self-destruct if I took a single bite.

"Christmas Eve tomorrow," I said quietly. "What should we do?"

"Eat sugar all day," Bryce insisted.

"Part of the day." I nudged his leg. "We could play a couple games."

He gave me a shy look. "And you don't have to work . . . at all? Not even a little?"

"None," I promised. "Film can wait until after the holiday."

He tried to smother his pleased smile, but it broke free anyway. "Maybe we could play Monopoly or something? You don't usually have time for a long game like that."

It was almost impossible to speak over the guilt screaming in my head. "Monopoly would be perfect."

Bryce jumped off the couch. "Sweet, I'm gonna go pick games for tomorrow," he called, tearing off toward the storage closet at the end of the hallway.

"Can we go to that church down the street?" Maggie asked. "A couple of my friends at school said they do one of those candle services." She frowned. "It doesn't sound very safe to have open flames in church, but I kinda want to see it."

"We can do that if you want. We can make all new traditions, if that sounds good."

With Rachel, Christmas was always over the top. She wanted black tie parties and spectacle. It wasn't about movies and games and quiet evenings at home. A decorating company came in and made our house look like something out of a magazine.

Maggie stared at the half-decorated greenery in the corner. "I love our little tree."

"That *little tree* is nine feet tall," I said.

"Yeah, but it's not perfect. I like that." She hopped up from the floor and dug through the box to find another ornament. *Baby's First Christmas*, it said, with a small blurry picture of Bryce. "It feels like a *family* Christmas tree."

When she was done, she made her way over to the couch and curled up against my side. I closed my eyes, tightening my arm around her shoulders. "Yeah, it does, kiddo."

She was quiet for a minute, playing with the edge of the blanket covering my lap. "Do you think it would be sad at Christmas without family around?"

They spoke to Rachel a couple times a week. But outside of that, they didn't ask about her much. Finding a new normal, just the three of us, was both easier and tremendously more difficult than I'd imagined. The kids seemed to know that they were better off with me, as did Rachel. All their early childhood years had been run by nannies. The maternal gene had skipped Rachel, as did a few other traits I thought I'd seen in her early in our relationship. Candor being one. Vulnerability another. And the ability to love, most of all. I wasn't entirely sure she was capable of it.

But my kids had all those traits, and it didn't surprise me that Maggie might be worried about her mother being alone during the holidays.

I dropped a quick kiss on the top of her head. "Yeah, kiddo, it would be hard to be alone."

She nodded. "What if—what if you're in the position to make someone feel better? Shouldn't you do it?"

"Of course," I told her. "What do you have in mind? A call on Christmas Day or something?"

Maggie lifted her head, giving me a look like I was crazy. "No, I was thinking of inviting her over."

"Honey, your mom's in California," I answered slowly. "She won't be flying here tomorrow."

Maggie rolled her eyes. "I wasn't talking about Mom."

"Then who are you talking about?"

"Lily. She doesn't have any family, so she'll just be alone tomorrow." She gave me a beseeching look. "Please, Dad."

It was astonishing how your kids could back you into a corner of your own making. Without realizing what she was doing, Maggie had me completely at her mercy, asking me to voluntarily spend time around the biggest threat to my sanity, the one woman I needed space from. And she was doing it because she had a huge heart. Because she cared about people and was asking for my advice about how to put that care into action when it really mattered.

I'd rather swallow hot coals than stifle the girl's kind nature. Yes, she was smart as hell and scary in a way I didn't know how to define, but she was good. That goodness could be snuffed out so easily, from a place of selfishness, of being too busy or too stressed, a million different reasons that might seem small at the time. Might seem inconsequential. Wasn't that often the way with most parenting decisions? *It's just one time.* But one turns to two, turns to a dozen, and then a pattern is formed before you realize what you've done. It made me wonder if someone hadn't stifled Rachel's heart when she was Maggie's age.

"How do you know she doesn't have any family?" I asked quietly.

"She told me a couple days ago. I asked her what she was doing for Christmas, and she said nothing," Maggie answered. "Because she doesn't have any family."

"Maybe she just means she doesn't have any family *here*."

"Maybe," she hedged. "But I don't think so. I think she's alone." Maggie's eyes welled up, and I was a fucking goner. "I really like her, Dad. I don't want her to be alone. Can we please invite her over tomorrow? I've always wanted to decorate cookies at Christmas, but Mom never wanted to make a mess in the kitchen."

It didn't matter what I wanted or didn't want. It didn't matter whether I needed space, or that Lily got under my skin so effortlessly that it felt like all she had to do was breathe and my agitation went sky high. What mattered were moments like this, where my daughter felt like the things she wanted were important. Backing up the things I told her, about how to be a good human being, how to be kind and thoughtful and true to our principles.

No matter how often I felt like I was failing, as long as I didn't fail her *here*, I was doing all right.

I cupped the side of her face, speaking over the knot in my throat. "Yeah, kiddo. We can invite her over tomorrow."

Her smile was huge. Happy. "Can I do it now?"

"It's late," I answered. "Why don't you send her a text in case she's already in bed. She can answer tomorrow."

"Okay," Maggie called, running into the kitchen to get her and Bryce's shared cell phone. It was basic, only allowing for texts and calls from preapproved numbers. If I could swing it, I'd keep them off social media until they were thirty. Knowing my daughter, however, she'd find some corner of the dark web that would tell her how to circumvent any protections I could put in place.

Being a parent for kids their age was impossible. They were being pushed by the world to learn more, to experience more. A world that was telling them things that were both wildly inappropriate and entirely educational. They felt older and more mature than they really were. And it was impossible to protect them. No matter how badly I wanted to make their lives easier, to remove their obstacles and stress, I couldn't.

Nights like this were like watching sand escape the hourglass in real time. Still so innocent, still naive to the toughest lessons I'd had to learn, but in a lot of ways, smarter and more aware than I was ready to give them credit for.

She was already tapping on the screen.

"I want to see the message before you send it."

Maggie nodded, typing three times faster than I'd be able to manage on my own. "Okay. How's that?"

The message was enough to melt any reserve that might be lingering.

Hi Lily. Happy Christmas Eve Eve. I loved the cookies from your last batch. Can you help me bake some tomorrow? No one should be alone on Christmas, and Dad said if we have the ability to help someone who is, we should do something, so we're inviting you over tomorrow. We're playing games and going to church and eating. You can even choose your favorite Christmas movie. Please come?

P.S. This is your friend Maggie.

My voice was rough when I told her, "It's perfect."

She beamed, hitting send with a nervous little exhale. "So now what?"

"Now you wait to see if she says yes." I gave her arm a gentle squeeze. "And if she says no, then we respect her answer, okay?"

Maggie nodded solemnly, but I could see in her eyes she was not prepared for that to be the case.

Bryce came back in the room, arms loaded down with board games, the top few wobbling dangerously. "I think I've got enough. Can someone help me?"

Chapter Ten

Lily

"What the fuck am I doing?" I breathed, my hand poised in the air, unable to make contact with the front door of the King house. "It's just . . . people. People hanging out together in a house. And he's not going to give you shit in front of his kids."

I was about 84 percent sure of that fact, but the sheer number of times I'd replayed our little *thing* at the concert was reaching sickening heights. It hadn't been like the other times we'd interacted. It'd held tension. Tension meant things I didn't particularly want to uncover.

Except wasn't that the point of a good ol' mental spiral? We uncovered like a motherfucker, over and over and over, until the scab was well and picked open.

The moment I'd gotten his text saying I didn't need to watch the kids the day after the concert thing, I knew that man was full of shit if he said he wasn't thinking about our *thing* too.

My own musings were trapped in a three-part loop.

First, I had gotten arm tingles when he touched me. In general, I avoided tingles from complicated men like him.

Second—and a somewhat problematic second point it was—I had *flirted.* Denying said flirting was stupid, because even when I did it, I knew what the hell was happening. He may not have, though. Some people had the gift of subtle flirting, and I was one of them. There was a fine line between being mean, giving someone harmless shit, and actual flirting. I straddled the fuck out of that line. But I couldn't help it. Me being nice would've made his head explode.

Third, and most important, he had not flirted back. What he *had* done was react in such a perfectly grumpy way that a sick little thrill shot up my spine whenever his eyes met mine.

After Maggie's concert, we didn't converse further. After effusively praising Maggie's performance and giving both kids a hug, I escaped back to my car—safe from any more loaded Barrett eye contact or interactions with spineless married dweebs.

Which was good, because that man with the wandering eyes and skinny arms was not my type.

What my type *was* was not a concern I needed to deal with at the current moment, because this sweet little invitation from the kids, who were rapidly becoming my favorite people in the world, had nothing to do with my . . . type.

Not that Barrett was anything of the sort. The muscles were fine. Big and defined and clearly well maintained. The jaw and the dark eyes were . . . whatever. Anyone could have a cut jawline, and it didn't make me want to remove my undergarments. Trust me, a good profile wouldn't make your life easier.

That was the other part of my spiral that I didn't want to touch with several ten-foot poles. I didn't even know what my type was. It felt impossible to think that anyone would want to deal with me—long term, at least. But the thought of only having short-term dealings for the rest of my life . . .

That left me feeling like my chest was strangely empty. Like all I'd ever hear were echoes of the things I didn't have, clanging around against my ribs. The worst part was, it would somehow be even scarier if he was sweet and thoughtful and saw through the worst parts of me.

Hissing at new people and slamming doors, like he'd said. Not too far off, all in all, and if he—if *anyone* with muscles and jawlines and dark, warm eyes—could peek behind that particular curtain and not run screaming . . .

That seemed significantly worse.

Or it would, if I was worried about Barrett King being my type. But I wasn't.

Because *he* wasn't.

My hand clenched as I held my fist aloft. I was doing this for Maggie. For Bryce.

It was enough to bring myself to knock. Firmly, decisively, like I was *totally* fine being here. With my stomach in regrettable knots that made my nerves impossible to ignore—those little dicks—I let out a deep breath and centered my chi or whatever I needed to do in order to face Barrett for the next several hours.

The sound of thundering footsteps coming toward the door made me smile. Not the owner of the house letting me in, then. I highly doubted he'd sprint in my direction, unless the house was on fire and I was blocking the exit.

It was a good thing I braced myself before the door whipped open, because Bryce and Maggie flung themselves at me like they hadn't just seen me two days earlier.

"Whoa," I laughed. "Hey, you two."

Bryce pulled back first, his eyes shining. "Do you like Monopoly? Or any game? We can play Scrabble too. I love Scrabble."

"I—"

"She's baking with me," Maggie reminded her brother, grabbing my hand and pulling me into the house. "I already told you that."

"You can't just claim all her time, Maggie," Bryce huffed.

"We can do both," I assured them. "But we should bake cookies first. Let them cool before we decorate."

Barrett was nowhere to be seen, and the knot in my stomach eased a little. What kind of Christmas dad was he? There was a cartoonish version in my head when I tried to imagine him navigating a lighthearted holiday. He'd have a schedule, color coded and militant. Fifteen minutes to eat cookies. Then fifteen minutes to drink eggnog. Not a single piece of wrapping paper would touch the ground, lest it create a mess.

A hysterical laugh threatened to spill out of my mouth, because the fact that I was here made me question my own decision-making skills. But despite all that, and the looming, unseen presence of Hot Scary Christmas Dad, the house smelled good—like a pine tree farm and mulled cider had exploded in the main room.

My eyes tracked over the space, drinking in all the details. I hadn't made it this far inside the other night, and I didn't even try to hide my curiosity now.

The kitchen was big, stretching along the back wall of the house, an island with four stools in the middle. In the living room, there were a few support columns behind the long L-shaped couch that faced the TV mounted on the wall, and in the corner was a Christmas tree with twinkling colored lights.

It was the only nod to the holiday that I could see, but the space underneath it was filled with prettily wrapped presents. In the bag slung over my shoulder was one for each of the kids.

"You look pretty," Maggie told me.

Elastic waistbands and forgiving fabric were the real MVPs of the holiday, which was why I'd gone for my softest pair of leggings and the Celtics sweatshirt. Despite a quick swipe of mascara before I walked over, *pretty* was not the look I'd been going for, so I gave her a wry arch of my eyebrow. I touched the sparkly headband holding her hair back. "So do you."

"We went to church this morning," she sighed. "And we don't really ever go, so I wasn't sure what to wear. But I felt like I needed to dress up a little bit." She paused. "For baby Jesus."

I nodded seriously. "Of course."

Bryce started peeking in my bag. "What's in here?"

I smacked his hand away. "Hey, do you normally go through people's stuff? Away, little man. Nothing for you to see."

He laughed, running off to the dining room table, where a messy stack of board games took up half the surface. "How long will it take you to get the cookies in the oven?"

I set my bag down on the counter and fished out the container of chilled dough. "Twenty minutes, maybe? Unless your sister has real problems using cookie cutters."

"Oh, we bought some at the store this morning," Maggie said, opening up a bag sitting on the counter next to the fridge.

"You went to the grocery store on Christmas Eve? You must be out of your mind," I said, tapping her on the tip of her nose.

"Dad's fault," they said in unison.

"What's my fault?" the man in question said, appearing at the end of a hallway on the other side of the room. He was looking down as he rolled the sleeves up his forearms. It was basic—a plain white button-down I'd seen on hundreds of men in my life, but I cursed the sudden pitch in my belly at the way it fit him.

Good. It fit him good. Fit him *well*?

Whatever. The grammatical construct of that sentence aside, Barrett King was doing his button-down shirt some serious favors. Apparently, he'd also dressed nice for baby Jesus.

"Lily brought cookie cutters," Maggie pronounced. "We didn't even need them. I *told* you she would."

His eyes lifted slowly, like the air was thick and made everything sluggish, and when they met mine, it seemed as though he was just as apprehensive about this as I was.

"Ah. You're here."

"Merry Christmas," I told him, and I almost winced at the sound of my voice. It was half an octave too high, and my nerves were now a blinking neon sign over my head. "Thank you for inviting me."

All morning, I'd promised myself that I could be polite to him. That I could be kind and sweet . . . okay, well, maybe not *sweet*, because I hadn't undergone a personality transplant recently, but we could be in the same room without snipping and snapping at each other.

The pressure of his gaze was so tactile, I almost took a step back, but I forced myself to stay in place. There would be no backing down from this man, thank you very much.

When his gaze made it down to my feet and then back up, I merely raised an eyebrow. "Do I pass dress code, Mr. King?"

Only the slightest flicker in his eyes gave him away, even though his mouth stayed even. A low, scraping hum was his only response. "No scary little beast by your side today?"

I smiled faintly. "No, Larry was content to nap on the couch, as it turned out. I asked him if he wanted to come, but his response was to burrow under some blankets and growl."

Barrett made a small noise in the back of his throat. "So he doesn't just growl at me?"

"Oh no. That dog loathes my very presence, make no mistake." I turned on the faucet, pushing my sleeves up to wash my hands before Maggie and I started. "Thank you for getting cookie cutters, though. You have some shapes that Patty didn't."

"Which ones?" Maggie asked.

I leaned toward the selection she'd pulled out. Barrett was still watching me, even as Bryce asked him for help setting up a game. "I don't have a snowman or a reindeer or a bell. Let's pick six shapes and make four of each. Sound good?"

Maggie did the little bouncing move on her toes she always did when she was excited, and as we parsed out the shapes we liked best, she did it again. It was little things like that I'd remember when I left, and my heart squeezed for a moment before I could stop it.

When she'd made her final selections, she looked up at me for approval.

"Those will be fun."

"You might need to decorate the reindeer. I don't think I'll be any good at it," she said.

"We all have to start somewhere—and even if it's an unholy mess, that's better than going nowhere at all."

The words were out before I knew what I was saying, and I could hear my father's voice as if he were standing next to me. The breath I sucked in was shaky at best, everything spinning topsy-turvy in my brain for a split second. I turned, pretending like I was looking in the bag again.

Maybe I should have stayed home.

Maybe this was too much.

What was I *thinking*?

"What do you need next?" Maggie asked, pulling me from the absolute *no thank you* of my thoughts.

"A rolling pin and some flour, if you please."

"Yes, Chef." She saluted. I exhaled a short laugh under my breath while she set the flour on the counter, then started pulling open drawers and paused. "Dad, do we have a rolling pin?"

Barrett's eyes locked on mine as he nodded. "Drawer right behind you. Don't think it's ever been used, though."

"Thanks, Dad," I said, batting my eyelids.

He leveled me with a supremely unamused look. God, he was so good at those. It wasn't even fair.

"What?" I asked innocently. "I could've said *Daddy*."

"Lily," he warned.

I sighed. "Fine. Christmas truce?"

Maggie appeared next to me with the rolling pin.

As I hefted it in my hand, Barrett made a small noise of concession. "Does that mean you're going to be nice?"

"I'm always nice," I pointed out. *God, this thing would make a great weapon.* "Ask your children."

"The nicest," Bryce said. "Why would you call him *daddy*? You're not related to him."

"I wouldn't," I told Bryce firmly, attention drifting briefly over to the man in question. "Not my thing."

The set of his jaw and the glint in Barrett's eyes were just about my undoing, and I swallowed, tearing my gaze away as I took the container of flour from Maggie and began sprinkling a thin layer across the counter's surface.

She leaned in next to me. "Why is the dough cold?"

"Because if we don't chill it for a few hours, the butter melts and we get big blobby shapes for our cookies—and I promise, no one wants that." I tilted my head toward the table. "You think your dad will eat a blobby reindeer? I don't think so."

"So I am allowed to eat these?" he said. "That's a surprise."

I gave him a quick look. "That's your Christmas present. See? I said I can be nice."

For a second, we stared at each other across the room, the reality of spending this holiday together draping a blanket of tension thick in the air. He broke first, and a hairline crack slipped down the center of my chest.

Feeling the crack was harder than defining it. It was an awful lot like regret. That I'd said yes. That I'd felt lonely all day—sick of my company and a grumpy little dog who kept ignoring me—and was somehow unable to maintain any sort of distance from this family.

Me. With a family—*this* family—on Christmas. The me from even six months ago would've called present me a lying ho.

Maggie and I rolled out the cookies, and I found her to be a perfect baking assistant. She followed directions, wasn't bothered by correction when it was necessary, and before I knew it, we had a dozen in the oven and another dozen waiting to go.

Bryce and Barrett were engaged in a surprisingly even round of Monopoly, and even though I didn't want to, I found myself watching them from the corner of my eye.

There wasn't a single comment made about the mess we were making in the kitchen—and believe me, we were making one. There was flour on the floor, in Maggie's hair, and a little bit in mine too. It seemed he was watching that out of the corner of his eye, too, both of us circling how the other interacted with our two pint-size buffers. He was patient with his son, correcting him gently when he'd make a decision, but instead of telling him what to do, or that Bryce was wrong, Barrett managed it in a way that never came off heavy-handed.

Which . . . shock of the century, right? I thought *heavy-handed* was his middle frickin' name.

"Think about the properties you didn't buy when you landed on them," he said. "If you hoard all your cash, it makes it harder down the road."

"But I have more money than you," Bryce said. "Isn't the goal of the game money?"

Barrett nodded, hooking his arm over the back of the chair next to him. The muscles in his biceps did things to the stretch of the shirt, and when I found myself staring, I gave myself a mental bitch slap.

No, Lily. His sleeves are no business of ours.

"You grow your money with investments. We haven't played this in a while, and I probably went easy on you the last time, but make sure you're thinking about how to win long term, not just right now."

Bryce sighed. "This game takes forever, doesn't it?"

Barrett smothered a smile as he stared fondly at his son. "Yeah."

The look in his eye held more of my attention than any single part of his body in that damn shirt. The way he loved his kids was *right there*—like I could scoop it up and hold it in the palm of my hand. The dichotomy of how he was with *me* twisted my brain a little bit. A Christmas truce with this version of Barrett was about seventeen kinds of dangerous.

"How do these cookies look?" Maggie asked, leaning in front of the oven window. "Should we take them out?"

I blinked out of my stupor, wiping my hands on the towel slung over my shoulder. Joining her by the oven, I set my hand on her shoulder and squeezed. "Perfect. See that tiny little bit of browning on the edges?"

"Not really."

"I'll show you when I take them out. That's how you know they're done. We still want them to be soft." I slipped my hands into oven mitts and nudged her backward. "Careful."

With the first dozen settled on the top of the stove, I found myself smiling when Maggie took a deep, appreciative whiff. "Those smell so good."

A pang of nostalgia almost took my legs out from underneath me, the reverberations seeming to go on and on, only weakening when I closed my eyes and took a deep breath too.

"I haven't made this recipe in a long time," I told her.

She looked up at me. "How do you know it so well, then?"

I turned and found a spatula in one of the drawers, setting it beside a cooling rack next to the finished cookies. "It was my mom's recipe. She swore these were the best sugar cookies in the world."

"Did the two of you bake these every year at Christmas?"

The pressure on my chest was overwhelming, the squeeze of it on my bones making it hard to keep my face even while I slid the next batch of dough into the waiting oven. "No, we didn't," I answered quietly.

It was impossible not to think about all the years I'd sat in the next room and not asked if I could help. Hadn't asked what she could teach me. It was the kind of thing that haunted me if I wasn't careful, and I made it a firm point not to be haunted over things I couldn't change.

Maggie handed me the spatula, then watched carefully while I tested the bottom of the cookies still on the pan. They needed to cool just a bit longer before coming off.

"Does your mom still make them?" she asked cautiously.

Even though a Christmas movie was playing in the background—one of the versions of *The Grinch*—it felt like everyone went quiet waiting for me to answer.

I kept my eyes down on the cookies, then gave her a tiny smile. "No, honey. She doesn't."

When I turned to do . . . something, anything, to keep my hands busy until I could move the cookies from the baking sheet to the cooling rack, my eyes shifted up and over.

Barrett was staring right at me, a thoughtful expression on his face that scared the absolute shit out of me. After a beat, I tore my gaze away.

"Okay," I said before clearing my throat. "Let's get these cookies moved."

Chapter Eleven

LILY

"I think you're cheating."

"I would never."

Barrett scoffed. "If it meant winning, of course you would. I'm starting to think you have a weird addiction to humbling me."

I laughed, and Barrett's eyes dipped briefly down to my mouth. Well, since he was already there, I picked up another cookie—I'd lost count at this point—and pointedly bit the head off a gingerbread man. I finished chewing the bite, then licked the crumbs from the corner of my lips.

"Sore loser?" I asked when he stared down at the board with a slow shake of his head.

"That's *not* a word," he insisted.

The kids watched us with wide eyes, because the game of Scrabble after the Monopoly round where Barrett wiped out his son had gotten much more competitive than anyone could've foreseen.

"It *is* a word, you just don't know it," I told him. "I told you I was good at this game."

"She did," Bryce whispered loudly. "And we looked it up; it counts."

Barrett sat back in his chair and pinned me with a fiery look. I merely smiled, settling my folded hands on the table in front of us. "*Q* is on the triple-word score too." I sighed. "Brutal."

"Definition," he bit out.

"Sorry?"

"I want the definition," he said, enunciating the words. "I think you found some cheater Scrabble loophole, and my kids are ganging up on me because they love seeing me lose this game."

Maggie giggled. "We do. We can't ever beat you."

Bryce moved around to Barrett's side of the table and cuddled in under his dad's raised arm. The easy affection was killer on my resolve. To my utter dismay, he was not a scary militant Christmas dad. We'd gone the entire day without a single mention of the time. He'd let his kids pick the movies—we'd moved on to *A Christmas Story*—as well as the games being played. The mood was chill. And dare I say, fun?

Until this sweet, delicious moment right here, he was a levelheaded competitor who did a great job patiently herding his kids through whatever was in front of them. Honestly, who needed drugs when there was winning at Scrabble against Barrett King?

"Q-A-T," Bryce read slowly. "It refers to the leaves of a shrub." He leaned in and whispered to his dad, "I can't pronounce the scientific name."

"I can see it," Barrett said patiently, sending me a quick glare.

Again, I smiled. Just a little one. Enough to make his glare intensify.

Bryce continued, "You can chew them like tobacco or make them into a tea, and it, um, it gives you a eu-euphoric sensation. What's that?"

I leaned back and spread my arms out over the chairs on either side of me. "Buddy, *this* feeling right here is euphoric," I said, holding Barrett's gaze. "Winning against someone who badly needed to be beaten. There's nothing better in the world."

Barrett exhaled steadily, and the sheer annoyance in his eyes made me fucking giddy.

"Fine," he said, raising his hands and letting them drop. "I concede. You win."

Maggie whooped, giving me such an enthusiastic high five that the skin on my palm stung. "That was awesome. I'm using that on everyone now."

"Too bad this was our last game of Scrabble ever," Barrett said lightly.

"No," the kids wailed, laughing as their dad started picking up the pieces of the game.

"Yup. New house rule: No Scrabble, no weird leaf names."

I bit down on a grin and picked up my tile board, fingers brushing lightly against his when I handed it over. He glanced at me, then back down at the box as he put everything away.

"Can we do one present tonight?" Bryce begged. "We'll save everything else for tomorrow morning."

"Please," Maggie also begged. "Then Lily can see us open something."

Barrett and I traded a quick look, and when he gave a subtle arch of his eyebrow, I turned to his daughter. "If your dad says yes, I might have brought something for you and your brother."

"Really?" She bounced on her toes, gripping her dad's arm. "Daddy, *please*. Just one. I'll never ask again."

He laid a big hand on the top of her head, and his mouth almost pulled into a visible smile.

Almost.

"What have we said about making promises we know we can't keep?" he said evenly.

She let out a heavy sigh. "Fine. I won't ask again *this* year."

I covered my mouth with my hand to hide my smile. Barrett noticed.

"One," he said.

The kids shouted, running over toward the tree and settling on the ground to study the pile of boxes. I picked up the top of the Scrabble box and handed it to Barrett. His eyes were fixed on the tattoo on the inside of my forearm, visible now that I'd pushed up the sleeves of my sweatshirt.

"Have a problem with tattoos?" I asked lightly.

Here we go. Here's where grumpy Barrett would come back out. He'd say something about marking your body permanently and how unwise it was, how it sent a bad message to his kids or something. My loins were *girded* before he even opened his mouth, defensiveness making the hairs on the back of my neck stand up.

"Just wondering what it is," he said, giving me a brief look. "You've got a few of them."

Oh. The neck hair settled as his simple answer deflated the response cocked and ready to go. Even that made me feel prickly, the unexpected reactions.

"I have more that you can't see." His hands stilled as he closed the box, and he didn't lift his gaze to mine, but the air thickened all the same. Briefly, I touched the simple outline of a car on my skin next to the bend of my elbow. "They each have a story," I told him. "But I don't usually share them."

Barrett straightened, his handsome face inscrutable.

"Then why get them if you don't want people to understand?"

His eyes weren't a simple dark brown at all. They were gold and hazel and a touch of green, and I never would've known that unless I got close enough to see.

So I stepped back. Added space. Provided distance where it was badly needed.

"Because I didn't get them for anyone else," I told him. "They're just for me."

Barrett hummed in response, the low pitch to his voice raising the hair on my arms this time. Not a defensive reaction at all. It was awareness, tugging at a neglected part of my brain, and the pleasant reverberations of that awareness had me breathing a little unsteadily.

If he noticed, he didn't show it. There was nothing to be gleaned from his facial expressions.

What a pair we were, because I imagined my face held a similar look. Like two Sphinxes staring each other down.

What secrets were held behind his walls? I knew what was guarded behind mine. Which was why, in typical Lily fashion, I desperately searched for a change in subject.

"Do you have fifteen-minute gift-buying breaks during your day too?" I asked, picking up my bag from where I'd set it on the floor. "That's an impressive pile for a single dad who works a million hours a week."

He paused, holding my gaze for a moment before answering. "No. I have a very thorough executive assistant who knows my children well, and shops for me because she knows I don't have time."

"Ah yes, Bridget." I smiled. "We've texted."

"I heard."

The grump made his first appearance with that growly, annoyed response, and my smile spread.

"And she puts up with you full-time? You must pay her a lot."

"I do," he answered. "Though she'd argue I can always do more, especially on the days I drive her crazy."

"Daily, then?" I asked sweetly.

"Dad, come on," Maggie begged. "You can pick up later. You said we have to be in bed in thirty minutes, and if we get something really cool, I'm going to want to play with it."

Barrett nodded toward my empty glass of ice water. "Sorry, I'm not a very good host. I don't have any wine or beer to offer."

I shrugged. "I don't drink, so water is fine with me."

He paused, giving me a thoughtful look. "I don't either."

We walked into the family room, his shoulder brushing mine before he stopped, allowing me to choose a seat first.

Nothing about this man was what I thought it would be. He chose a seat a respectable distance from mine, a full couch cushion open between us. There was no manspreading into my space, and I tucked my legs underneath me while I studied him.

Before Scrabble, he'd changed from the button-down into a well-loved black sweatshirt with a yellow *O* on it. He caught me staring while the kids poked and prodded at the gifts. "What?"

"Nothing," I said, blinking away. "Just wondering what the *O* stands for."

"Oregon," he answered. "My brother and I played college ball there."

I nodded. "The fun uncle," I said lightly. "I've heard all about him."

Barrett's smile was faint, hardly even a real smile—more like a begrudging softening to the normally firm line of his mouth. "I'm sure you have. Kids don't see him as much as they'd like, but he's just as busy as I am." He rolled his neck. "He plays for Denver."

"Parents must have one hell of a gene pool."

He huffed a small noise of amusement. "I guess. I never really thought about it."

"Lily, can we open your presents tonight?" Maggie asked.

"Sure, if that's the one you pick, but it doesn't have to be just because I'm here."

Bryce pursed his lips and stared between the box I'd brought for him and the other presents marked as his under the tree. "I think I'm going to open my present from Mom."

Barrett raised his eyebrows. "You sure?"

He nodded. "Then I can tell her thank you when we talk to her in the morning. Is that okay?" Bryce asked me. He looked nervous.

"Of course," I assured him. "It's your Christmas, bud. Open whatever you'd like."

His shoulders dropped as he exhaled. "'Kay, cool."

"I'm opening Lily's," Maggie announced. "I get presents every year from Mom, and they're *never* good."

"Maggie," Barrett admonished gently.

"What?" She shrugged. "I'm not saying anything bad about Mom; I know that's not allowed. I'm talking about her gifts."

I cut him a quick sideways glance and was surprised by how exhausted he looked at the topic shift. It was human nature, to want to know more about what had happened between him and his ex. The kids didn't talk about her much, and I didn't want to pry.

That was a lie. I totally did.

The important part was that I had *restraint* and, like a mature adult, I managed to use it when it mattered. Sort of.

As oldest, Bryce went first. The gift was meticulously wrapped, shiny silver paper and a black ribbon crisscrossing over the top. He took his time opening it at the edges, until Maggie groaned.

"You're so slow. Just rip it."

"I don't like ripping it," he argued. "Rip your own."

Inside the box was a button-down dress shirt with a designer pattern, the brand expensive enough that my eyebrows lifted of their own volition. That shirt probably cost five hundred dollars.

Bryce put on a brave face, lifting it up out of the box. The pattern was a large repeat of the brand logo. I rolled my lips between my teeth, imagining Bryce, the kid who always wore sports T-shirts and jerseys and athletic pants, throwing that on before school.

He winced when the shirt was fully exposed. "It's . . . nice."

Maggie fell over in helpless giggles. "You're not going to wear that, are you?"

Barrett rubbed the edge of his jaw, eyeing the shirt. "Maggie, enough. Maybe he likes it."

"I really don't," Bryce said under his breath. Then he set aside the shirt and saw a five-hundred-dollar bill on the bottom of the box. "Whoa. I'm rich."

Next to me, Barrett let out a barely contained sigh. "I'll put that in your bank account, bud. We're not going to keep that much cash for your wallet."

"Aw, why not?" At the look his dad gave him, Bryce sighed. "Fine. It can go in the bank."

"You can still buy something. It's your money, but we just want to make sure we take care of it."

Bryce perked up. "Whatever I want?"

"Within reason. You come up with a list, and we'll talk it over."

That seemed to appease him.

Neither of the kids commented on the lack of card with the present, so maybe they were used to it. But I noticed, and it plucked at some sad little chord inside me that I preferred to stay . . . unplucked.

It was Maggie's turn next, and as she started tearing into the wrapping paper, I said, "Just to temper your expectations, I did not slip five hundred bucks in there."

She breathed out a short laugh, and even though I could feel the weight of Barrett's gaze on the side of my face, I ignored it. Maggie carefully opened the envelope attached to the top of the box, her eyes skimming the card.

The moment awareness hit, I saw it in the widening of her eyes, her mouth going slack. The card was carefully set aside, and then she took a deep breath and ripped off the final piece of paper covering the label.

Maggie squealed when she saw the picture on the side.

"No way," she breathed. "It's yellow?"

"How else are we going to know it's yours?"

Barrett leaned forward as his daughter unearthed her present. Carefully, she pulled out the first layer of Styrofoam until the pale yellow of the mixer was visible.

"You got me a real baking mixer?" she said, eyes filling immediately. She dashed at her cheeks when tears spilled over, and I felt a pinch of panic in my chest that I'd overstepped.

"Oh, honey, I didn't mean to make you upset."

She shook her head furiously. "You didn't."

Then she launched herself into my lap, and for a stunned second, I looked helplessly over at Barrett as I rubbed his daughter's back.

He stared down at the mixer, his brow furrowed.

My hands felt tingly. Bad tingly. *Really* bad tingly—anxious *what the fuck did I do* tingles, and a few deep breaths did not make them disappear right away.

Maggie sniffed and pulled back, color high in her cheeks. "I love it, thank you," she whispered.

My heart was in my throat when I answered. "You're welcome. It's going to take practice to figure out how to use it. You'll make a few messes, but that's why it's good to have your own. You get the feel for it."

She nodded, immediately pulling out the different hooks and attachments. "Will you show me what these do?"

"If your dad's okay with it," I said, not willing to look over at him again.

"Daddy, can she? Maybe after Christmas?"

"Yeah, sure," he answered. His voice—that deep, goose bump–inducing timbre—gave nothing away. "It's time for bed, kids."

They groaned, but with a simple look from Barrett, they stopped. Which . . . highly impressive, if you think about it.

I stood, feeling a little self-conscious that I was still present for the whole "bedtime routine" part of the night. The day had been so much easier than I'd thought it would be, and in some ways, a lot fucking harder.

It was being part of someone else's family traditions that had the inevitable effect of making you think about your own. Or lack thereof. Of the consequences of moving around so much that you didn't have time to create traditions somewhere.

My only tradition—for any holiday, any part of the calendar—was movement.

There was an emptiness present in my life that was filled by theirs, especially in moments like this. Watching movies and playing games and eating cookies. Yes, I could do some of those things on my own, but wasn't sharing it with someone else what made it special?

I wasn't sure there was a clear answer. If that empty space didn't bother me, then it wasn't wrong. Just like forcing yourself to be part of someone's traditions wasn't automatically right. But I hadn't been forced into being here.

I'd chosen it. And after giving the kids a hug, wishing them a Merry Christmas, thanking Maggie for the invite, and then watching Barrett walk them down the hallway and up the stairs, I knew I would've chosen it again.

I thought of my bags and suitcases, tucked away in a closet at Scott and Patty's, and the weariness of having to fill them again made my entire body feel heavy. Tired. Could I do this forever?

I wasn't sure anymore. And for so damn long, it was all I'd wanted.

Nervous energy had me pacing into the kitchen, unable to leave the mess I'd helped create. I moved quickly, stacking cookies into a plastic container and then soaping up a washcloth to wipe down the island. There was still a bit of flour on the floor, but I was able to get that wiped up too.

The cookie sheets, washed and dripping, went onto the drying rack to the right of the sink, and I searched through a few drawers until I found clean dish towels so that I could dry and put them away.

There were still muffled noises from upstairs, so I knew I had time to sneak out before Barrett made his way downstairs. My mind conjured the image before I could stop it. Running into him in a dark kitchen, without the kids to distract us. My stomach pitched with nerves, a persistent fluttering behind my ribs that really pissed me off. That was the last thing I fucking needed.

But I still couldn't bring myself to bolt, and I dug my proverbial heels in when the question of why poked at my subconscious.

Everything about him—*them*, really—had me feeling a little off-kilter. Did he hate me? I wasn't sure anymore. On my end, at least, there'd been no flirty energy, because honestly I did not need those kids picking up on any subtext. Knowing Maggie, she'd *Parent Trap* the shit out of us. Find some clever way to lock us in the house together for a weekend, hoping I'd emerge with a ring on my finger and her dad hopelessly in love with me.

I snorted, drying the last cookie sheet and tucking it away in the correct cupboard. The counter was clean again; no dishes remained in the sink after I'd loaded everything into the dishwasher. With a quick exhale, I folded the towel and hung it neatly over the handle of the oven door.

My bag was empty save for my unused cookie cutters, and when I slung the handle over my shoulder, I paused before leaving the kitchen, looking back at their tree.

A Christmas Story was playing on TV again, and when Ralphie opened his Red Ryder BB gun, his face reminded me of Maggie seeing her mixer.

It was too much, I scolded myself. The present went too far for a temporary babysitter. A temporary neighbor. Bryce would love his gift too; I'd found a vintage jersey of a British football team he'd told me he loved. But I couldn't deny that Maggie's gift was different, that I'd picked it out for her knowing exactly how much it would mean. And that maybe, *maybe*, a small part of me would be remembered after I was gone.

It was the first time that particular thought was allowed to take root in my head. After a decade of movement, a decade of outrunning my own shit, I was thinking about what would be left behind. Selfishness took many forms, and that withered part of me that missed companionship blossomed under the self-centered thought that maybe, just maybe, someone would *miss* me when I was gone.

Maybe Maggie and I could maintain a friendship . . .

Maybe this time, I could keep in touch with someone. I could find postcards at a new location and have a place to mail them. Write down more than just my favorite things and hide them in a book. I could share a piece of my life with someone.

My hands were trembling, my head down as I started to walk away.

Leave. Leave now. You say you don't want to get caught, but you are a cookie-eating, Scrabble-winning liar, Lily Marie Townsend.

I blew out a slow breath and paused, closing my eyes while I tried desperately to ignore the truth of that while it blared in my head. When my eyes opened, I found myself face-to-face with Barrett in the arched entrance to the room.

"Oh," I said on a shocked exhale, my heart banging around inside my chest. "How are you so fucking quiet when you walk around?"

His eyes moved over my face. "Been holding on to that swear word all night, haven't you?"

"Yes."

He shook his head, mouth softening. A little. "I suppose this means our truce is over."

I cleared my throat. "I suppose."

Barrett didn't move away. Neither did I.

Then he moved, just half a step. Closer, though, not farther away.

The sudden nearness of him had me jumpy, my hands unable to fidget properly because they were empty, and I didn't think he'd appreciate me using his soft-looking sweatshirt as an outlet for my repressed sexual energy.

Besides, what was I going to do? Yank on the front until he was two inches away? No thanks.

Knowing my luck, he smelled even better the closer he got; then what would happen? Chaos. Anarchy. Probably some really great sex, if he'd let himself relax long enough to break a few rules.

My skin tightened at the thought, adding to the unrelenting noise in my head that I couldn't get a handle on. It would be good. There was no doubt in my mind that it would be incredible.

Biting kisses. The kind that felt like a fight.

Torn clothes. Slow wouldn't happen, not between us. It wouldn't be reluctant or hesitant.

Knocked-over furniture. Held up by walls and tables because moving to a bed would take too long, would allow for second-guessing and more rational heads to prevail.

Sex that allowed anger to hold the reins. Attraction that pissed both of us off, because I was quite sure neither of us wanted to be attracted to the other, but it was there, had been there from the moment I slammed the door in his face, and we both fucking knew it.

This was something I could leave behind, too, a different sort of legacy, comprised of dirty words and greedy hands and Barrett's undoing in a way that felt like another win.

Even thinking it caused a rapid-fire deterioration of my verbal filter, which had been firmly in place after the regrettable *daddy* comment. There were no kids watching now, and yes, there was a teensy little devil on my shoulder—wearing a Santa hat and looking a little bit like one of the elves from the movie—and that little sucker was begging to be heard. To see if Barrett felt even an iota of the leashed energy I had coursing through my veins.

Proximity to him, it seemed, was the impetus for all my worst impulses to come out to play.

"Lily—" He paused, seemingly searching for words. Then he looked up. "Oh."

"What?" Then I looked up, too, my heart lodging itself right in my fucking throat. *"Oh."*

Hanging directly above us, in an inconspicuous little bundle of bad decisions and inevitable regret, was mistletoe. My lips curled in a pleased smile.

Perfect.

Chapter Twelve

Barrett

"This is interesting."

She was still staring up at the mistletoe when she said it, a casual tilt to her head that sent her long hair spilling over her shoulders. Only during the cookie-baking process had it been tied back, but as soon as they were done, she let it down again.

The sight of it gave me the most irrational reaction. Chiefly, a skin-tingling curiosity that needed a mute button because I patently refused to give it any headway.

Was it soft? It looked soft.

My hands curled up in helpless fists, and I sucked in a breath. "Is it?"

Her eyes—that dark-navy color—flicked to mine. "You're saying you didn't put it there?"

My head reared back. "*No*. Why would I?"

"God, Barrett, if you wanted to kiss me, you could just say so." Lily bit down on her bottom lip, casually surveying my facial expression. "Not what I expected for a Christmas present, but I suppose I can consider this part of the truce."

"I did not put that there to try and kiss you, Lily," I said evenly. Fucking miracle, that, because my pulse was entering dangerous territory—thready and fast and roaring in my ears. Panic made me lightheaded, and I tried to back up, but there was a wall directly behind me, and when my back hit said wall with an audible thud, Lily's eyes lit up.

"No tongue, then?"

"Lily," I practically growled.

"So you don't want to kiss me," she said seriously, taking another step closer. "I feel like . . . like I might be a little bit offended."

My throat was bone dry as I tried to swallow, and fucking hell, I was hard as a rock behind my jeans. "Please, I couldn't offend you even if I tried. You'd have to care what I thought first."

Her lips pursed into an amused little pout. "True. But what if *you're* my type?"

I blinked. "What?"

Slowly, she licked her lips, her teeth biting down on the shiny, wet bottom lip before she took another step closer. "What if, after a day without bickering and snarling at each other, I find myself attracted to someone who's a little bit quiet?" she whispered.

Her hand reached out, one finger winding into the material of my sweatshirt, raising goose bumps along my arms. Thank God she couldn't see them.

"Very serious. Kinda growly. *Sucks* at Scrabble." Her lashes fluttered, a shaky inhale through open lips. I was transfixed. "Maybe I want someone who's a little mean to me," she whispered. Then she lifted her eyes. "What then?"

Every muscle in my body screamed to do something. To snatch her behind the neck and slant my mouth over hers, lick against her tongue and see how her ass felt underneath my hands.

It was all I could do to keep breathing, to not let her see how unmoored I felt by her unexpected proximity. There was no control to be found here, no discipline, unless I wrenched it up to the surface with bloodied nails.

Just when I opened my mouth to speak, Lily let go of my shirt, her lips curling into a secretive little smile. "No matter," she said airily. "It must be all the cookies going to my head, because I'm pretty sure my dog fits that description too."

As she took a step back, ready to pass by me, I pushed off the wall and my hand shot out, palm anchored on the wall next to her head.

Lily reared back, her eyes wide.

Rapid breathing had her chest rising and falling, and simply because I knew they existed, my brain focused in on one searing fact: Underneath that baggy sweatshirt, she was hiding incredible curves. It didn't make her any less attractive because she wasn't showing them. In fact, this side of her, the one I'd seen all night—sweeter than I'd imagined, almost unbearably kind with my kids, filling the house with a warmth that by all rights shouldn't have come from this prickly, surprising woman—simply made her even more attractive. Dangerously, hopelessly attractive, because both sides of her existed in one stunning package.

"What are you doing?" she snapped, the defensiveness back in full force.

The sudden flip in her demeanor wasn't upsetting or surprising. If anything, a switch flipped in my head, clarity flooding my brain.

"Don't play," I told her, my voice raw, and even to my own ears it sounded dangerous. She must have heard it, because she sucked in a quick breath and lifted her chin. A show of strength, pulling up on her backbone, much like I'd done when she'd prodded me in a very different way.

Lily scoffed. "Who's playing now?" she asked, tilting her head toward my hand on the wall, where I'd effectively caged her in.

"I don't have the time or inclination for games." I held her gaze unflinchingly. "And you know that's not what I'm doing. So you better think really carefully before you try something like this with me again."

Her throat worked on a swallow. Then her eyes dropped down to the floor. It was as close to an admission of guilt as I'd get. When she lifted them again, they were carefully blank, like she'd slammed a wall over whatever she was feeling.

"I don't really know what I expected you to do," she said quietly. "I didn't . . . I didn't mean to be disrespectful."

The honesty had me dropping my hand but not moving back. One step and her chest would brush mine, so I held carefully still.

"I think you know exactly what you expected me to do."

Lily sucked in a breath. "Most men would've taken advantage of that moment," she said, eyes still on my face.

"Most men might have," I told her. "Believe me, if I wanted to kiss you, I wouldn't need a fucking plant to make me do it."

Her eyes flickered. "Take-charge type, are you?"

I pulled in a slow breath through my nose. "When the moment's right, yes."

God, who could remember? Not me.

She hummed. "But this moment isn't right?"

We were dancing a line, tiptoeing around the edge. By calling her bluff, I'd stepped over it into her space before she'd known what was happening. There was nothing to be gained by going any further, but the uncomfortable tightening in my stomach, the overwhelming need to inject honesty into whatever this was—it pushed me there anyway.

"You don't even like me," I pointed out quietly.

This time, it wasn't a coy smile that spread. It wasn't teasing or meant to entice. It was pure amusement. The sight of it left me a little stunned, and I fought not to let my mouth fall open.

"I don't know about that," she said cryptically, then walked away to slip her feet into her boots where they sat by the door. "You're growing on me, Barrett. Like a barnacle."

I rolled my eyes. "Lovely."

Instead of tugging on her coat, she draped it over her arm. "Thank you for inviting me. It was nice—and weird—not to be alone tonight."

A million questions threatened on the tip of my tongue, but I swallowed them. "It's cold outside. You should put your coat on," I said, unable to help myself. Her eyes gleamed, and I gave her a stern look. "Don't you dare call me *daddy* right now."

She sighed, sounding terribly put out. "I told you, that's not my jam. I mean, no kink-shaming or anything if it's yours."

"It's not," I said dryly. Not that I knew what my kinks were anymore.

Other than long-legged brunettes with mysterious tattoos and a mean streak.

Lily opened the door, sending me one last smile over her shoulder. But when I followed behind her, she paused, the edges of her smile dropping. "What are you doing?"

"Watching until you get inside," I explained. My cheeks were hot, and I felt a little—a lot—stupid. But the urge was there, and ignoring it would only make things worse.

She blinked. "I live next door."

"And it's slippery out," I barked. "What if you fall and hit your head?"

"Oh my." She sighed. "You really are a pessimist, aren't you?"

We walked side by side down the driveway, and when we cleared the edge of my garage, I stopped. "Hard habit to break," I admitted gruffly. "You telling me you don't watch my kids when they come home in the evenings?"

"Of course I do," she said, completely affronted. "But that's different."

I held her gaze, and my tongue. The quickest way under her skin, I'd learned, was my silence. If she expected a big reaction, she wouldn't get one, and when she screwed up her lips, impatiently waiting for me to attempt the last word, a flicker of satisfaction burned bright under my chest.

Maybe I *was* playing a game of sorts; it just wasn't a game I was used to.

I expected Lily to scoff and march off, but she stood there instead, her breath visible in puffy little clouds from the frigid air. For a moment, she glanced at Scott and Patty's home, then looked back at me. There was no wall anymore. Her eyes were big in her face, and she blinked a few times like . . . like she was nervous.

"It's a car," she said quickly.

I tilted my head. "What is?"

She licked her lips, the movement quick and jerky, nothing like when she'd done it earlier. With one hand, she pushed the sleeve of her sweatshirt up and gently tapped the small tattoo just beneath her elbow. "It's a car," she repeated quietly. "My . . . my dad loved working on old cars. When I was little, I'd always find him tinkering on one. The smell of a garage still reminds me of him."

Somehow I was able to tear my stunned gaze away from her unexpectedly vulnerable expression to glance down at her arm. The silhouette was a simple line, graceful and small, and unless you studied it closely, you might not notice what it was.

"That's one," I said quietly, unthinkingly. How many more did she have?

She let out a small laugh. "I guess."

"Why'd you tell me?"

Lily shrugged one shoulder, tugging her sleeve back down until the ink disappeared. What other stories did she hold on her skin? The curiosity might drive me mad before she left, but this explanation felt like a strange gift.

The sky above us was ink black, a thick cloud cover blocking out the moon and the stars. Instead of answering, she stared up at it for a long moment.

Then she looked at me, her face open and direct as she smiled. A real smile. Genuine but small, and I felt it in my lungs. In my stomach too. "Merry Christmas, Barrett."

"Merry Christmas." I hardly spoke above a whisper, but she heard me, nodding at my response before crunching through the snow between our houses. Lily let herself in the front door without looking back in my direction. When the lights went on inside the house, I let out a slow breath.

It had been so long since I'd felt the aching, unnamed thing swirling around my chest, I could hardly recognize it long enough to give it a name.

Scarier than attraction. Bigger than lust. It wasn't about wanting her. If I was being honest with myself, I'd wanted her the moment I saw her wrapped in my favorite blanket, wearing my slippers.

What was larger than want? What eclipsed simple desire?

Nothing I had time for, that was for damn sure.

I ran a hand over my mouth and stared at the house for another moment, refusing to label anything. Unearthing new impressions of someone took a certain level of humility. You had to set aside what you knew of them before.

When I went back inside my house, I locked the door behind me and shook my head, thinking of all the different things I'd thought of her from that first exchange.

Rude.

Cold.

Prickly.

Impertinent.

Surprising.

And what now? The sight of my daughter's present, something thoughtful that would likely be her favorite gift of the year, tugged at that empty spot in my chest that was feeling things long unfelt. On top of the box was the card she gave Maggie, and with a sigh, I bent down to pick it up.

Her handwriting was neat and small.

> Maggie,
> You are one of the best gifts I've gotten this year. Thank you for climbing through the fence and making my life just a bit sweeter. Please self-destruct this letter before my hardcore reputation is ruined. Merry Christmas, my favorite little wild thing. I hope you never lose who you are right now.
>
> Always,
> Lily T.

Emotion tightened my throat as I thought of what something like that would mean to my daughter, but I swallowed it away. To feel seen and appreciated during a stretch of time when we were ironing out so many kinks in our new life—it was something Maggie would remember forever.

Slowly, I sank down on the couch, my head reeling. All it took was one day, and so many carefully constructed barriers could be irrevocably shaken. I wasn't even sure how to go about erecting them again.

It was good that I hadn't kissed Lily. Only madness would've followed.

It was good because I didn't want to kiss her.

I didn't want to know what sounds she made. Or if her lips were sweet and soft. It was entirely possible that all this time with no female companionship had simply forced my brain in her direction because I was mildly curious. There was no big, dark, unnamed thing swimming under the surface, no matter what it had felt like standing in the cold with her.

Like everything else in my life, I could slot her into the space where she made the most sense. Define her in a way that was clear so that the way I defined myself remained the same.

Yes. I could do that. I'd made a living being able to do that with every other facet of my life. It was why I was successful.

Redefining Lily was the only course of action. That was why, as I laid my head back and stared up at the ceiling, I thought about dark-blue eyes until I fell asleep.

Chapter Thirteen

Lily

"I think I need new friends."

Larry sighed, a disgruntled little sound, and merely burrowed farther down into the fuzzy blanket close to the fireplace. His buggy eyes were barely visible, but he was at least looking at me, so there was that.

"I'm serious, you're terrible at this. It's Christmas Day and you won't even listen to my predicament."

I picked at the edge of my pajamas—yes, I was still in pajamas because no one could tell me not to be on Christmas Day—chest heavy and stomach unsettled as my overthinking reached wild new heights. I probably had bags under my eyes the size of lemons because that overthinking had elbowed right into my REM cycle.

Normally, I slept like a baby. Every night.

But last night? I had my own Ebenezer Scrooge moment. Haunted by the ghost of me. Past Lily, who did not think through what she was doing. This was what happened when you didn't people very much. All it took was two cute kids and a Captain von Trapp fantasy come to life, and I was going around acting like a wild animal. I couldn't take me anywhere, and that was a good lesson for the future.

"I don't know why I did it," I said quietly. "It's like I can't help myself sometimes, you know? He's just so . . . just so contained. I can never tell what he's thinking. And I just wanted to make him do something. React."

Larry blinked.

"I used to do this a lot, you know." I stretched my feet out closer to the fire, sighing happily when the heat penetrated through my socks. "Push at people to try and get a reaction. It drove Mom and Dad crazy, didn't it?" I laughed quietly, swallowing the lump in my throat. "The Button Pusher. That's what Aaron called me. You probably remember, don't you?"

The dog closed his eyes and sighed.

"Fine. We don't have to talk about it if it makes you uncomfortable." I wiggled my toes. "What should we do today? I can't sit here and talk about Barrett all day. That would be . . . embarrassing. And silly. Wouldn't it be silly?"

He was unmoved, his eyes still shut.

"Larry," I said. Whined. Whined petulantly.

I could call myself a lot of names, but that was the first time in my entire adult life I'd used *petulant*.

It looked like my Christmas present to myself was an absolutely untenable new situation with Barrett King. Because for a split second, just one teensy little second, when his arm had caged me in, I almost sort of, kind of, wanted him to kiss me. *Really* kiss me too. Wrap his big hand behind my neck and tease my lips with his, slide his tongue into my open mouth and make one of those really great noises at the back of his throat—a deep, satisfied noise at the taste of me.

Just for a second, of course.

It hadn't really been a teensy second, though. It had been a big one. It had been many seconds that made up many minutes. Then, when I lay in bed later, revisiting the horrors of those minutes, I swear I could feel the ghost of him, pressing me up against the wall behind my back. He'd tower over me, his body so much bigger than mine.

I don't know what universe I was living in that a man towering over my anything sounded like a great fucking time, but regardless, it was where I found myself.

If I wanted to kiss you, I wouldn't need a fucking plant to make me do it.

I laid a hand on my chest, the thundering of my heart the only distraction.

"I need a hobby. Or I need to go sightseeing." An errant thought occurred to me. "Maybe I just need to get laid," I whispered. "It's been a while. That's gotta be my problem, right? Any slightly attractive, non-smelly man could've trapped me under some mistletoe and I would've felt the same way. And I beat him in Scrabble, so my brain was already wired toward best possible outcomes in that house. It was just . . . chance. Proximity." I chewed on my bottom lip. "It's not really personal to him at all. That makes sense, doesn't it?"

I looked over at the dog.

He started snoring. Loudly.

"Whatever. Besides, it's not like he's sitting at home talking about *me*."

Barrett

"She cheats at Scrabble."

The dish beneath my hand squeaked as I scrubbed the glass mercilessly.

"Uh-huh."

I added more soap, flipped the water all the way to hot, kept my eyes laser focused on the casserole pan from dinner.

"She constantly tries to push my buttons. From the moment I met her, actually." I gripped the sponge, the veins in my arms popping out as I scrubbed into the corner. "Don't ask me how she's so different with the kids. I think Christmas Eve was her idea, you know? Maybe Maggie didn't even come up with the idea. Maybe it was Lily. And it worked."

"I'm not sure—"

"And then," I interrupted, "she tells me that *I* must have hung the mistletoe. Like I'd ever hang mistletoe. Trapping people under some silly plant, forcing them into situations they don't want to be in. Non-consent hidden under the facade of a horrible tradition."

"Right."

Two days.

It had been two days and I couldn't force that woman from anywhere. Not from my brain. Not from . . . other parts of my anatomy that were still very interested in thinking about her. Not from my—

No.

Once the gifts were finished—after Bryce opened up his gift from Lily with an awe-filled expression that made my throat tight—I'd made it through Christmas Day just fine. Watched football with the kids. Played a few more games—not Scrabble—and never once did I ask them about her or look next door or wonder, even the slightest bit, if she was sitting home alone that day too. Good for fucking me.

Not only that, but I survived one more day of my kids terrorizing the front offices before they went with Bridget to pick up my parents from the airport.

They were still awake when I got home from the office around ten p.m.

"And do you know what happened today at work?"

"It is very hard to say at this point."

I kept scrubbing and scrubbing. "I was late to a meeting because I started looking up words for Scrabble." My voice rose in volume with each consecutive word, and for the first time in my life, it felt like I was strapped to a runaway train. "Now she's ruining my first day back to the office when I have the last game of the season against a division rival on Sunday—and if we lose, it's going to be because I was thinking about mistletoe and Q words and how the hell she smells like cookies all the time!" I yelled.

The dish slipped out of my hands, clattering into the sink. Chest heaving, I braced my hands on the edge of the counter and hung my head.

"Fuck," I muttered under my breath.

When I finally looked up again, my parents were staring at me like I'd lost my mind. My dad still had one of Lily's cookies in his hand, frozen halfway to his mouth. My mom kicked him under the table.

"I just . . . I just asked how she made these cookies taste so good," my dad said. "I didn't know all *that* would happen."

My mom tried to hide her smile.

It would've been so much easier to brush it all off, to change the subject, but I couldn't bring myself to do that either. The decision to dismantle whatever softened feelings for Lily that had emerged had been a good one.

Smart and wise and logically sound. I didn't have time to feel things. Didn't have time to think about her tattoos or why she was alone or the color of her eyes. But there had been a slow deterioration of that decision over the course of the forty-eight hours that followed. When I stopped to think about that deterioration, the only thing that made sense was because *Lily* didn't make any logical sense.

I couldn't make her fit into a single, neat definition, and ultimately, it was proving to be my undoing. Helpless frustration, as it usually did, made me feel like the worst version of myself. Control clawed to the surface, a desperate bid to ignore the one thing—the person—making me feel the most out of control.

The dish towel sat next to the sink, and I snatched it up, then wiped down the casserole dish until it was dry.

My mom cleared her throat. "I'd already washed that, you know."

I rolled my lips between my teeth, praying that the heat crawling up my neck wasn't visible.

"Well, now it's extra clean," I said gruffly.

Dad was finishing the cookie when I turned around, sneakily reaching forward for another one when my mom reached over and smacked his hand. "You've had four," she admonished.

"It's Christmas," he stated, shooing her hand away and getting a fifth. "And they're really good."

I crossed my arms, leaning up against the counter. "Kids okay while I finished up work?"

Mom nodded. "Perfect as always."

I snorted.

"Perfect for us, at least," my dad said. "Maggie's gonna run the world someday, you mark my words."

My shoulders relaxed at the change in subject. I just . . . I needed to stay away from the topic of Lily. Needed to stay away from *Lily* until I had a better handle on whatever this was.

"How was practice today? Archer getting in line for the last game of the season?"

I pinched the bridge of my nose. *Was* Archer getting in line?

He'd skipped all film-review sessions that morning. Hadn't taken a single note in the offensive meeting. Hadn't joined me for lunch with his receivers. And in practice, he'd said the game plan for Sunday was something his grandma could've planned better.

"Practice was fine," I said tightly. "He'll . . . he'll be fine by Sunday."

There was a beat of silence, and I ignored the wordless glance shared by my parents.

"You okay, son?" my mom asked. "You're not really acting like yourself."

Not being the perfect son who never stepped out of line. Not being the guy who never lost his grip on the leash of his legendary restraint. She was right—I wasn't acting like myself, and there was only one person to blame. It didn't matter whether I wanted to be around her. I shouldn't. Couldn't.

I held her gaze and sighed. "I'll be fine. I just need to get a few things under control."

Chapter Fourteen

Lily

"Larry, I beg of you. We're a hundred feet from home. You can make it."

He sat down on the asphalt and stared up at me, unmoving even when I gave his leash a gentle tug.

"Dude, it was one block. Don't you remember that really nice vet in Phoenix? He said that walks would do wonders for you."

He licked the tip of his nose, giving me a stubborn look. Then he shivered, and I let out a deep sigh.

"Fine." I leaned over to pick him up, and once he was tucked under my arm, he let out a disgruntled groan. I gave him a look. "I put dog mittens on your paws even though there's no snow on the road. Your coat cost more than mine. I'm not sure your complaints have a leg to stand on here, buddy."

The look he gave me was as close to a doggy eye roll that I'd ever seen, and my lips tugged in an unwitting smile.

"Come on. Let's get the mail, and I'll bring you back in, where you can turn back into a couch slug for the rest of the day. And yes, I'll put on the diaper before you start bitching to me about having to pee in the snow."

The walk in question wouldn't have taken very long, but, like it always did, Larry's little gremlin face had neighbors crossing the street to say hello. The dog stared at each and every one of them like they'd done him personal injury.

Did that deter them?

Not in the slightest.

"Oh, isn't he cute? What's his name?"

My head snapped up because I'd been thinking about too-friendly neighbors and their obsession with the dog, but unfortunately, this voice had come from outside the confines of my head. A taller-than-average woman with short curls in a light-silver color was standing at the end of Barrett's driveway.

I blinked, then glanced down at the dog.

Not fucking again, I could hear him say. I shifted his slight weight in my arms. "Larry," I told her. "Unfortunately, his personality doesn't match his looks. One can only be so blessed, you know? If he had both, it would be unfair to dogs all around the world."

She laughed, folding her arms tight around her middle and walking toward me. Internally, I let out a heaving, massive groan, and it probably sounded a lot like Larry's.

Two peas in a pod, we were.

But instead of asking about the dog, she was studying me. "If that's Larry, then you must be Lily."

"Oh God," I groaned. "I'm scared to ask how you know that."

She laughed under her breath, and for a split second, I thought I saw something familiar in her face. "My grandchildren have done nothing but talk about you for the last two weeks."

I let out a big puff of air. "Ah. Maggie has been texting me updates of the things you've been doing over break. You're Barrett's mom."

"You can call me Robin. And yes, most days, I'll claim him," she said, eyes sparkling with humor. Not like her son in that way, then. "From what I hear, I owe you a thank-you on multiple levels."

"For what?"

My short response didn't deter her in the slightest—but then again, if she'd birthed Barrett King, she was used to less-than-stellar people skills.

"Well, my husband would thank you for the best cookies he's ever eaten." I exhaled a short laugh, briefly looking down to the asphalt because my cheeks were probably pink as shit. She wasn't done, though. "For helping with my grandkids and taking such good care of them." She tilted her head back toward the house. "Maggie, in particular. She has a tendency to get into trouble when the wrong person is in charge."

"You know, Barrett said that, but I thought he was exaggerating because he was so pissed at me."

Her smile was huge. "No, he was telling the truth. Did he tell you about the time she forged paperwork so she and Bryce could fly to Colorado to visit their uncle?"

My head reared back. "She did not."

"Oh yes," Robin sighed. "Barrett came home from work and found a note. They'd already landed and found their way to his brother's house. She's skilled in many, many ways."

"Little troublemaker. No wonder I like her."

She was delighted by this answer, but the way she studied my face was disconcerting at best.

I moved Larry from one arm to the other, and he let out a low growl, which I ignored. Robin looked concerned, taking a step back. "Oh, he won't bite," I told her. "Literally can't bite. He only has half his teeth left, and I'm not sure he could muster the energy to move that quickly."

She smiled again, and I realized what looked familiar. It was the same smile as the kids'. Maybe their dad had it, too, I'd just never actually seen it.

"And you're welcome," I told her. "For the cookies and watching the kids. It was no trouble, really."

Effusive praise for both of the children threatened, but I swallowed it down because she probably already thought I was weird. There was a slight pause, and I could only imagine that she wanted to get back inside; she was wearing a sweatshirt, whereas I had my puffy black coat, gloves, and winter hat on. Actual waterproof winter boots.

Why I'd bought them was a mystery I did not want to delve into, but they were just there on the shelves when I went shopping the day before, and I thought about Bryce's little face when he'd been so concerned about my feet getting wet, and they'd hopped their ass right into my cart.

"It was nice to meet you," I told her. "Tell the kids I said hi."

Her face fell. "Oh, you're leaving already?"

My brow furrowed. "Did you want to stand outside in the freezing cold much longer?"

Robin laughed. Like it wasn't a serious question. "I don't mind the cold. We might live in Arizona now, but our whole lives we were in Michigan. That's where the boys grew up. Got the same lake-effect snow in the winter that they do here, so not much about hard winters faze us."

I leaned closer. "Everyone keeps saying that, and I genuinely don't understand the difference."

Her eyes gleamed. She found me funny, and I couldn't figure out why. "You've been here a couple weeks, right?"

I nodded.

"The Great Lakes are amazing, Lily. Absolutely nothing like them in the summer. But in the winter, they can be merciless too. All of a sudden, you get these great big fluffy flakes, flurries that seem to come out of nowhere. Or a storm front that you hardly get one day's notice, and all of a sudden a foot or two of snow gets dropped right past the lakeshore."

I wrinkled my nose. "Ew."

"It's an acquired taste," she said as she smiled. "We love it in Scottsdale, but I do miss winter."

"Why?"

"Because it's beautiful." She shrugged, looking around. There was still snow on the ground, but with a few days of above-freezing temps, a lot had melted too. "I've always thought it was a little bit magical to sit and watch it snow. Everything slows down. You have the perfect excuse to cuddle under blankets and watch movies and play games. Not go anywhere. Not rush from place to place. Just . . . enjoy that magic for a few days."

To my horror, my eyes felt gritty and my nose burned. I coughed, looking down at Larry while I blinked rapidly.

"You okay, honey?"

I glanced up, not really able to make eye contact. "Fine. Yeah, I'm . . . I'm fine. I think I got something in my eye, is all."

"Lily!" Maggie came running down the driveway, and she was also not wearing a coat.

"Where is your coat?" I asked her.

"It's not even that cold out." She scratched the top of Larry's head and smiled when he sniffed her fingers. "I think he missed me."

"Undoubtedly," I murmured. "He's sick of *me*, that's for sure."

Maggie laughed. "You met my grandma?"

Robin wrapped an arm around her granddaughter. "We were just getting to know each other a little bit. I can see why everyone likes her so much."

Robin must have low standards for conversations with strangers. Instead of telling her that, I nudged Maggie's arm. "You use your mixer again?"

"A little," she said. "We made some muffins the other day; I forgot to send you pictures. And I tried cookies yesterday, but they were really crumbly."

"Ah. You probably added too much flour."

Robin clucked her tongue. "I told you that might be the problem. I was never the baker, unfortunately. I can make a mean casserole, and I love my Crock-Pot, but I've never quite mastered cookies. It's too precise."

"Can you come over tomorrow and help me?" Maggie asked.

"I could, yeah."

She grinned. "You're not too busy? I, um, I saw you come and go a lot the last few days."

Robin gave me a soft smile.

"I was playing tourist," I told her. "I was feeling a bit cooped up in the house, so I decided to see a few of the sights."

"We've seen a bunch of cool stuff. Mostly in the summer, though. Dad's not at work quite as long during the spring and summer, so we actually see him more then." She smiled. "Do you want to come after lunch? You can tell me about everything you saw while we're baking."

Robin gave her granddaughter a look. "Your dad—"

"Won't care if Lily is coming over," Maggie finished. She turned and gave her grandma a guileless look. "He invited her over on Christmas Eve, didn't he? Tomorrow's just a random weekday. Why would it bother him?"

I pushed my tongue against the inside of my cheek and decided now wasn't the appropriate time to list the multitude of reasons why he wouldn't want me there.

Robin stared at Maggie for another second and then sighed. "I suppose you're right. He'll be just fine with it."

I smiled. "Great. After lunch, then?"

Maggie nodded. "What kind of cookies do you want to make?"

"How about I surprise you?"

Her face lit up. "Okay."

"I'll go to the store in the morning and get everything we need. Do you want to learn baking more or how to decorate?"

"Mmm, how about baking right now? Maybe we could do decorating next time?"

Next time. I had a feeling this girl would keep me busy until the day I was scheduled to leave.

Robin must have seen something in my face. "We can talk about that tomorrow, Maggie Moo."

A big black truck came down the street, slowing as it reached their house. My stomach flipped around when the window opened and Barrett's face appeared. His eyes weren't even on me, and just the sight of him felt like someone laid a big, warm hand on my throat and squeezed. Just a little.

A good kind of throat squeeze. The kind that came with kisses and naked bodies and multiple orgasms. I slicked my tongue over my teeth and prayed to every deity in existence that my face wasn't flaming red.

"Where's your coat, Maggie?" he asked.

She rolled her eyes. "That's what Lily said too."

I didn't look up at first, studiously fixated on the tuft of hair on the top of Larry's head. He really needed a good brushing or something. Finally, I raised my eyes, and he was watching me, face expressionless.

Maybe mine was too.

Yes, avoidance was best. Avoidance was great. Who needed to act like things were different? Just because he'd done the arm thing and I'd tried to goad him into kissing me, and then I'd told him about one of my tattoos. There was no need to pretend like any of that existed.

It didn't feel like my face was expressionless, though. My cheeks were warm—tellingly warm, a spotlight on all my biggest vulnerabilities. What did he see now, when he looked at me? Did I give too much away?

There was the slightest flicker in his eyes, but it disappeared just as quickly. Barrett pulled his gaze from mine, and I felt a tear in my chest when he did.

"I got pizza for dinner," Barrett said. "If you don't want it to be cold, you better come inside."

Maggie turned to me. "Do you want some pizza?"

"Maggie, we should—" Barrett said.

"Oh, I don't—" I said at the same time.

My eyes locked on his again. What was he going to say?

"Not tonight," I continued, softening my answer with a smile. "But thank you for inviting me."

Her shoulders slumped. "Okay."

Barrett's jaw twitched, and, shifting his face forward again, he rolled up the window, pulling his truck into the driveway without another word. The man from Christmas Eve was seemingly gone, the wall put firmly back in place.

"You'll still come tomorrow, though, right?" Maggie asked.

I winked. "It's a date."

Her relieved smile wiggled its way under my ribs, and instead of trying to ignore it, I decided that maybe, for today, it was okay to let it stay there.

Robin and Maggie waved goodbye, then followed Barrett, and it took me a moment before I turned and walked back to my own place.

The entire family—right up to the grandparents—seemed as if they'd been sent into my life just to unnerve me. To unseat me from the place I'd always felt safest: being alone.

Chapter Fifteen

Barrett

"Goodness, how long have you two been up?"

Mom found Dad and me sitting on the couch watching film, her robe wrapped tight around her body. My second cup of coffee was in my hand, and at his wife's entrance, Dad stood to give her a sound kiss on the mouth. It was the way he'd greeted her every morning for my entire life.

"Best part of waking up," he said, then smacked her on the bottom.

He'd also done that every morning.

Their easy affection wasn't necessarily something I took for granted; I was fully aware it wasn't normal. Especially after a decade with someone who, as it turned out, had a healthy amount of loathing for me.

"You didn't hear me come in and wake Dad?" I asked.

"No." She yawned, patting Dad on the stomach before going in search of her own coffee. "I assumed that you working from home today would mean that you'd be able to sleep in a little bit."

I exhaled a quiet laugh. "Unfortunately not. My body wakes at four thirty whether I want it to or not."

"You woke your father up at four thirty?" she asked, eyes darting between us.

"No, I was generous and gave him until five thirty." I rolled my neck. "I did my run on the treadmill and some weights first."

The basement of our home wasn't anything fancy, but it was partially finished, at least enough that I'd built a serviceable home gym so that I could get my workouts in when I was home. Bryce liked using the treadmill in the winter, keeping his conditioning up before soccer started again in the spring.

"Now, that is something he should be joining you for." Even though Mom said it pointedly, Dad ignored her, waiting until she'd finished filling her mug before holding his out for a refill. She paused, eyeing him carefully. "How many have you had? You know your doctor wants to limit your caffeine intake."

"Two small cups, and he only said that because he didn't know my son would be waking my ass up at five thirty in the morning." When she hesitated, he motioned for the carafe and filled his own mug. "My ticker is fine. It can handle a little extra oomph."

I smiled faintly.

Mom took a seat with her coffee, tugging a blanket over her legs while I cued up the next section of film. My eyes lingered on that blanket—it was the same one Lily had wrapped around her shoulders when I'd found her snooping in my office.

"What are we watching?" Mom asked, a life preserver from my own thoughts, something I desperately needed. My tablet was casting to the screen, and I tapped a few buttons, pulling up a new game since we'd already finished reviewing a different one.

"Denver versus San Diego a couple weeks ago. We play San Diego next. Denver runs a similar offense; it's good to see how they handled this game," I said carefully, glancing over at Mom's expression.

Mom's eyebrow lifted slowly. "Did you watch the game when it was on? It was a nail-biter."

"I didn't." I took the last sip of my coffee, grimacing since it was lukewarm. "Saw some highlights later, though." When I didn't say anything else, Mom and Dad traded a quick look. "Griffin played well. He always does," I added gruffly.

It couldn't be easy for them, watching their only sons, identical twins who'd been joined at the hip growing up, being slowly pulled apart by our own competitive natures, even though Griffin's looked a lot different from mine. Not just how competitive we were, but contradictory. My brother might look exactly like me, but the ease and carelessness about life that he carried around like a trophy chafed every single part of who I was.

If not for me, he would've been kicked out of college, but I'd begged Coach to give him a second chance. For years, Griffin held that against me, that I'd fought a battle for him that he didn't ask me to fight. Time passed, and we both took shots at each other that inflicted pain. By the time we were both drafted, we hardly spoke.

My injuries, career-ending and devastating in a manner that I hadn't anticipated, pitted my brother and me against each other in a different way once I retired and shifted to coaching. Suddenly, I wasn't just the King brother who played quarterback—I was the youngest offensive coordinator in the league. A couple years later, I was the youngest head coach in the NFL. The Brain, they called me. Griffin was the Brawn.

He was the life of the party. Constantly getting tabloid attention while I was home with a wife and two young kids, trying my best to stay out of the spotlight. In the only meeting we had on the field—me on the sideline with a headset and a giant play card, him playing the game—I came out the victor.

My divorce came shortly after that, which was ugly and public and a second type of devastating because it felt like another place I'd failed. Couldn't keep a relationship with my brother. Couldn't keep my wife. At least, that's how it looked from the outside.

Archer's words from the office replayed in my head, the truth of them getting uglier and uglier with each pass.

You wouldn't risk your job—or your reputation—to prove that point. You want everyone to think you're perfect.

That was what Archer didn't understand. I knew I wasn't perfect. But holding myself to high standards wasn't bad, either, because it meant the people around me could trust that I'd lead by example.

When we were younger, Griffin hated that side of me as well because it made him feel like the *bad twin*. He wasn't, he just . . . he couldn't control his impulses, and I'd smothered mine so deeply that I forgot they existed. Neither was healthy.

Because of two meddling children who were too smart for their own good and a new girlfriend who had flipped Griffin's life upside down, our relationship was better. Not what it used to be, and not where my parents probably wanted it, but it was still progress. A handful of texts and that was it. But to my parents, moments like this—where I'd sit and watch his game, acknowledge his talent—were a relief after years of absolutely nothing. They never pushed either of us too far, just quietly supporting us in the way we needed most.

The three of us watched the first drive, and I had to pause only a couple of times to write down notes while I studied San Diego's offensive movements. Griffin lined up on the right side, which wasn't typical for him, but I saw the shift in San Diego's offensive setup and knew why. Their right side was weak, a rookie tackle lining up opposite Griffin, and my brother was taller, bigger, and faster.

The center snapped the ball, and I leaned forward, watching Griffin execute a spin move that shouldn't be possible for someone his size. He was on the quarterback before he could even attempt to evade the sack, and as he wrapped his arms around the guy, Griffin knocked the ball clean from his hands long before the quarterback's knee ever touched the ground.

One of his teammates scooped it up and ran it back forty-five yards for a touchdown, Griffin providing a crucial block when a tight end chased after the defender. I watched my brother sprint down the field to celebrate with his teammates, and found myself swallowing an unusually potent pang of nostalgia.

Years ago, we used to celebrate like that too.

"Do you usually watch his replays?" Dad asked casually.

I blinked, shifting my focus back down to my notebook, and I scrawled out a few notes. "When I think about it, yeah. Caught his first game back after his arm healed."

Mom snorted. "It wasn't healed. I swear, three doctors told him he should've rested it another two weeks, but you know your brother. He hates being kept off that field. Ruby tried too," she said, referencing my brother's fiancée—a whip-smart librarian who we'd known growing up. "She gave up, though. Said he was driving her crazy being stuck at home."

"I bet."

"Speak of the devil," Mom muttered, lifting up her phone to answer an incoming call. "Hello, youngest son of mine."

"Mother. Just calling to make sure Maggie hasn't run you out of the house yet," my brother said.

"You've got it on speaker, honey," Dad whispered.

She rolled her eyes. "You're up early, Griffin. Just like your brother. I'm sitting here with him now. He and your father were watching your game footage when I came down for coffee."

I sat back on the couch and closed my eyes, allowing the smallest shake of my head. So maybe she pushed *a little*.

"Oh yeah?" Griffin asked. "Which game?"

"San Diego," Dad answered. "Hey, Griff."

"Pops," Griffin said. "Barrett make you get up at the crack of dawn with him?"

I opened my eyes, barely stifling an eye roll. "Isn't it, like, five a.m. there?" I asked.

At the sound of my voice, Griffin made a small little humming noise. "Touché. Ruby loves it when I force her to get up with me too—don't you, birdy?" he called out. There was a muffled noise in the background, and Griffin laughed. "She just threw something at my head, so I'm going to take that as a no."

Mom and Dad smiled, and I tried to imagine my playboy brother settled down but couldn't quite do it. Yet he was. He was happy. Happier than he'd ever been, according to Mom and Dad.

"Tell Ruby we said hi," Dad said.

"Will do. Anything new and exciting happening out that way?"

Mom cleared her throat. "I met your brother's neighbor yesterday," she said. "Beautiful. He didn't tell me how beautiful she was when he was complaining about her for *hours* the other day."

"Mom," I said in a warning tone.

Griffin whistled. "No shit. Tell me more. What's she like?"

I sighed, pinching the bridge of my nose. "There's nothing to tell," I said loudly. "She's my neighbor. She helped with the kids for a little bit. That's all."

The lie was so easy to say, a lot less easy to believe.

"She cheats at Scrabble, apparently," Dad filled in. "Your brother has a lot of feelings about it."

I stood up. "I'm leaving."

"Makes amazing cookies. Best I've ever had. He doesn't like it when I eat those either."

"She beat you in Scrabble, didn't she, Barrett?" Griffin asked. "Hot damn, I wonder if she'd give me some tips."

I wasn't even sure where I was going, but once I was out of the room, I shoved my feet into my boots and snatched my coat before I could second-guess anything, marching into the garage as my chest heaved.

Was I so transparent?

No one had ever called me that in my entire life. It was always the opposite. Every inch of me felt hot, my family's notice of the last thing I wanted anyone to notice ratcheting up my internal temperature by a solid fifteen degrees.

Next to the door was the big snow shovel I'd bought in the fall. We had a snowblower, but I'd always preferred the act of shoveling the driveway myself if I had the time and we weren't talking a foot of snow.

Overnight, we'd accumulated a few inches, the flurries done by the time the sun rose. It was as good of a distraction as any, even though I'd already worked out that morning. I punched the button to open the garage door and peered out at the fresh blanket of snow, a deep sigh escaping my pursed lips, resulting in a visible cloud in the brisk air.

It was perfectly still, perfectly quiet, the branches of every tree coated in white. The sun was up, the cloud cover broken up enough that the snow glittered. I almost hated interrupting such a perfect moment.

Thump.

Scrape.

Thump.

"Son of a *bitch*, this should not be"—a pause, a grunt—"so fucking hard."

I closed my eyes. Apparently Lily did not have those same feelings.

I walked a few steps until I could see the front of the house next door. She stood in the middle of the driveway, one squiggly line of cleared driveway behind her, a dinky little plastic shovel in her gloved hands.

With her face screwed up in a determined expression, she shoved the plastic edge down into the snow.

Thump.

Using her arms, she lifted the snow and dumped it straight ahead, then dropped her head back and groaned. "Why do people *live* here? This isn't normal."

Retreating back into the garage held no small amount of appeal, but the sight of her was too much to resist. Admitting that felt like a certain kind of victory, after days of finding myself unable to unscramble my thoughts when it came to her.

Maybe I couldn't define Lily. Even worse, maybe it was a fool's errand to indulge whatever I felt climbing through my chest when she came into my head. That I'd end up hurt and missing her when she inevitably left.

Every other part of my life felt like a struggle, but while I stood there watching her battle with the snow and curse up at the sky, the answer was surprisingly simple.

Go. Talk to her. Get to know her.

It didn't have to be anything more than that, and it didn't have to be perfect.

It was easy to take a step in her direction. Then another. And another. Easy to admit to myself that this was what I'd wanted almost the entire time. Sometimes fighting an inconvenient truth causes us more suffering than just living with the fallout of saying that truth out loud. Of taking action to make it part of our reality.

And I should've known that my struggles, my inability to uproot her from my mind, stemmed from a different kind of truth. I was just a guy who didn't remember how to approach a woman. Flirting was a language I didn't speak, and I didn't really have the inclination to try.

Her back was turned, attempting her inefficient snow-removal technique in a different direction, but at the sound of my boots crunching through the snow, she froze.

"Morning," I said. My voice felt loud with the snow muffling everything around us.

Lily straightened, fidgeting briefly with the white knit hat on her head before she turned to face me. "Morning," she said, eyes not meeting mine. "Do you often lurk around the corner like that?"

"Only on Thursdays," I answered evenly.

She didn't appreciate my attempt at humor. See earlier statement about flirting. Somehow I had a feeling that she'd jab me in the throat before she'd be receptive to any attempt in that department.

I peered out by the road, then lifted my chin toward the shovel, if you could call it that. "What's that?"

She arched her dark eyebrows. "I believe some people call it *a shovel*," she answered slowly.

I hummed, keeping my face even, holding out my hand and gesturing for her to give it over.

After the slightest pause, Lily sighed and passed it to me. I tilted my head as I stared at the red plastic handle. The shaft was made out of flimsy wood, and as I imagined saying *that* out loud, heat crawled up the back of my neck.

"This is not a shovel." I held it out to her, but she didn't move to retrieve it.

She looked at it in my hands. Looked at my face. Looked back at the shovel. "Then what the fuck is it?"

"May I?"

"Uh . . ."

I gripped it with both hands and snapped it clean in half.

"You broke my shovel!" she wailed.

"I'll give you mine," I told her. "That was a toy. Not any sort of effective tool for . . . whatever it is you were doing."

"You know, you winter people are awfully judgy," she huffed, taking the broken pieces and walking them over to the garbage bin. "Look, I couldn't find the real one, and all Scott had was this giant scary machine with a lot of buttons and knobs, and there's no way in hell I'm gonna try to use that thing." She slammed the lid shut and wiped snow off her gloves as she walked back in my direction. "I grabbed the first one I saw at the hardware store. It was cute."

I gave her a look, and she rolled her eyes.

"If you say one stupid man thing about buying something because it's cute . . ."

"Wouldn't dream of it. You've got that violent look in your eyes."

"Of course I do. I paid five bucks for that thing."

"Also a sign it wasn't a real shovel."

"I cannot tell you how glad I am you came all this way to say hi." She crossed her arms, and with a mutinous tilt to her chin, she studied my face. "When are you leaving again?"

"I can help, if you want," I said. Attraction spread like wildfire once you gave it the right conditions. What mine for Lily needed was something exactly like this: permission to grow.

"You broke my shovel," she said, like I hadn't heard the first time she said it.

"Better let me make it up to you, then."

The offer had an unintended subtext to it, and her eyes flickered briefly. "What's that supposed to mean?"

I glanced into the garage. Scott had the same machine I did. "I can teach you how to use the snowblower, if you want."

"If that's a euphemism for something else, you might want to work on your game," she said dryly, but her glittering eyes gave her away. They flicked to my mouth and then away again.

Somehow I managed not to smile. "I think you know by now that I have no game to speak of."

"Lord, if that ain't the truth."

"May I?" I said, gesturing to the open garage.

She blew out a harsh breath. "Is it hard?"

"Nope. It is loud, though. And your arms might feel a little wobbly when you're done, if you're not used to the feel of it."

Lily shook her head, peering over my shoulder toward my house. "I'm sorry, I'm not sure I can continue this conversation. My mind is too dirty."

"What?" Then I thought of what we'd just said, and I cleared my throat. No wonder I was single. "Ah. Up to you, if you need to go somewhere and need the driveway cleared out."

"No. Just . . . trying to get some energy out, and apparently exercise is good for you. Or whatever they say."

I studied her face, a smile tugging at the edge of my lips. "They do say that," I murmured.

"Does it ever snow during daylight here?" she asked, staring up at the sky. "I swear it doesn't."

The change in subject had me blinking. "Um, yeah. But I guess maybe not since you've been here. Why?"

She sucked in a deep breath, avoiding eye contact again. "Nothing."

"You sure you don't want me to show you?"

Lily glanced at the snowblower, then back at me. There was nothing to glean from her expression, the curtains carefully drawn again. "No, thanks. Me and big machines don't really mix, no matter how hard and loud they are."

I held her gaze. "You always react this way when someone tries to help you?"

"Yes," she answered with a tight smile. "Especially your version of *help*, which is both unhelpful and mildly destructive."

I cleared my throat and broke eye contact. "Right. Sorry."

Just before I turned to go, she took a step closer, and I found myself holding my breath. "You're not working today?"

"I am," I said. "Just finished watching some film with my dad, but I've got stuff to do at the office later today."

Her teeth dug into her bottom lip as she stared at the house, eventually giving a distracted nod.

Before she could say anything else, I turned and marched back into my own garage, staring at the line of shovels mounted on the wall. A couple were older, that I'd taken from our old house, even though we rarely needed them there. The brand-new one leaned against the wall next to the garage door.

I grabbed it and strode back over to Lily.

Her eyes widened as I approached, and her jaw went slack when I thrust the new shovel in her direction.

"Take it," I said gruffly. "Use your legs when you lift the snow, and toss it farther out of your way."

She blinked. "Oh."

My cheeks felt like they were on fire, and her stunned eye contact only seemed to make it worse. I nodded, cursing my own ineptitude, which multiplied whenever she was around. Then I spun around and marched back home, wondering, not for the first time, if I'd ever get laid again.

Chapter Sixteen

Lily

"I did it. I actually did it."

The counter was covered. An absolute mess remained. Sticky circles of lemon juice. Powdered sugar clung to places it shouldn't cling. One batch had gotten a little too crispy, and that was already in the trash. The pile of discarded lemons was much bigger than I'd thought it would be (and the reason I'd bought half a dozen, when I knew we really only needed two), but Maggie and I stood by the island, my arm slung over her shoulders, as we stared down at the most perfect batch of lemon meltaway cookies.

"Maggie, honey, they're beautiful." Her grandma clapped her hands together, taking in the finished product with awe.

"And they're *yellow*," Maggie said, smiling so huge that I felt it like a punch to my chest.

"Why do you think we started with these?" I asked.

She exhaled, swiping her hand over her forehead, leaving behind a streak of lemon glaze. "I should eat the first one, right?"

Barrett's dad, a tall, wiry guy with thinning salt-and-pepper hair, strolled into the kitchen with Bryce tagging right behind. "Cookies ready? I haven't had one yet today."

Robin rolled her eyes at her husband. "You had three OREOs with your breakfast."

That stopped him short. "Well, those don't count."

"Why not?" she asked.

"Because my granddaughter didn't bake those." He winked at Maggie.

Bryce elbowed in by the island, eyes wide as he surveyed the two dozen cookies in front of us. "You made those?"

"All by myself," she proclaimed. Then she gave me a bashful look. "Well, sort of."

"Claim it," I told her. "I just supervised, but you did all the important steps by yourself."

Her brother leaned in to inspect the cookies. "What's that yellow crap on the top?"

She scoffed. "It's lemon zest, Bryce."

He wasn't impressed. "They look like worms."

"Fine, then you don't have to eat any." She looked up at me. "And you've really never taught anyone to bake before?" Maggie asked.

"Nope." I ruffled her hair. "You're my first student, and I'm afraid you've spoiled me. I won't be able to teach any others."

Robin watched us with a small smile hovering on her lips. "Thankfully you've got time to teach a little more, I hear."

"She leaves in February," Maggie stated, her smile dropping at the edges. "We better make a few more cookie dates before then."

Someone had shoved a wad of sandpaper down my throat, and I could not make that sucker budge, even with a hard swallow. "We will," I said, voice slightly strangled.

Robin was watching me carefully. That woman was just a little too perceptive, if you asked me.

Maggie picked up the first cookie, studying it intently. She pulled her bottom lip in with her teeth and then shoved the cookie at me. "You have it."

She reminded me so much of her father heaving that damn shovel toward me that I almost lost my breath. The jerky movements and lack of eye contact was . . . adorable. On both of them, really, which was just a little obnoxious for a man his size to do anything that was adorable. I found it much more palatable coming from his daughter.

"Big honor," Robin said, winking subtly at me.

Was I blushing? God, how embarrassing. It was a cookie. But it was, like, symbolic or something. Because it wasn't just a cookie.

In ten years of moving around, I'd never experienced anything like this. Hadn't let it happen. More than once now, I'd spent time in this kitchen with her, and that made it a pattern. Patterns, no matter what they were, were hard to break. Good ones, bad ones—it didn't really matter.

The only pattern I'd ever managed to form was never letting myself look back.

But with my heart in my throat, I accepted the cookie from Maggie and took a small bite. The bright burst of lemon had me humming, and the cookie melted on my tongue. I closed my eyes and finished chewing. When I opened them, everyone was watching me.

And yet again, Barrett had entered the room without making a single fucking sound.

After licking the crumbs off my lips, I looked down at Maggie and nodded slowly. "Perfect," I told her.

She smiled, exhaling loudly. "Good." Then she looked around the room. "Does anyone else want one?"

Bryce and her grandpa had one in their hands before the words were even out of Maggie's mouth, and I laughed into my second bite, finishing the cookie with another small sound of appreciation.

I squeezed her shoulder while she watched the other two inhale their first cookies, then go for another one.

"Good job, kiddo," I told her.

"This is the best feeling *ever*."

I smiled, but it was only a moment later that my attention shifted to *him.*

Across the room, Barrett slid his laptop bag off his shoulder and set it on a chair, and damn it, I couldn't help it—I just watched. Had I watched for his truck to leave before coming over for cookie baking? Maybe.

Did that stop me from wondering what the fuck this man was thinking with his weird, strangely destructive displays of thoughtfulness? Nope.

I didn't know what to make of him, not after what had happened that morning. And now the thought of teasing him didn't hold nearly the same appeal that it had on Christmas Eve. A shift, invisible though it was, still registered in the back of my head.

Robin went for her first cookie, moaning when she took a bite. "You two are dangerous in the kitchen."

"Everyone tells me I'm dangerous everywhere," Maggie muttered.

I laughed, and so did Barrett's parents. Barrett's expression was hidden, only his profile visible. But there was a slight softening in his cheeks, a hint of a smile, and I found myself unable to look away.

But his head moved, so I did as well.

"February, huh?" Robin asked.

Barrett was watching me—I could feel it—but I kept my eyes on his mother, nodding in answer. "They'll be home middle of the month."

"Must be hard to move around so much," she said.

The kids chattered with their grandpa, and Barrett joined them, but Robin spoke loudly enough that I could tell he was listening.

"Sometimes," I admitted quietly, picking up a dishcloth to wipe down the counter. "But it's all I know."

She was quiet, coming around the counter to help clean up.

Wouldn't it be easier if she annoyed the shit out of me? If she was intrusive and rude and pushy, and I could run out of the room, desperate for a quiet house and my own space?

Alas, she was none of those things.

Barrett's parents, much to my absolute dismay, were completely delightful. Friendly without being overbearing. Chatty without dominating conversation. A bit curious, yes, but I never felt like I was being interrogated.

"I suppose it must be fun to see the country this way." She smiled, all nice and warm and sweet and motherly. What the fuck was I supposed to *do* with that? "And you've probably done a lot of different jobs, haven't you?"

"I have," I answered, trying to keep the wary tone under control but failing miserably.

"Usually house-sitting?"

"About half and half. I've been a barista, a dog walker, a temp, a digital marketer . . . I tried my hand at being a travel influencer, worked at a small tourist farm for a while and some clothing boutiques—though I am not nearly nice enough for retail . . ."

She chuckled. "A temp? I can't picture you stuck at a desk, honey."

"It was actual hell." I smiled. "I hated every single second."

"And you've seen the country while doing it," she said kindly.

"I have."

"How long have you been traveling like this, sweetheart?"

Later, I'd blame it on the easy way she used the endearment, something I wasn't sure I'd earned. The Mom Energy was strong with this one, and it decimated my ability to lie. To brush her off and pretend like this wasn't a really fucking hard question to answer. I pulled in a sharp breath through my nose, fully aware of Barrett's eyes on me while I did.

"Ten years. Three months." I swallowed. "Two days."

His mom was quiet. So was Barrett, his watchful expression from across the room more than I could handle.

"That's a long time," Robin said slowly. Her eyes were so kind. So warm. Both things tied me up in knots inside. "And you saw some of Buffalo recently, isn't that right?"

I nodded, not trusting myself to speak right away.

"What did you like seeing most yesterday?"

Barrett's eyes were heavy on the side of my face as I cupped my hand underneath the edge of the counter and swept a small pile of powdered sugar into my palm. "Niagara, actually."

"In the winter?" he asked.

The sound of his voice, deeper and lower than his father's, made the hair on the back of my neck stand up. I met his eyes carefully and nodded. "It wasn't busy, and a lot of it is frozen over, but . . . it was amazing."

Magical. Everything about it was magical. The movement of the water underneath the sheets of ice. The water churning mightily, the air filled with a mist so cold on my face that it was hard to breathe sometimes. But I had stood there as long as I could handle, until my nose felt like ice and my teeth started chattering.

His eyes were on me, their unrelenting heat twisting my stomach into a weightless knot.

"Get everything done at the office?" Barrett's dad asked him.

Barrett pulled his gaze from mine and nodded. "Had to sneak in and out so too many people didn't stop me, but most everyone knows I was working from home today."

Bryce sidled up next to his dad, nuzzling against his father's chest. Barrett returned the embrace, absently dropping a kiss on his son's head. His phone started vibrating, and he pulled it out, looking at the screen.

"Isn't that the GM?" Bryce asked.

Barrett nodded.

I waited for him to pull away, but instead he ignored the call.

"You don't need to take that?" Bryce asked.

Barrett touched his son's face and shook his head. "Not right now. I'll tell him my son was hugging me voluntarily. He'll understand," he answered with a wryness to his voice I'd never heard.

Bryce grinned, hugging his father tight. That would've been enough. Enough to do me the fuck in. It was already a battle not to melt right there on the kitchen floor, but with Barrett's face when he returned the hug—the way he closed his eyes, pressed his nose into Bryce's hair—I was in mortal danger of bursting into tears.

Naturally, I grabbed another cookie and shoved it right the hell into my waiting mouth, because if anything could stem a hormone-induced meltdown, it was copious amounts of sugar.

Bryce pulled away and snatched another cookie, the entire thing disappearing in one bite. His cheeks puffed out as he chewed.

"How many have you had?" Barrett asked.

Bryce blinked, then swallowed the cookie. "I lost count."

He sighed. "Last one, okay?"

Maggie perked up. "Did you bring home that stuff Bridget told me about?"

Barrett nodded. "Boxes are in the back of my truck if you want to go grab them."

The kids tore out of the kitchen, and Robin whispered something to her husband, shooing him toward the hallway that led to the guest room.

"Did you try one?" I asked, nodding at the cookies.

"I don't eat many sweets, but I'll wait until she's back in here." He eyed the remaining cookies. "Thank you for doing this." His wide chest expanded on a deep breath, and God, he was wearing that black quarter-zip like he was doing it a favor. "It means a lot. To Maggie." His eyes met mine and held. "And to me."

My pulse spiked, an erratic thudding in my ears that had me worried I might stroke out if this man and me and his kids had any more sweet little meaningful exchanges. Breaking shovels. Baking cookies. A girl could only take so much.

I licked my lips and pivoted toward the sink, where the mixing bowl was soaking in soapy water. "It's no problem," I said, grabbing a sponge and scrubbing the absolute shit out of that bowl.

"You do this often?"

The soapy water splashed up my forearms. "Wash dishes? Almost every day."

He sighed, and I fought a smile, smothering it immediately as he came to join me at the sink. This close, I could smell him. Masculine and clean. Warmth emanated from his frame as he carefully picked up a dish towel and held out his hand.

I finished rinsing the bowl and handed it over to him, my throat tight and my brain all wobbly.

"You know what I was asking."

It was the steady assurance in his voice, completely devoid of sarcasm, that ultimately did me in.

I did know what he was asking.

What is life like for you? Have you let anyone else in like this?

While he methodically dried the bowl, I scrubbed the remaining bits of dough off the mixing paddle, rinsing it carefully before handing that to Barrett as well.

"No," I said quietly. "I've never done this before."

He didn't say anything right away, and for that, I was grateful. For some, opening up felt a lot like relief, but it wasn't that way for me. A tight, uncomfortable ache bloomed somewhere under my ribs, and this was no different.

It was exposure, and just like yesterday, when I'd stood in front of the harsh, cold elements of Niagara, if I lingered too long, there was only so much I could handle before I cracked. The fact that they were beautiful didn't matter, didn't lessen the possible outcome of staying too long.

"What kind of bird is that?" he asked quietly as I turned off the faucet.

My hands froze, water still dripping from my fingers into the sink.

Plink, plink, plink.

For a minute, I stared down at the ink near my wrist, this one on the opposite arm from the outline of the car.

You don't have to tell him anything.

You don't have to.

You don't.

But what if I did? What if I told him just a little bit more?

What would happen if I left this piece behind? Could I walk away unscathed knowing that Barrett King had possession of a part of my soul? He wouldn't be aware, of course, but he'd still hold it all the same.

"Swallows," I whispered. "We, um, we had a lot of barn swallows in our area, and my mom loved to make nesting boxes for them."

More words crowded the back of my mouth. About how she'd used to watch them from the deck off the back of our house. How my dad had made as many of those boxes as she wanted because it made her feel better knowing they had a safe place to land, no matter how far they'd fly. About how I could look back on that now and see the heartbreaking irony that had escaped me as a rebellious teen who wanted nothing more than to fly past that horizon myself. About how she'd let me.

My throat felt raw, and the sudden intimacy of the moment made it hard to breathe.

Barrett folded the towel, placing it on the counter with precise movements. Then he stilled before slowly turning his face toward me.

"Why you'd tell me?" he asked.

Something cinched tight around my lungs, a quick, hot rush of panic only making it worse. I couldn't breathe through it. There were no more words wanting to be said, only a driving urge, the crack of the proverbial whip in the back of my mind spurring me into flight.

Leave. Now.

The last time I'd been in the kitchen feeling unmoored and unsteady, I played games with a man who admittedly didn't deserve it. I didn't want that to be my default anymore. Not with him.

"I, uh, I should get back home," I said in a rush. "Larry needs to eat, and . . . he's been really finicky lately."

Barrett only nodded, and there was a desperate urge to look at his eyes. Could I get a sense of what he was thinking if I did that?

No. That was too dangerous. I left the kitchen, a deep breath punching from my lungs. But I didn't make it far, pausing when the kids came inside with arms full of boxes.

"I have to go," I told Maggie. "You did amazing, kid. I told you that, right?"

She grinned. "A couple times."

Bryce sighed heavily. "She's going to be unbearable after this."

The laugh I let out helped ease some of the tension building in my chest.

"I'm serious," Bryce said. "They're giving her a *show*, and she can bake. It's terrible."

I smiled. "I heard. Don't worry, I'm sure you'll find a way to humble her in no time."

Maggie sniffed. "If you're nice to me, I'll let you cohost."

He perked up. "Really?"

"Occasionally. But I'm the boss."

Bryce rolled his eyes. "Never mind."

After saying goodbye to the kids, I set a hand on my trembling stomach and fumbled with my boots. When I straightened to remove my coat from the hook on the wall, I didn't have to hear anything to know he was standing behind me again.

"What?" I asked, my natural defenses already kicking in.

"You know the drill," he answered easily.

I glanced over my shoulder, taking him in with a small scoff. He was waiting, hands tucked into his pockets, biceps testing the seams of his sleeves. It was on the tip of my tongue to ask him to start wearing his shirts a size bigger, but I didn't think it would help anything.

"Seriously?"

Barrett didn't answer. He simply watched me with utter stillness, endless patience, as I yanked my coat on.

My steps were fueled by the teeniest amount of embarrassed female rage, but I didn't say anything else as I crossed the yard separating our houses. When I was on the front porch, I paused, my slightly more rational, less-bitchy defensive side finally taking the reins.

"You gonna do this every single time?" I asked.

Only, it didn't come out snappish, and to my horror, it didn't even sound all that bothered. It sounded like . . . oh God . . . it sounded like I was asking for reassurance.

"Yeah," he said.

That was it. No explanation. Nothing.

"Why?" I asked raggedly.

Across the yards, Barrett watched me for a moment, his frame expanding on a deep breath. "I'll answer that when you tell me why you explained your tattoos."

Oh, *fuck* him. My eyes narrowed dangerously, and because I was too far away to tell, it almost looked like Barrett smiled.

"Good night, Lily," he said, then disappeared into his house.

Chapter Seventeen

Lily

Pretty much from the moment I walked in, I was gaping like a little kid. Absolutely no chill—which was never my favorite look.

Look! We spend money on all the things! every inch proclaimed.

Everything was big. And shiny. And no matter where I turned, that logo from his quarter-zip was right in my fucking face. While a very serious man with a very serious badge checked my ID, I pursed my lips and looked around the sprawling lobby.

"You sure he knows I'm here?"

Bryce shrugged. Maggie turned a cartwheel in the middle of the lobby, garnering the applause of a few massive-looking guys who passed by.

"Exactly how sick are your grandparents?" I asked him. The text from Robin had been scant in details, which didn't help someone of my skeptical nature.

He shrugged again. "I dunno. Grandma just said they were super contagious and couldn't drive and we needed you to take us."

"Huh."

While Mr. Security Guard typed up my information for some official-looking guest pass, I glanced over my shoulder, doing a double take at the sight of a massive photo of Barrett on the opposite wall, shaking the hand of a white-haired woman in a white Chanel suit.

Speaking of suits.

His frame, large and broad, was fitted in a charcoal suit tailored to absolute fucking perfection. Whoever had cut that thing deserved a raise—several of them, in fact. My heart fluttered behind my ribs at the proud tilt of his jaw, the confident gleam in his eye.

"Here you go, Miss Townsend," the security guard said, sliding the visitor badge across the desk. That was big and shiny, too, attached to a red ribbon, BUFFALO printed on a repeating pattern in blocky white letters. God, I bet they all saw that word in their sleep. "This will get you access throughout the building."

"Everywhere?" I asked. "Like, I can break into Barrett's office with this thing?"

His eyes never left the screen in front of him. "You can try."

"Hmm. I think I'll pass."

"Probably wise."

"Thank you." I pulled it over my head and let it drape over my Dolly Parton sweatshirt, which he eyed, bushy eyebrows rising briefly.

I straightened the hem where it hung over my jeans and combat boots, then nodded at Maggie. "Let's go, superstar. You're going to have to lead the way because I have no friggin' clue where anything is in this monstrosity."

The guard cleared his throat.

I gave him a small smile. "Sorry. It's very lovely."

He shook his head and turned back to the computer at his desk.

"This way," Maggie said, skipping off to the right and down a gleaming hallway lined with more giant pictures. Players and coaches from the past. Iterations of jerseys and snapshots of very large men holding trophies over their heads. Everything in white and red and silver.

We passed a few employees who knew the kids by name, and every single one of them gave me a curious once-over. God, they'd think I was the nanny. Or they'd think I was the fiancée.

A groan got trapped in my throat because I wasn't even thinking about how people might pay attention to *me* in this whole little favor.

We took a few more turns, and I was hopelessly lost, when a striking woman with curly brown hair and killer curves came out the double doors at the end of the hallway, her face softening into a smile when she caught sight of the kids.

"There you are," she said. "We're getting everything set up for you, Maggie." The kids sprinted down the hallway, eliciting laughter from both of us. She paused, tilting her head as she looked me up and down. "I'm sorry, I was expecting Coach's parents. You are . . . ?"

"Lily." I cleared my throat. "I'm the neighbor. They're, um, sick or something. I'm just playing chauffeur today."

"Got it." She glanced at the watch on her wrist and blew out a harsh breath through puffed-out cheeks. "We need to head in there. You ever watched a practice?"

"Never watched anything about anything." I shrugged. "Sports aren't really my thing."

She smiled, deep dimples appearing in her cheeks. "Then this should be fun." She stuck out her hand. "I'm Wren, by the way. If any of the guys bother you, please let me know."

"Eh, should I expect that?"

Wren looked me up and down again. "Yes."

"Oh, goodie."

She laughed at my dry response, and I let out a beleaguered sigh and followed her toward the large double doors. When she pulled one open, I stopped short, mouth falling slack.

It was massive, which . . . duh, it was a fucking football field, but the sheer scope of the space—filled with absolutely huge men running and laughing and lining up and throwing things and *wow*—was so much more than I'd expected.

People were everywhere, players in ripped T-shirts and tight white pants, some in helmets, some not. Cameras were set up off to the side, and a white backdrop covered in pastel-colored flowers held up a fluorescent-pink sign that spelled out MIDFIELD WITH MAGGIE. Two chairs sat in front of the backdrop, yellow velvet wingbacks with a small yellow enamel table between them. It looked more professional than a fucking movie set.

And this was for a ten-year-old because they thought she was funny. The sheer amount of money that went into an operation like this threatened to make my head explode.

"This is not normal," I said under my breath.

Wren glanced over her shoulder. "What's that?"

"Nothing."

A football whizzed overhead, and instinctively, I ducked, covering my head with my hands, even though it cleared the top of my head by five feet and bounced harmlessly onto the emerald turf of the field.

"Holy fuck, death by football," I muttered. "That's how I'm gonna get taken out, isn't it?"

"Heads up," someone called about four seconds too late.

"Oh, no shit?" I called back.

He looked suitably chastened. "Sorry."

Wren laughed. "You'll be just fine, I think."

In the center of all the organized chaos was Barrett, wearing that fucking quarter-zip that did unholy things to the shape of his biceps, along with a dark hat molded to his head. His eyes were locked on to a clipboard. Another tall man in a backward cap, with a long black beard and tattoos on his neck, stood to his side, pointing at something that made Barrett nod. His jaw was covered in stubble, which I'd also never seen, and a flurry of ticklish anticipation had me dragging my feet as I followed Wren.

Maggie got to Barrett first, and his mouth softened at the sight of his daughter. They talked for a few seconds, Maggie excitedly pointing things out on the set. Then she pushed up on tiptoe and cupped her hand around the side of his face as he leaned down. Whatever she said made his entire frame go still.

Then his head snapped up, eyes locking on to mine even though they were under the shadow of his hat's brim. His jaw tightened, and in response, so did my stomach.

Barrett had *not* known I was going to be there, then. That always made our interactions extra special, didn't it? And now it was public. Even better.

He said something to the man off to the side and passed him the clipboard, then settled a hand on Maggie's shoulder before she scampered off to the set waiting for her.

Wren glanced from Coach's inscrutable face to mine as he strode purposefully in our direction, then cleared her throat. "Right. I think I'll . . ." She gestured to the set and took her leave.

I swear, I almost clutched her elbow and swung her around to shield me from the intimidating approach of the massive man commanding this massive space.

It wasn't until he came close enough to touch that I got a clear view of his eyes under the hat, and I fought the irrational urge to knock it off his fucking head because I didn't like that I couldn't see him clearly.

I glared at it instead.

"What are you glaring at?" he asked.

"Your hat. It looks terrible on you."

His sigh was loud and long, but he must've been feeling charitable because he didn't call me on my bullshit. Nothing Barrett had worn thus far made him look anything other than stupid hot.

He crossed his arms. "You're here."

"Astute as always."

"Why?"

I gave him an incredulous look. "You expected your sick parents to drive them here?"

"My—" His face froze. "My what?"

I grabbed my phone and held it out for him. "This is the text I got."

Barrett's face disappeared again as he tipped his head down to read the text, his chest expanding on a deep, measured inhale that sounded a whole lot like annoyance. I knew what he was reading, because I'd stared at it all morning before deciding that I could, in fact, handle seeing Barrett in scary, growly coach mode.

Robin: I'm so sorry to do this, but my husband and I are terribly ill. Would you be willing to take the kids to the team facilities? Maggie is needed there for her show, and she'd be devastated if they had to reschedule.

Me: Oh, I'm sorry to hear that. It must have hit you fast, you were both okay yesterday.

Robin: Really fast. Just . . . knocked us completely over. Do you think you could pick them up at 3 PM? Maggie will have the address to the facilities.

Me: Sure, I can do that. Do you want me to bring you any soup or anything?

Robin: Oh no, that's fine, thank you, sweetheart. We're just going to hide in our room so we don't get anyone sick. Tell Barrett we'll see him when he gets home from work.

A rock had more expression than his face reading through the text thread, but a muscle twitched ominously in his jaw. Before he returned the phone, Barrett muttered something under his breath that I couldn't understand, and when our fingers brushed, his eyes flashed dangerously.

"You seem surprised by this turn of events," I said slowly.

His gaze traced over my face. "Astute as ever."

"Oh, goodie, the man has jokes today."

He ignored that. "My parents were perfectly fine this morning when I left for work."

I blinked. "Your mom lied?"

"Apparently."

"Why?"

He gave me a pointed look, and I felt the heat crawl up my cheeks.

"Oh."

"Yeah. *Oh.*"

"Coach, who is this lovely creature and why don't we know her?"

Barrett's eyes never left mine. "Go away, Justice."

"Nope. Can't." He approached with a wide white-toothed smile and dimples deep in his cheeks. The guy was easily six five, muscles on muscles, his thick arms covered in ink, and so freaking gorgeous that I couldn't help but stare. "I'm Justice Tyler. And who do I have the pleasure of meeting?"

Barrett sighed. He was doing that a lot today. Maybe he had breathing problems.

I raised my chin and held out my hand. "Lily Townsend."

Justice took my hand and turned it, raising it up to his mouth to drop a kiss on my knuckles. I couldn't help it—my cheeks were on fucking fire. *Anyone's* would have been. Imagine Michael B. Jordan walks up and kisses your hand. You'd be blushing, too, okay?

Barrett cleared his throat pointedly, glaring at my hand in Justice's until the man dropped it, giving me a tiny wink as he did. "How do you know Coach? He never brings friends, so this is a very exciting day for all of us."

"I am going to make you run sprints across this entire field for the next hour," Barrett snapped.

"Worth it. Now, I'd like to hear the lady answer, if that's all right."

The heat in my cheeks slowly started to ebb, and I arched an eyebrow slowly at the pissing match playing out in front of me. "We're not friends; I'm his neighbor."

"Interesting," Justice mused.

"Go back and run the play, Tyler," Barrett warned. "You owe me those sprints tomorrow."

"He's in a bad mood," Justice explained. "I'm sure he'll tell you why."

"He's very forthcoming about his feelings," I said. "I can't get him to shut up most of the time."

Barrett looked up at the ceiling and sighed while Justice let out a hoot of amused laughter. "Oh, I like her, Coach. You better lock this one down."

"Go run the play, Justice," I said, giving him a warning look of my own.

He saluted crisply, then jogged back over to the other players.

For a few moments, we watched the players line up facing each other. I didn't know what the fuck I was looking at, of course, but after a quick glance at Barrett's facial expression, I knew he was dissecting something I couldn't see.

"Watch the line, Carson," he yelled. "See the blitz before it happens."

Every single guy was tall and muscly and fast, a veritable ocean of testosterone as far as the eye could see, but one in particular stood off to the end of the group of players not lined up, glaring over to the man at my side. He had a bruise on his cheekbone and jaw, muscles popping on his arms where they were crossed over his big chest.

"Oh my."

"What?"

"That one," I said, lifting my jaw toward Grumpy Face. "If looks could kill . . ."

"I'd have been dead a long time ago," Barrett finished. "My quarterback is mad at me."

I pursed my lips and studied the gentleman in question. Like Barrett, he was tall, with long legs and a sharp jaw. "Did you make him cry in practice?" I tilted my head. "Wait, there's no crying in football, right?"

"Wrong sport. There's no crying in *baseball*, and that's a great movie."

I lifted my brow in concession, allowing my arm to brush against his as we watched the play unfold. The guy who yelled a bunch of random words caught the ball when some other dude snapped it from between his legs (like, *what*?), held the ball in his hands, and danced to the side when someone tried to tackle him, then heaved the ball down the field, where it landed perfectly into the hands of a waiting receiver. Justice picked the receiver up and yelled, the celebration unfolding like I was watching a game and not a practice.

Grumpy Face turned and stalked away, and Barrett watched with slightly narrowed eyes.

"They always get this worked up for throwing a ball?"

Barrett shook his head. "No. I have our backup quarterback in on this play."

"I don't know what that means."

The edge of his lip tugged up, and my chest tightened in anticipation of a smile that never came. Damn him and his stingy, non-smiling soul. I'd perish if I ever saw one for real.

"Between my players—backups, starters, practice squad—and my staff, I've got a lot of personalities to balance. Big egos too." He scraped a hand over that stubbled jaw, and my mouth went dry at the sound it made as it dragged over his skin. "I've been accused of being a perfectionist."

"No."

He gave me a long-suffering look, then turned back toward the players as they milled around the field, discussing the previous play with the other coaches. "That I care more about my reputation than anything else."

My brows furrowed at the unexpected turn in the conversation. Did we share things now? Were we . . . friends? Maybe the broken shovel had been a bizarre friendship ritual I wasn't aware of and now we were stuck with each other for life. "I don't know if I believe that," I said carefully.

"No?"

"I mean, if you only cared about your reputation and looking perfect to everyone, you'd be fake as hell. You'd try to be everything to everyone. Match *their* definition of perfect. And *fake*, Barrett King, is not a word I'd ever use to describe you."

His eyes settled on my face again, their searing weight making me wish I hadn't said anything.

"It's not?"

Keeping my expression as close to unaffected as I could muster, I allowed myself one fleeting look in his direction, and when our eyes locked, I felt a powerful little shock all the way down to my fucking toes. "No. You were too much of an asshole at the beginning. You didn't give a shit what I thought."

"Quite true," he murmured, keeping his gaze on my face even when I looked away. "I guess I could use that as my proof if he ever says it again. *Go ask Lily,* I'll say. She'll vouch for my dick-ish tendencies."

"I can be counted on for many, many things," I said sagely. "Who's not listening to you? Mr. Grumpy over there?"

He hummed, and I decided to take that as a yes.

"Just tell him to fuck off if he doesn't listen. You're the boss."

"Simple as that, huh?"

"Totally. But as you can imagine, I'm not a perfectionist and I don't care what people think of me."

The lie hung in the air, low-hanging fruit that must have been so hard for him to ignore. But he did. The man had every opportunity to call me on the second round of rampant bullshit, but instead he let it be.

How nice to be in possession of such epic restraint.

Barrett glanced over at Maggie—they were still getting her hooked up to mics and messing with lighting—then he turned contemplative eyes toward me.

"What? Why are you looking at me like that?"

"I'm curious about something," he said, all slow and thoughtful. It made my skin itchy.

"It better not be about me."

At my snappish tone, his eyes softened, and I might not have noticed if we hadn't been so close.

"Can I ask you something?"

"Oh God."

Another almost-smile, and my lungs cinched tight around absolutely nothing. "Nothing bad. No tattoo questions."

My shoulders relaxed an inch or two. "Okay."

"Tell me what you'd do," he said in a deep pitch that felt all sorts of intimate, speaking as if we were the only two people in the room. We weren't even close to alone, but as we stood off to the side, I could almost pretend that we were. Dangerous, dangerous thing, that.

"About what?"

"You have someone who's important to the team. Supposed to be your leader. But he's rash. Reckless. Stubborn. Doesn't like to listen. Hates being corrected. But he's talented. Smart. Not performing even close to his potential. You can see it, but he doesn't want to dig deep enough to get there. He thinks he's untouchable. That there will never be consequences to his actions. That he can keep shoving himself forward in life without ever stopping to look back at where he could've reacted differently." My brow furrowed, heart inexplicably racing as he spoke. He tilted his head and watched my face. "What do you do to get through to him?"

I adopted an airy tone. "Buddy, if you need me to help coach your team of big man-babies, you've got bigger problems."

"Tell me how you'd handle someone like that," he said again, and his coaxing tone was my undoing. "Someone who looks at the world in a completely different way than you do."

There was no way I could look at Barrett again, because he was dangerously close to prying back a layer of carefully constructed armor. Something bolted down and hidden from view. Instead, I closed my eyes and pictured a different face. As a teenager, I assumed it was frustration, but now, as an adult, I could see the weariness. It couldn't have been easy, dealing with me.

Someone rash and reckless and stubborn and who looked at the world in a completely different way. The situation was vastly different, but the similarities were striking enough that I couldn't ignore them.

If I could go back, would I tell her to do something different? Impossible questions like that could never truly be answered, because the truth couldn't always be distilled down into a clear yes or no. My heart screamed yes. A million times. But I couldn't, and entertaining a different reality was a fool's errand.

"There are always consequences to our actions," I said, then cursed the slight unsteadiness in my tone. "No one can protect us from those, and I don't think they should. Even the best people in the world—patient and understanding and full of the best intentions—can't save someone from themselves."

I pried my eyes open and risked a look up at his face. He was watching me so intently that it took my breath away.

"And I don't think you should try to save him. Even if it makes you look bad. Let him feel the weight of his own consequences, because no matter how badly we want to, we cannot change someone who doesn't want to be changed. It's pointless to try," I said, voice tapering off to a thready whisper. "We have to want to change." My cheeks flushed with heat. "He. *He* has to want to change."

Barrett nodded slowly, eyes searching mine. "I agree."

"Did he do something really bad? Or just sorta bad, like giving you attitude in practice?"

He let out a short huff of amusement. "Well, a couple nights ago, he was at a party with players from an opposing team that we played recently. He got into a fight at that party—I'm told he instigated—and because of that, it's up to those opposing players to press charges or not." Barrett sucked in a quick breath, focusing on the men in front of him. "But I told him this morning I was benching him unless he could show me that he was ready to take this seriously."

"A little coach tough love, huh?"

He hummed. "Sort of."

"What else would it be?"

In the bright lights of the cavernous space, there was no hiding the warm streaks of gold in his eyes, especially not when he looked down at me the way he was now. "No one can make us change unless we want to, right?"

I managed a jerky nod.

"I needed to change too. Because he wasn't wrong, you know. I've tried to save people because, deep down, I worried how their mistakes might reflect on me. That's a level of arrogance that I don't particularly care to hold on to anymore." Barrett searched my eyes, and I found it hard to breathe. "Change is never easy. But the hardest part is having to look in the mirror and know that no one can do it for us."

Through the quaking of my ribs, completely unmoored by this forthcoming side of him, somehow I managed to speak. "How will you know if it works?"

Barrett let out a small noise. Not quite a laugh. Not quite a huff. He did that a lot. Made those quiet little sounds, a tell that he was listening but wasn't ready to speak. Then his face softened, a glint of rare humor in his eyes. Inside my chest, something melted right along with it.

"Either he'll pull his head out of his ass, or I'll get fired for benching the franchise quarterback without the permission of the team owner."

"Is he nice?"

"*She* is smart and intimidating, and I'm not sure I'd ever trust you in a room with her because you'd gang up on me mercilessly."

A surprised laugh burst out of me, and Barrett's eyes lingered on my mouth. "I should make a point to meet her, then."

"God help me," he said fondly.

"Oh my *gosh*, are you Lily?"

At the sound of my name, I tore my gaze from Barrett's but still caught a glimpse of his face flattening.

"Bridget," he said, voice low in warning.

"Ah, the woman who runs his life," I said.

She was petite, with thick red hair and a bright expression. "I got a text from him a few minutes ago that I wasn't allowed down here, and he never says that stuff to me, which is why I came down immediately. Plus, if I listened to everything he said, life would be incredibly boring."

"I'm going to fire you," Barrett growled.

"No, you're not." She stuck her hand out. "Bridget. Absolute *pleasure* to meet you."

"You too," I said hesitantly. Why did it feel like I was shoved onto a stage, naked, anytime I met someone from Barrett's life? Friendly curiosity felt like I was being poked and prodded, up on display so they could study the recipient of his weird shovel-friendship gestures.

"I hope I didn't interrupt," she said.

Barrett crossed his arms. "You did. And I'm pretty sure you have a meeting right now."

"I canceled it." Bridget looped her arm through mine. "Please tell me everything awful he's ever done to you, and feel free to go into detail."

My eyes flew up to Barrett's, and after a prolonged beat, he looked away, the slightest flush in his cheeks that was so stupidly attractive, I felt it in my wobbly knees. "I'm not sure you have enough time, Bridget."

She laughed. "Trust me, I'll make time."

"I'm leaving," Barrett called.

Bridget shooed him off. "Great. Bye. Have an excellent day." As he stormed off, the anticipation that had been bubbling through my chest since I arrived suddenly and violently popped, and instead of wondering why, I let Bridget steer me away.

My stomach was in knots, as I assumed this tiny, terrifying woman would actually press me for details. It would be messy—so very, very messy—if thoughts and feelings were divulged to someone other than Larry the canine vault.

"He's such a pain in the ass, right?" she said easily.

"It's a gift, truly." I cleared my throat. "So . . . this whole show with Maggie—is this normal?"

The change in subject didn't fool her for a fucking second, because she gave me a sidelong look. "No. This is a first for us, actually. Barrett had his reservations, but I think he'll love it by the time they edit everything together."

Maggie, all mic'd up and with a stack of note cards in her hand, looked like a seasoned pro as she settled comfortably in the big yellow chair and waited for the first player to join her.

Someone even larger than Justice approached, and he grinned widely at the sight of Maggie waiting for him. "What's up, girl?"

"Hello, Keshawn. Welcome to *Midfield with Maggie*. You're my first guest because you're my favorite."

His face lit up. "No shi—" Wren cleared her throat loudly, and Keshawn winced. "No kidding," he finished.

Maggie smiled. "It's fine. I've heard worse."

Keshawn winked. "What are we talking about today? You're not gonna ask me anything crazy, are you?"

She studied her first note card, then fixed an eager expression toward Keshawn. "What's the most annoying thing my dad does?"

The man's face went slack with shock, while Wren choked on a sip of her coffee. I slapped a hand over my mouth to stem a burst of laughter. Bridget let hers ring out, nodding slowly as everyone tried to contain their laughter.

"Still think Barrett will love it?" I asked Bridget.

"I don't care," she said with a huge smile on her face. "This is going to be the best thing I've ever seen."

Chapter Eighteen

Barrett

No one noticed me walk into the locker room after the last game. They were too busy celebrating.

Stopping shy of exploding champagne bottles, the music was loud, players danced around, stripped down to just their pants and a T-shirt. In the center, Keshawn lifted his hand up.

"Hey, hey," he yelled. "Zip it!"

Eventually, his teammates noticed he was trying to get their attention, the veterans shushing the louder players around them. The music was turned down, and after a few seconds, everyone circled around.

"Floor's yours, Coach," he said, tilting his chin in my direction.

The team turned, everyone smacking my back as I walked into the middle of the circle.

I set my hands on my hips and turned slowly, looking at everyone around me. "You know I'm not the guy who's gonna yell and scream or do a victory dance that'll end up on social media for everyone to make fun of," I said. "But if there was ever a game that would make me want to, it was that one." Through their proud murmurs, I shook my head as I exhaled a laugh. "I still don't know where I threw my headset after the game."

They laughed.

I let out a deep breath. "That wasn't easy. We had to work for every inch of that win." I looked at our defensive line, pointed to the five guys in front of me. "What you did today was incredible. You had the best—the *best*—running back in the league coming at you, and you didn't flinch. Held him to forty-two yards the entire game, and not a single run longer than five. No team has done that this season."

The room swelled with a chorus of *hell yeah*'s and *yeah, they fucking did*'s. Waiting for the cheers and yells to quiet down, I motioned for a ball, and when my assistant coach tossed one in my direction, I caught it easily.

For a moment, I stared down at it, let the feel of it in my hand bring me back to moments like this, when I was the one bruised and tired and proud of what my teammates had accomplished.

Palming the ball, I held it up for everyone to see. "Leadership is born in games like this. And when you see it happen, it's fucking incredible." Guys nodded and murmured in agreement. "I've got one game ball today, and even though I don't need to say why, I'm going to." I swallowed and turned to the other side of the room, seeking out the face I was looking for. "Get up here, Carson."

The team erupted as the backup quarterback made his way from the back of the room to the front, a few shoving him good-naturedly as he passed by. His eyes met mine, and his chest expanded on a deep breath. It was his first game ball.

"There's no playoff run for us this year. We knew that by halftime." I took a moment, allowing that to sink in. Two games in our division hadn't gone our way, the last wild card spot slipping past us through no fault of our own. "In the end, we had nothing at stake in this game. Nothing except our pride. Nothing except the need to prove ourselves. This season challenged every single one of us, but I think you and I had the most to prove today, didn't we?" I asked him.

He lifted his chin. "Yes, sir."

"You played your game today, Carson. Messy and tough and incredible." I handed him the ball. "Three hundred and seventy-two passing yards. Four passing touchdowns and a rushing touchdown. No interceptions, and the gutsiest performance I've seen under center in a long fucking time."

His jaw clenched, cheeks still bright red from the game, and he took the ball from my outstretched hand. "Thank you, Coach. I, uh, I wasn't sure I'd ever get one of these."

The guys around us laughed, and I couldn't help but smile. "You got one today, and that's what matters."

There was dried blood on the bridge of his nose, streaks of green on his arm, and, if I had to guess, the beginnings of a nasty bruise on his thigh from when he got rocked late in the fourth. Goose bumps popped on my arms as he turned, looking at the rest of the team.

"Everyone said we'd lose," he said quietly. "When I left the house today, my wife said, 'Just don't get your ass kicked, okay?'" Everyone laughed. "But we didn't lose. We proved that we can win when it matters." He paused, eyes searching out the players all around the room, and I saw the moment his gaze landed on Archer, who was leaning against the wall and watching with a conflicted look on his face. "If this is the only game ball I ever get . . . this is the best fucking win in my entire career."

He put his hand in the middle and met my gaze. I set my hand on top of his.

"All in," I said evenly.

Everyone crowded in, hands overlapping hands, and I nodded at Carson.

"Grit on three," he yelled.

When the team broke apart, I let out a deep exhale, feeling the weight of another season passing. It would never get easier, but moments like this sure as hell made it worth it.

I hugged a few of the guys as I walked through the jubilant crowd, making space to allow them their celebration. When I pulled away from

Justice, Archer was standing in front of me, arms crossed. The only reason he'd suited up was in case Carson got injured, but he'd spent the entire game on the sidelines, wearing a headset and watching film on the tablets with his offense when they were off the field.

He didn't speak at first, probably because he was holding his jaw so tight, words physically couldn't escape. I lifted my chin, angling it toward a slightly quieter part of the locker room.

The bruise on his jaw was still visible, and I had plenty of time to study it while he tried to work up the courage to look me square in the eye.

"I didn't think you'd actually bench me," he said, finally pulling his gaze up. "I thought . . . I thought you'd text me this morning. Tell me to get ready to start because you wanted to win."

"I *did* want to win. Coaches always do." I set my hands on my hips and shook my head. "It gave me no pleasure to do it, Archer. And I promise, if we'd lost—and lost badly—I'd be in Pearl's office right now getting my ass chewed."

He nodded. "What about next season?" he asked.

"I don't know if I can answer that right now."

I refused to let him look away. There was no saving Archer. He wasn't my brother, who I used to swoop in and save when he pulled something stupid, hoping to spare us both the embarrassment of him getting kicked off the team. And in the end, my brother had saved himself.

"Show me, Archer. Show me how bad you want this and that you're willing to work for it, because I have a guy who *is* if you're not. He's a good guy too. Team respects him. So do the coaches."

Archer's cheeks flushed, and he looked down at the ground, suitably humbled. "I know. I can't . . . I can't hate him, even if I want to." When he looked back up, there was a fire in his eyes again. "But I hate sitting on that bench."

"Then make it right."

Archer's throat worked on a swallow. "What if I can't? What if . . . what if I did peak in college and I can't be what this team needs?"

I set my hand on his shoulder and squeezed. "You can. Take the offseason and figure out what that looks like to you, okay?"

Eventually, he nodded. As he walked away, I rubbed the back of my neck and let out a deep sigh.

The door to the locker room opened, and Bridget poked her head in. "Is it child appropriate?"

"I think so." I looked over my shoulder. "Kids incoming!" I yelled. "Keep it clean, guys."

Bridget smiled, pushing the door open fully. Maggie and Bryce ran in, heading straight to me for a hug.

"Enjoy the game?" I asked them.

Bryce nodded. "Carson was awesome! That twenty-yard run for a touchdown? He shook three defenders."

"Impressive," I said.

Maggie held up a container. "Can I hand these out?"

My brow furrowed. "Where'd those come from?"

"Lily helped me make some this morning after you left for the stadium. Double chocolate chip with a little sea salt on the top." She shrugged. "She said that makes 'em extra good, but salt on cookies sounds a little weird to me."

I smiled. "You didn't try one?"

"Not yet. I have just enough for the team. Grandpa tried to sneak one, but I caught him."

I ruffled her hair. "Go ahead."

Carefully, Maggie opened the lid to the container and looked around at the celebratory chaos around the room.

I leaned down. "Want a little help getting their attention?"

She nodded.

I asked my assistant coach for something, and he handed it over with a grin. Maggie hopped up onto a chair, put the silver whistle in her mouth, and blew. Loud.

The entire team quieted immediately. Her eyes widened. "Um. You did really good today, and I made cookies if you want one." She paused. "And there's no peanut butter because I know Justice is allergic."

"My girl!" he yelled.

With bright eyes, she held out the container.

Guys shoved each other out of the way, tripping and elbowing their teammates as they rushed toward my daughter. Keshawn started the chant, and soon the entire team was involved. It grew louder and louder, and Bridget pulled out her phone to record what was happening.

"Maggie, Maggie, Maggie!"

Her cheeks were flushed pink, and when she handed out the last cookie and thrust the empty container over her head like a trophy, they let out a raucous cheer.

"And then, and *then*, they all yelled my name," Maggie said. "Did I tell you that part?"

"Yes," Bryce groaned, pairing it with an over-the-top roll of his eyes.

"Mr. Archer said they were the best cookies he's ever had in his life. His *whole* life."

My mom smiled. "That's amazing, honey. When am I going to be allowed in a locker room?"

"Never," Dad said. His eyes remained closed, and his hands were folded over his stomach as he rested on the couch. They'd been in the box with the kids, and Bridget and her wife. "I'm sure they would've been the best cookies I'd ever had in my life, too, if I'd been allowed to try them."

"Everyone feels very sorry for you, honey." My mom patted his shoulder, only a little bit condescendingly.

The kids snuggled on the couch—one of them next to my mom and the other next to my dad—and I smiled as I watched them.

The best part of having the early game was being home at a decent time, and today it felt even sweeter. For a while, at least, my days would be a bit shorter, have a lot less meetings. I could have dinner with my kids. Not really tuck them in at night, though, because they'd both proclaimed themselves too old to be tucked in anymore.

Needing to let go of that was a loss of sorts, something I hadn't really thought of when they were younger. One random night—I couldn't even remember when—was the last time I'd tucked them in. Leaving work early enough to be able to do that had been so important to me, and there was no warning when those things suddenly went away.

The thought of missing them, especially on a voluntary basis like Rachel, was absolutely unfathomable. There hadn't been a fight over custody because she didn't want to split anything. I was already dreading the two weeks in the summer they'd be with her. And next Christmas, I'd be alone.

We'd already taken down the tree, the corner of the room now filled with a floor lamp and a basket that held a couple of blankets. Next year, I likely wouldn't even put it up—and it was that thought that sent my eyes over to the spot on the wall that had held the mistletoe—a gift from my daughter, I'd later found out.

That was gone too.

Where would Lily be next Christmas? Absently, I rubbed at my chest. Even though it wasn't mine to worry about, the question gnawed at me all the same.

My phone buzzed in my hand, and there was a punch in my chest when I thought it might be Lily, irrational though it was. I had her number and she had mine, but now that she wasn't watching the kids, there wasn't much reason for me to text her.

But the text wasn't from her.

It was from someone just as surprising, though.

Griffin: Your win didn't suck today.

I shook my head, quickly deciding I couldn't do this with an audience, especially if my parents had any idea that there was some form of reciprocal conversation happening between us. Then there was pressure, expectations. And more than anything, my brother and I needed space to figure out what a relationship between us looked like.

I didn't answer until I took a seat in the den, which also served as my office.

Me: Neither did yours.

Griffin: You feel as tired as I do right now?

Me: Probably not. You had four sacks and played every defensive snap with a half-healed arm.

Griffin: It's not HALF-HEALED. I'm fine. That mother of ours is running her mouth, isn't she?

Me: It's possible.

For a moment, three dots appeared on the screen and then disappeared, only to reappear again. It was good to know I wasn't the only one stumbling through these occasional interactions.

Griffin: I wanted to ask you something if you've got a minute.

Me: No, I don't think you're better looking than me.

Griffin: Holy fuck, did you just make a joke?

Me: I'm funny.

Griffin: Uh-huh.

Griffin: Anyway . . . would you be okay with the kids coming to spend a few days with me and Ruby now that the season's done? We'd love to spend some time with them.

Griffin: Intentional time. You know, when you're aware they're flying to see me. I already told Maggie she's not allowed to forge paperwork anymore.

I rubbed the back of my neck and sighed, thinking of how my kids would want me to answer. They'd beg and plead. Promise all sorts of things in exchange for a long weekend with Griffin and his fiancée.

The selfish part of me wanted to say no. My schedule had just freed up, too, breathing room that would allow me to see them more. Clinging tight to Maggie and Bryce would be so easy. More than anything, I wanted to keep them near me after such an exhausting season.

But it wouldn't be fair.

Me: Give me at least a week with them now that I can breathe again, but after that, I'd be open to letting them visit.

Griffin: Thank you. I know you have every reason to say no, but I miss them.

Me: They miss you too. And you're welcome.

Griffin: I don't want to sound like a sappy asshole . . .

Me: Dear God, then don't. I already said yes, you don't have to suck up to me.

Griffin: First, I would never. Second, there's only two reasons I get sappy. Ruby and your kids, so trust me, it has nothing to do with you.

Me: Okay.

Griffin: It's just, I know this is hard for you. To let go of them like this. Especially to me. I know I've changed a lot, mostly thanks to Ruby, who is a thousand times too good for me, but I think maybe you've changed too. I'm proud of us, you know?

Griffin: Fuck, don't tell mom and dad I said that. They'll cry. It'll be a whole big dramatic thing.

Me: My lips are sealed. I'll text you some dates that work.

Griffin: Thank you.

I sucked in a deep breath and sent one more text.

Me: Maybe you and Ruby could fly here to get them. I'd love to spend some more time with her.

Griffin: Yeah, we'd love that.

Me: One night maybe?

Griffin: Fucking baby steps. I think two days with your ass and I'd run back to Colorado.

When my screen went dark, I was smiling to myself. It was messy and incredibly imperfect, but it was something. It reminded me of our win today. For so long—my entire life, really—I'd sought out perfection. There was a certain kind of insulation that came with it.

If I do this exactly right, everything will be okay.

My grades.

My play on the field.

Then it was proposing to Rachel, even though every single red flag existed early in our relationship.

When playing football was gone, my marriage dissolved shortly after. Then coaching. If I studied more film, if I gave up just a bit more sleep, if I had the perfect game plan . . .

But it was impossible. All of it. I couldn't do any of it perfectly.

And now it was becoming increasingly clear that parenting, especially on my own, would fall far short of perfect as well.

Even the appearance of Lily in our lives, my interest in her that wasn't going anywhere, was as imperfect as it could get too. There'd be no flirting with her. No wooing her. Underneath that shell—and it was a tough one—there was something incredibly vulnerable about her, and more than anything, I wanted to dig deeper. Wanted to know why she protected herself so fiercely.

I just . . . wanted more. Whatever that looked like, really. Even if it was messy, even if it was clumsy and uncomfortable to put myself in a position with this woman where she might hurt or reject me.

There wasn't always failure waiting behind the release of perfection. Sometimes it was moments like this. Acceptance that I was willing to mess up.

My brother was willing to do that when he texted me. The guy who never took anything seriously outside of football.

I opened up my phone again and started a new text thread, attaching a video with a simple caption.

Me: You've created a monster.

Her response was immediate, and exactly what I'd been hoping for.

Lily: This is the best thing I've ever seen! Omg, you just made my night.

Me: Then I'm glad I sent it.

Now it was Lily's turn to make the bubbles appear. Disappear. Appear again.

Me: I've rendered you speechless. I had no idea I was that powerful.

Lily: Fuck off, I just wasn't sure how you meant it.

Me: I meant it how I said it. No ulterior motive.

Lily: Huh. What a novel concept.

Lily: So . . . did you win your game today?

Me: We did.

Lily: No wonder you're in such an accommodating mood.

Me: Now would be the time to ask me to shovel the driveway. I'd probably say yes.

Lily: I can clear my own driveway, thank you very much.

Me: . . .

Lily: I swear, if you're smiling right now . . . You know what I mean.

Me: Indeed I do.

Lily: I'm not even sure you're capable of a smile.

Me: Is that your way of asking for a picture?

Lily: Fuck. Off. Like I'd give you the satisfaction.

Me: Does that mean I can't ask for one?

To my delight, Lily attached one. I could see her eyes, staring dark and direct into the camera. The rest of her face, though, was obscured by her middle finger.

In the dark of my office, with no one to see, I smiled, laughing under my breath as I saved the picture to my phone.

Chapter Nineteen

Lily

It was possible I needed therapy. A lot of therapy.

Though that was nothing new; it had been an errant thought over the years, but I'd dismissed it easily because, ugh, then you need to sit and unload all the big bullet points in the first hour.

An expensive hour that could be titled *What's My Villain Origin Story?*

But I was considering it again, as I found myself lying belly down on the floor, trying to hand-feed my dog, who hates me. It was expensive food, the kind that had to be kept in the fridge and was supposed to cure everything that could possibly ail him. Except, in my case, his horrible disposition—that wasn't going anywhere. Much like me, in that way. Cookies hadn't cured my bad attitude, either, so I guess we were even.

"Come on, Larry," I coaxed gently, easing my hand closer to his mouth. "Even I think this smells good."

He leaned forward, sniffing the food balancing on my outstretched fingers. He gave it a half-hearted lick and then retreated again, laying his head down between his paws with an old-man groan.

I sighed, flicking the food back into his ceramic bowl. It had his name on it and everything. Teeny black paw prints painted on the rim. It was cute. And expensive. And he still didn't want to eat out of it. "Fine. Be that way," I said, wiping my fingers off on a piece of paper towel.

Unable to stop the worry creeping steadily through my veins, I chewed on my bottom lip as I watched him fall asleep in a small patch of sun he'd found streaming through one of the front windows. He was fine, acting normal, other than not eating as much.

My phone buzzed, and *fuck.ing.hell*, I got a flutter of something in my chest. Could've been fear. Might've been excitement. To err on the safe side, we'd call it general nausea, because honestly, both of those feelings fit within that umbrella.

A football field heart-to-heart and one measly little text exchange with mildly flirty undertones, and I'd turned into an absolute overthinking wreck.

Had he sent anything else since then? No.

Did I want him to? No. Maybe. Except no.

I searched the Buffalo social media and found videos of him after the game. Like a moon-eyed schoolgirl who wanted to catch a glimpse of the popular boy. Surrounded by tall, strapping men with an overabundance of muscles, Barrett commanded the locker room with ease.

I liked that he wasn't over-the-top cheesy, shouting and screaming cliché catchphrases. Instead, he seemed to speak from the heart, every single person on the team listening intently to what he had to say. It was likely that some were older than him, too, but he was still undeniably in charge.

No wonder he was in such a damn good mood. Why he was being sorta flirty with unsuspecting neighbors who weren't mentally prepared? How was I supposed to react to that kind of bullshit?

I sure as hell wasn't going to initiate. Like I was begging for his attention or something. I'd never give him the satisfaction.

My phone buzzed again, and I pinched my eyes shut, finally screwing up the lady balls to look at the screen.

Not Barrett.

It was Patty, wanting to know if I had time to talk today. Please, all I *had* was time. I'd done nothing the last week except blow through three new fanfics and a binge of *Schitt's Creek* for the seventeenth time.

With a sigh, I pulled up her contact information and settled my back against the couch while I waited for her to pick up.

"Good morning," she said cheerily. "Is the house still standing?"

"So far."

"Oh good. I realized yesterday when I saw how cold it was there, we forgot to tell you how to change the whole-house humidifier on the furnace. Have you been getting condensation on the inside of the windows?"

"A bit, yeah."

"Just need to lower the humidity in the house when it gets this cold. There's a chart on the front of the box to tell you what to set it to; it's in the mechanical room back by the garage."

"You got it, boss." I had an actual person on the phone, and I wasn't quite ready to hang up yet. Maybe the state of New York was slowly breaking down my inner introvert. "How's Arizona? And please, feel free to describe the weather in great detail."

She laughed. "Beautiful. Sunny every day. Scott's playing pickleball, and I'm reading about some sexy dragons in the sun. Have much snow right now?"

"Not too bad," I admitted. "Sometimes I wake up and we got a couple inches, but I really can't complain. It's just cold as shit this week, so I haven't gone out much."

I scratched the top of Larry's head, and he opened his eyes in a doggy glare. I pulled my hand back and raised it in apology.

"Seen the kids much this week?"

"No. They're back at school."

My glum response made her laugh again. "They're great, aren't they? They used our pool a lot last summer. It was wonderful having a little life back there again."

"They are."

"And Barrett's parents are still there, right?"

I nodded, then remembered she couldn't see me. "Yeah. I'm . . . I'm not sure for how much longer. Maggie told me they leave this week." My fingers played with the edge of Larry's blanket. The ragged edges were so faded, it was hard to remember what color it used to be. My thumb dragged along the raised pattern. Yellow. It used to be yellow and blue and white.

The fluffy hair above Larry's eyes twitched as he watched me touch his blanket. There was no growling or groaning, though, and he didn't move away.

"So," she said decisively, "are you wishing you'd said no to my little job offer?"

I let out a quiet laugh and stared at the snow. The sun's appearance made it all sparkly and shit, like the earth was coated in jewels. It was beautiful—there was no denying that, and I never would've known that if I hadn't seen it myself.

There were a lot of things I wouldn't have known if I hadn't made the decision to come here.

"No, I don't regret it," I said softly, allowing the admission to come out painlessly. There was no point in fighting it, so I didn't even try. "It's been a pleasant surprise."

She hummed. "Where will you be going next?"

I laid my head back and stared up at the ceiling. This admission wasn't so easy.

"I'm not sure."

Patty made a noise of surprise. "How come? Don't you always have the next move planned?"

"Usually," I hedged. Always. I *always* had my next move figured out by this point. A destination, if nothing else. Or I was asking my current job if they knew of anyone who might need someone with my particular skill set.

I really hoped no one asked me to list those skills, because I wouldn't look great on paper.

She hermits well, but please don't ask her to have surface-level conversation. Also wears disdain and general disgust clearly on her facial expressions.

I'd joked about those things for so long, and it's because they had a basis in truth—but wasn't there room for our personalities to change as we got older? That the things we wanted, the things we craved, could change too? Allowing those changes was often the hardest part. It made me think about what Barrett had said about not wanting to hold on to the way he used to do things. Arrogance, he'd called it.

I wasn't sure I'd ever met a man so willing to admit his own flaws.

"It's getting harder," I admitted in a hushed voice, "to keep moving like this. But I'm not sure I know how to stop."

Patty let out a quiet sigh. "I may not have a great answer for you, Lily. I'll say this, though: No one's making you leave. Not yet. The guest room is yours if you wanted to stick around Buffalo for a while after we get home."

Her offer moved me far more than I dared admit, and that emotion built in the back of my throat. "Thank you. I'm not sure I'd make a great roommate, though. I don't have very much practice."

"It's hard to change when we're used to doing things a certain way," she said carefully. "But I have a feeling you'd be better at it than you think."

There wasn't a whole lot to say after that, so we said our goodbyes after I promised to change the humidity thingy on the furnace. Larry was sound asleep when I disconnected the call, and I pushed to my feet with a groan, wandering down the hallway to the mechanical room. I found the knob and had to rise on the balls of my feet to be able to read the tiny print. Once the knob was moved, I dropped back down and shut the light off, a lingering sadness hovering like a cloud after my conversation with Patty.

I'd felt it all week, if I was being honest with myself.

It wasn't the kind of sadness that weighed me down completely, but I just couldn't get it to *go away*. It had settled at the back of my mind, found a tiny foothold in all my thoughts. A thin wisp of fog that couldn't be swept away. If I tried, if I waved my hand in front of me or shifted my thoughts elsewhere, it simply crept back up, drifting in and out of my day-to-day.

It being the thing I was feeling. It did have a name; I'd just refused to use it the entire week.

I missed them.

I *missed* them.

What a horrifying discovery to make, because holy shit, there was no turning back from that.

On the dresser in my room was the postcard I'd picked up when I visited Niagara Falls. For the last couple of weeks, I'd left it sitting there, unable—or unwilling—to write anything on the back. The cloud, though . . . the cloud of sadness pushed and prodded until I couldn't ignore it anymore.

Carefully, I picked up the ballpoint pen I'd left next to the postcard and slowly wrote three things across the back.

Maggie.

Bryce.

Barrett.

My eyesight blurred when I closed the pen.

For the first time in over ten years, I wrote names. Not a place or a restaurant or a sight that I'd visited. Living, breathing human beings—who'd provided memories to take with me, moments to miss and replay. A gift. One they weren't even aware of.

With a heavy chest, I opened the closet to put the postcard away where it belonged, tucked in a clear page of a book full of pieces of paper just like it. But I didn't close the closet, deciding instead to pull out my suitcase. The small one that I hardly ever opened, and simply kept bringing with me from place to place. Somewhere in Texas, there was a storage unit that held all the items I couldn't bring myself to get rid of. But as I moved around, I took a select number of sentimental items with me.

They hadn't seen the light of day in at least a year. Maybe longer. Why? Because it fucking hurt to look at them, and I made it a habit not to hurt my own feelings.

Except when I felt like this, I supposed. When I needed a tangible reminder of why I was avoiding this very thing. Why missing anyone was the last thing I needed. Why missing memories and moments and traditions should be avoided at all costs. Forget heaven and hell—*that* was purgatory. And I'd already spent enough time there to know how much I hated it.

My hands shook as I opened the suitcase holding the small white box. The edges were smudged and banged up, but the clasp still held tight. When I opened it, a small creaking sound filled the room, and I had to shore up all my defenses before I cracked the lid.

Larry's paws made a pitter-pat sound on the floor in the hallway, and I tilted my head, waiting for him to appear. He stopped in the doorway of my room and plopped his butt down, his own head tilted like *Well . . . what are you waiting for?*

"You're so pushy," I said, and my voice sounded thick and rough, no hiding the emotions I'd been shoving down all week. The dog walked over to the bed and looked up at me, letting out a weary sigh. I rolled my eyes and leaned down to pick him up. When my hand curled under his belly, he groaned. Once safely on the bed, he sat down, then stared at the box.

The pictures on top were faded with time, even though they hardly saw the light of day. A single glimpse of the top picture was enough to make my hand freeze in midair.

A much younger Larry, maybe only a year old, was cuddled up in a brighter, more vibrant version of the blanket he slept on every day. And the face above his . . .

My lungs burned, so did my eyes—but I couldn't blink. Couldn't breathe. A wildfire swept through my entire body while I stared at the smile. The dimples. The rosy cheeks and the bright smile.

That was enough.

I slammed the box shut and set it aside, trying to pull air into my lungs while my heart raced.

Therapy, I thought again with a desperate laugh. *I need therapy.*

Larry looked up at me, and on a stack of Bibles, I'd have sworn he was tearing up.

"I know, buddy," I whispered. "I miss them too."

Carefully, I set my hand along his skinny back and gently pet him. He leaned in to the touch. Just a fraction. But enough that I noticed, and I smiled faintly.

There was a knock on the front door, and I deflated, not sure how much I could handle. For a moment, I thought about not answering it. Ignoring whoever it was. Guilt tore at my insides, and I knew that if it was Maggie or Bryce, I'd never be able to forgive myself.

I blew out a hard breath and caught a glimpse of myself in the mirror before I exited the room. My eyes were a little red, but hopefully not enough that anyone would notice. I'd rather let someone think I was on drugs than the actual truth. Lily Townsend, sitting alone and crying? No fucking thank you. The silhouette on the other side of the door was distinctly female, and my heart let out a puttering little sigh of relief-slash-disappointment that it wasn't Barrett.

At the moment, I could not handle that man. Because, so help me, if he gave me another shovel or offered up some strangely thoughtful version of help, I'd ask him to hug me. Or I'd cry. I wasn't sure which was worse.

The crying. Definitely the crying. My face got all red and splotchy, and nothing about it was attractive. A healthy amount of vanity was not the end of the world, okay?

It didn't *mean* anything.

I pulled in a fortifying breath and pulled open the door.

It was Robin.

"Oh. Hi."

She smiled, seeming genuinely amused by my confusion. "I'm sorry to intrude. I'm sure you're busy."

"Super busy," I said. "Just . . . the busiest."

Her eyes traced over my face and seemed to find the lie pretty quickly, even if she chose not to comment on it.

"I was wondering if you'd like to join us for dinner tonight. My husband and I leave soon, and we would love to spend a bit more time with you. Barrett's done with the season, of course, so we thought a nice family-style dinner could be a good way to spend our last evening."

Have you ever tried swallowing around an elephant? That was what it felt like. The idea of dinner with the Kings filled me with actual terror, the kind that made my limbs tingle.

"I can't," I heard myself say. "I'm sorry."

"Oh." Her face fell. "Of course. I should've known you might have plans."

It was on the tip of my tongue to correct her, but I just . . . didn't. The truth was . . . I *couldn't*. I could not sit at a table with all of them and pretend like I was okay when I wasn't. I couldn't watch Maggie tell stories and Bryce talk about his day. I couldn't meet Barrett's knowing gaze and pretend like it didn't shake me to my fucking core.

I tried to push a polite smile on my face, but based on her expression, it must have come off like a grimace. "I'm sorry," I said again. Not like I had anything to apologize for. It wasn't wrong to say no to someone, even if their offer was nice and kind and thoughtful.

At the moment, nice and kind and thoughtful would be my absolute undoing.

Robin paused like she was going to say something, then thought better of it. "If we don't see you before we leave," she said carefully, "it was a real pleasure, Lily. I hope this isn't the last we see of you."

The entire King family was going to fucking break me, I just knew it. Letting her see that would've ruined everything, so I infused as much strength as I could muster into my voice.

"Thank you," I replied, hardly above a whisper. "It was nice to meet you, too, Robin."

Her gaze was thoughtful, and I wondered if there was some Mom-radar going off in her head that I was real close to a mental breakdown. I swear, if she came in for a hug, I'd absolutely fucking crack, and then I'd never forgive her for making me snot all over her shoulder.

"If you ever get back to Arizona," she said, "feel free to look us up."

"I will," I promised. Even more surprising was the fact that I meant it.

She must have seen that on my face, because she finally let out a small sigh.

After another smile, she turned and left, and I watched her cross the driveway, then the yards between our houses. When she was safely inside, I closed my eyes and locked the door behind me.

Chapter Twenty

Barrett

It was snowing.

Normally I might not have noticed, but for the fact Lily mentioned it the other day. They were big, fluffy flakes, some of the largest I'd ever seen, and with the kids upstairs doing their final packing for their trip to Colorado for the weekend, I was alone in the kitchen, drinking my coffee, watching the snow fall through the windows.

Was she watching it too?

I tried to imagine texting her.

Just wanted to make sure you knew it was snowing.

I did know that, she'd say, *because my eyes work, you dumbass.*

"Maybe not," I muttered, taking another sip of my coffee and keeping my phone far out of reach.

My parents had extended their stay by a couple of days once they knew Griffin and Ruby were coming. Both of their boys under one roof . . . My mom had been crying all morning.

Happy tears, of course. When I tried to think about Maggie and Bryce not speaking for years, unwilling to be in the same place, it made my heart sink for what my parents must have felt.

I pushed up out of my chair and wandered over to the slider, fighting that ever-present feeling of guilt over the time we'd spent angry at each other.

For a few moments, I stared blankly into the backyard, watching the kids' footprints from yesterday fill with the snow falling lazily from the sky. Movement from next door caught my eye, and my head reared in shock.

Lily was flat on her back, unmoving, in the yard.

"Shit," I mumbled, slamming my mug onto the counter and jogging to the back door to grab my boots and my coat. "Mom, I'll be outside," I yelled. "Can you make sure the kids finish their packing?"

I didn't wait for her to answer, bolting out the door instead, my heart clanging noisily behind my ribs as I ran through the side yard and yanked open the gate that led into Scott and Patty's yard.

Her head lifted slightly at my noisy approach, brows furrowing. "What's wrong?" she asked.

I stopped short, my chest heaving, air coming out of my mouth in visible puffs as I tried to catch my breath. "What's *wrong*? You're flat on your back. I thought you passed out."

Lily blinked. "Oh." Then she laid her head back down and stared up at the sky. "No. I'm fully conscious, I promise."

If the ground opened up and swallowed me, I wouldn't have been sad about it. I licked my lips and rubbed the back of my neck, staring at her profile. A black hood lined with fur was pulled up around her face, her hair spilling out the edges. The blue looked brighter than usual against the perfectly white snow.

"Are you . . . are you okay?" I asked quietly. The loud breathing had stopped, but my stomach was still twisted with worry.

Finally, Lily blinked. Her jaw tightened and then relaxed. "It's snowing," she said quietly. "I've never seen it snow before."

"So you're going for a fully immersive experience, then?"

The edge of her lips curled up, but only for a moment. "I guess. Have you ever lay like this? Just to watch?"

"No. I, uh, I can't say that I have." I rubbed a gloved hand over my jaw and thought about it. "Maybe when I was a kid."

She closed her eyes for a moment. "Do you remember it?"

Briefly, I glanced over at the slider, making sure no one was watching. Or recording it on their phone for later. For the time being, we were unnoticed, so I took a few steps closer, tugged my hat out from the pocket of my coat, and pulled it over my head. Lily's eyes darted in my direction, then shifted back to the sky when I eased down onto the snow next to her.

We didn't speak, and I felt my blood pressure drop as I stared up into the sky. Everything was white. The spindly arms of the trees were visible in the edges of my vision, but other than that, everything was void of color. Trying to focus in on the snow as it fell almost felt impossible. The flakes landed on my face, but I didn't brush them away immediately.

Her hands were on her stomach, so I mirrored her pose, and even though my legs were going to freeze off and my testicles had likely taken up permanent residence inside my body, I'd lay there next to her for a while.

"I don't ever take time to do stuff like this," I admitted.

"Most people don't."

I turned my head to the side and studied the finely carved lines of her profile. Her cheeks were flushed from cold, as was the tip of her nose. "But you do?"

Lily didn't answer right away. "Not as much as I should."

There wasn't a sound anywhere around us—no kids out playing, no dogs barking, no cars on the street.

"What do you see?" she asked in a hushed voice.

My throat was dry from staring at her, but she didn't seem to notice or care. I shifted my gaze away, moving it back to the sky. There was probably some poetic way to describe it, but when I tried, everything fell just a little short.

"I'm not . . . I'm not good at saying things in a pretty way," I admitted roughly. "But it feels peaceful, I guess."

Lily made a small humming noise, her chest expanding on a deep breath.

"What about you?" I asked. "What do you see?"

Her face stayed perfectly still, and I wasn't sure she'd heard me. Wasn't sure she was planning to answer. But then she closed her eyes, and it wasn't until her brows furrowed and her lower lip trembled that I knew something was wrong. That even if she was physically fine, Lily wasn't okay.

"Magic," she whispered. Her eyes opened, and they were glossy with unshed tears, but not a single one fell. "I see magic."

She held her hand up, and when a few fat, fluffy flakes landed on her glove, she brought it closer to her face. Watching her study them was fascinating, and it tore me apart how badly I wanted to know more about her. Wanted to know what was making her so sad. Wanting to fix it. Take it away, if I could.

If she'd let me.

"It's like the sky is breaking apart," she said. "Doesn't that sound scary when you think about it?"

"I guess."

"It's not, though. Each piece that pries away from the others, it's different from the one next to it. Isn't that incredible?"

I looked back up, watching the mesmerizing descent of the snow. She was right. It did look like that. Slowly, I turned my face back toward her. "Beautiful."

She didn't say anything right away, and that was fine with me.

I wondered how long it would take for frostbite to set in when you lay on the snow wearing jeans. My calves were numb. So was my ass. Hers couldn't have been any better since she was wearing leggings.

But I was fairly certain that, until she moved, I wouldn't either.

"I'm surprised you're out here."

"I thought you were unconscious. If I didn't come out, then I've got even bigger problems to contend with."

"I'm not, though." She looked over at me. "Unconscious."

"Appears that way."

After a moment, Lily turned and stared back up at the sky. "And you're still here."

My lip hooked up in a wry grin that she didn't see. "Is that your way of asking me to leave?"

She blinked. "No."

I brought my gloves up to my lips, cupped them around my mouth, and blew. Lily mimicked the action and made a small humming noise when the warmth hit her fingers. "That's nice. I don't know those tricks."

"You've never gotten cold anywhere else?"

"Not like this." She blew on her fingers again. The gloves she wore were black, and too thin to be out in the snow. Her fingers were probably already frozen solid. With a sigh, I tugged mine off and laid them on her stomach.

"Wear those," I told her.

She glanced at me. "What about you?"

"I'll be fine." I gave her a quick look. "Unless you foresee this exercise going for the next couple hours, in which case, neither of us are prepared."

Wordlessly, Lily wiggled her fingers into my larger gloves and sighed when they were covered by the thicker, warmer material.

From inside the pocket of her coat, her phone started ringing, and she bolted upright, the movement so startling that I almost jumped.

Using her teeth, she yanked my gloves off and answered the call, bringing the phone up to her ear. "This is Lily."

As I sat up, I couldn't hear who was on the other line, but watching Lily's face was enough. The color drained from her cheeks, and her nostrils flared slightly, her eyes unblinking as she listened.

"Okay," she said. "Yeah, I'll be there as soon as I can."

For a moment, she stared forward, even as her hand slowly lowered into her lap. The hood had fallen off her head, and her hair was slightly tangled in the back from however long she'd been lying in the snow.

"I hate that dog," she whispered, the slightest catch in her voice.

My brow flattened. "What happened?"

She let out an incredulous laugh, then stared up at the sky again. "He's dying." She rolled her lips together and her chin trembled. "What a jerk."

I sucked in a breath and angled toward her. "Where is he?"

"I brought him in to the emergency vet late last night. He . . . he hadn't peed or anything in days. No eating. No drinking water. They told me to go home and get some rest while they monitored him." Lily sucked in a sharp breath and pinched her eyes shut. "Oh God," she said, clapping a hand over her mouth to stifle a sob before it escaped.

There was no time to question whether I should lay a hand on her back or even attempt to comfort her in any way, because with quick, jerky movements, she stood, snow falling off her back as she did. I joined her, watching her face carefully in case she crumpled.

"I have to go," she said unsteadily. "They . . . they told me I have to come in if I want to say . . ."

Then she covered her face with both hands and took great, big shuddering breaths to try to compose herself.

Moving slowly, I reached out, wrapping my fingers around her wrists until her hands were away from her face. "Let me come with you," I said slowly. "Let me help you."

Lily's eyes were bright with tears, but she held them in, unblinking as she studied my face with the slightest look of confusion. "Why?"

Moments like this didn't happen very often. Where even the air between us, as it fell in pieces from the sky, felt fragile and precious. Lying to her did me no good. And I didn't want to.

"Because I want to be there."

The waiting room at the emergency vet was quiet. Only one other couple was off in the corner, laughing at something they were watching on their phone. The room was clean and bright—black-and-white photos of cats and dogs on the wall. Paw prints painted in a crooked line underneath.

I sent my mom a text letting her know why I was gone with no notice, and she promised they'd explain to Griffin and Ruby when they arrived from the airport. Resting my elbows on my knees, I leaned forward and set my head in my hands.

On the drive over, Lily had stayed quiet.

Not just quiet—she was dry-eyed as she asked me to wait in the lobby, dry-eyed as she followed a vet tech down a hallway, disappearing behind a glossy black door with the number 5 painted on the placard on the wall.

She'd shut down, and I couldn't blame her.

Discomfort sat like an anchor on my chest, like my insides were being stretched in two very different directions. There was no foundation between us that might warrant my presence in that room, but damn if I didn't want to be there.

My mom sent a text not long after Lily went into the exam room. She'd told the kids, and they were sad, but Griffin and Ruby's arrival helped. They were settled in the guest room, and she'd order pizza for dinner. Enough for Lily, too, if she wanted to join, she said.

I shook my head. Subtle as a freight train.

A door opened, and I lifted my head, but it was a redheaded woman cuddling a black-and-white puppy on a leash. My shoulders fell, and I had to cover my mouth with one hand as I waited. Patience, in moments like this, was not my strong suit.

Doing nothing was even worse.

But sometimes doing nothing was the best thing you could do for someone. Being there was doing something. Even if it meant waiting. Even if it meant being perfectly fine that she didn't say a single word.

Another door opened. The soft murmuring of voices reached my ears.

It was door number 5.

Slowly, I stood, waiting for her to leave the room. The vet tech came out first, her eyes downcast. Lily was behind her, face pale and her coat clutched in her hands. When her gaze lifted, she looked so empty, so unbearably fragile, that my chest ached.

"Hey," I said softly. "You ready to go?"

Lily tucked her hair behind her ears, attention shifting to the front desk. "I need to pay."

"I already did," I told her. "I didn't want you to have to stay any longer than necessary."

Her throat worked on a swallow. "Thank you," she whispered.

When she looked up into my face—looking so fucking lost, so devastated—I almost did something really stupid, like pull her into my arms. But doing nothing . . . I couldn't.

I laid my hand on her shoulder and squeezed. Underneath my fingers, her hair was silky and smooth. Lily pinched her eyes shut and then walked past me, my hand falling back down to my side.

A vet tech came around the corner with a bag in her hand. "Here. She forgot to take these from the room."

All it took was a quick glance over my shoulder to know she was long gone. Lily was already in the parking lot, arms crossed tightly as she strode to my truck. I gave the employee a small smile. "What is it?"

"The dog's collar, and the blanket she had him wrapped in when she arrived last night. It looks like it was well loved; I thought she might want it back."

"Thank you." I tucked the bag under my arm and sighed. "Is there anything else we need to do?"

She shook her head. "We'll take care of everything. She didn't want the ashes after cremation, so there's not really anything left to do."

"Okay. Thanks again."

"Have a good day, Coach." She smiled shyly.

Lily was waiting outside the truck, and the lost look was gone from her face. In its place was stoicism. Her chin was lifted, and she still held that coat in her hands despite the snow flying and the blustery wind.

Without a word, I held out the bag, watching her face carefully. For a moment, she stared at it, then removed it from my grasp. I unlocked the truck and opened her door. She stared at my hand on the edge of the door, her chest rising and falling on a deep breath before she grabbed the handle and pulled herself into the passenger seat.

Once she was in, I closed the door and walked quickly around to the driver's side.

She was quiet on the drive home, but unlike last time, she didn't stare out the window.

Lily was staring at me.

Instead of fidgeting underneath the weight of that stare, I hooked my wrist on the top of the steering wheel and simply let her look.

For a while, at least.

At a red light, I glanced sideways with a raised eyebrow. "Got any incoming questions, or are we just going to have a staring contest every time I stop?"

"I'm not sure I'm ready to ask you any questions," she said, tucking her leg up against her chest and wrapping an arm around it. She'd toed off her boots before I got into the truck. "You never answer them anyway."

I hummed. "Seems to be the theme of our relationship, doesn't it?"

"I answer some."

"Not all."

"Well, no, what fun is that? Once the mystery is gone, you'll stop acting as my personal chauffeur for traumatic moments, and then where would I be?"

If bantering with me made Lily feel better, I'd do it all fucking night.

"I'd imagine you'd be driving yourself," I answered evenly. "You didn't need me to come with you. You'd have handled it."

For a moment, she was quiet; then, finally, she shifted her gaze to the front windshield as we got closer to our neighborhood. "Yeah, but I would've been mean to the staff," she said quietly. "You were nice, I think."

"No, you wouldn't."

Her head snapped toward me. "How do you know?"

The light in front of me turned yellow, and even though I could've made it, I eased the truck to a stop, then turned and caught her eye. "You're not as mean as you proclaim to be. And if I hadn't been there, you would've been polite. Kind, even. And I have a feeling if I hadn't been waiting for you, you would've finally let yourself shed a tear over that grumpy little beast, who you don't actually hate."

Lily rolled her lips between her teeth and stared down at her lap, where her fingers turned white at the knuckles from how tightly she held her hands. "You don't know me," she whispered.

"Yeah, but I wouldn't mind changing that," I said easily.

Her jaw went slack, and she let out a shocked laugh. "So this is, what? An elaborate seduction technique? You say no to kissing me under the plant of doom, but you think a first date at the emergency vet will really seal the deal?"

I leaned in slightly, my elbow easing onto the console between us. Another inch and our arms would've touched. "Is that what you think I'm doing, Lily?" I held her gaze. "Truly?"

Her eyes darted between mine, and eventually she shook her head.

After a beat, I moved back into my seat, pressing my foot on the gas when the light turned green. "Sometimes people don't have ulterior motives. They help because they want to help. They get to know someone because that sounds better than not knowing them at all."

"And that's you?"

I sucked in a breath through my nose and gave her a quick look as I exhaled. "Yeah. It is."

"Hmm."

The disbelief in her tone had me fighting a smile. Nothing about this—about *us*—made much sense. And I just couldn't find it in me to care.

As I took the last turn onto our street, I saw the kids waiting on the front porch of Scott and Patty's place, and I glanced at Lily to gauge her reaction.

The lightness that had briefly shifted our exchange was long gone, likely because it was a flimsy sort of defense mechanism over what was really happening inside her.

"How'd they know we were almost home?" she asked quietly.

"Oh, uh, Maggie knows how to track my phone." Her lips curved in a smile, but it disappeared quickly. I cleared my throat, slowing down before I turned into her driveway. "Do you want me to ask them to go?"

Immediately, she shook her head. "It's okay." She gave me a quick look. "You gonna open my door on this shitty date, or am I allowed to do it myself?"

Affection swelled under my sternum so fast, it almost took my breath away. "You can do it yourself." I paused as I turned off the truck. "This time."

Lily muttered something under her breath, but I didn't hear it. Probably better that way.

The kids were alone, and I had a feeling my mother was to thank for that. There was no way Lily could handle a crowd right now. But just in case I was wrong, I laid a hand on her forearm before she exited the truck.

"If you want, you're welcome to come over for dinner tonight. Just . . . pizza. Nothing fancy. My brother and his fiancée are here; they're flying the kids to Colorado tomorrow for a long weekend, but I know they wouldn't mind if you joined."

Her eyes were so big in her face again, like she wasn't even sure how to process my offer. She inhaled slowly, gaze moving briefly to where Maggie and Bryce stood by her front door, both of them holding something in their hands. Her face softened. "You enjoy your time with your family," she said as she stared at them. "Pretty sure I'm going straight to bed anyway. I'm tired."

"Okay."

Lily slipped out of the truck without another word, and I noticed she left the bag holding the blanket and the collar on the floor. With a sigh, I picked it up again and hopped out.

Bryce and Maggie approached her cautiously, and my heart fucking broke in half when I saw their eyes. Maggie had already been crying, and she ran her hand underneath her nose, tears tracking down her cheeks.

Bryce was trying to hold it together, his lips in a firm line as he thrust a piece of paper at Lily. "I-I'm not really an artist. But I wanted to make you something." His chin trembled while she studied it. "He was a good dog. I'm . . . I'm really sorry he died."

Lily cupped the side of his face and bent down so she was closer to his height. "This is perfect, thank you." She wrapped him in a tight hug, her eyes red again. Bryce let out a quiet sob and then turned immediately into my arms when Lily pulled back.

I kissed the top of his head while he cried.

Maggie held out a plate of slightly burned cookies as tears streamed down her cheeks. "I kinda burned them. But I didn't want anyone to help me, be-because I wanted to do something that would make you feel better." She hiccuped around her words. "And I forgot to set the timer, and then I started thinking about Larry and when he licked my hand that one time, and you s-said he didn't usually do that."

"He didn't," she whispered shakily. "He didn't like very many people, trust me."

Maggie's smile was wobbly, and tears dripped down her chin. "But you really think he liked me?"

"Yes," Lily said genuinely.

Maggie's face crumpled, and she flung her arms around Lily's midsection for a hug. While Maggie cried, I watched Lily's face. She'd set her chin on the top of Maggie's head, her eyes closed and her breathing slow and steady. In through the nose, out through the mouth. Again and again.

I remembered lying on the gurney while they strapped me in place after I'd torn my MCL and ACL. The pain had been excruciating, and all I'd allowed myself to focus on was my breathing. Not the people watching me. Not the eyes glued to this horrible moment. Not what it meant for the future.

I'd turned inward, refusing to allow a single crack of emotion show through. *Time for that later,* I'd promised myself. And what I saw in Lily's face now was what I felt back then.

Discipline to an unfathomable degree.

Maggie pulled away, wiping at her face. Lily gave her a small smile and held up the plate of cookies. "Thank you. I have a feeling this might be my dinner."

"That's not very healthy," Maggie said in a thick, watery voice.

Lily smiled. "No. But I think it's all I can handle."

I ran a hand over Maggie's hair. "Why don't you two head back home, okay?"

"Thank you," Lily told them. Then she looked at me. "All of you. I can't—" Her voice cut out, her jaw tensed, and for a moment, she stared at the driveway. "Thank you."

The kids each gave her another hug and walked back home.

I held out the bag, and Lily's shoulders deflated. Her fingers brushed mine as she took it, then turned to walk away.

"It doesn't feel right," I said, watching as she froze.

"What doesn't?" she asked, eyes finding mine over her shoulder.

"Leaving you alone right now."

Something more crept into my voice. More than I wanted. More than I should have allowed.

If Lily had heard it, she didn't comment on it, and maybe that was for the best.

"It's okay," she said. "I'm used to being alone."

And then she turned and walked into the house. I stood rooted in place, then looked up at the sky and, for a moment, simply watched it snow.

Chapter Twenty-One

Barrett

The leftover pizza had been put away; my parents and Ruby were on the couch, watching the meteorologist make dramatic sweeping gestures with his arms—a lake-effect system was moving in just after they were set to take off with the kids the next day—and me and my brother were locked in a battle of Scrabble, with my innocent children reluctantly taking part.

Maggie and I leaned our heads together so Bryce and Griffin couldn't hear.

"I have an idea," she whispered, pointing to our opponents' last move, a craftily placed *waterhen*.

The validity had been challenged, my brother issuing a smug grin when it was upheld.

"Whatcha thinking?" I asked her.

Maggie tapped the *q* on our tile holder, then the *t*.

I gave her an unamused look. "On principle, I'm not sure I can use that."

She giggled, then sent a mock glare at her uncle when he leaned in and pretended to listen. She cupped her hand over my ear. "Do you want to win or not?" she whispered. When she pulled back, her eyes widened meaningfully.

I did.

I really did.

"Fine," I murmured quietly. Maggie sat back with a smirk, and I nudged her under the table. "Poker face," I instructed.

Her expression smoothed out immediately, and we waited patiently for Bryce and Griffin to make their next move. As long as they didn't touch *waterhen*, we'd win.

I'd also have to eat major crow, but we'd win.

Dinner had been fine. The addition of my parents, plus Ruby and the kids, meant that my brother and I hadn't really had much occasion to talk. Certainly not by ourselves.

Before I set the tiles down, I looked at the board again, then up at my younger-by-two-minutes brother.

He raised a challenging brow, and I couldn't help but wonder how on earth people ever got us confused. To me, he looked so different. It was the slightest difference in the slope of his jaw. Something in the shape of his eyes. Griffin always needed to shave, and today was no different; the dark stubble on his jawline was thicker than mine usually was.

I ran a hand over my own jaw. I hadn't shaved in two days, and I supposed it was possible I looked just a bit more like him. As much tension as our relationship had held over the last decade, I'd be lying if I said I didn't see the difference in my brother now.

He was happier. Lighter. Undeniably settled.

Throughout the evening, he'd found his way back to Ruby's side, tucking the petite woman under his arm, leaning down for a kiss when he thought no one was looking. For the first time in his life, my restless, wild brother was at peace.

Jealousy knotted deep under my skin the longer I watched them together. I wasn't jealous of his relationship with Ruby, per se. I was jealous that he knew what it felt like. A partnership in every sense of the word. No matter how different they were—and good Lord, were they different—they were evenly matched.

The jealousy didn't eclipse my happiness for him. All I'd ever wanted was to see Griffin happy, even if I never quite knew how to go about it.

The curse of the oldest brother, I supposed. Which went hand in hand with the unshakable need to beat him in every single game we ever played for the rest of our lives.

Griffin said something to my son, who nodded, grabbing tiles as he leaned forward. Maggie and I held our breath, exhaling slowly as he built a different word elsewhere on the board. He counted the tiles.

"Seventeen points," Bryce said.

Griffin wrote it down, then gave me a look. "You're gonna lose. Might as well start your concession speech now."

I elbowed Maggie lightly, and she made a happy sighing noise. "Read it and weep," she said, placing the *q* on the triple-word score, and the *t* below the *a* of *waterhen*.

Bryce's mouth fell open.

Griffin nose wrinkled. "That's not a word."

"Yes, it is," I said firmly. "Trust me."

He pointed at the board. "That's not a word." Turning in his chair, he motioned for his fiancée. "Ruby Tate, come look at this sh—" He paused, looking at the kids. "Crap," he finished. "He's cheating."

She rolled her eyes but left the couch, sliding her arms around his shoulders as she stared at the board. "That is a word," she confirmed.

"*What?* How?"

Maggie steepled her hands together and smiled. "It's a leaf on a shrub that we don't know the name of. Go look it up."

Griffin was out of his chair before I could blink. "You think I won't. Bryce, don't give up."

My son sighed. "It's a word, Uncle Griffin. Just let it go."

"No way," my brother yelled. His voice came from the den, and I tucked my hands into my pockets and followed. He'd taken a seat at my desk and tapped my computer to life.

Panic made my chest go cold. "Why can't you look it up on your phone?"

"It's in the bedroom," he said, eyeing me strangely when I tried to swipe the computer. "See? I knew you were fucking cheating."

"Give me my computer." I used my scariest coach voice, and Griffin rolled his eyes. I lunged forward again.

He held it out of reach. "This is just like when we were in high school, and I was trying to show Dad that one play in practice and you didn't want me to because it made you look bad."

"Grow up," I snapped. "That was a million years ago. Give me my laptop."

Ruby appeared behind me. "What is going on in here?"

"He won't give me my computer," I said tersely.

Griffin held it over his head. "He won't let me prove he's not cheating."

Her face was frozen in shock as she glanced between the two of us. "How old are you two?"

"He started it," we said in unison.

She held her hand out. "Griffin, give it to me."

He scoffed but did as his fiancée asked. The screen flared to life when her hand swiped over the mouse pad, and her eyes narrowed imperceptibly. When the words registered, her gaze snapped in my direction.

I set my jaw and held my hand out.

"Right," she said primly, then tried to hand it over to me.

Griffin got it first.

"You dick," I muttered. "I take it back. You can't sleep here tonight."

"Too late," he said absently, turning the screen in his direction. "*How to flirt with a woman*," he read. His eyes flew to mine, a wide smile breaking open over his face. "You googled it? You had to *google* this?"

"Give me my fucking computer," I said, snatching it out of his hands.

Griffin bent over, hands resting on his knees, while he laughed. My cheeks were red, no doubt, and even Ruby, polite as she was, gave me an apologetic look.

"Griffin, shut up," she said, smacking his shoulder.

My brother's laughter eased, and when his fiancée gave him a sharp look, he held up his hands. "Sorry. I just . . . I never thought I'd see the day."

"Are you going to be good now?" she asked.

"Yes," he promised, then tipped her chin with his finger and gave her a soft kiss. "You can go back and catastrophize about the weather now."

"It's not catastrophizing," she said hotly. "I just want to get our flight out before the snow hits, okay? Up to eighteen inches, they're saying."

"Only eighteen?" he teased. "It's like it's not even trying."

Ruby rolled her eyes and went back into the family room. With a weary sigh, I sank down onto the couch and set the closed laptop next to me. My brother moved back to the desk, the creak of my chair the only sound I heard, since I wasn't willing to make eye contact just yet.

"Go away," I told him.

"Nah. This is too fun."

I pried my eyes open and leveled him with a look. "I fail to see what's fun about any of this."

Griffin's face went uncharacteristically serious. "You like her. The neighbor."

"You going to give me relationship advice now?"

He shrugged, folding his hands over his stomach, stretching his legs out in front of him. "Why'd you feel like you needed to look that up? It's not like you haven't been married before."

"I'm not sure my relationship with Rachel counts for much," I answered honestly. That was the thing I hated saying out loud. "I never had to flirt with her, that's for damn sure."

Silence filled the room. My brother and I looked at each other for a moment.

"We ready to talk about her yet?" he finally asked.

I winced. So did he.

"No," I answered.

"So what's the deal with Lily, then? Why do you feel like you need *that*," he said, gesturing to the computer.

For a moment, I stared at it and tried to consolidate my thoughts into something simple, something that made sense, until I came to the conclusion that that might not be possible.

"You know what it feels like when you watch film and you break down every angle of it until you can pick it apart?"

He nodded.

I rolled my neck until it popped. "I can't read her for the fucking life of me. Can't figure her out. Sometimes I think she hates me. Sometimes she seems hell-bent on pushing all my buttons. She's grouchier than me most of the time," I said. Griffin's eyes widened dramatically, like it was impossible to imagine. I rolled mine, and he cracked a small smile. "But she's so good with the kids. There's something about her. And I just want to know more."

He rubbed his jaw and shrugged. "So ask her out. It's not hard."

"She's leaving in a month, Griffin." Even saying it made my stomach curl unpleasantly. "That's what she does. She moves. She leaves. No home base. It's not how she lives."

"Fuck," he muttered. "That complicates things."

"I can't ask her to give that up because I want to take her out on a date."

Griffin got this look on his face. Something I couldn't decipher. It was a little smug. A little affectionate. And it made me want to punch him in the face a little too.

"What?" I snapped.

"You have a crush," he said knowingly.

"No, I don't."

"You do." He stretched his back and groaned, settling back in my desk chair like he owned it. "I recognize these signs from when I was first dating Ruby. She didn't know we were dating yet, but it didn't take long for my presence to overwhelm her."

"Yeah, I can imagine you do that on a daily basis. I didn't miss it."

"Yes, you did." He leaned forward, bracing his elbows on his knees. "Having a crush isn't emasculating. You can adore the shit out of her. Think she's the most beautiful woman in the world. Desperately want to hold her hand because it's the prettiest hand you've ever seen. Want to have serious, grouchy little babies with her, and also want to fuck her brains out because she's hot and pisses you off."

I closed my eyes. "Stop talking. I can't do this."

Griffin let out an easy laugh. "As usual, brother, you are overthinking everything. You don't have to ask her to give up a life she loves. But you can still show her all those things you told me. It's not either-or."

"Isn't it?" I asked seriously. "I don't . . . I don't do casual. I'm not wired that way. It's okay if you are"—I paused when he gave me a stern look, and held up my hands in concession—"or used to be, before Ruby. And I don't know how Lily is wired. But if I know someone doesn't want to put down roots, how do I start anything knowing there's an hourglass over our heads and half the fucking sand is already gone?"

"You have time," he said, uncharacteristically serious. "Until the moment she leaves and says she's never coming back, you have time."

"I don't know how to do this. I feel like I'm going to screw it up," I admitted. My voice came out a little tight, a little strangled, some invisible hand trying to cinch my throat shut so that words wouldn't escape.

Griffin's eyebrows rose incrementally. "How'd that feel coming out?"

"Awful."

I'd never said that before. Never even felt it. Even when my career had collapsed around me, I felt so certain about what to do next. That certainty had been one of my guideposts.

And it was possible, looking back, that I'd fooled myself into thinking that being certain about something always meant it was right. One of the greatest examples of that was sitting in front of me.

I held my brother's gaze. "I shouldn't have tried to take care of you the way I did. Or tried to tell you what to do. And I'm sorry for that."

Griffin didn't ask me how the apology felt coming out. My answer would've been different from the last time he'd asked. Because it felt an awful lot like relief, like I'd been choking on some invisible knot that finally unraveled until it disappeared.

"It's okay," he said. "I forgive you." Then he sucked in a breath. "And I'm sorry for not listening when you were giving me good advice. And . . . telling the press that you're boring and . . . all that other shit I said."

I smile wryly. "Forgiven. I *am* boring, so it wasn't all that offensive."

"Listen," he said, tilting his head toward her house, "you were there for her today, right? That shit matters. Show up. Don't tiptoe around the way you *should* act. That's your problem, Barrett. You proposed to Rachel because you thought you should, not because you loved her. You stayed married to her even though she was a miserable snake, because you thought you should.

"There's no list of rules in starting any relationship, because everyone's different. You like her? Then act like it. Do nice shit for her because it makes her smile. And if she doesn't like it, I bet she'll tell you. If you two have been sniping at each other since the beginning, don't fucking stop. Ruby loves it when I piss her off."

"Does she really?"

"You want to try saying that to my face, Griffin King?" Ruby called from the kitchen.

My brother laughed. So did I. And it felt good.

"When did you get so smart?" I asked him after a beat of silence.

He leaned back in my chair, folding his hands behind his head and smiling smugly. "Probably right around the time you stopped being such a stubborn asshole."

I smiled, shaking my head. "That may be. But I didn't cheat at Scrabble."

"I will prove it if it's the last thing I do," he said.

He tried to grab my laptop again.

I kicked him in the shin.

Chapter Twenty-Two

Lily

Everyone at the grocery store seemed very chill, considering the apocalypse was descending upon us.

I'd braced myself for empty bread aisles, no water to be found, yelling and fighting over supplies. A statewide shortage of nonperishables. I'd even pumped myself up to box someone out if I caught sight of some peanut butter. But there was no line. No fighting over the last can of beans.

They were acting normal.

What was *wrong* with these people? Did they just walk around ready for seventeen feet of snow at any given moment? I tucked my mouth against the zipped-up collar of my coat because, I swear, ever since I heard that shit was heading our way, I'd been unable to warm up.

"That everything, honey?" the cashier asked me, eyeing the items on the conveyor belt with visible confusion.

What? She'd never shopped for *lake effect* before?

"I think so." I chewed on my bottom lip. "Do you think I need more?"

Her pencil-thin eyebrows arched, and she let out a quiet, "Uh, no?" Then she regrouped. "How many people are you feeding?"

My chin rose a notch. "Just me."

Her eyes widened, her mouth quivering as she tried to stifle her laugh, and I wanted to chuck my shopping cart at her judgy little face.

"I think you'll be fine," she said carefully. "For the next month."

I rolled my eyes. "Whatever. I've never lived through a blizzard before."

She scanned the items, shuffling them toward a bored-looking teen who bagged them unseeingly. *He* wasn't judging me.

Then he blinked down at the items as he set them in the paper bags, clearly seeing a pattern. And he gave me a weird look.

I pursed my lips and mulishly set my jaw, staring him down until he relented, cheeks flushed pink.

Just before he started loading my items up on his little cart, set to bring them out to my car, I held up my hand. "Just put them back in my cart. I'll do it."

"You sure?" he asked, voice squeaky and high despite his tall, long-limbed body.

"Yeah. Thanks, though."

He shrugged and pulled my cart around to the back of the counter to do as I'd asked. I shifted restlessly, staring down at my boots before glancing at the next person in line. The elderly woman behind me was watching my items too. All she had in her basket was a couple of cans of soup and a bag of coffee.

Great. Even the old people weren't panicking.

My cheeks were hot when the woman told me my total.

I handed my card over to the cashier with a tight smile as the teen bagged up the last of the groceries. Receipt in hand, I kept my head down and pushed the cart out to the car, slowing down when the slush accumulating on the parking lot surface impeded my speedy getaway.

"Ugh," I said, pushing the button to open the hatch on the back of my SUV. Groceries loaded up and safe, I decided to take pity on Mr. Squeaky Voice and bring the cart back inside. The magic of the snow wasn't quite as magical today, and I glared at every fucking flake that had landed on the car while I was shopping. There was probably some fancy tool to remove it, but even if I'd owned one, I couldn't have stood out in that shit for a moment longer, relying instead on the windshield wipers to give me enough visibility to drive the five minutes back home.

My phone buzzed and I yanked my gloves off to open the text from Patty.

Patty: Met someone at the pool today. She's looking for a dog/cat sitter for about six months while they go on a world cruise. They live in Florida, and if you're interested, I can pass along your information. My offer still stands, of course, if you don't want to leave. But if you do, there's another option. She said she doesn't even need to interview you, because she's gotten rave reviews from the people who met you here last year.

There it was. The exit strategy I'd been missing. I should've been ecstatic. Should've sighed the biggest sigh of relief known to humankind—but it never came.

Neither did the urge to send an immediate yes in response. My fingers were stiff. Unable to type anything back. Probably the cold. It was definitely, 100 percent the cold that made my insides feel all empty and echoey and terrible.

My side itched, evidence of my errand before the grocery store making an absolute mockery of me. I laid my hand over the spot on my ribs and let out a deep breath. That itch turned into a burn. Pressing my hand down harder didn't stop it, and my blood seemed to pulse under my skin, concentrated in one regrettable spot.

Damn, damn, damn my impulsive streak. One must never make big decisions in the throes of grief. I should've just cut some fucking bangs.

Then I sent a text.

Me: Tell her I'll take it. Thank you.

As I shoved my phone into the center console, I struggled to take a deep breath. A nasty little voice in the back of my head kindly pointed out that I was still being impulsive, but I really didn't feel like hearing that shit, so I ignored it. Just . . . ignored all the things that were making my insides feel tight and squeezy.

Rash.

Reckless.

Stubborn.

You can't change someone who doesn't want to change.

What if I did, though? What if I did and I just didn't know how? What then? It was like taking a first step out into space when all you'd ever known was the familiarity of solid ground. Fear had a way of doing that, leashing you somewhere because it felt safe.

My hands trembled while I pressed them against my eye sockets. But there was no forcibly removing Barrett's voice from my head. If the man ever found out, he'd be insufferable, knowing he'd laid anchor somewhere in my subconscious, like a hot Jiminy Cricket trying to teach me all sorts of life lessons.

While I waited for the car to warm up, and the defrost to kick in and remove the fog from the glass, I pressed my fists up to my mouth and blew warm air onto my fingers.

Barrett doing the same thing flashed in my head, and I had to pinch my eyes shut to ban the memory. My hands fumbled with the knobs on the dashboard, and I cued up some female rage music.

There.

I sat my head back on the seat and nodded along to the beat. After a few seconds, I opened my eyes, watching the fog dissipate and my view to the outside clear up.

The snow was still magical. Any other thought to the contrary was just my epically bad mood talking. If I closed my eyes again, I'd see him.

Flakes landing on his face. Catching on his hair.

Catching on mine. The warmth of his gloves when I slipped my fingers inside.

I pressed my hands to my face and let out a deep breath.

No. No, no, *no*.

We didn't need happy, sweet thoughts about the way he looked at me while the snow fell soft from the sky. My heart was still too fucking broken for any of this.

It was all I could do to get out of bed that morning, and I'd stared blankly at Larry's food and water bowls until my eyes turned all gritty and dry. I could pick that shit up later.

Larry should've given me a little heads-up, you know? Tapped something out in Morse code.

Ready for doggie heaven. I is tired and you talk too much.

Everything about this sudden life change really just pissed me off.

Anger was easier. I wasn't actually mad at that little grouch, but if I didn't stay firmly camped where I was, I'd start thinking other things.

Sad, heartbreaking things.

Crying things.

Soon I'd be waist deep in chocolate and eating cookie dough straight from the bowl and sobbing until my face puffed out.

Between the snow and Barrett and the dog, I was a lit keg ready to freaking blow.

I put the car in reverse and slowly made my way out of the slushy parking lot. The roads were slippery, and as my hands clutched the steering wheel, I cursed my past self for all sorts of things.

"Lying out in the snow," I muttered, then squealed when I hit the brakes too hard approaching a red light and the back end of the car fishtailed a little. "Making cookies and standing under mistletoe. Ugh. Keeping the dog in the *first* place. What was I thinking?"

But there was no one to listen.

My stomach trembled, a slow reverberation that worked its way up to my chest. My throat. My hands, which would've shook if I wasn't white-knuckling the wheel.

There was no one to listen.

Larry, for all his many faults, was a great listener. All these years on my own, he'd been the one to hear everything. The things I didn't want anyone to hear.

Oh, but at the back of my head, something terrible happened. A voice whispered, prying through the dark webs of grief, until I had no choice but to listen.

Barrett would.

Barrett would listen.

I shook my head furiously, my breaths coming in sharp and fast through my nose.

How had he managed this? How had he weaseled his way into this position over such a short amount of time?

It was some mind-boggling man magic that I didn't want to think on too deeply. That pissed me off too.

I eased down the street, glaring at his house like it had kicked me in the crotch, when the man himself walked through the front door and put a couple of suitcases into the back of a black SUV. Even with a glare already fixed on my face, my eyes narrowed even farther, until I could hardly see.

Didn't even look over at me. No wave; no serious, restrained little nod like, *Yeah, I see you. Yeah, we had some moments recently, and I just wanted to acknowledge your presence.*

Even as I pulled into my driveway, he never glanced my way.

I scoffed. Loudly. Kinda sounded like I had a hair ball.

"Who the fuck does he think he is?" I hissed.

There was a moment just after I punched the button to turn the car off when blind anger, frustration, and grief coalesced into a screaming pile of wreckage. I shoved at the door, shouldering it open and marching between the yards before I could talk myself out of it.

Steam was probably shooting out my ears.

Displaced steam, but it was there nonetheless. Logic had no place. The sight of his indifference kicked that shit right out the fucking window.

Barrett's head was covered by a ball cap, his broad shoulders in a black hooded sweatshirt as he set a suitcase on its side in the back of the vehicle.

"You have some nerve," I said hotly. "You can't even wave. Or look at me. After yesterday?"

Abort! Abort! another voice in my head screamed. Especially when he froze and turned in my direction, his eyes wide and his eyebrows lifted.

"Um—"

"No," I cut in, my hand making a dramatic stabbing motion in the air. "No, this isn't fair. I don't know what to do with you, Barrett. You make *no* sense. I'm leaving, and you know that, but you keep doing these things and I don't know why. You give me a *shovel.* And sit in the snow and listen, and you carry the bag of horribleness for me, but you're . . . you're so . . ."

He winced, holding up a hand. "Wait, hang on, I don't think you want to do this."

I crossed my arms, hip jutting out as I pinned him with a lethal stare. "Don't tell me what I do and don't want to do, you bossy asshole. And that's the other thing, you know. You are not in charge of whatever . . . whatever this is! Whatever *you* think is happening here. The gestures and the . . . conversations and the flirting, if you can even call it that—because honestly, I think you're really bad at it, if it is."

He swiped a hand over his mouth and looked me up and down, but without the usual lingering heat. "Lily, right?"

Oh, okay. So that's what it felt like to have someone stab you in the chest.

My mouth hung open, and I blinked. Repeatedly. *"What?"* I said in a horrified whisper. "Is this a fucking joke?"

He blew out a slow breath. "Trust me, I am not the one you want to be saying this to."

Something wasn't right.

In fact, something was very, very wrong.

"What do you mean?" I asked, arms tightening around my waist, an anchor in whatever insanity was about to explode in my cranium.

But before he could answer, the door to the house swung open. A pretty, petite woman with messy blond hair and big gray eyes stopped short at the sight of me.

"Hi," she said, taking in my slightly aggressive posture warily. "What's going on?"

"Who are you?" I asked, horror creeping up my spine like ice.

Her brows bent in. "I'm his fiancée, Ruby."

"What?"

He held up his hands again. "You have me confused with someone else," he said to me.

The woman's mouth fell open. *"Oh."*

"'Oh' what?" I snapped.

Someone else joined her in the doorway—and my fucking knees went weak, comprehension dawning like a kick to my face.

"Griffin, you forgot Maggie's—"

Barrett froze at the sight of me, eyes swinging between me and . . . oh God, oh holy fuck me over the rails . . . he was a twin. He was a *twin*. "Lily," he said cautiously. "Are you okay?"

My entire body slumped, and I covered my face while my heart turned out a slow, lethargic beat. Maybe I was having a nightmare. With snow and judgy cashiers and two Barretts to make my life a living hell. Or maybe I was stroking out. Yes, that was a great option. I was officially choosing that.

Unfortunately, it was all very, very real. And I could not pinch myself into waking up. I'd just go hide for the rest of my life. Heat crawled up my neck, into my cheeks, and when my hands dropped, I drew myself up to my full height and made scathing eye contact with the real Barrett.

Was I mad at him? No.

Was I embarrassed as all get-out? You bet your ass.

That embarrassment, to my dismay, came out looking a lot like rage.

"Of course there are fucking two of you," I hissed. And without saying another word, I turned and marched right back through the yards, praying desperately that the ground would open up and swallow me whole.

Chapter Twenty-Three

Barrett

No one moved.

My mind raced, battling between running after her, and not making a complete spectacle of what had just happened.

"She seems . . . nice," Ruby said carefully.

Griffin nodded, catching my eye with a smug smile. "I get it." Ruby whacked his chest, and he rubbed at the spot. "Ouch. I don't mean it like that. There's not a single woman on earth who would ever top you, birdy—but for him . . ." he said, gesturing toward me, still frozen in place, staring after where Lily had stomped off. "I get it," he finished.

Ruby was appeased by this, and I'd witnessed enough of their teasing to know she wasn't really mad at him in the first place. With a growing sense of hysteria, I thought about what my brother had said. About how Ruby loved it when he pissed her off.

Well . . . I'd gone and done that.

"Wait," I said, setting my hands on my hips and turning toward Griffin. "What did she say before I came out?"

His face went blank. "Nothing."

"Bullshit, what did she say?"

"Nothing," he said slowly, "that I'm going to tell you," he finished in a rush. He winced. "Pretty sure she'd rather die than repeat it at the moment, so I think you should give her a little breathing room—"

"No way," Ruby interrupted. "Go over there. She's embarrassed. You could see it on her face."

"Just give me a hint," I told Griffin. "Was it good? Bad?"

"Eh, a little of both? She's not happy with you. Well . . ." He paused to consider, tilting his hand back and forth. "She's not happy with me because she thought I was you. And that is all I'm going to say about it."

"Shit," I whispered under my breath. "When do you guys need to leave?"

Griffin glanced at the watch on his wrist. "Less than five minutes. I thought we'd have more time, but the roads are getting worse, so we should head to the airport."

I nodded wearily. "I'll try to talk to her after you leave. I need to say goodbye to the kids."

Griffin leaned in and tapped me on the chest. "Snowed-in weekend. No work. No kids. Don't fuck this up, Barrett. This might be your best shot at getting laid in the foreseeable future."

Ruby pinched the bridge of her nose and muttered something under her breath.

My brother grinned. "She does that a lot."

"Thank you," I said flatly. "That's helpful advice, while she's over there plotting my death."

"I am here for you, brother." He winked, and I wondered how he might respond if I punched him in the throat.

With a sigh seemingly born from the depths of my weary soul, I pulled myself together enough when the kids jogged out of the house, hopped up on adrenaline for their long weekend in Colorado. They both hugged me fiercely.

"Be respectful, use your manners," I told them. "Listen to Uncle Griffin, and make sure you abide by the house rules."

"Pfft. We don't have any house rules," my brother said.

Ruby just shook her head and mouthed, *Yes, we do.*

I smiled.

The kids promised all manner of things—that they'd be perfect and never get in trouble again and I was the best dad in the entire world for allowing this. Their eyes were bright with excitement, and it tempered the sting of missing them. They weren't even gone and I already did.

"Will you get bored?" Maggie asked.

"Are you kidding? I can't wait to be bored."

Griffin and I shared a look, and he wisely decided not to call me on my bullshit. I didn't know how to be bored any more than he did. I'd be working within fifteen minutes of them leaving the house. At home, due to the storm, but working nonetheless.

The kids gave me one last hug and piled into the car with Ruby. Griffin paused, holding out his hand, which I grasped in my own.

"Maybe, uh, maybe next time you can come with them," he said casually, belying the brief flash of intensity in his eyes.

"You'd want me to?"

He shrugged, tucking his hands into his pockets. "I guess." Then he stopped and looked up, his eyes clear and direct. "Yeah. I'd want you to come next time."

My chest clenched. "Okay."

"Okay."

I managed a small smile. "Text me when you land."

He snorted. "Like you won't be tracking our flight."

I laughed easily. "You're right. I will."

"Unless you're busy," he said with a meaningful look next door.

"Aren't you leaving yet?"

Griffin grinned. "Yeah. But, uh, I don't think you have anything to worry about. You only get that worked up about someone when they're really under your skin."

Anticipation had my stomach in knots. To talk to her. To find out what she'd said that had her so upset. Just . . . everything. I anticipated Lily, in every way she'd allow me to have her.

After the car left, I walked over to the house and knocked on the front door.

Nothing.

Hands cupped around the glass, I peered in through the side windows, but there was no movement. The TV was dark, only one lamp on in the living room, but the lights were on in the entryway. I reached over to press the doorbell.

"No, thank you," she yelled.

"Lily, open the door. Please."

The entryway lights turned off.

I knocked once more and tried the doorbell, but then I heard the slamming of a door inside the house, and I looked up at the sky.

The flakes weren't big and fluffy anymore, instead coming down sideways, swirling in the gusts of wind. I wasn't wearing a coat, and my hands were absolutely frozen.

"I'm going back," I yelled at the door. "But only because I don't really feel like getting hypothermia. I'm going to call you, okay?"

There was a loud thumping noise on the other side of the door, then a muttering sound, and I wondered if she'd kicked a wall or something. I jogged back over to my house and stomped the snow off my boots before walking in the front door, toeing them off onto the mat and going straight for my phone where I'd left it on the kitchen counter.

The phone rang and rang; eventually the sound of her voicemail picked up.

"Hi, this is Lily. I don't listen to voicemails, but I do answer texts. I trust you can make the right decision with this information."

A sigh burst out of me, and I scratched the back of my neck.

Me: Will you please talk to me?

Lily: Nope. Can't.

Me: As happy as it makes you to yell at me, I'd think you'd leap at this chance.

Lily: Sorry. I've reached my word quota for the day.

Me: Lily, please.

And then nothing. Our text thread showed a message that she'd silenced her incoming notifications, and I let my phone fall out of my hand with a loud clatter. Hands braced on the counter, I allowed my head to hang down while I tried to figure out what to do.

Maybe she did need some space.

But it felt wrong to just let this go. I picked up my phone again and sent her one more text, then forced myself to go do some work while the snow continued to fall.

◆ ◆ ◆

Three hours later, the house shook, buffeted by the relentless wind as it howled outside. Glancing up from where I sat with my laptop, I was stunned at how much snow we'd gotten since I'd settled in with work.

Pushed around by the wind, the snow had formed serpentine drifts along the back of the house, coming halfway up the slider by this point in the day. My phone remained quiet, but I checked my messages anyway.

Another gust of wind kicked up, and I watched the branches of the trees bend to the merciless force. A large branch snapped off the oak tree in the corner of our yard, immediately disappearing into the snow. The kids would've gotten a kick out of that.

I heard another crack of a tree branch—this time coming from the front of the house—and when the lights flickered but held, I thanked my past self for installing a whole-house generator as soon as we'd moved in, just in case the power eventually went out.

My thumb drummed on the table as I stared in the direction of the house holding the woman currently ignoring me. She'd never lived through a major winter storm and didn't own a home. Would she know how to hook up a generator? If they even had one . . .

Picking up my phone, I shot a quick text to Scott asking if he had a generator, and he replied immediately.

Scott: Hey, Coach. We don't, unfortunately. Starter button died on the last one and I never got around to replacing it before we left. How is it up there?

Me: Cold. Snowy. Wind is pretty angry. Lights flickered but didn't go off.

Scott: Yet.

Me: Yet.

Scott: Thanks for keeping an eye out. I'll make sure to get a new one when we're back.

I thought about trying to call her again, but I knew she wouldn't answer. The lights flickered again, and I looked up, holding my breath.

Everything went dark.

"Shit," I muttered.

In less than thirty seconds, all the lights came back on, the whirring of the generator attached to the back of the house hardly noticeable over the sound of the wind. The temps outside were brutal; the windchill on my phone showed negative five.

Without pausing to think about just how pissed off she'd be, I yanked my coat on, shoved my feet into my boots, and snatched the key to their house off the hook on the wall in the mudroom. The wind was biting, and I kept my head down as I trudged through the snow, trying to find paths that weren't as tall because of the drifting.

With my gloved fist, I pounded on the door. "Lily!" I yelled. "Open up."

"I'll be fine," she called back, voice on the other side of the door.

"Lily," I said, worry getting the best of me, the anxious feelings gnawing at my gut, turning it into something churlish and restless. "Open the fucking door; this isn't the time to be stubborn."

The door whipped open, her face barely visible through the two inches she allowed. "I'm fine. You don't have to take care of me."

Before she slammed it shut, I wedged my shoulder into the opening and pushed her back easily.

"You fucking caveman," she said through gritted teeth, trying to use both hands to close the door on me.

When I was through, she stumbled back, and I eyed her head to toe. She was wearing a hat and gloves, thick woolly socks on her feet, and two blankets wrapped around her shoulders.

"Is your heat not working?"

"It was," she hedged. "Before the power went out. But just looking at this shit made me cold."

I pushed my tongue against the inside of my cheek. "You need to come with me."

"The hell I do," she said, head rearing back. "The power will come back on. Any second, I bet."

I pulled out my phone and brought up the outage map. There were outages all over, and her brow furrowed, deeper and deeper the longer she stared at it.

"Well . . . that doesn't mean anything."

I tapped on the area over our neighborhood. "No restoration timeline is available. If they've got downed lines all over because of trees, it could be one night. Could be two. But I promise, if you're cold now, you're in for a rude awakening when the temps start dropping in here."

Her eyes flickered. "Let me guess, your house is toasty warm."

"I have a generator, so yes, it is. So either you're driving to find a hotel . . ." My pause gave both of us enough time to glance outside, and I could practically hear her whimper. "Or you're coming with me."

She scoffed. "I can't believe I thought you were turning nice," she said, trying to brush past me. "Feel free to add *kidnapping* to your résumé."

"I know that you're embarrassed and you've had a really shitty couple days," I said, tone low and urgent. I had roughly thirty seconds before she either bolted or took a swing at me. Lily froze, her eyes flickering back up to mine, and despite the chill in the air from my less-than-subtle entry, her cheeks were flushed pink. "I'm being nice now, and you know it."

"What if I want to stay here and freeze?" she said. "What if that's preferable over having this conversation with you?"

My temper ignited. "Then you're even more stubborn than I thought."

She let out a harsh exhale and started striding away. I grabbed her elbow—or tried, through the thick layers of blankets—and she ripped her arm away.

"Go back to your warm house with your fucking twin. I have blankets and . . . more blankets. I'll be just fine right here without being tormented by you and your mirror image."

Lily couldn't even look me in the eye when she said it, the color climbing higher in her cheeks.

"I'm sorry you found out about my brother that way. We will talk about this, one way or the other," I told her in a rough voice. "Doesn't matter if it's now. Or tomorrow. Or next week." My volume increased. "But you are *not* staying here with the power out."

By the time I'd finished, I was yelling, and Lily sucked in a deep breath, eyes lit with emotion. God, she was beautiful when she was pissed off. She shucked off her blankets and poked me in the chest.

Anger caught fire the moment she touched me. Anger and something else. Something hotter, and much, much harder to control. A high I'd never felt in my entire life.

"What the hell are you going to do about it?" she said, leaning until I almost grabbed her face and used my mouth and my hands to shut her up. "I fucking *dare* you to try and boss me around right now."

My molars clenched together so tightly, I swear my jawbone creaked.

That slight pause must have looked like defeat to Lily, because she stepped back, a smug smile pulling at her lips.

That was when I bent at the knees, braced my shoulder in her midsection, banded my arm tight around the backs of her legs, and straightened to my full height.

"Put me down!" she yelled.

"Not a chance."

The door slammed behind me, and with Lily pounding ineffectually against my back, cursing my existence to the angry, swirling sky, I marched us right back through the snow to my house, a grim sort of satisfaction flaring to life in the empty parts of my chest.

Keep pissing her off, my brother had said.

No fucking problem.

Chapter Twenty-Four

Lily

From my upside-down view, two things were abundantly clear.

First, Barrett's ass was fantastic.

Second, the man had a death wish.

"Put me down!" I yelled, smacking ineffectively against his back. I almost went for the ass, but the thought of adding *any* sort of spanking dynamic to whatever was happening here blurred way too many lines, and the sudden addition of the cavemen carry was already doing that quite effectively.

"Once we're inside, I'll be happy to."

A foot of snow had already fallen, and for the last few hours, I'd watched the piles outside grow with increasing alarm. Even the food on the island had started to seem insufficient.

"My food!" I cried, trying to push up but failing miserably. God, I needed to do more ab work.

"What food?"

"I got groceries this morning. A lot of them."

Barrett grumbled something under his breath that I missed.

The wind on my cheeks was brutal, and I tucked my face against the warm wall of his back until he shoved open the door leading into their garage. Was that betraying my principles? Possibly. But I hated being cold more than I hated being annoyed at the manhandling.

To be honest, I wasn't even all that annoyed, because it was fun as hell to get mad at this guy. Weirdest kind of foreplay I'd ever experienced.

Once we were inside the house, the world flipped, and as soon as my feet were on the ground, I scrambled back, trying desperately to fix my hair. He thrust his hand out, my hat tight in his grip. What with all the flinging of my body, I hadn't even noticed it had fallen off.

With as much dignity as I could muster, I tugged it back in place.

"You've got some nerve," I said, chin raised.

Of course, his face was even. Patient. So was his voice when he said, "And was it preferable to letting you freeze over there?"

"Well, no. But you could have talked me into it like a normal person."

He leaned in, gaze so unflinchingly potent that I felt it tug behind my belly button. "Because you were so keen to listen."

I ignored that, gesturing between us. "And while we're on the subject of *talking to people*," I said, enunciating the last three words with just a little bit of extra oomph, "wouldn't it be nice to reveal a certain little factoid about yourself ahead of time? Like, *Oh, hey, Lily, there's fucking two of me in this world. And you won't be able to tell the difference between us even if you're staring the other one right in the face*?"

Was I yelling?

I was yelling.

While he tilted his head, eyes studying my face, I rolled my lips together and tried to dredge up some sort of calming ritual. Deep breathing. Something.

"I told you I had a brother." He crossed his arms. "I even told you my brother was here. *And* invited you to dinner last night, where you could have met him. I wasn't trying to keep it a secret. I just don't . . . I don't know, walk around proclaiming it to people."

"Why not? You should." Hysteria crept into my voice while I replayed all the absolute nonsense I'd spewed at his brother. Had he told Barrett? If he did, I was just going to lock myself in his guest room and not come out until the power returned. "I feel like the universe is punishing me. Can't handle one Barrett King? Too bad! Behind this curtain, there's another one," I said, holding my hands out like some cheesy game show host.

His eyes gleamed. His lips twitched.

"Don't," I said in a low voice, even stepping closely enough that I raised a shaking finger and poked it into the hard expanse of his chest. "Don't you *dare* smile at me for the first time about *this*."

"Why not?"

The slight bend to the corners of his mouth was driving me out of my mind. It was *almost* there, and my chest almost fucking caved in imagining it.

I'd lose it. I'd . . . I didn't even know. Would I slap him? Would I kiss him? Honestly, it was a toss-up. But I was already driving the anger train straight through this storm—why stop now?

"Would that drive you crazy?" he asked, taking a step closer to *me* now. My breath hitched, and he heard it, his gaze shifting heatedly to my parted lips. "It's only fair, given your mouth has driven me out of my fucking mind since the moment we met."

Oh.

Oh.

We were admitting things. Not dancing around them or skirting the edge of a line.

"Are you thinking about kissing me right now?" I whispered, head spinning like a top.

"Yes."

"Oh." I licked my bottom lip.

"Oh."

"Do . . . do you have an angry-woman fetish or something?"

His eyes, dark and fathomless, stayed right on my mouth. "No. I think it's just you."

"That's interesting, and I'm not entirely sure what to make of that, now that we're stuck in your house with no kids or family to distract us." Barrett's gaze moved up to mine. But I couldn't stop. Words spilled out even though a blaring siren in the back of my head was telling me to shut. The fuck. Up. "Are you just thinking about kissing me because I'm here, or do you *want* to kiss me?"

That asshole didn't answer my question, simply kept his broody sex eyes right on mine and spoke in a ragged sex voice that all went very nicely with his big, tall sex body. "I've racked my brain trying to figure out what would happen if I did." His tongue darted out, licking *his* bottom lip in the same way I had, and I realized exactly how much of a tease that was. "Why don't you tell me?"

My fingers curled into fists at my sides. "We'd probably have sex," I whispered. "M-maybe even right in your kitchen because we couldn't wait. On the floor. Or the counter. Or . . . maybe the couch since it's easier on the joints."

A noise came from the back of Barrett's throat, like he was urging me on.

My verbal filter was gone, and if I'd stopped to think even for a moment about how good that kitchen sex might be, and how pleasant this weekend could turn out for my lifetime orgasm count, I might not have said what I said next.

"But you know I'm leaving. And this can't be anything, and . . . and I get the feeling that's not enough for you."

Barrett's eyelids dropped in a slow blink, and he took a step back, seeming to gather himself as the promise of kitchen sex disappeared in a poof with two poorly timed sentences from me.

He rubbed the back of his neck as he stared at me. "I didn't bring you here for this," he said, shoulders deflating on a sigh. "And I shouldn't have . . . I shouldn't have antagonized you that way. Forgive me."

There was no rebuttal to what I'd said. No denial that it was true or not. But given that his hands weren't up my shirt and his tongue wasn't in my mouth, I had a feeling it *was* true. That I'd pegged him exactly right. As slightly old-fashioned. That he wanted to respect me in the way he knew how. Only start something he could stick with. That he could commit to in a meaningful way.

That he wanted me.

I was right about that too.

Somehow that made it even worse. Everything I'd said to his brother came rushing back, because this was the kind of thing that made me want to yell and maybe shove him a little bit. Not a mean shove. The kind of shove you do when you actually hope a man will forget he doesn't have casual sex, and that shove is the last straw before he kisses the hell out you.

"Forgiven," I said softly.

Barrett nodded. "There are blankets on the couch, and I've got the fire on. Go warm up."

I wrapped my arms around my middle. "What are you going to do?"

Again, the firm line of his mouth softened, that damn almost-smile that would probably haunt me in my dreams. "Go rescue the groceries."

"I can go get them," I told him.

"Are you cold?"

I blinked. "Yes."

"Then I'll do it."

Inconvenient things were happening in the pit of my belly. Not butterflies, per se. More like pleasant little bursts of heat. Warm and comforting in the midst of a very cold, very shitty week. I wanted to hold them in my hand and let them melt against the skin of my chest.

"Can you, um, can you grab the small blue bag on the bathroom counter while you're over there? *Someone* didn't really give me time to pack, and I'd like to have my toothbrush."

His cheekbones washed with pink, and the sight of his embarrassment was more than I could handle. It was so fucking endearing, I wanted to cry.

"Anything else?" he asked in a rough voice.

"Maybe, um, the laundry basket on the kitchen island. It's clean, I just never got the chance to put it away. You could use it to carry the other stuff too."

Before I could say anything, he was out the door again, leaving me with no clarity, more confusion, and a raging crush that seemed doomed from the start.

Barrett was gone for less than ten minutes, but I swear I'd started to doze underneath the weight of the blankets on the couch. My feet were shoved into his slippers, because if the man was going to leave those puppies lying around, then I could not be blamed when I used them for myself. I buried my nose into the blankets and inhaled. They smelled like him. Had he used them before the power went out?

A gust of cold air preceded him into the house, and my eyes flew open when he slammed the door shut. Based on the sounds coming from down the hall, I could track his movements. The laundry basket getting set on the floor. The thunk of his boots on the tray next to the door. The shift of the material of his coat as he hung it up on the wall, and then a small noise as he picked up the laundry basket after he'd set it down.

I hadn't been sure he'd be able to fit it all, but as he came into the kitchen, I smothered my embarrassed smile at how many bags of groceries were clutched in his hands, on top of everything in the basket. Barrett set everything down on the counter and then stood back, hands on his hips.

"May I ask you a question?"

"Mmm-hmm."

His eyes flicked over to mine. "What happened at the grocery store?"

I scoffed, flinging the blankets off my lap. "Listen, everyone knows when there's a big storm coming, you get water and canned food and bread and peanut butter."

As I started unpacking the grocery bags, Barrett's eyes were unwavering, and I just *knew* he was counting the loaves of bread as I yanked them out. Then the jars of peanut butter.

"So you got . . . five loaves of bread. And six jars of peanut butter," he said slowly. "Eight cans of peas and carrots. And . . ." His eyebrows rose on his forehead. "Four massive jars of applesauce."

It was on the tip of my tongue to tell him that the peas and the applesauce were for *nutritional value* and wouldn't go bad, but instead, I pushed that tongue into the side of my cheek, because he hadn't gotten to the inexplicable boxes of Fig Newtons yet. I didn't even *like* them. "What would *you* have gotten?"

"Not this." He opened another bag. "That's something, at least."

I snatched it from him and pulled out four bags of chocolate chips. "You won't be complaining about my choices when I make cookies and they're full of these."

"Do I get to eat them?"

Oh great, now he was teasing me.

I sniffed. "Undecided."

He braced his hands on the counter and peered down at the pile titled *Lily's Irrational Grocery Store Adventure*. "How about if I make dinner? Will you share the dessert?"

My eyes narrowed in a glare. "Do you purposely make everything sound sexual?"

His eyebrows lifted slightly. "No. You did say you have a dirty mind." Barrett rubbed his hands together. "How about grilled cheese? Might as well use up some of that bread."

"You're really going to make me dinner?" I asked, giving him a sidelong glance as I riffled through the laundry basket to see what pajama options I'd ended up with. My nose wrinkled. Two baggy

T-shirts, and that was about it. Where was a girl's fleece pajama set when she needed one? I was *never* going to warm up again.

"That seem strange to you?"

"Yes." A balled-up pair of socks was wedged into the bottom corner of the basket, and I yanked them out for layering purposes, careful not to fling any underwear around. "No one ever cooks for me. Unless I'm paying for my meal."

"Oh, you're paying, all right," he said, walking around the counter to stack the groceries in a neat pile next to the fridge.

"With what? You already took sex off the table."

The moment the words were out of my mouth, I regretted it.

Barrett's movements slowed. "Do you think I'd make you pay for meals with sexual favors?"

If there wasn't a dangerous glint in his eyes, I might have thought he was offended.

"No." I watched his face as he turned again, continuing to put away the food I'd bought. "I think you're a gentleman." His hands paused, but he didn't face me. "I think that you equate sex with serious relationships. And you've probably never dated casually in your entire life. That's probably why I can't figure you out." I swallowed, pushing down my nerves, ignoring the bursts of warmth that came with accidental eye contact and a brush of his skin against mine. "You flirt with me. You seem to be unbalanced by me, I guess."

Eventually, he did turn around, but his expression was guarded. I chose my next words carefully, well aware that the two of us were walking a very fine line. At the edge of the cliff, a dizzying fall just on the other side.

Now that I was warm and the fight had drained out of me, down the proverbial drain alongside my embarrassment, I could see how we'd arrived at this place. How each seemingly insignificant step had gotten us right here—where he risked my anger to take care of me. Where I risked honesty even through the fear that had always held me back.

We'd begun this relationship—for better or worse—with our weaknesses on display. Under a blinding spotlight, every wrinkle, every imperfection harshly lit and up for dissection. But instead of feeling worse for it, I found that I liked Barrett's weaknesses. I liked his imperfections. Even more surprising was that I could fully believe he'd say the same about me.

Which was why saying the rest of it out loud, the truly important part, didn't fizzle and die behind any of the conversational filters I'd spent over a decade cultivating.

"And you want me," I said quietly, my own voice hardly audible over the loud clanging of my heart. "I can see it in your eyes right now. But I don't believe that you'll do anything about it knowing there's an end date. And that makes me very curious, Barrett King."

For a moment, he did nothing but stare. Puzzling me out. Just like I was. There was a flicker in his gaze, the shifting of his thoughts, and I saw the moment he came to a decision.

"Let's play a game," he said.

My brow flattened. "What?"

"Twenty Questions," Barrett continued. "You want to know more? Great. So do I." His arms spread out wide. "We have nothing but time."

Time had nothing to do with it. I could've spent my time learning jujitsu or how to speak Mandarin. I could do laundry (no) or math (absolutely fucking not) because I had *time*.

This was a bad, no-good, horrible idea. There was a one million percent chance I'd regret it. The thought of someone digging into my past—even if it was him, even with the detestable soft spot I'd developed for this man—made those warm bursts turn to ice.

"What kind of questions?" I asked warily, easing myself into one of the stools at the island.

"We can start easy." His thumb tapped the edge of the counter, like he was keeping time as he thought of where to start. "You go first."

"Can't we play Scrabble again?"

His eyes warmed, and the breath caught in my throat when his lips twitched. The corners moved up a little farther. Barrett leaned in, lowering his voice like someone might overhear us in this big empty house where we were the only occupants. "Guess what word Maggie and I used to beat Bryce and Griffin last night?"

"No." I leaned back in my chair, appraising him openly. "Does that mean you officially recant your cheating accusations?"

"Maybe."

There was no smothering my smile, especially when a sweet ache took residence under my skin. If someone were bored and wanted to give that sensation a name, it might be something like *longing* or *affection.* But I wasn't bored, and I certainly wasn't looking to name anything at the moment. Barrett's eyes dropped, locking in on an unconscious movement, and when I looked down, my fingers were brushing against the birds inked on my wrist.

"How about this," he said simply, eyes still locked on the absent brush of my fingers against my skin, "you ask me whatever you want."

I arched a brow. "And you're not asking me anything?"

"Later. When you're ready."

"No questions about . . . about yesterday," I said, an invisible fist closing around my throat. I forced a swallow, watching his profile carefully.

"Deal." He pulled butter out of the fridge, along with a couple packages of sliced cheese—sharp cheddar and gouda—and then two plates from the upper cabinets. "Just one for you?" he asked.

When he didn't press, I let out a deep breath and nodded.

Barrett set out a large skillet and turned on the burner beneath, then buttered three pieces of bread, laying them face down.

I folded my leg up against my chest, setting my chin on my knee while I watched him flip those grilled cheeses like he'd been doing it his whole damn life. Maybe I had a competency kink. That had to be it, right? Because it was ridiculous to be this impressed by a man toasting me some bread with a little cheese in the middle.

My standards were higher than that. Too high, some might say, considering my ass was still unmarried and there'd been no one who tempted me to do anything of the sort. But someone had tempted him, once upon a time.

Curiosity rose up, swift and fierce, slamming past my hefty reserve.

There was no pale ring on his finger, no leftover sign that there'd been a Mrs. Barrett King. What had she been like? What had they been like together?

"I'll play," I told him.

The glance he gave me over his shoulder was quick and impossible to read. "Hit me."

Questions about the ex danced on the edge of my tongue.

No. Not yet.

"Favorite movie."

He flipped the sandwiches again, giving each one a quick tap with the spatula. "*Cinderella Man*." Then he paused. "Or *Rudy*."

I shook my head, and he must've caught it in his peripheral.

"What?" he asked. "You think I'm predictable?"

"A former football player turned coach who loves *Rudy*? Yes."

"You're telling me that movie doesn't inspire the hell out of you?"

"Never seen it," I replied.

He hummed briefly, like he was thinking about something. "Good thing we've got time, then."

A brief, vivid image popped up in the back of my mind—me and Barrett and a dark room and a couch and blankets. It was so date-like. Dates involved movies and questions and food and intention. According to him, his intentions were pure: keep me from freezing to death and whatnot. It didn't explain why my brain didn't get the memo. Those images went from PG to fairly explicit very quickly.

I cleared my throat.

"And now he's forcing a movie night," I drawled. "Who says I'm not going to lock myself in the guest bedroom after this?"

"You scared, Townsend?"

For a second, his words didn't register. He said it so lightly. So easily. Somehow the power dynamic had shifted during the course of my knowing this man, and I didn't like it one little bit.

"Of answering some questions? Hardly."

God, how easily I could lie when the situation demanded it. If I were strapped to one of those lie detector machines, that baby would be *screaming.*

"To watch a movie," he said slowly, and my face heated at the implication that I'd just given myself away.

"Oh."

He glanced knowingly down at my fingers, where they still touched my wrist. My hand dropped instantly, and I slicked my tongue over my teeth, a crawling sensation wiggling under my skin. I knew what it was too.

Damn him, he was right. And if I tried to say it out loud, I just might choke on the words.

Barrett checked the bottom side of the sandwiches, sliding them easily onto the two plates he'd set out. From the fridge, he grabbed a bottle of ketchup.

I stared at it when he handed it to me first.

"What's *that* for?" I asked.

His brows furrowed. "You dip the sandwich in it."

"Since when? Where's the tomato soup?"

Barrett flipped open the bottle, squirted a small pile of it next to my sandwich, and pushed it back toward me. I eyed the ketchup warily but figured I couldn't bitch since the man had just made me dinner, and that hadn't happened in years.

"You're very pushy today," I told him. "I'm not sure how I feel about it."

His eyes warmed, but he didn't say anything right away.

"No tomato soup," he answered. "Some of us chose not to clear out the grocery store today. My parents always served it this way when we were growing up in Michigan." He lifted his chin. "Try it." My nose wrinkled. "Oh, come on," he coaxed gently. "I thought you were the adventurous one."

"That's emotional manipulation, sir."

He watched me quietly for a moment, studying my face in a way that made my hairline sweat a little bit. "Is it working?"

I scoffed but dipped the corner of my sandwich into the ketchup. Barrett gave himself some, watching me from across the island as I moaned through the first bite. After I finished chewing, I licked the corner of my mouth. "'S good."

He took a wolfish bite, damn near half the sandwich, and my eyes lingered on the movement of his jaw while he chewed. Watching *anyone* chew should not be a moment for sexual tension, but what the hell did I know?

Barrett set down his sandwich and gave me an inscrutable look.

"What?"

He took a drink of water, then handed me a napkin when he realized he'd forgotten. "That can't be it."

I took another bite, begrudgingly swiping the sandwich through the ketchup again. It was pretty tasty. When I swallowed, I met his gaze. "Maybe all I ever wanted to know from you was your favorite movie, and now all my Barrett-related questions are satisfied."

Barrett hummed, and it was such a low, pleasing sound that I almost shivered.

"Come on. Don't be a chicken shit," he said, ignoring the dangerous glare I leveled in his direction. "Hit me. And make it a good one."

"Fine." I wiped my fingers on the napkin and pursed my lips. He wanted to play? Not a problem. "Tell me about your wife. Why'd you get divorced?"

Chapter Twenty-Five

Barrett

The expectation for me to run, to balk at her question and close the drawbridge, was right there in her eyes. I wished the light was brighter, that the sun was out and I could see every single variation of blue when she stared at me like that.

I fucking dare you.

Her voice was in my head, whispering it to the part of me that didn't want to talk about Rachel right now. Didn't want anyone else to intrude upon this opportunity with the wild, wily creature sitting in front of me.

But instead of meeting her expectations, instead of avoiding her thrown gauntlet and watching the challenging glint in her eyes fade, I took a deep breath, picked up my plate, and moved to the other side of the island, choosing the stool next to hers and turning it so that I'd be facing her.

Wariness creased her eyebrows as she watched me, but she angled toward me as I took a seat and kept my legs spread.

Lily chewed on her bottom lip, watching me get settled, eyes drifting to where the inside of my leg almost brushed against hers where it was dangling down. The other was still bent against her chest, and I didn't think she'd drop it. Her armor, flimsy though it was.

"You want the long or the short version?"

Her teeth released her bottom lip, which turned it the prettiest pink color as she regarded me. As she weighed whether I was being honest or not.

"I get a choice?"

"Of course."

Lily swallowed, then dropped the leg against her chest. Her knee rested on the inside of my thigh, and the contact made my blood sing.

"Tell me whatever version hurts the least," is what she settled on.

That had me tilting my head because I couldn't help but wonder if she knew how telling that was.

What's hurting you? I wanted to ask. *Let me help. Let me take it away.*

It was a rare sensation, to want to dive headfirst into something like this, and instead of fighting it, like I might have even six months earlier, I let it fill me up.

"I think it's good when our stories hurt to be told," I answered evenly. "Doesn't that mean they were real?"

"I'm sure most people would say that, yes." Her fingers toyed with the edge of her plate, only half of her sandwich eaten. "Personally, I don't like reliving the worst parts of my life."

An urge gripped me, painful in its intensity, to reach forward and slide my hands along the sides of her face, brush my thumbs over her cheekbones, and tell her that she wasn't alone tonight. That my shoulders were big enough to carry her pain if she wanted help, even for a little while.

Instead of doing that, I folded my hands and kept them in my lap. "Rachel and I dated in college. She approached me after a shared class and asked to be my study partner. It didn't take long after that for her to let me know what she wanted. She was beautiful. Sharp. Smart. Incredibly driven." I kept my eyes on Lily. "She was also selfish. Cold. Calculating."

Her eyes flickered. "Did you know this prior to her taking your last name, or after?"

"After she came to me in tears and told me she was pregnant with Bryce. That her father found a pregnancy test and was going to disown her. I proposed on the spot." Lily's face softened, and I pulled in a deep breath. "Not long after that, she informed me she'd also been sleeping with my brother, Griffin. My brother wasn't aware either. She was just . . . hedging her bets, I guess."

Lily's mouth fell open. "Bryce . . ."

"Is mine," I finished. "Griffin was gone for a few months when he was conceived." I smoothed my hands down the tops of my thighs. "After we got married and I got drafted, she told me I was the safer choice. The boring one, of course. Too cold for her. But I'd take better care of her than Griffin would."

"Oh, Barrett," she whispered, rubbing at her chest like it hurt. "And this is the same woman who chose not to fight for more time with her kids?"

I nodded. "If she'd tried, I would not have made it easy. The less time they spend with her, the better. I have a feeling in a couple years, she'll let them decide if they want to come see her. And they won't."

"They don't seem to miss her," she said carefully.

"She didn't really raise them." I took a sip of water. "Nannies did. I helped when I could, when work allowed." Then I shook my head. "I'm not perfect, though. We were incompatible from the start, and I did shut down on her when Maggie was young. Always put the kids and my job before her. I don't blame her for hating me."

The color was high in Lily's cheeks. "She's not going to randomly show up here in the next month, is she?"

"No. Why?"

"I might have to break her fucking nose," she said calmly.

"That so?" I murmured, adoration wrapping around my heart like a vine. "Rachel's pretty scary when she wants to be."

"I am so scrappy in a fight. You have no idea."

I leaned forward, bracing my forearm on the counter, my fingers a hairbreadth away from her arm. The space between us disappeared, and Lily sucked in a breath at my nearness. "Tell me why you'd want to do that."

Her eyes locked on my mouth. "Is that one of your questions?"

"If that makes you feel better, sure."

"Your kids are incredible and I think I hate her a little bit." Lily inhaled sharply through her nose and lifted her gaze to mine. The sincerity I saw there made it hard to breathe. "And you're not boring. You're a really good man, Barrett."

My heart hammered against my rib cage, each messy thrash forward testing the limits of what those bones could endure.

"You're patient and loyal and thoughtful, and a woman like that doesn't deserve to have a man like you."

When I was capable of speech, my voice came out ragged, every fiber of my restraint fraying at the edges. "If you're trying to test my control right now, you're doing a very good job of it."

Lily's exhale was shaky, and when she raised her hand, fingers trembling, I stayed perfectly still. The tips of her fingers landed on the side of my jaw, a tentative, testing brush along my unshaven skin. "I'm not," she whispered, and her eyes followed the motion of her fingers until they briefly touched the bottom edge of my lip. "I just . . . felt like touching you. It's probably been a long time, hasn't it?"

"Yes." My voice was hardly recognizable, coming out as a coarse whisper.

I didn't realize how much I'd missed affection like this. Had I ever experienced it with Rachel? I wasn't sure I had. It was entirely foreign, entirely wonderful because of how unrecognizable it was. For years, I'd ignored the absence out of necessity. There hadn't been time to think about what a gaping hole it left inside me. That I wasn't just a father, I wasn't just a coach. I was a man, and knowing a woman like this wanted me sent heat spinning through me so fast that it was fruitless to try to extinguish the flames.

Discipline and control warred mightily with my baser urges. In less than a minute, I could have her on the counter. Could have her panting and moaning in less than five. Lily, naked and at my mercy, sweet and supple in my arms, would fill every empty space I'd felt over the last few years. The last decade, if I was being honest.

If I let myself have it. Tearing through the cracks of the absolute fucking high of her hands on my skin was that whisper of caution. Not because I didn't want it, or because she didn't either.

The strength of my desire was what let it slip through.

This was *important*. What we were doing was important. The things I was allowing myself to share mattered. Especially to Lily, who, by her own admission, was always alone. I didn't want her to feel like that anymore. I wanted her to feel seen. Like someone, somewhere, cared about what she had to say and cared about the things she kept locked tight in her head.

"What's your favorite movie?" I asked raggedly, keen to touch her, the urge so strong that it sliced a path straight through my better judgment.

Lily exhaled a quiet laugh, which snagged in her throat when I gently clasped her wrist and brought her palm to my mouth.

"I—I can't think," she said unsteadily.

I kissed the skin just above her wrist, and her fingers curled in, brushing against my cheek. I dragged my nose over the center of her palm. She smelled so good. The thought that she'd smell like this everywhere—clean and sweet—had my mouth watering.

"I can stop," I rasped.

"*M-Mary Poppins*," she finally answered.

My eyes opened, my mouth hovering over her skin as I looked at her in surprise. "Really?"

Lily nodded, her gaze still slightly unfocused as she watched me. "Gives zero fucks about what anyone thinks. Lives life on her own terms. You can tell she's been through some shit, but she's got a spine of steel. Kids love her. Men don't know what to do with her. She's my fucking idol."

I couldn't help it—I laughed. I laughed deep and loud, and, keeping my fingers wrapped around her wrist, I laid our joined hands against my chest, just above the place where my heart beat hard and fast.

Lily smoothed her hand out, pressing against that spot, and when my laughter faded, she inched forward, her eyes locked on my smile.

Her hands slid up my chest, and my smile slowly faded. She looked drugged as she got off her chair and stood between my spread legs. Something slipped through my veins, too, a euphoric buzzing that turned my head around.

"That's not fair," she whispered.

"What's not?"

Her palms cradled my jaw, and I closed my eyes, gripping her wrists without pulling, instead easing my hands up and down her forearms. Her fingertips, cool and light, danced along the lines around my mouth that only appeared when I smiled. I wanted to stay here forever. Just like this.

When she didn't answer, I finally opened my eyes.

"Look at you," she whispered. Her eyes traced my face, fluttering shut when I dropped my hands from her arms and anchored my palms around her waist, dragging my thumbs along the space above her hip bones. "How am I not supposed to want to eat you alive when you smile like that?"

My head was reeling, and I couldn't make heads or tails of what I should say. What I should do. All my better intentions were reduced to ash by this unyielding force of nature underneath my hands.

"I didn't mean to make you feel that way," I managed, voice tight. My palms skimmed around the curve of her ribs, fingers dancing along the edge of her leggings where they sat high on her waist. The skin on her back was warm and firm, and when I touched it, she let out a short burst of air. My hands kept going, and her forehead dropped to my temple, her labored exhales hitting the side of my face as she wrapped an arm around my shoulders, her fingers dragging through the hairs at the back of my neck.

"I know," she said, her lips brushing the shell of my ear. "That's what makes it so, *so* much worse." She arched her back when my hands coasted higher underneath her shirt. Her chest pressed against mine, and I let my forehead rest against her collarbone, where the silky strands of her hair brushed against my face. "You don't even know you're doing it, and God, I want to show you what that does to me."

God, I was wrecked for this woman and we hadn't even kissed yet. What devastation would she cause when this was through? I wasn't sure I cared anymore. Kissing her, touching her, taking her to bed—it wasn't simple lust, and it was far more than important. My heart might stop beating if I didn't know the feel of her.

Skin. Underneath her shirt, the entire expanse of her back was just skin.

"Lily," I murmured, my lips brushing her collarbone, then moving into the notch at the base of her throat. I pulled in a greedy inhale, lungs expanding on the sweet scent of her skin. She emitted a nonsensical response just next to my ear, and my hands pressed harder, my fingers dragging along her ribs as she shivered. "You're not wearing a fucking bra."

"I hate them," she groaned. "You have no idea how much."

I tipped my chin up and watched the shift in her face as I turned my hand, dragging the back of my knuckles along the front of her ribs, inching them up and up. Her mouth opened on a tiny *o* and her long, dark lashes fluttered shut when I found the curve along the bottom of her breast.

Her skin was impossibly soft and warm, and even as my entire blood supply rushed south, directly between my legs, where I was quite possibly harder than I'd ever been in my entire life, I had enough rational thought left to go slow.

This descent into madness was meant to be savored.

Lily's fingers at the back of my neck tightened, the tips of her nails digging into my skin when I brushed over the hard tip of her nipple.

"Barrett," she moaned, her nose dragging over my cheekbone. My other arm tightened around her waist, holding her firmly in place.

Gently, I kissed the side of her neck, then sucked lightly on the skin underneath my mouth, tugging a whimper from the back of her throat. I wanted to swallow that sound, feel the vibration of the noise with my tongue against hers, with my hand between her legs as she broke apart in my arms.

There was no stopping this. I was too tired to try, and resistance melted away with very little effort. I stood, the stool behind me shoved back with a noisy clatter. I filled my hand with her breast, pressing her back against the counter as my other palm anchored against her backside, my thigh slotted between hers as she gasped.

Lily gripped the side of my face, and in the next breath, our mouths slammed together.

No finesse. No savoring, despite my best efforts. We were driven by something else, desperation and a snapping of the restraint that had held us back for the last few weeks.

Her tongue was soft and wet as I licked into her mouth, her lips firm and sweet, and she went up onto the balls of her feet as I groaned into this bold first kiss. She did, too, a disbelieving, relieved sort of sound torn straight from her lungs.

I tugged on her bottom lip with my teeth, and she shoved her hands up underneath my shirt, raking her nails along my stomach muscles. Her fingers were cool and nimble, wrapping firmly around the buckle of my belt.

My hand tore at the hat on her head. I wanted that hair—that fucking glorious hair—wrapped tight between my fingers. I cupped the back of her head, tilting my own to deepen the kiss. But I couldn't. Our mouths were fused together as deeply as they could go, tongues winding and teeth clacking and lips melded together. I couldn't hold her tight enough. I couldn't get her any closer to me, her body already locked in my fierce embrace.

My entire frame trembled from the force of how much I wanted her, and when she wrapped her hand around the tented fabric at the front of my pants, we both groaned.

Hours. I had hours and days with her. My mouth dragged down the line of her stubborn jaw, and I placed a sucking kiss there.

"Please," she begged.

In my life, I'd been asked for a million things, maybe more. Nothing sounded as sweet as that single word falling from her lips.

I'd give her anything. Anything she asked for.

I wrenched her shirt up and tugged her closer with both hands, ducking down to suck that hard, pink nipple into my mouth, laving it with my tongue, then biting down gently with my teeth.

Lily moaned, clutching my head to her chest, her back arching underneath the pressure of my lips on her body. I moved to the other breast and sucked on the bottom edge, hard enough to mark her skin, and her stomach trembled where I held her firmly in place.

My lungs heaved as I lifted my head and took in her mussed appearance. Her lips were pink and abused. Her cheeks flushed. Her hair tangled around her shoulders from my hands. Underneath her collarbone was another tattoo, closer to her shoulder. I dragged my thumb over it, a delicate design against her flawless skin.

Lily's gaze absolutely leveled me, the heat buried there enough to take down a city block. Certainly enough to knock the breath from my lungs.

Had I ever been looked at that way?

I wasn't sure I had. And what a heady feeling that was.

I gripped the sides of her face and dragged her mouth to mine again, groaning when she brushed her tongue against the tip of mine in a slow tease.

A shudder racked my frame when she tightened her hand around my hardness, then started undoing the belt buckle as we kissed.

Yes. Yes. I wanted her hands on me. Wanted it more than breathing. Needed it to survive.

Bzzz. Bzzz.

We both froze, the jarring sound of my phone on the counter slicing through the thick tension clouding the room.

I rolled my forehead against hers and sighed. "It's the kids," I said, voice absolutely shredded. "I told Griffin to have them call me when they got to his house."

Lily nodded, covering her mouth with her hand as she pulled away. I adjusted my shirt, watching through heavy-lidded eyes as she did the same. She ran her hands through her tangled hair, and I had to turn away as I did the same.

I let out a deep breath and pressed the button to connect the video call.

Their faces were smushed together in the camera, and I found it easier to smile than I thought. "How was the flight?"

"Good," Maggie said. "The flight attendants gave us fries and pizza and dessert. Not as good as Lily's cookies, but they weren't bad."

My eyes met Lily's, and she smiled softly. "Yeah?" I said. "I'll have to tell her that."

"How's the storm?" Bryce asked.

"Pretty bad. Power went out a while ago, so we'll probably be hunkered down here for a couple days."

"'We'?" Maggie asked.

Lily's eyes widened, but I gave her a reassuring look. "Yeah, Lily didn't have a generator at her place, so she's hanging out here to stay warm."

Lily's eyebrow arched as she glanced meaningfully down to where I was still hard as a rock. I gave her a stern look, which made her grin.

"Can I say hi to her?" Maggie asked.

Lily walked closer, holding out her hand for the phone. She smiled when she was in front of the camera. "There's my favorite troublemakers. How's the Rocky Mountain State?"

"I can't believe you're sleeping over and we're not there!" Maggie wailed. "Can you do it again when we get home?"

Lily's face was guarded as she glanced back up at me, and it was like I watched the fog of lust clear the room. "We'll have to talk about it," she answered diplomatically.

"Okay." Maggie sighed. "How long will we have with you when we get home?"

The line of her throat worked on a swallow, and she couldn't meet my eyes. "Scott and Patty get home before Valentine's Day."

"That's not very much time," Bryce said sadly.

The change in Lily's face made my stomach drop. "I know, buddy. It's not."

"Where are you going next?" he asked.

Lily sucked in a deep breath. "We don't need to talk about this now, okay? You go have fun with your uncle. I'll be here for a few weeks after you get back."

She handed me the phone, eyes locked somewhere around my chest, and she turned away as I made small talk with the kids. Lily cleaned up our dinner plates and washed the skillet as Maggie and Bryce gave me a tour of their bedrooms at the massive house Griffin owned outside Denver. Ruby's big dog was there, too, and I got a very close-up introduction to his panting mouth, as well as a play-by-play of all the tricks he knew. But the kids were so happy, I didn't mind their rambling, no matter what it had interrupted.

In the background, I heard Griffin say something, and the kids nodded. "We're gonna go out to dinner, Dad. We love you."

"Love you too," I told them. "Don't forget to call me every once in a while."

"We won't," Bryce said. "We know how bored you'll be without us."

I smiled faintly. "Bye, buddy."

As I set the phone down, I kept my gaze firmly on Lily's back. She finished drying the skillet and bent down to open the bottom cupboard where they were stored.

When she was done, she set her hands on the counter and let out a heavy sigh, her head hanging down. Defeat was written all over her posture.

"Lily," I said, aching to go over to her. But I wasn't sure she'd welcome it. The chasm had opened back up between us—what I wanted and what she wanted on two completely different sides. There was nothing to bridge this gap except complete truth. Inconvenient truth. "Look at me."

"If I look at you, I will forget why we can't do this."

The heartbreak in her voice had my hands curling into fists. "Talk to me."

"Ask me why I always move around," she said in a voice so quiet, I barely heard her. "Ask me why I can never force myself to stay."

A panicky swell of emotion filled my chest, so big that it threatened to fill the room to the brim. "Why?"

Slowly, Lily turned. Her face was full of sorrow. Devastation was stamped in her eyes so deep that I felt it like a blow to the chest.

"Because I cannot—I will not—ever let myself love something so much that losing it will kill me," she whispered, her eyes glossing over. "You and your children are not casual to me. I do not have the strength anymore to pretend like you are."

I couldn't sit still, not while I was watching her heart break right in front of me. "Lily," I said urgently, "just talk to me. I can help."

She held up her hand when I came around the island, and I forced myself to stop.

"No, you can't," she said.

Helplessness left me paralyzed. If I wanted to respect her space, I couldn't force anything right now. And it was that impotence that had me raking my hands through my hair, tugging at the strands while I stared at her.

A reckless impulse took root, and I held her gaze as I weighed the risks of asking.

"How long has it been since you've seen your family?" I asked carefully.

Her face went pale, and her chin trembled. But before my eyes, I watched her gather herself. Pull up some internal reserve, an invisible well of strength that defied any explanation.

"Ten years." She let out a slow breath. "Four months." She closed her eyes. "Six days," she whispered brokenly.

I said her name, but it felt like a plea more than anything. She backed away.

"I . . . I have to go to bed." She strode around the other side of the island. "Guest room is down the hall, right?"

I nodded, my heart battered and weary as she fled at the first sign of emotional intimacy.

Wordlessly, I watched her grab the laundry basket. She paused at the end of the hallway and glanced over her shoulder. "Thank you for dinner." Her smile was sad. "And for not letting me freeze."

I waited until she was in the bathroom to pull the electric blanket from the linen closet and lay it carefully on the foot of the bed where she'd be sleeping.

Then I walked back down the hall and sank onto the couch, my elbows braced on the tops of my thighs, head in my hands as I sat in the silence of my house, thinking about how close she was. Knowing she was within reach. Knowing she was completely unreachable. The parts of her that mattered, at least.

Touching her body was only part of what I wanted. It was the glimpses of everything else that had my head and heart tangled up in knots. I wanted that too.

Blankly, I stared out at the relentless snow and wondered if I'd ever see it again and not think of her.

A couple hours passed. *SportsCenter* flickered on the TV, not really doing a good job of distracting me from any of this. But I couldn't focus on anything worthwhile, and probably wouldn't for as long as she was under this roof with me.

It was dark outside, finally late enough that it was acceptable to go to bed. As I turned off the lights, a noise came from down the hall.

I paused to listen and heard it again.

It was Lily, and when I strode quickly toward the room, I heard her shout someone's name. I didn't pause to consider the ramifications, simply opened the door to wake her.

She was already sitting up in bed, her face flushed, chest heaving, her hair tangled, and her eyes wide and frightened.

I crouched next to the side of the bed, reaching out to lay my hand over hers. "Are you okay?"

Her breathing came quickly, her eyes still clouded with sleep and terrorized confusion. I pressed my fingers along the underside of her wrist to check her pulse, watching her face carefully as I counted the beats.

"Barrett?" she whispered. Her chest glistened with sweat, as did her forehead.

"I'm right here." I ran my palm up her arm. "You had a nightmare."

Even though she was clearly still disoriented, she nodded, but her face crumpled, the first tear slipping down her cheek. She dashed at it with her hand, still breathing unsteadily.

"What can I do?" I asked. My chest ached with a force I'd never felt in my entire life, a bruise that spread over my entire skin, a hurt with her name on it.

She turned to me, eyes wide in her face, tears spilling over her cheeks. "Will you stay with me?"

Chapter Twenty-Six

Lily

The moment the words were out, I could breathe. A sweet rush of oxygen filled my lungs when he didn't hesitate.

I couldn't bear to be alone, not for another second. Sadness could be held at bay for only so long before the dam broke, and what I needed now was his steady, quiet strength to hold me together.

Silently, Barrett stood and pulled back the covers as I shifted to the side. He peeled off his sweatshirt, which left him in a thin T-shirt and the gym shorts he must've changed into after I escaped to the bedroom.

His scent—warm and masculine, like clean skin and musk—filled my head as he eased into the bed next to me, settling his arm underneath my pillow.

Then he waited.

Waited for *me*.

My ribs shook as I tried to hold everything in, only the quiet tears escaping down my face giving even the slightest hint as to what lurked underneath.

"Come here," he said in a low voice.

My chin trembled, and he gently pulled me down into his arms, folding one behind my back and the other tight around my waist. I pressed my face into his chest and let the first sob escape.

His hands moved up and down my back as he let his chin rest on the top of my head.

"I've got you," he said quietly.

And he did.

To feel wanted by him was something heady and dangerous. But this . . . this could crack my world open. A devastating consequence I hadn't seen coming.

It had been countless days, months, years since anyone had held me this way. I wasn't sure I'd *ever* been held like this. Like he was keeping me tethered to Earth. I gripped his shirt in my fists and let the tears come.

He didn't ask me why. Didn't ask for anything I wasn't ready to give.

Because I knew if he did ask, he'd want nothing less than my entire heart. He deserved that too. Someone who could give him a future. Who could love him with reckless, wild abandon and not expect him to change who he was.

Planted in front of me, as I wept in his arms, was nothing more than my own fear. It stood dizzyingly tall. Thick as a redwood. Impenetrable for the last ten years, four months, and six days.

To climb it, to destroy it, I had to trust more than just him.

Trusting Barrett was effortless. Trusting myself was a little more difficult.

He held me like I was precious, like he wanted to absorb my tears. When they started to ebb, my throat raw and my nose almost completely plugged, he reached over to get a tissue off the nightstand.

I took it wordlessly, wiping underneath my eyes and discreetly blowing my nose. In the dark room, it was hard to make out his features, but what I saw was heartbreak in the bent *V* of his eyebrows and the serious set to his mouth. I kept the tissue balled up in my hand, tucking it between his chest and mine where we were pressed together, and eventually felt my pulse settle.

Barrett's big hands never stopped their soothing motion. Up and down, up and down, until my muscles relaxed and my breathing steadied.

"I've got you," he whispered once more against my temple. Tears welled again, and I closed my eyes to keep them from falling. "You're safe."

Instead of letting myself drown in embarrassment or shame or worry about how I'd explain this with the rising of the sun, I simply snuggled closer to the broad heat of his chest.

Barrett sighed, his arms tightening around my back. "I'm not going anywhere."

As sleep claimed me, exhaustion pulling on my body and my heart expanding with the relief of this sweet moment, I decided to believe him.

◆ ◆ ◆

I woke before Barrett, our position similar to how we'd fallen asleep. We were facing each other, his arm still underneath my neck, the other slung over my waist, fingers dangling over my lower back. His shoulders rose and fell on deep, even breaths. Under the covers, one of my bare legs was tucked between his.

The light in the room was weak and gray, filtered through the edges of the curtains that didn't quite cover the windows. But it was enough to study the handsome angles of his face. The straight, proud nose; the lines of his lips; the hard edge to his jaw—dark now with stubble, lending a dangerous air to his already attractive features.

Everything about him made my heart hurt, and I didn't have much time to figure out what to do with that. Less now, as he began to wake. His eyes didn't open right away, but he attempted to stretch his shoulder where it lay underneath my neck.

His patience with me defied anything I'd ever known, and as I waited breathlessly for him to wake, to take stock of the intimate way we'd slept, I felt an undeniable urge to give him something in return.

I didn't want to make him work so hard. Didn't want him to feel like he had to beg for scraps of what my life looked like. More than that, even, I didn't want to make him ask something that he was afraid to ask. Afraid to upset me or push too hard.

The truth was, I was the one who'd enforced that invisible line. Erected boundaries that neither of us had ever named. And he'd respected every single one. Even when I didn't make it easy.

Barrett's eyes finally opened, his gaze on mine and a soft smile tugging at his lips.

"Morning," he said, and the rough scrape of his voice lifted the hair on my arms.

"Thank you." I didn't want anything else said before that. "Thank you for staying."

He adjusted his head on the pillow but didn't move to take his arm back. There was no way it wasn't numb as hell. Slowly, he curled it up, easing a hand over my shoulder and upper arm.

"You sleep okay?" he asked, studying my face carefully.

I didn't even really want to think about what I might look like. A cry-headache bloomed behind my sinuses, and I could only imagine how big the bags under my eyes were.

I nodded, absently playing with the T-shirt covering his chest. He couldn't have known the way anxiety tightened an invisible screw in the center of my heart, or how my body braced for impact as I tried to unearth my nerve.

"It's early," he continued. "If you want to go back to sleep, I can get up."

My hands tightened in his shirt, anchoring him in place, and his brow furrowed as he studied me with a million questions in his eyes.

I licked my lips.

"The tattoo beneath my collarbone," I said quietly. "You touched it last night." Slowly, Barrett nodded. "It's . . . it's three stars." I tugged the neckline of my shirt so he could see it. "It's for my family."

He sucked in a sharp breath, dropping his gaze to my exposed skin. His thumb brushed over it. That gentle brush of his calloused finger solidified my resolve, made it easier to find my voice.

"The biggest star is for my dad. His name was Robert. He liked fixing cars and spending time in his garage. He was always trying to teach me things. Even if I didn't want to learn, he was so patient." A tear slipped out of the corner of my eye, and Barrett brushed it away.

"The second star is for my mom. Kathleen. She was always in the kitchen. She and I used to butt heads all the time," I said, my voice trembling now. "But she's the reason I know how to bake. That's how she showed her love to people. Even when she was upset at me because I didn't want to live in a small town like they did. When all I could talk about was leaving and traveling and seeing the world. She'd make me a plate of my favorite cookies, and they always made me feel better. She never tried to change me, never made me feel bad for the way I was."

His eyes were red rimmed, but he simply listened.

"The smallest star is for my little brother," I whispered raggedly, a sob climbing up my throat. "Aaron. He was eight." I had to stop and try to catch my breath, tears flowing down my face again. "They were on the way to the airport to pick me up from a trip I took when I turned eighteen. A drunk driver crossed into the middle of the road." I stopped, rolling my lips in and letting his perfect little face fill my mind. Gap between his teeth. Freckles over his nose. Black hair, just like mine. "Aaron never saw snow before he died. He always wanted to. H-he told me that it probably looked like magic in the sky."

Barrett's eyes were glossy with unshed tears now, too, and the sight of them was the only thing holding me together. I'd been alone in my grief for so long. Been *alone* for so long.

He kept using the edge of his thumb to wipe my tears, even when it was clearly a losing battle. He never stopped.

"Larry was his dog," I said, my voice wet and full and thick. "My parents got him as a puppy right after Aaron turned three. My dad named him after Larry Bird because the Celtics were his favorite team. He and Aaron . . . they were inseparable. Only person that fucking dog ever really loved." I pinched my eyes shut as the loss of that little furball turned my chest inside out. "He was all I had left of them."

"Oh, baby," he breathed, tucking me against his chest while I wept. Grief, kept locked away long enough, had a devastating consequence when it was finally given a chance to breathe. My entire body shook as I cried. Saying their names, telling their story, was like breaking my head through the surface of the ocean. I'd been drowning for years, without really trying to reach out for help.

I wrapped an arm around Barrett's back and held him as tightly as he held me. When I finally pulled back, he got another tissue and I managed a tiny smile before emptying my nose of the ungodly amount of snot blocking my breathing passages. Barrett finally pulled his arm out from underneath me but wove his fingers through mine so he could bring my knuckles to his mouth.

He shook his head and simply breathed me in. "I am so sorry. I can't . . . I can't imagine, Lily."

"There's nothing you can say." I tightened my grip in his. "I don't like talking about it, as you can imagine."

He pulled one hand from mine and smoothed it over the top of my head. "This is the third time you've finally told me about one of your tattoos."

I exhaled a quiet laugh. "Yeah, it is."

"You going to tell me why now?"

His eyes were soft, full of understanding. And I had a terrifying moment where I thought, *I want to look at them forever.*

"I've never met a man like you, Barrett King." I adjusted my head on the pillow, tangling my legs further with his as he kept our hands anchored tight against his chest. "And you keep surprising me. I guess I felt like you deserved a piece of me no one else has ever had before."

Oh, he liked that. His eyes did this warming thing, and his lips curved, and I wanted to lean forward and kiss them. A soft, sweet kiss, just because I could. Because he was close enough and would let me.

This wasn't the moment for a kiss, and we both knew it.

"And that scares you?"

I let out a short, dry laugh and nodded. "The thought of putting my heart anyplace where it might get hurt again is the most terrifying thing I could imagine." I licked my lips. "I don't know what to do with you."

With his free hand, Barrett cupped the side of my face, gently tracing the shell of my ear with the tip of his finger. "You don't have to do anything."

"No?"

He shook his head and gathered me close again, laying a gentle kiss on my forehead. "No. Right now, you just let me hold you. Okay?"

"Okay."

Chapter Twenty-Seven

Lily

"You're terrible at this."

"You were a lot more patient of a teacher with my daughter."

I swatted his hands away from the mixer. "Yeah, because she wasn't terrible." Barrett didn't budge, even when I tried to shoulder him aside. Like moving a fucking tree. I gave him a brief annoyed look, and he conceded a few inches of space, allowing me to glance inside the mixing bowl. "Quit hovering over my shoulder like a creep; you're not going to intimidate me."

"Not trying to."

I snorted, then used the spatula to scrape down the sides of the bowl. "See? You're missing half the ingredients here. I told you to do this while I was getting my socks."

"You're already wearing socks," he pointed out.

"*More* socks. Looking at the snow makes them feel colder."

With a sigh, Barrett kicked off his slippers and nudged them in my direction. As I shoved my double-socked feet inside, I wiggled my toes and sighed happily.

Barrett motioned for the spatula, and I handed it to him, glancing quickly at his face.

On day two of our snow-pocalypse, we'd traded in for a very different vibe. It wasn't so much *rampant sexual tension* as it was *sweet and innocent because we're not sure what to do with each other now that all the proverbial cards are on the table.*

After we dozed for a bit longer, I took a quick shower and tried very hard not to make eye contact with my reflection because I did *not* want to see the collateral damage of my little mental breakdown in the midnight hours. When I was done, face cleaned and damp hair slicked back off my face, Barrett was busy in the kitchen making french toast.

Two meals in a row, folks, and I didn't even have to take off my underwear. It was some kind of new world record.

He did some work at the dining room table after breakfast, talking to Bridget more than once. Two other men called him, and they discussed things like draft picks and plans for the combine, and it all sounded incredibly official.

It was a nice morning, all in all. Without being asked, Barrett pulled the electric blanket off my bed and transferred it to the couch, where I blasted that sucker up to high and curled up with my Kindle to read. Fine, half the time I was staring at him over the edge of my Kindle, gaze darting back down to the screen anytime he raised his from his laptop and tablet. There was no lingering eye contact. Just a guy doing work and a girl reading steamy fanfiction about the same two idiots falling in love.

At least, until he brought out the glasses.

They had dark frames—black, maybe—and he pulled them out of a nondescript leather case before sliding them onto his face. My throat went dry, and my Kindle was slowly lowered all the way down into my lap, lest it interfere with the untapped professor fantasy playing out in front of me.

Barrett noticed, doing a slight double take when he caught me gawking.

"What?"

Intelligent words seemed a bit beyond me at the moment, so I settled on, "Glasses. Why?"

His mouth softened in a wry grin, which absolutely twisted my stomach in knots, and he adjusted them on his face. "Staring at screens most of my day. Makes my eyes tired after the season is done. I know, they probably make me look older."

"Yeah, practically geriatric," I said airily. At least, I tried to say it airily. It came out all choked and wonky. Even though his mouth didn't move, I'd swear it in a courtroom, the man's eyes smiled. "It's not attractive. You should take them off."

Barrett hummed, then went back to work, glasses still very much on his face.

I rolled my eyes and tried to focus on my story.

After a few hours of relative peace, he forced me to watch *Rudy*, sitting at a respectable distance away, still wearing those fucking glasses. When I surreptitiously wiped my cheeks at the end of the movie, he didn't gloat, just handed me another tissue.

I swiped it from his hand. "How many tissue boxes do you have around this house? They keep popping up everywhere." I blew my nose and wadded up the tissue in my hand. I wasn't going to admit this just yet, but watching that movie made me feel like I'd run through a brick wall for Rudy.

"Two." Barrett stretched an arm over the back of the couch, his fingers coming dangerously close to my braid. If he kept looking at me like that with those damn hot-teacher frames on his face, I'd mount him like a *bike*. "I just keep moving them wherever you are, just in case."

That one comment was the only time we'd danced around what happened the night before, just innocuous enough that it didn't make me want to hide under blankets all day.

"Funny," I said, peeling off the blanket. That was about the time I informed him he was helping me make cookies. It was either that or ask if I could sit in his lap and stare at his face, and I wasn't sure he'd agree to that just yet.

The TV remained on in the background, Barrett having switched it to a sports talk show after the movie was over, and with the sides of the bowl finally scraped and the dough acceptably mixed, I caught him watching the talking heads discussing his first season as a coach in Buffalo.

"You know what I'm gonna say," the first guy said, leaning back in his chair. "I thought he was too young to be a head coach at his last job, but he did all right because the system and the players were established. But starting over in Buffalo, with a new quarterback he didn't draft, was a recipe for disaster. When he benched Archer Evans, I thought that man had lost his mind." He shook his head. "End of the Barrett King era before it could even start."

His coanchor tossed a piece of wadded-up paper in his direction. "Go ahead, say you were wrong. I want to hear the words coming out of your mouth. My man Barrett did his thing, and there's no arguing it. That guy needed his ass benched. Not many coaches would've had the stones to do it."

"I reserve the right to change my mind." The first guy held up his hands. "That's all. I'm not *saying* I was wrong, but I need to see what they do next season before I actually admit he can hack it as a head coach."

I narrowed my eyes at the screen, wondering who the hell these guys were and why they got to talk shit.

Barrett continued scooping dough onto the cookie sheet. "This is a good size?"

"Little bit bigger," I told him. "No one wants a dinky chocolate chip cookie." He scooped another one, and when he glanced up, I nodded, continuing to study him when he made another ball of dough exactly the same size as the last one. "Is that weird?" I asked.

"What?"

I tilted my chin toward the TV. "Hearing them talk about you like that?"

Barrett shook his head. "Used to it by now. This is pretty tame. They had a field day whenever Griffin and I used to play against each other. 'The Brain versus the Brawn,'" he said dryly. "I won that first matchup when I coached, and it took weeks for the chatter to die down."

From my perch sitting on the counter, I picked up a clean spoon and filled it with dough, pulling it off with my fingers and popping it in my mouth. Barrett watched me, his gaze heavy and soft.

"Want some?" I asked.

"And get salmonella? No thanks."

"Please. I've eaten my body weight in cookie dough the last decade. I think they just made that shit up to keep the cookie companies in business." I got another spoonful and hummed happily upon eating that, too, which made Barrett shake his head. "So. These dudes think you're too young to be a coach?"

"Some of them." He used his finger to slide the dough out of the spoon onto the sheet, carefully getting more. The man was meticulous in everything he did, and for such a bossy asshole, he really did take instructions beautifully. "But if I let other people's opinions sway all my decisions, I'd be stuck. I do what I'm good at and let my performance speak for itself."

He and I were more alike than I ever realized, even if we went about living life in very different ways. His convictions allowed himself to be anchored in one place—not only visible in what he chose to do but also under immense pressure. Mine kept me anchorless, drifting along with the tide. No pressure. No one watching.

Until him.

"Did you like playing better? Or coaching?"

"Playing," he said quietly, staying focused on the task at hand. "I miss it all the time. But . . . my knee and a few big concussions made that decision pretty easy. The faster I wreck my body, the less time I have with my kids. I wasn't willing to make that trade, no matter how much I love the game."

Well. Wasn't he just . . . perfect. If his worst flaw was the dedication he showed to his job, I was in a world of trouble walking away from this man. Knowing my luck, he'd have a beautiful penis *and* know what to do with it. Seriously, if he was as good in bed as he was at everything else, I'd weep.

I blinked, clearing my throat as I brought my thoughts back to more polite conversation.

"Do you ever get sick of it?" I asked.

"My job?"

I nodded. "Watching football all day. Dealing with cocky athletes. Living your life fifteen minutes at a time. Being beloved by millions," I teased.

His smile was barely there, and flutters bloomed in my stomach at the sight of it. "I'm only beloved as long as I'm doing my job well." He scooped up the last of the dough and handed me the bowl so I could scrape the edges. "That's what you accept the moment you say yes. It can end badly, and in this league, it often does. If I make poor decisions, or don't have the right staff in place. If my players don't buy in to the way I run the team. We all know the risks, but we do it anyway."

For a woman who'd spent her entire adult life avoiding risk, I didn't miss the subtext of what he was saying. But he wasn't being preachy. If he were, it would have been easy to dismiss it.

"Why?"

Instead of answering right away, Barrett turned and washed the cookie dough off his hands, using a towel left on the counter to dry them before he turned, gently prying the spoon from my grip. My face heated as he stood between my legs, one hand braced on the counter just to the side of my hip; the other, he used to scrape the spoon into the bowl again, collecting no more than a teaspoon of remaining dough.

He held it up to my mouth. After forcing a swallow, I licked my lips and opened my mouth, waiting for him to set the spoon against my tongue. His eyes were locked on my mouth, but instead of giving it to me, he turned the spoon and fed it to himself.

I scoffed, smacking him in the stomach as he ate the dough. He gave a lopsided grin that echoed in the unsteady thud of my heart.

When he pulled the spoon out of his mouth, I had to fight the urge to lock my thighs around his hips, wrap my ankles around his ass, and make him stay right where he was. The counter height in this place was *perfect*.

"What point are you trying to prove, other than you're a criminal tease?" I said icily.

It said something about Barrett that my bitchy little outburst didn't deter him in the slightest.

"When things are good enough, important enough"—he held my eyes unflinchingly—"when we love them enough, we take the risk, because we damn well know the reward is worth it." Like he hadn't just tossed out the fucking L word, Barrett held up the empty spoon and gently tapped the tip of my nose with it. "You do it too. It just doesn't feel as scary because you've never gotten sick. Doesn't mean it doesn't happen, or it's not real."

I snatched the spoon out of his hand, and he emitted a quiet laugh, nothing more than a pleased little rumble in his chest, and oh, how I wanted to press myself up against his body to feel it. I knew what it was like now, to be held by him, and his little risk/reward speech was feeling very real as I considered the ramifications of shifting forward a few inches.

"Have I rendered you speechless?" he mused.

"No. I'm just thinking."

He hummed.

Unthinkingly, I laid my hand on the side of his throat. "Do that again," I commanded quietly.

The look in his eyes made my stomach tremble, but he lifted his chin and did as I asked. Lower this time, and longer.

I closed my eyes and dropped my hand.

"Do you get sick of the hard parts of your life?" he asked, his thumb gently rubbing the side of my thigh, back and forth, back and forth. It was an absent-minded touch, almost like he wasn't even aware he was doing it.

Because it was easier, I kept my eyes closed while I answered. "Sometimes," I whispered.

"When?"

It would have been simpler for him to reach inside me and pull the words out himself, In front of him, after last night, this was the most difficult thing he could've asked of me.

"It keeps getting harder to pack up and leave. To find somewhere new and feel that excitement. Sometimes I'm just . . . tired. But I don't know how to stop." My hands curled up into fists in my lap, a last-ditch effort to keep from reaching out to him. "That's all I ever wanted growing up. To see everything. My parents didn't have much, so living simply wasn't hard for me. And I saved and saved and saved to take a trip as soon as I turned eighteen, right after I graduated from high school. It was the first time I got on a plane. First time I saw the ocean."

Barrett's fingers drifted over my cheekbone, gently tucking some hair behind my ears.

Holding up my body was too hard; my spine collapsed like wet cardboard under his gentle touch, and I sank forward, allowing him to hold me up for a little while. My forehead rested against his shoulder, and Barrett curved a strong arm around my waist, his hand moving up and down again.

Being able to hide in his embrace allowed me a moment to open my eyes.

"Then when they died, I couldn't stay." My tears were gone after last night, and for that, I was thankful. "I sold their house, put some stuff I couldn't part with in a storage unit, collected what life insurance had been left to me, packed the dog in the car, and took off."

Barrett remained quiet, his nose dipping briefly against my temple as he inhaled slowly, then let it out again.

"Stopping feels like I have to face everything I've lost." Summoning whatever courage I had left, a hidden reserve that should've been long gone, I lifted my head and looked him full in the face. "Sometimes I want to," I admitted in a broken whisper. "And sometimes I don't think I'm capable of it. That I'll run from it for the rest of my life."

Barrett cupped my face in his hands, and I closed my eyes again, overwhelmed by the warmth and strength in that hold.

"Then stay somewhere," he said urgently. His thumbs brushed over my cheekbones, and my eyes couldn't stay shut anymore. "Just for a while. How are you going to know until you try?"

The flutters in my stomach turned to giant wings—panic spiking with each great big whoosh along my insides, so intense that it stole my breath. "Don't do this."

His eyes were bright, intense in a way I hadn't seen before. "Don't what? Don't tell you that I want to see more of you? That I want to take you out on a date? That I want to watch movies and explain football and see you with my kids and take you to bed? That I want to wake up next to you and let a hug from you be the best part of my day? I want *more*, Lily, and I cannot let you leave here without knowing that."

The heavy press of overwhelming emotion made my throat close up, and I pinched my eyes shut again, shaking my head until his hands moved from my face. But he didn't drop them, and he didn't back away. He simply shifted them down until they held each side of my neck, his thumb underneath the line of my jaw.

Barrett was unmoving in the face of my fear.

"Look at me," he said gently, firmly. "Please."

Everything he'd listed sounded like a life someone else was meant to live. Movies and kids and football and baking cookies and snowstorms and letting him take me to bed. Simple hugs at the end of the day. Warmth and family and affection and . . . and love. There was a part of me screaming for all those things.

I wanted to be the one he came to when the whole world questioned him. Wanted to sit at school concerts with him by my side. Letting him hold me every night the way he held me before.

And bed. Yes, I wanted Barrett to take me to bed. I wanted to finish what we'd started last night, so much so that my heart screamed itself raw, hissing wildly to scare away the fears still holding my brain prisoner.

But it was those things—the memories of goodbyes I hadn't been ready to say, coffins and stupid flowers and empty words from people trying to make me feel better, knowing I was facing down a lifetime of missing the people I loved—that were the loudest. I didn't want them to be, but they were. For ten years and four months and seven days, they'd driven all the decisions, and I wasn't sure how to pry them away from the steering wheel.

When I forced my eyes open and saw the way he was looking at me—the heart in his eyes—I did the only thing that felt right.

I told him the truth.

"I just took a six-month job in Florida," I said unevenly. "I *can't* give you what you want."

I expected him to step back. For his hands to drop from my skin. His eyes to shutter and his mouth to form a firm line.

But none of those things happened.

"Don't run from this," he said evenly. "I'm not going to hurt you, Lily. I'm not going anywhere."

My hands fisted in the fabric of his shirt, anger and frustration—at him and at myself—fused with a white-hot bang inside my chest. I wasn't mad that he was so unfazed. I was furious that, more than anything, I felt a desperate itch to believe him.

Eclipsing it all was head-spinning desire, and instead of running away from it, from trying to justify why we couldn't, I leaned all the way in and let it crash over my head.

Barrett's eyes flashed when he clocked the change in my face.

Which was why I made a small noise of annoyance, gripped his shirt tighter, and pulled him down toward me, one hand sliding up behind his neck while his mouth slanted over mine.

Chapter Twenty-Eight

Barrett

As a distraction technique, it was effective.

My hands dove into her hair, and I took control of the kiss in the span of time it took for my heart to expand in my chest. Her tongue, soft and warm and wet, twisted around mine, and I groaned into her mouth.

I tightened my fingers, and Lily let out a short whimpering sound as I gripped the strands of her hair to tilt her head. Her legs wound around my hips, tugging me flush with her center, and I rocked against her mindlessly, shocked at how quickly we'd arrived here.

I shouldn't have been.

This woman had the stunning ability to bring me to my knees with nothing more than the crook of her finger, and I wasn't even sure she was aware of it. She bit down on my bottom lip, and I untangled my fingers from her hair, cupping her face to roll my forehead against hers.

"Are you kissing me just to shut me up?" I asked, unable to keep my hands from sliding along her waist and back, down to the curve of her ass, keeping her tight against me. Even if she said yes, I wasn't sure I'd be able to stop.

Lily's cheeks were flushed pink, and her hands slid underneath my shirt again, palms coasting over my sides, up over my chest. "Baby, if I thought that would work, I would've done it the first night we met."

I laughed against her mouth, and she pulled back. After a slow, dazed blink with her eyes locked on my lips, she surged up, kissing me again with a helpless sigh. I wound my arms around her and held her tight to my chest.

"It drives me crazy when you laugh," she moaned, gripping my hair in tight fists as she rolled her hips over my blood-draining hard-on. "You don't even know."

"Yes, I do," I breathed, pushing my hands under her T-shirt, finding her braless again. God bless her hatred of that particular undergarment. "What do you think it does to me when you smile? When you laugh? When you tuck yourself against my chest, all soft and sweet? You're no better."

Lily leaned her head back, and I kissed down the line of her neck, sucking on her skin, driven by a throbbing urge to mark her. Not once in my life had I felt that way, the desire to leave a bruise or a bite mark. But with her, it was all different. Better. Heightened in a way that should have been frightening.

Everything about her had me off-center, and I couldn't find my way back to solid footing.

She was leaving. She'd taken another job. Six fucking months. And instead of making me want to pull away, I simply wanted her more. Because no matter what she said, Lily Townsend wanted this with me as much as I did with her.

If I had to single-handedly dismantle the towering wall of her fear, tearing it down until my hands were bloody, I'd do it. One day at a time. Even if it took weeks or months or years.

"Barrett," she said in a breathy voice, gently pushing on my chest. I pulled back, heaving breaths in and out while we stared at each other with only inches between us. "What if I can't?" she said again.

I shook my head, brushing her hair off her face. "What if you can? And what if it's amazing? Then what?"

Her eyes were huge, her lips red from our kisses, and it was clear she didn't know what to say. "I'm not very nice," she blurted out. "I'm not . . . friendly. I don't really have friends."

I held her gaze. "Neither do I."

Lily blinked. "You don't?"

"No. I have my kids and my parents. I can't tell my brother he's one of my only friends, because it'll go to his head. Bridget would say she is, but she scares me too much for me to call her that."

Her lips twitched, hands twisting absently in my shirt as she tried not to smile.

"And I have you," I said quietly.

Lily's eyes flew to mine. "What?"

"I have you." I smoothed my hands up her arms. "I like having you around, Lily Townsend. You don't talk just to hear your own voice. You're funny without trying. Smart as a whip. You are thoughtful and kind with my kids, which says a lot about who you are as a person. And I think, if you let yourself, you'd be an incredible friend."

"I'm selfish," she said, tilting her chin up. A challenge to argue, maybe. "I've only lived for myself for a long time. I'd be the worst girlfriend. I'd hog the bed and the remote because I've never had to share. I'd tell you to turn down the TV because I'm used to quiet when I read. I'll probably get restless. I'd be terrible at football games with all these people expecting me to be perfect and sweet and outgoing."

"I'm a perfectionist," I countered. "I work too much. Bridget had to put up Christmas trees in my office so no one thought I was a Grinch." Her lips twitched again. "And during the season, I have *no* downtime. You would hardly see me during the week." She stared down at where her fingers were twisted in my shirt. The tips of her thumbs rested on my skin, but she didn't move them. "Everyone tells me I'm too serious. That I wouldn't know fun if it bit me in the ass."

Her eyes lifted again, wide and serious. "I'm terrible at dealing with my feelings."

"You don't say," I said dryly. She let out a quiet laugh, sobering again as she stared into my face. "Remember what I said to you at practice the other day?" As her brow furrowed, I sucked in a deep breath. "I care what you think, Lily. How you view me as a person—and not because I need to be perfect, but because you matter to me. Your opinion matters. Your respect is something I want to know I've earned." I cupped her face again, chest constricting when she didn't drop her gaze in this nerve-racking moment of vulnerability. "That probably scares you, doesn't it?"

"Sort of," she whispered.

"That's okay." My thumbs swept over her cheeks. "What else?"

"I might try to run if I'm afraid to get hurt. Just for a little while."

My heart swelled, affection almost taking me out at the knees.

"Then I will always be waiting when you come back," I told her fiercely. "You need to go to Florida for six months to warm your stubborn ass up after this winter? Do it. We can talk on the phone. I can charter a flight to come see you. Take the kids, too, if I'm feeling like sharing." My hands slid over the sides of her neck. "But I don't know that I will. I've never been possessive of a woman in my entire life, but I think I will be with you."

Her eyes welled up, but no tears fell.

"I am not scared to wait for you. To give you time to be ready." My fingers wound through her hair. "And we could sit here all day talking about all the shit we've done wrong, the ways we're not perfect, but I'm not scared of that either." I kissed her once, a sweet, lingering kiss. "I have waited my entire life for someone who feels like my best friend. My partner. I'm not giving that up so easily now that I've found it."

I kissed her again, the resistance melting from her frame. I pulled back, nose brushing hers while I spoke against her lips.

"Fight for this with me, baby. Even if it's hard. Even if we have to piss each other off from time to time. Fight for something good, Lily, because you deserve that after being alone for so long."

A tear slid down her cheek, and I brushed it away with my thumb.

"So do you," she whispered. "Maybe . . . maybe we could stop being lonely together."

If there was a sound to falling in love, then it was buried somewhere in the sweet sigh she let out when I kissed her again. I wanted to hear it every day for the rest of my life.

I deepened the kiss, warmth flowing through my veins as her hands roamed over my chest and tugged at my shirt. I broke away to yank it over my head. She stared hungrily at my upper body.

"God, look at you," she breathed. "A man who sits at a desk should not have a six-pack like this." Her fingertips dragged over my arms, her eyes following their path. "Or arms like this. How?"

I dipped my head and kissed the skin just beneath the line of her jaw, letting my lips whisper over the shell of her ear when I said, "All the better to fuck you with, darling."

Lily was practically panting as she tugged my face to hers, our mouths clashing in a furious kiss. The barriers—emotional and otherwise—were gone, and my hands tugged at her shirt, trying to peel it over her head before I had to break away from the decadence of her lips on mine.

"Bed," she begged against my mouth. "Bed, now."

I gripped my hands under her ass as she wound her legs around my waist. I couldn't kiss her and navigate through the house at the same time, and when I tried to ascend the stairs with her in my arms, she tugged on my earlobe with her teeth and I bit out a growled curse, spinning to press her back against the wall the moment I cleared the landing at the top. With her back braced against the wall, I could free one hand for more important things.

With a groan, I sucked her tongue into my mouth, filling my palm with the warm weight of her breast. Lily rolled her hips against my stomach, and I wanted those leggings gone. Wanting everything between us fucking vanished with nothing but a flick of my fingers.

Our kiss was a fight for dominance, and I loved that she didn't just let me take control. I didn't want to tame her. I wanted scratches on my own skin in the same way I wanted to leave marks on hers.

Then she pulled back, staring at me with a delectable flush over her chest and neck. "Wait."

"What?"

She stared at my mouth, then seemed to gather herself. "Let's move this to a bed first. I have something to show you."

I grinned, ducking down to tug on her bottom lip with my teeth. "Is it something I get to put my mouth on?"

Lily let out a breathy laugh, her eyes bright, pupils blown wide with desire. "Technically, yes."

"Then tell me where you want me."

She hummed, easing her legs from around my waist until her feet touched the ground. Having the use of both of my hands meant I could touch more, and touch her I did. Her breasts were high and full, and I skimmed my fingers over the tips until she shivered, her eyelids fluttering shut.

"You're such a shit," she sighed. "You make me think I'm in control, but I'm not."

I dipped down, my hands coasting over her hips until her backside was firmly in my palms. I wrenched her tight against me until I could talk against her lips. "You're not," I whispered. We kissed again, so deep and so wet, my appetite for her ratcheting up to a dangerous degree as our bodies pressed together.

When she broke away, Lily's eyes flared with the unmistakable light of challenge, and she gripped my hand, marching us toward my bedroom. Then she paused. "Wait. Which one is yours? I've never been up here."

Since my mouth was busy skimming over the line of her shoulder, I laughed quietly against her skin. I gripped her hips and propelled her forward. "Second door on the left."

"Big bed," she said as we cleared the door. "Not much else."

"Don't need much else." From behind, I cupped her breasts in my hands, and Lily arched her back with a sigh, her hands pushing at her leggings until I had no choice but to let go.

Worth it, though, as she shimmied them down her long legs, and I got my first look at the incredible sight of her long, lean body. There was a flash of ink on her shoulder blade. When she turned, I could hardly tear my eyes away from the impossibly small lace scrap of underwear cut high on her hips. There was ink there, too, just underneath the strap.

So much to discover. I shoved at the waistband of my joggers and pushed them down my legs.

Lily's lips curved into a smug smile and she licked at her bottom lip. "Oh yes. This works for me. I can deal with all your aforementioned flaws if you know what to do with that."

My muscles tensed from the restraint it took not to throw her on the mattress and wrench her legs open.

"On the bed. Time for show-and-tell, pretty girl."

When she reached the foot of the bed, she spun around slowly, her hands coasting down her body in a sensual way that spoke of comfort in her own skin, especially as she carefully tugged off the lace underwear.

"I'm on birth control," she said conversationally, like she wasn't standing stark naked in front of me for the first time. *God, look at her,* I thought. My gaze lingered over every inch, every curve, slowly making my way back up to her face.

"Good," I said roughly. "Because I don't own condoms."

Her lips curled up in a secretive little smile. "And if I told you I wanted you to wear one?"

My eyes didn't move from hers. "Then I'd go out in the storm of the fucking century to get them."

Lily's gaze burned bright and feverish when I took myself in hand, her tongue darting out to wet her bottom lip. "That wouldn't be very neighborly of me. Let's not do that."

"Let's not," I managed. "You said you had something to show me."

"Why don't you try and find it?"

My eyes locked pointedly on the space between her legs, and she tipped her head back, a throaty laugh filling the room and warming my chest. "Not that, you fiend."

I strode toward her, catching her in my arms as we toppled onto the bed, our mouths fused in a searing kiss, one with tongue and teeth and the trading of breaths from her lungs to mine. My hips worked restlessly, my hardness pressing against her stomach as I stretched out on top of her.

Slowly, I worked my way down her body, stopping to kiss along her collarbone. Then between her breasts, lingering on the right breast, then the left, blowing first on the tips until she arched her back; then I kissed each one. Soft, sucking kisses. Worshipful kisses.

I followed the line of her ribs, my hands pressing her thighs open so I could slide my fingers between her legs.

"You . . . you're not looking hard enough," she gasped, gripping my head as I sucked on the skin over her belly button.

"Sure I am," I said. I bit the curve of her hip bone, and she flinched as a breathy laugh escaped her perfect lips. My fingers worked between her legs slowly, where she was wet and soft and hot, and when she moaned my name, I had to close my eyes to fight the snapping urge to push up and inside. To rut and claim and listen to all the ways I could make this gorgeous creature say my name. All the ways she could scream *yes* and *more* and *right there*.

I wanted to hear it all. Wanted to make sense of all the things building in my chest at the sight of her in my bed. I pressed my forehead to her trembling stomach and breathed her in, then added my thumb between her legs, and she raked her fingernails along my shoulders. I set my chin on her stomach and watched.

Watched as she tipped over the edge. Watched as her eyes glazed over and her chest flushed pink and pretty.

"Beautiful," I whispered. "You're so beautiful."

She sighed as she came down, her hand threading through my hair. Still, I watched the play of emotions over her face. The way she licked her lips, her slow blinks as her body settled after such a violent burst of pleasure. My eyes tracked over her heaving chest, the pink flush over her breasts, and the rise and fall of her stomach as she caught her breath.

And it was as I watched that I saw what she wanted to show me: reddened skin underneath her ribs, the side I hadn't kissed, hadn't touched. Reddened skin and *ink*.

Slowly, I smoothed my palm over the soft skin of her thigh and up her waist, dragging my fingers underneath the newest mark on her body.

She hummed in satisfaction. "You're getting warmer," she sighed. "Much, much warmer."

I leaned up on one elbow and carefully ghosted my fingers over a delicate silhouette of new ink.

A snowflake.

Lily cupped the side of my face, her thumb rubbing lightly over my bottom lip.

"That's for you," she said, her eyes full of something she might not want to say yet. But I saw it. I saw it so fucking clearly that my ribs pinched. "I got it before I went and yelled at your brother," she said sheepishly.

"Lily," I said, completely undone by this woman, "I don't know what to say."

She took my hand and laid it over her heart. "Do you even remember what you said to me? When I got the call from the vet?"

I shook my head, let my palm absorb the steady thrumming of her heartbeat under her skin.

"Let me come with you," she said. "*Let* me. Like it was for you. You stepped into something you didn't even understand, showing up

for me in a way that no one had in a very, very long time." She closed her eyes and pulled on my arm until I was eye level with her again. "I didn't ever want to forget that moment." She cradled my jaw and pulled me down for a sweet kiss. "Didn't want to forget you," she murmured against my lips.

She wouldn't. I wasn't letting her go, not after this. There was something unbelievably precious about the way she'd allowed herself to tiptoe into these feelings. At her own pace, in a way so uniquely her. She did it not knowing if I'd ever be aware, and somehow that made it even more humbling.

I kissed her again. Slower and deeper. Then again. And again. The weighty emotion turned a corner, heat nipping at its heels until flames licked at my spine. She clutched at my back as I held her to my chest and slid my tongue into her waiting mouth, her leg hitching up on my side.

There was a time for words, and this wasn't it. Everything inside me screamed to take this moment, to make her mine, let Lily make me hers.

I already was. God, I was already hers.

Did she know? I wanted her to know she owned me, in all the ways that mattered.

I reached between us and lined myself up, stealing her mouth in a slow, tongue-heavy kiss as I worked my hips forward. She whimpered into my mouth as I pulled back and then pushed in farther.

Heat and warmth, tight and perfect, had me gritting my teeth, and I let my weight settle on her, gripping her wrists and holding them on the bed above her head. Lily tossed her head back as I thrust in again, deeper this time. Harder this time. Each sharp roll of my body wrenched sweet moans from her throat, had her breasts rubbing against my chest. Her skin was so warm and firm, her body sweet and responsive.

A possessive urge caught at the back of my throat, words I'd never said to another woman helplessly seeking a release.

"Mine," I growled, unable to stop myself.

"Yes."

I snapped my hips forward. "Mine."

Lily arched underneath me eagerly, her hips rolling to meet the motion of my own, her hands clutching at mine where I held them down.

Everything I felt about her crystallized, the world going slow and soft as I let those feelings pool steadily in my chest, bleeding out through my entire body as I worked her into a writhing mess against the mattress.

This was worth waiting for. No matter what I'd been through or what I'd missed over the years, every minute, every day had been worth it to get to this place with her. I'd wait another decade for this woman and she'd still have me on my knees.

In the cradle of her thighs, I pitched forward. Harder again. And harder. She let out a sobbing moan that set my blood on fire. Sex had never felt better, sharper, clearer, more perfect than it did right now.

"Fuck, Lily," I groaned. "It's so good. You feel so good."

"Yes. *Yes*, Barrett."

My body screamed to go faster and harder, to let sweat pool on her skin until she broke apart, until I did too. But my heart wanted to draw this out, to move slow and let the pleasure linger, let it build until she was incoherent for a release.

Wanting both sides of that coin—the driving urge for raw, sweaty sex crashing against the part of me that wanted this to last forever, wanting her in all the ways I could have her—came with a lucid burst of truth.

"I love you," I said tightly, knowing it might be too soon, knowing she may not say it back, but I didn't care. The words came from someplace right and true, tied to my heart as we kissed through each snap of my hips. "I *love* you."

"More," she gasped. "Right there. Oh, right there."

I held her tighter, releasing her wrists so I could brace myself. Through heavy-lidded eyes, sweat gathering at the base of my spine, muscles burning, I unleashed all the things I wasn't able to say in the smack of my skin against hers.

That I wanted her forever. Wanted her with my ring on her finger. Wanted to see her round with a child someday. It was nothing more than a flicker of a thought, no longer than a heartbeat, but heat licked up my back and chest, a territorial flame that caught and spread.

She was practically mindless now, bracing her hand on the headboard while I worked ceaselessly between her legs.

Her breath caught on a ragged moan, and I felt the moment she tipped over, her body a trembling, needy, whimpering mess beneath me. Her legs shook around my sides as she sobbed my name.

That was all it took. The heat gathered in my hips, sharp and blinding, a roar of sensation so big that I felt the tremor in my bones.

"Lily," I groaned, my lips dragging over her skin as I slowed my thrusts, came down from the dizzying peak.

Moments later, drained and exhausted and so fucking satisfied that it was amazing I was conscious, I buried my head into the curve of her shoulder, and her hands smoothed over my back as my weight slumped over hers.

I gathered her in my arms and turned us onto our sides, unwilling to pull from her body just yet. We kissed softly, the sweat cooling on my back as she dragged her hands over my skin. Her expression was bliss, and it made me smile as I pushed the tangled hair off her face.

"Oh yes," she sighed, kissing my cheek, the edge of my jaw, then the corner of my mouth. "This will work for me just fine."

I laughed, kissing her more deeply, coasting my hands up and down her back. "Good."

Lily grinned as she pulled away, a devious light in her eyes that twisted my heart with a pleasant ache. "You love me, huh?"

I let out a disgruntled sigh. "Maybe."

"Maybe?"

I kissed her again, lingering a bit longer this time. "Probably." Then I tickled her side. "And you got a tattoo for me. What does that say?"

Her eyes softened. "Oh, I can't tell you that yet," she said quietly.

My heart swelled, hope surging in my chest. "No?"

"No." She snuggled against my chest and sighed. "Can't make it too easy on you."

I smiled against the top of her head. "Yeah, I'd hate that."

Chapter Twenty-Nine

Lily

"Oh, come on, just one."

"I feel stupid."

I sighed. "What if I send you one first?"

The silence on the other end of the phone went thick, only the sound of his deep breathing for a few seconds, until his roughened voice filled my ear.

"What kind?"

"I guess you'll see."

"Sort of naughty or really naughty?"

"You tell me."

"Fuck, Lily."

I turned my face into my pillow and grinned. The power of Barrett King could not be underestimated. Two words and he gave me butterflies.

"Really naughty, then," I said breezily. "Hold please."

I was ready for this, which he should have anticipated.

Once I'd opened my camera roll, I chose the picture I'd snapped earlier when I was trying on my new bikini, a black strappy thing I'd picked up after I got to Florida. Before I'd tied the top on, I remembered that I had a boyfriend and he was across the fucking country. On a whim, I'd grabbed my phone and arranged my hair, all solid black now that I'd trimmed the last few inches off.

I was kneeling on the floor, facing away from the mirror, my naked back and the high cut of the bikini bottom on my hips visible as I took the picture over my shoulder. My free hand sat demurely in my lap. It was in the reflection of the second mirror across the room that the shadowy glimpse of my breasts were clear.

I clicked send, biting down on my bottom lip while I waited for it to go through.

"Holy fucking hell, Lily," he groaned. "Come back. Come back right now."

My cheeks flushed with pleasant heat as I snuggled into the bed. "See? I told you long distance would be sexy."

"It's been five days," he ground out. "I don't think we can state that with any certainty yet."

"You owe me a picture, sir."

"I will never be able to top that, and if you think I'm taking a dick pic, you're about to be disappointed."

I laughed. "Before I go to sleep, you owe me something good."

"I'll send you a picture of my bed. It misses you too."

My chest was tight and wonderfully achy. Being missed was a novelty that I found myself liking. A lot, actually.

"I'll just watch that video I took on Valentine's Day," I sighed. "That should tide me over."

"Deviant."

I grinned. "What was I supposed to do? You were just standing there, shirtless, cleaning the kitchen after ravaging me on the counter. I needed it to keep me warm on all these cold, lonely nights."

"The counter needed cleaning after the mess you made."

"Whose fault was that? I've *never* had that happen before."

"Mine," he answered, so smugly that I laughed out loud.

"Deviant," I teased.

He sighed. "That's your fantasy, huh? Me cleaning the counters?"

"After that performance? Yeah. It deserved to be immortalized. I'm pretty sure I blacked out."

Barrett made that little humming noise, and my eyes fluttered shut.

I missed him. I missed him so much that it was causing me physical pain. That was novel too. The newness of it coiled around my stomach—not an entirely unpleasant sensation.

"I miss you."

The way he plucked the thoughts straight from my head, feeling things exactly as I felt them.

We'd had a blissful month together in Buffalo before I had to leave. He took me on dates—real, grown-up, romantic dates. Being wooed was an absolute *delight*.

Kisses by the front door when he walked me home at night.

Sweet *good morning* texts waiting for me when I woke up.

Dirty ones when he was at the office longer than he wanted to be.

He'd come home from work with bouquets of bright, cheery flowers. One for me, one for Maggie.

He took me and the kids on fun, interesting outings on the weekends. Legit family shit that didn't even feel scary anymore.

Go me, right?

I started getting to know the people at the front offices in Buffalo because we had standing lunch dates on Tuesdays and Thursdays, where I brought takeout to his office. Once—and only once—I got him to screw me up against the wall where no one could see us, his hand over my mouth so I wouldn't make all those porny sex noises that he was exceptionally skilled at yanking out of me. I swear, if I wasn't experiencing the sex myself, I'd have thought I was faking it too.

At the end of the month, the temptation to say fuck it to Florida was huge.

But I'd made a commitment, and it was important to honor those. Or at least, that was the bullshit I'd told the kids when they asked why I still had to leave. Sometimes it had to be okay to cancel, right? Especially for hot, amazing boyfriends and their cute children who'd stolen my heart with equal force.

But in my gut, I'd known it was the right thing to do. Even though it was awful and heartbreaking and really, exceptionally shitty.

Missing him was important. Missing the kids too.

We talked every day, something he'd promised me when I left. Even if it was only for five minutes, he wouldn't let the day end without hearing my voice, he said.

This was the kind of pain that stretched my heart in incredible ways, and even though we were only five days in, I was proud of myself. I hadn't felt that in a really long time.

"I miss you too," I whispered.

Barrett: Maggie got suspended today.

Me: Omg who do I have to fight?

Barrett: Easy, turbo.

Barrett: She told a friend she figured out there's a way to hack the site where the teachers input the grades.

Me: Good God. She changed her grade??

Barrett: Oh no, she genuinely has straight As. She just wanted to see if she could do it.

Me: Ahh. And what's the punishment at home?

Barrett: Nothing. We just had a talk about integrity at school, and not bragging to friends when you figure out illegal things, especially when you have no intention of doing them.

Me: I love it when you talk about ethical shit. It's so teachery and hot. Will you put on the glasses and do a FaceTime with me?

Barrett: I knew you had a thing for those glasses.

Me: They're acceptable. Wear them the next time I see you, please.

Barrett: I saw you two weeks ago, why didn't you ask then?

Me: I was too busy trying to figure out how to ravage you without your kids hearing. Why are the walls so thin in this house? It's dumb.

Barrett: Maybe I'll leave them home next time.

Me: I don't know, I like them more than I like you.

Barrett: That so?

Me: You're all right.

Barrett: I miss you too.

Me: So fucking much. That's dumb too. Sometimes I feel like I'll die from it.

Barrett: You won't. It'll just make the next time that much better.

Me: Promise?

Barrett: Promise. You want me to call you before you go to bed?

Me: Yes. What do you want to talk about tonight?

Barrett: Will you tell me another story about when you were younger?

Me: Yeah. I can do that.

"It's impossible, Lily," Maggie sighed. "I don't know if I can manage these on my own."

"Nonsense. You've mastered everything we've tried so far."

"Macarons are way harder, though." She adjusted the camera where she'd set it on the counter. "Can you see now?"

"Yup." I held up my own silicon baking sheet. "See the size of mine? Try piping your circles a little bit bigger."

Maggie tucked her tongue between her teeth, brow furrowed in concentration as she did as I instructed. We'd mastered the art of FaceTime baking sessions pretty damn well.

Barrett's head popped into the background, his eyes locking onto mine as he sent me a devastating smile. "Am I allowed to say hi yet?"

"No," Maggie yelled. "It's my turn with her."

I blew him a kiss. "Later," I promised.

He winked. Just a tiny one. Not a big douchey one. That gave me butterflies too.

Maggie got batter on her hand and, in an unthinking motion, wiped it over her shirt, then groaned. "See? I told you I need an apron."

"We'll find you the perfect one," I promised.

Barrett reappeared with a washcloth, helping her get the mess off her shirt. Maggie's face was thoughtful when she picked up the piping bag again, pausing as it hovered over the baking sheet. "Remember when you told me about your mom's lucky apron?"

A gentle pang swept through my chest, and I let myself breathe through it as I nodded. "Yeah. It's in a box somewhere. It was pretty. She'd embroidered little flowers on it, and it had scalloped edges along the bottom."

Maggie pursed her lips, giving me a shy look. "Do you remember what color it was?"

I met Barrett's eyes in the camera, and the quiet support I saw in his face made it so much easier to answer than I'd thought.

"Yellow."

◆ ◆ ◆

Me: I feel like such an ass.

Barrett: You can't help that you're sick. No one's mad at you for not being here.

Me: I'm missing your brother's wedding! I wanted to see you in a suit. It does things to me.

Barrett: How about I skip the wedding and come feed you soup? I'll bring the suit for when you're feeling better.

Me: Tempting, but no. You cannot miss this. Plus, I'm all snotty and shivery. I'm not cute when I have a fever.

Barrett: You're always cute.

Me: You are the only person who's ever said those words to me in my entire life. Puppies are cute. Bunnies are cute.

Barrett: Fine. You're always scary hot. Better?

Me: Scary about sums it up. I miss you. I wish I could've seen you this weekend.

Barrett: I miss you too. We'll get something figured out once I get through the draft.

Me: Promise?

Barrett: I promise.

◆ ◆ ◆

"This is so stupid. Who thought we should do long distance? Not fucking me."

Pouting was not a good look—definitely not on me—but there I was, pouting like an absolute champ.

"How long has it been?"

"Almost three months. How the hell am I supposed to last three more?" I wailed.

"I meant, how long since he was supposed to call you?"

"Oh. He was supposed to call an hour ago," I said glumly.

Ugh. *Pouting.* I'd sounded like such a little baby bitch all day, and I couldn't stop, because now I was an addict. A Barrett King addict. Between me missing his brother's wedding due to the virus from hell and the draft, it had been six weeks since I'd seen him in person, our only visit happening after he and the kids had taken a whirlwind trip over a long weekend off from school. Not hearing his voice for a certain amount of time gave me withdrawal symptoms, for fuck's sake. Boyfriends like him should come with a warning label.

Caution: Prolonged exposure will result in a host of dangerous symptoms: inability to fall asleep without hearing him say good night; increased phone sex that makes you question your own sanity because of how good it is; tendency to engage in deep, meaningful conversations where he gently delves into your past and makes you feel okay talking about it; and an overwhelming, horrific urge to cry whenever you look at his pictures on your phone.

"Men are the worst." Miriam always thought men were the worst. But she had three ex-husbands who were pretty awful. "Why couldn't I be attracted to women? Marrying a woman would've been so much easier."

I smiled. "He's not the worst," I argued. "He's just . . . getting busier. They had the draft recently. We went three days without a phone call last week; he felt awful."

"This is what happens when you bang the coach," Agatha said, patting me on the head as she shuffled past. "They're important, and important people are always busy."

I wiggled my toes in the water and looked over my shoulder. The girls were in their usual spots by the pool. Agatha couldn't see anything today because she'd forgotten her glasses at home, but Miriam was always willing to share, even though her prescription wasn't as strong. Agatha slid them onto her nose and squinted in my direction.

"I like that swimsuit, honey. You look real hot."

"You don't think it's too much? I didn't want to give anyone a heart attack when I came down here." I adjusted the keyhole cutout between my breasts, which showed a generous amount of underboob. It was white, with thin straps that tied high on my hips and around the back of my neck. It had arrived yesterday in an expensive-looking box, along with a note from Barrett saying he wanted to picture me wearing it.

If I hadn't been late for the daily pool date with the neighborhood hellions, I would've sent him a new pic. I was getting *very* good at them.

"You kidding? I'd wear that in a heartbeat if I wouldn't fall and break a hip trying to put it on."

I patted her knee. "We don't need that."

The screen on my phone was still blank, and I let out a pouty bitch sigh.

"You tell him you love him yet?" Miriam asked carefully.

I knew I'd rue the day I'd been feeling all emo about that and found myself blabbing during pool time. Ruing had officially commenced, because now they *asked*. They checked in. They *worried*. And even stranger was that I didn't hate it.

Florida Lily was like a whole different person, and I was still coming to terms with that. I was in my first new job since Larry had passed on to doggie heaven, and even though I had Barrett—and God, did I have Barrett—and the kids, who also called me a few times a week, I found myself talking more. Chatting more. Turned out, opening your heart for someone made it easier for other people to sneak in.

Hell, even Patty and I texted. She was thrilled about this whole me-and-Barrett thing, and made me promise we'd do lunch sometimes when I moved back to Buffalo. Toss in Barrett's mom, Robin, who'd scheduled a phone date with me every Friday morning, and I was surrounded.

I had people now. A whole bunch of them. But more than that, more than friendly check-ins with people like Patty and the occasional text from Griffin's wife, Ruby, I had something else that I never saw coming.

I felt mothered.

After so many years without that role in my life, that sensation of being enveloped by someone's care and worry was one of the most incredible things I'd gained, outside of my relationship with Barrett and the kids.

But apparently, having a group of nosy surrogate moms meant they were all up in my relationship when I sort of admitted that I was scared to tell Barrett that I loved him.

"Not really," I hedged.

"You're nuts," Agatha said.

"Thanks."

Miriam always had a bit of a gentler touch. "You've never said it to anyone since your family died?"

Slowly, I shook my head.

"And he doesn't seem upset about it?"

"*No*. He's so patient. Probably more than I deserve, to be honest."

"Nonsense," Agatha insisted. "It's horseshit to act like you deserve less than anyone else simply because you went through something hard and ugly. We don't all pop up out of the dirt of our past smelling like roses, do we? Sometimes we smell like the dirt for a while, and there's nothing wrong with that because that's what makes us grow, honey. Not the other way around." She leaned forward. "Do you think Barrett deserves less from you because of what he went through?"

"Of course not." I ran my hand through the water, the distorted image of my fingers holding my attention while I sifted through my thoughts. "But hasn't he earned the right to know what's in my head?"

"*Do* you love him?" Miriam asked.

See? This was the problem. Even thinking it made my stomach all queasy, my chest heavy with a swirling mix of anticipation and anxiety and desperation. If I lost him, I'd be absolutely devastated. He and the kids were the axis of my world, and orbiting around them was as easy as breathing, even from all this distance. I couldn't wait to do it from close up. To have boring days and stressful days and everything in between.

When I was still in Buffalo, I'd thought of my burgeoning feelings for Barrett as a general sense of nausea. Love felt like that sometimes, didn't it?

He was so handsome and kind and thoughtful and sweet. And sexy. God, he was so sexy. Yeah, sometimes if I thought about the big-picture list of what kind of man he was, I did want to puke, but not in a bad way.

More like a *I cannot believe he's mine* way.

He was mine. And I was his. My new life goal was to make sure that never changed.

"Yeah," I whispered, so quietly I wasn't sure they could hear me. "I do."

"Oh, thank the Lord. Go tell him."

I let out a snort of amusement. "Eventually, I will. I don't want to do it over the phone."

"That's a relief."

I rolled my eyes. "Why?"

"Because he's here."

As my heart thrashed in my chest, my head snapped up, and at the sight of his tall, broad frame approaching the pool, a duffel bag in his hand and aviator frames sitting on his handsome face, I scrambled to my feet so fast that I almost fell over.

When my feet were finally under me, I blinked, hard, just to make sure he was real.

His lips curved in a smile.

Then I was running.

"No running by the pool!" the pimply lifeguard yelled.

"Fuck off, Robbie!" I yelled right back.

Barrett laughed, dropping his duffel bag just in time to catch me in his arms as I leaped.

He was here.

He was *here*.

My mouth covered his with a desperate groan as his hands held me up underneath my ass. I tightened my grip around his neck, my hands digging into the thick strands of his hair. Barrett moaned as our tongues slid against each other, his fingers tightening where he held me.

And my heart. Oh, my heart.

It sang.

I loved him. I loved him so much.

I pulled away on a short sobbing noise. "You're here."

His cheeks were flushed, the sunglasses askew on his nose. I ripped them off and cupped his face in both hands, tracing the grooves in his skin around his smile.

"I told you I wanted to see that bikini."

I laughed, happiness bubbling up like a popped champagne bottle, my heart racing at the mere sight of him. "Take me home," I whispered.

"Yes, ma'am."

He set me down and gave a sheepish wave at the whooping and hollering women I'd left at the pool, winding one arm around my shoulders so he could kiss the top of my head, then picked up his discarded duffel bag with the other.

The house where I was staying was a short walk from the community pool, and he was sucking at the skin on the back of my neck as I tried to unlock the door with shaking fingers.

"This should be illegal," he growled, hands already coasting up and down my sides, his fingers dragging over the exposed flesh of my chest. "I missed you so much, and I wanted to keep my head—but look at you, Lily. Look at you."

Once we were inside, he kicked the door shut and swept me up in his arms. We tumbled back onto the couch, Barrett underneath me as I straddled his lap and sighed into the deep, drugging kisses.

I wanted to snort this man into my bloodstream.

His palms dragged up and down my back while I rolled my hips over the intimidating length of his hard-on.

It would be so easy. A quick tug at his shorts, a snap of the meager little strings holding up my suit, and he'd be inside me. I loved when he was inside me.

Pretty sure I'd fight the entire world for the feeling this man gave me every time he took me to bed. And I'd survived without it for weeks. The impossibility of going longer set off a slight trembling in my hands, which held his face as we kissed and kissed and kissed.

It moved along my limbs as I wound them around his shoulders, trying to hold him as tightly as possible.

Barrett did the same, wrapping his strong arms around my waist as our kisses gentled and slowed. He tasted like mint. Smelled like heaven.

I'd climb a fucking mountain just for five minutes in his arms, just like this, even if there was nothing else.

After another luxurious, wet kiss, he moved his hands and slid them along the sides of my neck until he was holding my face in his hands. I pulled back and rolled my forehead against his, the crest of emotion finally catching up from the shock of seeing him.

"You're here," I whispered again, my lips brushing his as I spoke. "How long do we have?"

"Not long enough." He kissed me, deeper this time, tilting his head as our tongues wound together. I let out a short whimper when he pulled back again. "Forty-eight hours."

The trembling rolled through my frame, from my arms to my shoulders, and it spiraled as it found the length of my spine, until I was shaking in his arms, unable to hold him as tightly as I wanted.

He kissed the curve of my shoulder and dropped his head there, breathing in the scent of my skin with big, greedy breaths. "What's wrong, sweetheart?"

Now it was in my heart. I couldn't stop it. Couldn't stop the way it eclipsed every inch of my body, my mind, my fucking soul.

I cupped his face, pulling it up so I could look into his eyes. His warm, golden eyes.

A tear slid silently down my cheek. "I love you."

Barrett's face broke open into the most beautiful, perfect smile I'd ever seen on another person in my entire life. His heart was in that smile, and I couldn't believe it was mine.

He kissed me. So perfectly. So gently.

The trembling stopped.

Peace slipped in right on its heels.

"I know," he whispered.

I let out a watery laugh. "How?"

He traced the skin next to my eyes, studying every inch of my face. "I see it here. I see it when you smile at me. When you hug me so tight, like you want to sink into my skin. When you want to end every day talking." He kissed me again. "I told you I was okay waiting, Lily. I meant it."

"I should've told you sooner," I insisted. "I made you wait too long."

"You told me exactly when you needed to." He swept some stray hairs off my face, tucking them behind my ear. "But now I'll need to hear it every day."

"Oh yeah?"

He nodded, a grave expression in his face. "I told you I'd be greedy when it came to you."

"I love you," I said again. Barrett hummed, a delicious rumble that came from deep in his chest. As he closed his eyes, I leaned in and kissed his jaw. The corner of his mouth. "I love you."

His hands plucked at my bikini, and the strings loosened around my hips. "Again," he demanded gently.

"I love you," I sighed, as his hand carefully pulled the bottoms out of our way with a slight lift of my hips.

I pushed at his shorts, and we kissed—deep, deep kisses that I felt down to my toes, that raised the hair on my arms, that rewired my entire brain.

When Barrett pushed inside me, using his hands on my hips to pull me down, a long, smooth stroke that had us both groaning, he stole my mouth in a decadent kiss and told me he loved me too. He said it so many ways. Sometimes with words, and sometimes it was like this, with every push of his hips, with every gasp he pulled from my lungs, like I could breathe in the words and they'd stay there forever. I wanted to lock them in my bloodstream, let them cycle around my entire body until not a single piece of me was untouched by the truth of his love for me.

Eventually, he turned so I was on my back on the couch, and he moved slow and steady between my legs, pressing my calf up against his chest so he could hit the angle that made me see stars.

"I love you," he told me again. He always told me when he got close. It was one of the last things he said before his movements became sharper and harder.

My orgasm hit first. It wasn't a bright explosion. It rolled over my body, endless and mellow and so fucking perfect as I let it go with a moan.

And I watched as his finally crested, the tightening of his brow, like it was so good that it almost hurt, and underneath my hand, his heart thrashed in his chest while he groaned my name.

He wound his body around mine as we both came down, and he let out a great, heaving sigh when I kissed the space over his heart.

"Long distance is stupid," he muttered against my skin.

My smile was dreamy and sleepy and came straight from a blissed-out place in my mind. "It really is."

Barrett lifted his head and stared into my face. "How much longer?"

I swept my thumb under his lip. "You're the one who said it would be good for me to go."

"That was one of my worst decisions. You should never listen to me."

I laughed, and he dipped down to kiss me again, full of sweetness and longing.

"Don't worry," I whispered, curling my fingers into the back of his neck. "I'll be home soon."

Home.

Home. It slipped out so easily, felt so right.

"Yeah?" He nipped at my bottom lip, soothing it with a soft kiss after. "I've got two more years on my contract in Buffalo—more, if they want to keep me. I really like it there."

"I know."

His gaze was soft and heady. "You can handle the snow and the cold?"

"That's what I have you for." I snuggled into his arms, sighing happily when they tightened around my back. I was safe. Happy. And more than that, I was loved. "You'll keep me warm, right?"

He gently kissed the top of my head, burying his nose in my hair and breathing deeply.

"Always."

Epilogue

Lily

"You sure you want to do this?"

"Yeah."

Barrett hadn't come down to Florida for my last weekend there, but when I told him there was something I wanted to do in Texas, he told team ownership he needed thirty-six hours off. They gave it to him even though the beginning of the season was in full swing.

Before I'd even had the chance to ask, there was no question that he'd be there for me. He always was.

I handed him the key, shielding my eyes from the brutal heat of the sun while he unlocked the padlock that had kept the unit secure for the last decade. Not that long ago, I would've known exactly how many months and weeks and days it had stayed that way.

Counting that passage of time didn't help. Didn't make me miss them less. So I stopped. Now my countdowns involved the three members of the King family who held my future.

How many days until I'd see them. Until I could sleep in Barrett's arms. Until I could bake with Maggie after school. Watch Bryce play soccer and be that sideline mom who yelled at the refs until Barrett told me to calm down.

Barrett pulled the lock out and pocketed it, leaning down to yank open the rolling door.

My stomach had been unsettled all morning, my brain anxious, only settling slightly when Barrett got off the plane he'd chartered to come be with me. Banging the coach came with perks, and access to a private jet was definitely one of them. Pearl, as it turned out, was a closet romantic.

Before I opened my eyes, Barrett slid his fingers in between mine, holding them tightly in his grip as the stale smell hit me. I blew out a breath and finally pried my eyes open.

The unit was smaller than I remembered. In my head, it had grown into something big and intimidating, rows and rows of memories that I'd never dared touch. In reality, there wasn't as much as I thought. A couple of wardrobe boxes that held clothes I hadn't been able to part with. A leather chair my dad had often fallen asleep in. The covered body of the car he'd worked on for years, completed only about six months before he died.

He'd taken me on two drives in that car, and if I closed my eyes again, I'd remember the wind on my face and the songs playing on the radio. I walked closer, fingers dragging along the edge of the cloth covering the car. Barrett stayed with me, his eyes lingering on the vehicle, lit with curiosity when I glanced over my shoulder.

"What is it?" he asked in a hushed voice.

"You can look." My voice came out thick, tight with emotion that I'd kept bottled up all morning in anticipation of what we were doing.

Before he uncovered the vehicle, Barrett held my face in his hands and studied me closely. "Are you okay?"

After letting out a deep breath, I nodded. "Yeah. I'm okay." Then I smiled. "I'm ready."

Barrett dropped a kiss on my forehead, then turned to the low-slung car. With careful hands, he pulled the cover off, his face going slack when the beautiful blue was completely uncovered.

"Whoa," he breathed. "A Corvette?"

"1969 Stingray," I told him, eyes lingering on the sleek lines of the perfectly restored machine. "His dream car."

"It's incredible." His gaze locked on mine. "You should take this back with us. I think he'd like knowing you were driving it."

My eyes filled. I liked that idea. "Do we have enough garage space?"

"Sweetheart, I'll buy you a new house if we need to make room for this," he said, sliding an arm around my waist while we stared down at the car.

"I like that house," I protested.

"I do, too, but don't let that be the reason you leave it here." He kissed the top of my head. "This is too beautiful to leave hidden away."

I exhaled heavily. "Okay. We'll figure it out." I tilted my chin up at Barrett and he took the hint, leaning down for a soft kiss.

"Do you know which box you're looking for?"

Tucked in the corner were two small stacks of moving boxes labeled with big black letters in my handwriting.

Dad's garage stuff

Aaron's toys

Books

Paperwork

Office items and photo albums

The box on the top of the closest stack wasn't taped shut, just folded together.

Mom's kitchen stuff

My hands shook slightly as I pulled it open, silent tears coursing down my cheeks as I looked down into the box. Her cookie cutters. The rolling pin that was probably fifty years old. Vintage glass casserole dishes that she'd kept from her grandma—a burnt-orange-and-white pattern that was just kitschy enough to be cute.

Memories bombarded me, bittersweet and poignant, moments that had been simple at the time, but now they felt like everything. They didn't devastate me like I'd always feared. I rubbed at my pounding chest and took another breath as I shifted a glass dish to the side.

Folded neatly against the side of the box was a glimpse of yellow material.

I smiled through my tears. "Yeah. I've got it."

Two months later, I gave it to Maggie for her eleventh birthday, and she asked if I was okay as I cried when she put it on for the first time. I told her the truth: I was happy, but I missed my mom, and wished she'd been able to meet her. Then my sweet girl hugged me and cried, saying she wished that too.

Turned out, Bryce had the same reading taste as my brother, and he devoured the comic books Aaron had loved so much, losing himself in the fantasy worlds of animal kingdoms and wars and good versus evil. We read through them together, setting aside time every night before he went to bed to take turns reading.

My dad's car, which we named Blue, sat in the extra garage stall Barrett had added on to the house as soon as I moved in.

During the first regular season as the coach's girlfriend, I had a crash course in just how busy Barrett was. Much like when I'd first met him, he tried to be home before the kids went to bed, but it didn't always work out that way. On the nights when it was later, I waited up until he got home, greeting him with a long hug and a longer kiss. Sometimes he was asleep less than fifteen minutes after walking through the door, but it was always with me in his arms, and that was the only thing that mattered.

He was the hardest worker I'd ever met in my life, and I found that game day was one of my favorite things. Watching him get to do the thing he loved was almost sickeningly exciting. I especially liked his mood after they won. Celebratory sex was my jam. So was consolation sex after they lost. That was usually later at night, once we'd climbed into bed, and I'd wrap my arms around him while he talked about the game and what went wrong.

Like anything with us, all it took was one kiss—meant to be simply that—and it didn't take long to become more. As we neared the end of the season, closing in on a year from when we met, we were still insatiable. He told me he loved me every day. And I always said it back.

The first time the three of them drove somewhere without me, I didn't know where they were, and I had a panic attack when they were late coming home. He held me through it and told me it was okay. I started seeing a therapist a couple times a month after that, and to my surprise, all my emotional baggage actually could fit onto her couch.

Turned out, talking to people who could talk back really did help. No offense to Larry, but it was what I'd needed all along.

We argued on occasion. Because we were both stubborn as hell and always thought we were right. The makeup sex was worth it, though. It was over little things—like grilled cheese with ketchup, even when there was perfectly good tomato soup in the house. He was wrong, and I swore I'd get him to admit it someday. Or it was over larger things, like how we thought something should be handled with the kids—especially when it came to dealing with Rachel.

To my surprise, I did not break her nose when I met her. But we'd never be friends, that was for fucking sure. During an eternal Christmas break when the kids were at her house for a week, Maggie sent me a text saying she'd rather be home with us—her real parents—and I cried on and off for the rest of the day.

Barrett was more understanding toward his ex than I was, but even if we butted heads, he knew I'd take a bullet for his kids, and that was always where my intentions were rooted.

It was during that Christmas break, after a day of movies and snuggling on the couch, that Barrett pulled out a beautiful diamond solitaire and proposed to me under the mistletoe.

This time, he'd been the one to hang it.

When he got down on one knee, I couldn't stop crying.

"You're my best friend," he told me. "My partner. And every piece of my life is better with you in it." He kissed my hand as he looked up at me, his own eyes filled with tears. "Marry me, Lily."

I said yes, and we waited to tell the kids until they got home from Rachel's a few days later. Bryce wiped away a few tears that he thought we couldn't see, while Maggie proclaimed it the best day of her entire life.

Buffalo made it into the playoffs that year, winning their wild card game and then one more, and it was the saddest fucking thing in the world watching those players leave the field after they lost.

Two days later, Barrett woke me up with his mouth between my legs, and when he was done—or when I was done, rather—he said he had a surprise for the kids and me.

"That wasn't my surprise?" I said, still slightly out of breath, adjusting the sleep tank that had gotten all twisted around my chest.

He laughed. "Nope. Get dressed and come downstairs. We'll grab breakfast on the way."

"You're in a chipper mood," I said, eyeing him skeptically. "You didn't even get laid this morning."

He smacked a kiss on my mouth while he waited for me to stumble out of bed on still-shaky legs. "The day is still young."

I rolled my eyes.

We all piled into his truck and stopped for a fast-food breakfast, to the delight of his children.

Barrett took a turn and then instructed us to close our eyes.

Dutifully, I did as I was told, smiling when he curved a large hand around my thigh.

"Maggie," he said in a warning tone. "Close 'em."

"I *did*. Sort of."

He chuckled, and the sound of it made me shiver slightly. His hand squeezed, like he knew what I was thinking.

The truck came to a stop and when Barrett shifted it into park, he let out a slow breath. "Okay. Open your eyes."

Second Leash Animal Sanctuary

My mouth fell open. Maggie screamed.

"Are we getting a dog?" Bryce gasped.

Without waiting for an answer, Maggie hurled herself at her dad, uninhibited by the fact that we were still in the truck and she couldn't really get into the front without kicking me in the face.

"Thank you, thank you, thank you!" she said, peppering his face with kisses.

"Really?" I asked, smile spreading as I watched the unleashed joy in front of me.

He held Maggie to his chest and nodded, eyes warm on my face. "Really."

The kids were over the moon, even though Barrett gave them a steadying talk about how it might take time to find exactly the right fit.

But in the end, it took less than five minutes.

Maggie stopped at the first kennel, *ooh*ing and *aah*ing over what she found there.

Bryce looked carefully, slowly walking a bit farther than his sister, then stopped at one a few kennels down, crouching with a soft expression on his face. "Lily, look."

While Maggie and Barrett fawned over a wriggling black dog with white spots on his chest, Bryce read the sign in front of him, eyes darting back and forth between that and the dog inside the kennel.

He was skinny, with the coloring of a hound and massive floppy ears. Legs too big for his body. And he had big brown eyes that looked right into my fucking soul.

When I crouched down next to Bryce, the tip of the dog's tail started thumping against the ground. Then he edged forward to sniff

us, his tongue darting out to swipe over Bryce's fingers wrapped around the metal links on the door. Bryce and I smiled at each other.

"What's his name?" I asked, smiling gently when the dog did the same thing to me.

Bryce nudged my shoulder. "His name is Larry."

My heart turned over.

"Of course it is," I whispered.

Barrett squeezed my shoulder as he came up behind us. "And who's this?" he asked.

"I think this is our dog," I told him.

We did the grown-up thing and met four adult dogs and two puppies, spending time with them in a fenced-in yard area as patient shelter volunteers brought us each one, telling us their stories and helping us make the decision for our family. To no one's surprise, it was a unanimous decision—all four of us fell head over heels in love with Larry Jr., who we decided to call *Junior*, lest the original owner of the name think he'd been replaced and get pissed off up in doggie heaven.

In truth, they were nothing alike.

Junior wasn't grumpy, and he didn't growl. He was sweet and shy and loved to climb into our laps, even though he was long and gangly and wouldn't fit by the time he'd fully grown into his frame.

When we brought him home that night, the kids fought over who got to sleep with him, but in the end, we found Junior curled up in my and Barrett's bed.

My fiancé sighed as he wrapped his arms around me from behind and we stared down at the newest member of the family.

"Am I gonna regret this?"

"At least three times a day for a while."

He laughed, the sound warm and rich at my back.

Slowly, I turned in his arms. "Thank you," I told him.

"For the dog?"

I smiled. "No. Well, yes. But no." He traced his thumb underneath my bottom lip while he waited for me to figure out what I wanted to

say. He was so good at that. "For knowing what we need. The kids. Me. You always seem to know."

"I didn't always," he admitted. I kissed his chin, snuggling against his chest. "Not until you. That's when I really started getting things right."

"Good thing I'm marrying you, then, huh?"

"Good thing."

Barrett laughed, and I pressed my face closer to the sound, my eyes falling shut at the feel of it against my skin.

We got married that spring, a year after Griffin and Ruby's wedding.

Despite his twin brother's offer to do it, it was Pearl who officiated the ceremony in front of Barrett's family and a large gathering of players and front office staff. In the second row, Bridget wept unabashedly.

Maggie stood up for me, and Bryce for his dad. Tied to my bouquet with a blue satin ribbon was a tiny framed picture of my family.

My wedding dress—a simple ivory satin number with a high neck that draped over my body in one long column—couldn't really hide my bump, but we weren't trying to keep it a secret either. The entire town of Buffalo seemed to know as soon as we'd announced it to our family, and sometimes I'd get people congratulating me in the grocery store, wishing us well as we added to the roster.

Turned out, even though I wasn't sure I fit the mold of perfect coach's wife, they all *loved* me.

Barrett held my hands in his just before we said our vows, his thumbs brushing over my knuckles. I'd tattooed a small crown just underneath the ring he'd given me. Seemed fitting since my last name would be *King*.

I went into labor three weeks early, and even though Maggie made a valiant effort to be in charge of names, we settled on Jacob Aaron. Two minutes later, his sister, Julia Kathleen, was born.

Barrett wept openly when he held them for the first time. I'd never loved him more.

The first day we were all home from the hospital, four days after they were born, we found Maggie and Bryce sitting on the nursery floor while the twins napped in their basinets, Junior stretched between them.

"You guys okay?" Barrett asked the kids.

Maggie nodded, unable to tear her eyes away from the twins. "Just being happy."

The sweetness of it was almost more than I could bear. I leaned in to Barrett as he wrapped his arm around me, resting his cheek on the top of my head while we stared at our perfect little family.

"And you?" he whispered, nudging my chin in his direction with a gentle tap of his thumb to my jaw. "You okay?"

It would be so easy to think about how I might have missed all this. How I almost let fear deprive me of the best family in the world, the one meant to be mine.

But I didn't. And I wouldn't.

I gave him a lingering kiss, sighing as I pulled back to smile.

"Just being happy."

ACKNOWLEDGMENTS

Thank you to my family, as always and for everything.

To my author friends who continually remind me that I did not, in fact, forget how to write books.

To Maria Gomez for saying an enthusiastic yes to a grumpy-grumpy story when that was not what I pitched. To Kelli Collins, ME Carter, and Kathryn Andrews for helping with the story at different points in the process.

To my readers, for all the ways they make this job worthwhile.

Love is patient. Love is kind. It does not envy, it does not boast, it is not proud . . . It bears all things, believes all things, hopes all things, endures all things.

1 Corinthians 13: 4–7

ABOUT THE AUTHOR

Photo © 2018 Perrywinkle Photography

Karla Sorensen is the #1 Amazon bestselling author of the Kings series, the Wilder Family series, the Best Man series, the Washington Wolves series, and many other novels. Karla refuses to read or write anything without a happily ever after. When she's not devouring Dramione fanfic or avoiding laundry, you can find her watching football (British and American) or HGTV, or listening to Enneagram podcasts so she can psychoanalyze everyone in her life, in no particular order of importance. With a degree in advertising and public relations from Grand Valley State University, she made her living in senior healthcare prior to writing full-time. Karla lives in Michigan with her husband, two boys, and a big, shaggy rescue dog named Bear. For more information, visit www.karlasorensen.com.

CONNECT WITH KARLA ONLINE

Instagram

www.instagram.com/karla_sorensen

Facebook Reader Group

www.facebook.com/groups/thesorensensorority

Website

www.karlasorensen.com

Newsletter

www.karlasorensen.com/subscribe